TOURS OF THE BLACK CLOCK

TOURS OF THE BLACK CLOCK

STEVE ERICKSON

AVON BOOKS ▲ NEW YORK

Text from *The Rise and Fall of the Third Reich* by William L. Shirer, copyright 1959, 1960, 1988 by William L. Shirer, is reprinted by permission of Simon & Schuster Inc.

AVON BOOKS
A division of
The Hearst Corporation
105 Madison Avenue
New York, New York 10016

Copyright © 1989 by Steve Erickson
Cover art by Amy Guip
Inside cover author photograph copyright © 1989 by Victoria Mihich
Published by arrangement with Poseidon Press, a division of Simon and Schuster Inc.
Library of Congress Catalog Card Number: 88-23057
ISBN: 0-380-70944-9

First Avon Books Trade Printing: December 1990

AVON TRADEMARK REG. U.S. PAT. OFF. AND IN OTHER COUNTRIES, MARCA REGISTRADA, HECHO EN U.S.A.

Printed in the U.S.A.

OPM   10 9 8 7 6 5 4 3 2 1

I would like to thank the
National Endowment for the
Arts for their generous support
in the writing of this book.

S.E.

TOURS OF THE BLACK CLOCK

Geli was twenty, with flowing blond hair, handsome features, a pleasant voice and a sunny disposition which made her attractive to men. Hitler soon fell in love with her. He took her everywhere, to meetings and conferences, on long walks in the mountains and to the cafes and theaters in Munich. When in 1929 he rented a luxurious nine-room apartment in the Prinzregentenstrasse, one of the most fashionable thoroughfares in Munich, Geli was given her own room in it. . . .

It is probable that Hitler intended to marry his niece. Early party comrades who were close to him at that time subsequently told . . . that a marriage seemed inevitable. That Hitler was deeply in love with her they had no doubt. Her own feelings are a matter of conjecture. . . . Whether she reciprocated her uncle's love is not known; probably not, and in the end certainly not. Some deep rift whose origins and nature have never been fully ascertained grew between them. . . .

Whatever it was that darkened the love between the uncle and his niece, their quarrels became more violent and at the end of the summer of 1931 Geli an-

nounced that she was returning to Vienna to resume
her voice studies. Hitler forbade her to go. There was
a scene between the two, witnessed by neighbors. . . .
The next morning Geli Raubal was found shot dead
in her room. The state's attorney, after a thorough
investigation, found that it was a suicide. . . .

Hitler himself was struck down by grief. Gregor
Strasser later recounted that he had had to remain for
the following two days and nights at Hitler's side to
prevent him from taking his own life. A week after
Geli's burial in Vienna, Hitler obtained special permission from the Austrian government to go there; he
spent an evening weeping at the grave. For months
he was inconsolable.

Three weeks after the death of Geli, Hitler had his
first interview with [German President] Hindenburg.
It was his first bid for the big stakes, for the chancel-
lorship of the Reich. His distraction on this momentous occasion—some of his friends said he did not
seem to be in full possession of his faculties during
the conversation, which went badly for the Nazi
leader—was put down by those who knew him as due
to the shock of the loss of his beloved niece.

. . . He declared forever afterward that Geli Raubal
was the only woman he ever loved, and he always
spoke of her with the deepest reverence—and often
in tears. . . . In the Chancellery in Berlin, portraits of
the young woman always hung and when the anniver-
saries of her birth and death came around each year
flowers were placed around them.

For a brutal, cynical man who always seemed to be
incapable of love of any other human being, this passion of Hitler's for the youthful Geli Raubal stands
out as one of the mysteries of his strange life. As with

all mysteries, it cannot be rationally explained, merely recounted. Thereafter, it is almost certain, Adolf Hitler never seriously contemplated marriage until the day before he took his own life fourteen years later.

WILLIAM L. SHIRER

The Rise and Fall of the Third Reich

1

There was always a moment, sailing between the boathouse on shore and Davenhall Island, when neither was in
sight. There was nothing in this moment but his boat in
the fog on the water; there might as well have been no sun
in the sky or anything that called itself a country. He didn't
notice it when he first got the job working for the old man,
transporting the tourists from the mainland to the island
and back three times a day. Old Zeno died seven weeks
later. The young man's name was Marc. Marc took over
the business and sailed into that moment his first trip out,
when there on deck in the fog he almost said out loud,
among the unsuspecting tourists, Where in the universe
am I? Finally the outline of Davenhall Island emerged in
the gray. In the days to come the moment might arrive at
any point of the journey, halfway or when arrival was im-
minent, with the island appearing so suddenly Marc
thought he might run the boat right up the banks of the
river. Sometimes it happened so near the last moment he
thought the moment wouldn't come at all. There was
never once he didn't feel its fear and desolation. He'd look
around the boat at the tourists poring over their itineraries,
at this moment when no itinerary made any more sense
than a scroll from the Dead Sea of some other hour, stolen
from the clock of some other place. Perhaps the place that
preceded this moment or the place of the moment to come;
but not this particular moment anyway. Not this one.

2

This moment was the first lapse in a life of innocence. Marc grew up on Davenhall Island in Davenhall chinatown, the only white kid of the town's only white woman and, it had to be presumed, one of the town's fleeting transitory white men. One perhaps who'd come in as a tourist one night some twenty years before the night Marc left the island forever, or what he thought at the time would be forever. Marc's eyes were green. His hair was white as noon, not yellow, white; it never darkened. When he was small he sat in front of the mirror in his mother's room on the second floor of the hotel across from Greek Judy's in the middle of mainstreet, and pulled his eyes at their corners to narrow them like the rest of the eyes in town. As though there was nothing amiss in the genes other than his having been born into a darkness before which he never had to squint, a dark that sucked into itself all the color of his hair. A dark like his mother must have been born into too, though not so fuliginous and depthless since her hair wasn't the stark white of his, nothing of her was that white except the small scar at the upper corner of her mouth. Nothing about her came to characterize her for him so much as this small scar. He came to measure what she felt by it, or what he supposed the scar told him that she felt. When she caught him trying to look like a Chinese in the mirror of her room, the scar lifted to some expression between humor and alarm; he saw it and didn't do it anymore.

At night she warmed some milk and read to him in her strange accent, the accent of many languages woven into a jungle of one. She read from books in which neither of them had any interest except for the sound of her reading them. It was a rare gesture of motherhood though this isn't to say she didn't feel like a mother to him even when she made no gestures. The fact was she couldn't have been less prepared for him; when she had him she was at the age she could have been a grandmother. She had borne him after reaching a point where she supposed it was possible only in theory. Thus she regarded him as a bit of a theoretical child. She observed and considered him in the way she might observe and consider an extraordinary figment of her imagination. When she was most brutally honest with herself, she'd ask if, given this, it was possible she really loved him deeply; she was never so brutally honest she could bring herself to answer, though had she been that courageous it's entirely conceivable the answer would have been yes. At any rate the milk and reading were acts by which she stepped into her own imagination and took part in it, with conviction.

Then she'd fall asleep too, sometimes right there on his bed. There were times he thought she'd perhaps been drinking a little. On these occasions he'd lie awake thinking, just a kid staring at the black ceiling, and it was always then he heard the footsteps out in the hall. He'd sit up and look at the light through the crack beneath the door, and listen to the footsteps and how they paused outside the door. As far as he knew, nobody else lived in the hotel but the hotel's manager, a small Chinese lady who never spoke and was never seen; anyway the steps in the hall were those of someone big. Someone very big. For years, in the middle of the night, he heard right outside his door the tread of this unseen giant. There's someone else living in the hotel with us, he said to his mother. "Who?" she asked. If she'd simply said No, he would have known she was lying.

The sounds of his life on Davenhall Island were those footsteps in the hall at night, the trees in winter and the throttled din of the ice machine out behind the rice shop, a white and black unit that ran entirely on its own, blocks of ice spitting out onto the ground to the absolute indifference of everyone but Greek Judy who carved them up and put them in the bourbon she served in her bar. Judy was a young woman who had taken over the business some years before; her actual name was Garcia, nothing greek about her. Otherwise the ice sat like glittering glass fusing with the dirt of the town. Greek Judy's tavern served bourbon and beer, steak and onions to the tourists that came in on old Zeno's ferry. From four in the afternoon the concentrated red roar of life billowed from the bar in the middle of translucent oriental silence, and after the last ferry went back Marc, who sometimes saw other children in the bar with their parents, went around collecting their artifacts, which he hid under his bed upstairs in the hotel across the street. For years he assumed these things of an outside world were contraband before the will of his mother, who in fact knew all about them but recognized how necessary to a child was the glamour of his secrecy.

4

She knew he'd leave someday. When he was eleven he got it into his head he wanted to be a monk. Every day he built a small cathedral out of the iceblocks in the dirt; after a while all that was left of his monkdom were the ice cathedrals on which he would lie and listen to the crackling of the melting blocks. It seemed like the sound of ticking. It would be many years later, when he was sailing the boat back and forth to the island, that he'd forgive the men who found release in the legs of his mother. It would be many years before he forgave her, too.

5

The only negotiation Greek Judy ever had with the Chinese of Davenhall concerned the bodies in the trees out in the northern graveyard. The town could be crossed on foot in six or seven minutes walking up mainstreet, and the island in something between twelve and fifteen depending on the season. In the hard rains of autumn the graveyard flooded and the island diminished, shrunk at its northern border where Marc remembered seeing one afternoon, in a storm that came faster than any consideration of shelter, blue bubbles floating up around the tombstones; something unimaginable was gasping up from underground. The Chinese peasants of Davenhall routinely hung on the graveyard trees the bodies of the Davenhall dead, sometimes days, sometimes weeks, before interment. It was the peasants' conviction that if one died without speaking his or her name in the final breath, then to seal away the corpse that had been wrenched loose of its identity by death would exile the spirit to some netherbetween place. At each funeral witnesses would be called forth to verify that, before dying, the dead one had established without doubt his memory of himself. If no witness could attest to such a thing, the body would hang in the graveyard trees until the universe chose to write his or her name in the sky, so that he or she could read it and call the name out. Sometimes a body hung in the trees for quite a while. Sooner or later one of the peasants would wander into town and report to the others, "I heard him today, today he said his name," and with satisfaction the body was then buried. In the summer, especially when it was very hot, the bodies tended to remember their names much more quickly. It came to pass that the inhabitants of Davenhall kept on the tables by their beds small index cards with their names written in large letters so that should the moment of death come suddenly, and with it perhaps a paralysis of instant recall, they could read their names from the cards and cry them out in the night in order that someone walking by in the street might hear it. But when Marc saw the blue bubbles floating up around the tombstones, he realized that the interred had come to find they preferred crucifixion in the trees to slumber in the cold wet ground of the Davenhall marsh, and that they were casting out from under the rising river their very memories so that they might hang amnesiac and free before the sky and the pale rosy smear of sunset, and the writing of the universe. When Marc, huddled that day beneath a wood shack in the rain, saw the blue memories of a hundred ghosts drift off riverward to finally and vainly burst, he gathered up his innocence in all its fierceness and directed it toward the leaving of this town forever.

6

The night that Marc saw the stranger lying dead at his mother's feet, he was nineteen. He turned and walked down the hotel stairs, out into mainstreet, down to the dock in time to catch the last boat to the mainland. He'd thought about doing this many times but this was the first that his nerve caught up with his imagination. Over the years he'd watched old man Zeno with his red riverbitten face and his long blue coat with the dingy gold buttons sail his small human ferry back and forth each day, bringing over the years thousands of strangers to the black and amber lights of Greek Judy's tavern. Now in the dark Zeno didn't give a second look to the boy as he stepped onto the boat, crowding in with the others, huddling against them in the fog and reek of Judy's bourbon. But at some point during the twenty-minute journey, the old man looked Marc's way and said something to the effect of, "Boy, that hair's some kind of white."

They got to shore and the tourists piled out of the boat and onto the buses that were waiting to take them twenty miles northwest to the city of Samson. It's possible Marc wouldn't have gotten on the bus even if he'd had a ticket, nerve having lost ground to imagination once again. Nothing irrevocable had yet been crossed. But there was no boat back to Davenhall until the morning, and so he stood there in the dirt watching the lights of the last bus vanish down the highway and then looking over his shoulder at the river behind him, and Zeno's boathouse in the remaining desolation. Zeno sized things up. He stood in the doorway of the boathouse where he lit the gaslamp next to the window, and after blowing out the match and tossing it on the step he called out to the boy's white hair, "Just what is it you imagine you're doing?" I imagine, the boy answered, that I've lived on that island long enough, and am now about to put some real distance between us. "Not tonight, I'd say," the old man answered. After a moment he added, "Come on in and drink something stiff, and I'll take you back first boat of the morning."

I'll come in and have the drink, Marc answered. But I'm not going back.

They played cards in the boathouse, in the light of the lamp. The old man bet the gold buttons of his blue coat, since he plainly cheated and there was never the slightest danger of his losing them. He fell asleep against the wall while the boy made various accusations.

Marc did not go on to Samson the next day. Rather he did return to the island with the old man, much as the old man had figured, though he refused to step foot on it. Back and forth three times he sailed with the old man and more busloads of tourists, refusing to enter the town and waiting on deck as Zeno went to get some of Judy's beer. Once Marc glimpsed in the distance his mother walking up mainstreet in a tattered salmon-colored dress he recognized, her arms folded in that way of hers and her face set with a familiar and incomprehensible determination. He glimpsed her long hair in the rising dust of the town, the gray hair that once had been a tarnished panic of fool's-gold yellow. Marc lay low on the deck of the boat facing out toward the river, away from town and the island, leaning over the side and dragging his hand in the water, lunging for fish that he had no intention of catching.

7

Marc did not go to Samson the next day either, or the next.
He continued sailing with old Zeno back to the island,
hiding on deck and never stepping ashore. Zeno put him
to work collecting the fares; it also became his job to yell at
passengers who leaned too far over the side, and lie to them
about things in the river. It might be alligators one week
and piranha the next. The old man filled Marc in on how
to operate the boat through the sophistication of the currents. Sometimes, on the trip over, the fog would clear
enough for a moment so that Marc could see the whole of
the island as he'd never seen it. Beyond the island, beyond
the interminable river in which the island rested, he might
almost have believed he saw the river's other side; in the
distance a red train crossed on its tracks high above the
water. The dust out over the plains were the herds of shorthaired silver buffalo that had begun appearing out of nowhere at the turn of the century's final decade. "You don't
eat one of those," Zeno said, "however hungry you are.
Light you up like a city boulevard." Past the end of the
island was the old rubble of a small shelter that had been
built on wooden pillars out over the river; it was charred
black from a fire that had taken place before Marc was
born. The boy believed he could still see the smoke of the
inferno. It was something nobody, including his mother,
talked about. Know anything about that fire? he asked the
old man. "Not something I talk about," the old man muttered.

8

After several weeks Marc said to the old man one night, I'm not getting to Samson very quickly this way. "Don't say it like it's my fault," Zeno snapped back, "I'm not stopping you." Well, the boy said after thinking about it a moment, I don't have a ticket for the bus. "I'll give you the money for the ticket," said Zeno, "you can leave tomorrow. I'm not stopping you." You don't have any money, the boy said, those fares don't add up to anything, how do you get by with charging them four-bits anyway? What kind of business is that? "It's my business, that's what kind," the old man answered, "the fares don't mean puckey. Pocket money. I get my main cut from Judy on the island, a percentage of her take. I bring her the tourists and she provides a place for them to be brought. Don't worry about my business." He pulled a canvas sack from beneath his mattress. He pulled from it some ratty old bills and a lot of loose change. The boy turned away. He built a fire in the stove and lit the gaslamp, not looking at Zeno who stood with the money in his gnarly hands, affronting the boy with it. Marc's head was light and pounding from the final trip back—the liquor of the passengers and the fumes of the boat's motor. What about you? he muttered finally, still not looking at Zeno who by this time had dropped the money to his side. "Hell I got along forty years without you, punk," said Zeno. The two of them sat and had a drink together, and at last the boathouse began to warm though it never lost its dampness. The fire burned down and the boy fed and stoked it again, and when it burned down again, before they slept, Marc said, A couple more days. Then I'm gone. The old man nodded and muttered back, "Sure. You can leave tomorrow if you want." When Marc was sure Zeno

was asleep he added, You fucking cheat at cards anyway.
Closing his eyes he heard, "Sure, leave tomorrow. I'm not
stopping you."

A couple more days and Marc still hadn't left. It wasn't
long after that, on an afternoon when the sun broke glanc-
ingly through the fog, that the old man plopped with a
thump down on a fruit crate near the side of the boat; thirty
or forty quarters fell through his fingers and skipped across
the puddles of the deck. Marc instinctively knelt to retrieve
them, and only when he looked almost casually at old Zeno
did he see a face that was as white as his own hair. A fat
man with a hat and camera said, "Is he OK?" and began
picking up quarters. Marc shook Zeno's shoulder and said,
Hey. When Zeno didn't respond the boy said, Old man?
He still didn't respond. Oh Jesus, the boy exclaimed, torn
between attending to Zeno and steering the boat, which
was now beginning to veer wildly off course. Other passengers were looking around in confusion. Finally the old
man's breathing resumed, his head lifted and he peered
around, but he still didn't move and everything he said
was jumbled and without sense. When the boat reached
shore he couldn't feel his legs. Marc took Zeno into the
boathouse and put him on the mattress. He canceled the
rest of the day's schedule. He got into a fight with the fat
man in the hat and camera over the quarters he'd
pocketed. "Shouldn't have to pay to come back anyway," the man protested, "people should have the right

to go back where they came from." Not on my river, said
Marc.

Zeno was back out on the boat the next day for a couple
of trips over, but his legs still weren't right and things said
to him had to be repeated. Then he collapsed on the rail
and almost fell in the water. For the next several days the
business didn't run at all. Judy came over to see where
everyone had gone. "You could have let me known," she
said. Not on that island, the boy answered back. The two
discussed getting a doctor while Zeno lay on the mattress
listening. "Forget doctors," he croaked, in one of his more
lucid moments.

Marc woke that night when the light of the gaslamp was
only a point and the sound of Zeno's voice in the dark was
only a scrape of life against death. "I set it on fire," Marc
heard him, "are you listening? That house on the pillars
out over the river, forty years ago. . . ." There was a pause;
in the dark Marc, from his side of the boathouse, could
feel the old man struggling. He began to say, Don't struggle; but the old man said first, "Say nothing and listen. I
. . . are you listening? The hand that set it on fire was my
own and now I have to tell someone. Because a man died,
see. A man burnt up. City man, some kind of gangster or
private eye . . . your mother knows. He came looking for
her. He waited in that house over the river, and at night
when he slept I set it on fire. Never quite knew why I did
it. So I have his ashes on my soul now, now I have to tell
someone because your mother's knowing isn't enough.
She'll die with the secret the same way she hasn't spoken
to me since it happened, it's not a secret that should be
died with. . . ." Marc heard him gasp. He tried to keep the
old man talking, if only to reel him back from whatever he
was sinking into. Old man, called Marc. Nothing. Old
man?

10

It was obvious and appropriate that the old man should be given to the river; Marc wasn't about to let him hang in a tree for a week. So in the middle of the night he took Zeno into the river and bound him with rope to the bottom of the boat. He cried as he did this. The next day, wearing the blue coat with the dirty gold buttons, he opened up business; his first decision was to raise the fare to a dollar each way. As weeks and then months passed, he came to forget about Zeno tied to the bottom of the boat, except for those odd moments when his bones rattled in the currents of the river; the passengers would look curiously to their feet at the sound. But the new captain was certainly mindful of the old man that first trip across the river when the fog closed in and there was nothing but a world of water and vapor, leaving him to ask himself, Where in the universe am I? Which he might just as well have asked all those years his boat was only a floating chinatown. And that he asked it now without ever having asked it before was what made this moment the first lapse in a life of innocence.

11

Through this lapse streamed a hundred wanton nights, the first of which brought a slightly boyish blonde with straight short hair and glasses who worked in a bank three hundred miles away. She came to Davenhall Island looking for just such a moment when someone might leak his life into hers. She was on the last boat of the day. She had a wallet of androgynous men. He'd been anchored twenty minutes at the island and was lying on deck waiting the two or three hours until the passengers' return when the dark sense of her form fell across his eyelids. Since there was no sun it wouldn't be accurate to call it a shadow. He opened his eyes and looked at her. She was poised like a kitten who'd just seen her first bird and felt her first predatory instinct. "You can go on sleeping if you want," she said to him. Thanks, he said, and dozed for a bit until he realized the boat was moving and opened his eyes and saw she was still there, the anchor cut loose and the island about sixty feet away and drifting. She took off her shirt. "You can go on sleeping," she said again. She took off the rest of her clothes and then her glasses; she knelt for a moment, unsure. He got up from his place and went over to her. He wrapped his hands around her head and pulled her face up to his; as she groped for something to hold she fell back on the deck. Sprawled on her hands and knees in the middle of that moment when land was nowhere in sight she tried to rise when he plunged himself into her. As she pounded their small wooden planet with her fists, Zeno's bones beneath them clattered in response. After that the accomplices were endless. There was at least one every couple of weeks, secretaries and teachers, roaming housewives, beachgirls and therapists and communists, orientals looking for lost uncles, community representatives and neck-

lace saleswomen, photographers, film editors, South
American beauty contest runners-up. Pretty ones, plain
ones, goofy ones, neurotics, polemicists. For a while he
was seeing one constantly, a tough little Italian from Samson on a motorcycle. She was five feet one with wild brown
hair and starlet legs and a low voice. She lived with her
folks and refused to spend the night with him; later he
learned she was sixteen. On the deck of the boat, sheathed
in fog and cut loose from shore, they stripped and lay
across his blue coat; he took her into his mouth and drank
her. They dropped into the black river where they couldn't
see each other at all and he entered whatever part of her
his fingers could find. After three months she met a magazine writer one day on the trip back from the island and
put him on the back of her motorcycle and took him down
the highway to show her mother and father. For some time
after his wild little Italian girl left he was alone, then it all
started again, with girls he sometimes thought he remembered from before. He couldn't think of a way to ask tactfully if they'd met and they were always too shy for him to
be sure. He was sure he hadn't met Kelly and Cyrise; they
worked in a casino in a resort town two borders away. Kelly
was a plump strawberry blonde with lipstick so wet the fog
seemed to streak red when it wafted past her mouth. At the
dock when she gave him her dollar he could tell she'd already been drinking; her laugh held a drenched gurgle
somewhere in its middle and she had a hard time keeping
her balance. Cyrise was a melancholy blackhaired Iranian
so voluptuously beautiful the other tourists followed her
onto the island talking to her past her friend which only
seemed to make Kelly drunker as she contemplated everything she would drink at Greek Judy's in order to stand all
the attention Cyrise received. By the time the two women
returned at nightfall Kelly was having trouble getting on
the boat. The trip back to shore sobered her a bit, but when
the women reached mainland they wound up in the boathouse having a drink with their strange captain. The gas-

lamp burned low and the three played cards. Eventually Kelly spilled out naked onto the mattress halfconscious as Cyrise lowered herself onto him with almost willful compliance, riding him while he filled his hands with her spectacular chest. She rode after almost an hour to her morose ecstasy; but not his. She captained and abandoned him, and removed herself to the mattress. Kelly babbled in the deep corner of the gaslamp shadows. I'm not done, he said to Cyrise, erect; she shrugged and looked at her friend, cocked her head a moment and nodded at Kelly slithering across the floor. He took Kelly's plump pink body and rolled it over on its front and opened it up and mounted it. Kelly sort of gawked in surprise at the ravishment behind her. "I'll hold her down for you," said Cyrise, taking her friend by the wrists. After a while Kelly started to cry out; it was difficult to tell what she was trying to say. She thrashed beneath him against the mattress while Cyrise held her fast to the floor; at some point someone kicked over the bottle of brandy. "She'll forgive me later," Cyrise explained, "we'll talk about what a beast you were, and comfort each other." When she said this he looked at her face in the light and felt himself fall into the deep Persian heat of her eyes, and everything emptied out of him and for a moment he'd forgotten that it wasn't her into whom he emptied it. He stumbled off to the other wall and could only admire in terror how she'd fucked him and left the hot white consequences of it in some other body than her own. Later that night in the dark he woke to see Kelly crashing around the boathouse in confusion, opening the door and disappearing outside. A moment later Cyrise went after her. He didn't remember later if he heard them come back. He was aware however that he had just enough of a shred of innocence left to feel guilt-stricken about having cheated at cards. The next morning the casino girls were gone, the night's only evidence the empty brandy bottle rolling on its side.

1 2

Fifteen years passed. Darkness was all over his life now. It flooded in through a secret tunnel that began in Vienna and ended in one of the aortae of his heart. Every day through the years he sailed the boat back and forth to his home. He never stepped ashore or went into town. That he had directed his innocence toward the leaving of his home, and that his fate had become to spend his life on this river between home and irrevocable escape, transporting tourists, now stranded him in the country of self-betrayal. He became the muttering depraved rivermonk of Davenhall, his white mane and beard and the crazy blast of his green eyes adding age to his appearance by the epoch; the white hair on his arms grew like fur. After a while he didn't have the girls anymore. If one came to him as he lay on the deck of his boat waiting for the tourists' return, he sent her away. He'd simply raise anchor and drift off to that moment in the fog that had first terrified him when he was innocent but which he now called home or, if he couldn't recall the word, hell. Sometimes to pass the time, he sailed the river along the island's shore over to the western tip where he could see the old black and white machine still unmanned and burping out ice into the steaming dirt. He never ventured farther out into the open expanse of the river itself; somewhat like the ancients he was afraid of what was at the end. In truth he came to recognize he was afraid of venturing beyond the edge of his life altogether. He asked himself why he'd never been a tourist, then asked himself why he'd never been anything but a tourist. His blue coat lost its buttons one by one, not at cards but invisibly, when he wasn't looking. It was as though something was telling him that though he might suppose he was gambling nothing, in fact he was gambling all the time and poorly, just as everyone gambled everything in every moment; and he was losing. One by one the buttons disappeared. He dropped obscenities into the river one by one that the skeleton bound to the boat's bottom might hear them. He almost imagined the old man reaching up over the edge of the boat and clasping him by the ankle. He almost imagined he might look down and see the fingers locked to his foot. Once, earlier on, while sailing along the island, he saw his mother. Her hair was completely gray now. She walked along the banks of Davenhall silently looking at him. She looked as though she understood he wanted an explanation but she couldn't give it. He couldn't bring himself to call her. He would have asked how she was, and if they'd spoken long enough he would have asked who she was. She walked and he glided along in tandem silence, and in the light the small white scar at the corner of her mouth sparkled like a diamond in her tooth. It made him a little heartbroken. She finally stopped in the sand and, slowly, almost fearfully, raised her hand and gave him a little wave. A little wave goodbye. He waved back. Then she turned with her arms folded in that determined way, and walked away, and he didn't see her again after that. He sat on the deck of the boat and sobbed. The next time he thought of her was when he heard from Greek Judy that she was sick. "You should come see her," Judy called from shore. Tormented and racked with guilt, he nonetheless could not bring himself to step on the island; at the edge of his boat he stared at its shore as though it was the chasm beyond the edge of a cliff. Judy left him howling in the fog. In this moment amidst the fog he howled at the world of his mother and dropped into the black river where nothing could be seen, and groped for something or someone to enter where nothing would be entered. The next time he saw Judy, his mother had recovered; but though he was relieved, his guilt wasn't mitigated until much later, when everything was mitigated, the hymen of feeling worn away like innocence. One night he thought the feeling had returned when he lay on the mattress in the boathouse and something rumbled up from inside him: something's happening to me now, he said to himself with awesome hope; but the rumbling wasn't in him at all, rather it was the shorthaired silver buffalo sweeping across the dusty lot in front of his house where the buses parked in the day. He wrested himself from the mattress just in time to see the last of the animals disappear in the night. With this he lost all hope for the feeling. He lost it through the rest of his youth. He lost it into the years that he passed as a young man, on into the years when he neared the point he couldn't even call himself young, at least not young in any sense he'd ever understood it. He lost it right up until the day he saw her on the boat, in a blue dress; on that day he rediscovered not the hope of feeling life, but life itself. This was the day his life split in two. Her name was Kara.

1 3

He had no designs on her. He might have liked to put his hands on her hair and pull her gently into his chest, but he wasn't likely to do even this. She was probably not more than fifteen years old; she could have been born the night he assumed this post on the river. At this time he'd taken on an appearance that frightened these girls; she wasn't frightened. She stood alone watching into the water, the wet deck of the boat a dark mirror in which her blue dress shone. The ends of her hair stuck to the rail as she leaned across it; he touched her shoulder tentatively. I wouldn't like you to fall in, he suggested to her. She looked at him as though he'd said something strong and startling. I used to lie to people, he went on, that the river was full of alligators. Piranha sometimes. She laughed, And they believed you? On this river, he smiled, they believe everything. He said, Have you come far? and she seemed to think about it a bit, smiling at whatever she was thinking, and only nodded. She turned back to the water and the conversation seemed over; he settled his gaze back onto the island before him. He felt oddly moved and forsaken until he heard her say, And you? Have you come far? The water was lapping over the edge of the boat; he wasn't paying attention to his speed, and the other passengers were glaring at him. He said, I've sailed fifteen years between two points less than a mile from each other. The fog came in. They were swallowed up to the blithe indifference of tourists studying their itineraries. Only the girl looked around; she said, I always feel a little lost when I can't see the stars. The hair on her arms stood on end in the chill but she didn't appear to notice. I don't think, he said, I've ever seen the stars from this boat: maybe a patch of them. Do you know the stars? he asked. Yes, she said, I know them. Are you an astronomer? he said; they both laughed. The boat continued and the fog fell behind them and the island was there then. In the last few minutes he almost could think of nothing else to say until he said, perhaps more seriously than he meant to, But why have you come here? It was something he'd never asked anyone on his boat; but then she was the first person who, in that moment when the rest of the earth disappeared, noticed. And for a second it was almost as though she hadn't heard him; and he wasn't about to repeat it. The island approached and he brushed past her to dock the boat, when she answered, To bury something. She stepped ashore and he called out, to her alone among all the others, Boat leaves in two and a half hours.

14

But she didn't return in two and a half hours. He waited
for her as the others straggled back; he looked for her in
the distance. She didn't come. Occasionally this happened,
since there was another boat later that evening. After ten
minutes passed he took his other passengers back to the
mainland; he realized only later that he'd forgotten to collect the fares.

15

On the last run of the day, he was searching the edge of
the island for her as soon as it came within sight. But she
wasn't there; patiently he sat on deck staring at the island,
rather than away from it, the noise of the nightcrowd coming from town. At this point in his life he'd become too
locked in with the rhythms of resignation and instinct to
think profoundly upon the impact of this girl. He contemplated the frequency of destiny she transmitted and what
its exact nature might be; he mused that she might be his
daughter, or his future wife. But he didn't muse on such
things for long. He knew by now these frequencies were
unnamable, in a century that tried to name everything that
was particularly unfathomable. Time passed and the rest
of the tourists found their way back; of course they were
always drunker on the evening run. He kept looking for
her. There wasn't any doubt she'd appear; there was no

other way off the island, after all, and there was nothing to do other than leave it. In fifteen years there hadn't been a single instance when someone stayed, or had been left behind. So there just wasn't any doubt she'd appear. But when they were all back, and waiting to leave, and she still wasn't there, he delayed five, ten, fifteen minutes. "The buses are waiting for us," someone said, "when are we going back?" We'll go back when I say we go back, he said. Twenty minutes passed. The passengers became incensed. When he couldn't delay any longer, he took them back without her. After returning everyone to mainland, he did what he'd never done before—sailed back to the island and spent the night there, on the boat.

1 6

He had this idea she'd be there every time he opened his eyes. He had this idea she'd be there at sunrise, cold and frightened from her night on the island. But she wasn't there at sunrise and she wasn't there when he opened his eyes; and by late morning he was the one who was hungry and cold, and there would be people on shore waiting for the first run of the day. He went back. It was a sunny day. He loaded up the boat quickly and disembarked almost immediately; he found himself searching the island for her all the way across the river. He lost track of the speed with which the boat made its way over the water; people on deck were looking around anxiously and hanging onto the rail as the boat bounced along the surface. Two people actually toppled over; husbands looked at him in outrage as they scooped their wives up off the wet wood. "Do you think

you could slow down a little?" someone asked him; he ig-
nored it. At the island she wasn't there. Gratefully the passengers pried themselves loose from the boat and climbed
ashore, leaving him with abhorring looks and sarcastic
thanks. He didn't hear them.

He paced his boat, oblivious to everything else as he'd
been since her first failure to return the day before. Now it
seemed as though this had been going on not a single day
but many days, maybe weeks. He hastily sailed the passengers back a couple of hours later, even leaving behind one
or two latecomers calling from the beach; people began
tying themselves to the boat in the manner of Zeno's skeleton tied to the boat's bottom, so they wouldn't be thrown
over from the captain's assault on the river. "My God,
man," someone said to him, "do we have to go this fast?
Everyone's frightened." There was a girl, the boatman answered, she wore a blue dress. You see a girl in a blue dress?
All of them just shook their heads a little. He turned back
to the black water; he seemed to push the boat a little
faster. Passengers clung to the vessel whitefaced, teeth
clenched.

On this trip back, or perhaps the next, he realized it.
After fifteen years it was a little unthinkable he wouldn't
have seen it immediately; but it happened several times
before he noticed. Rather, it didn't happen. The Moment.
The Moment didn't happen. That moment in which time
and space belonged utterly to his boat, destination and
point of departure disappeared. And now that he thought
about it, he realized it hadn't happened this morning
either, when he woke at the island; and now that he
thought about it, he couldn't remember it happening the
evening before. For that matter he couldn't remember it
happening since she'd left the boat. And it didn't happen
the rest of the day; and for all the fear and desolation of
every time it had happened every day over the preceding
fifteen years, now the fear and desolation of it not happening were such as to trivialize everything he'd feared before.

And he began to fear that she was not going to come back to his boat. In the way he'd told himself before that there simply couldn't be any doubt about it, now he told himself there was nothing but doubt; now every time he sailed up to the island, and all through the time he waited there, he knew she wasn't going to come. It was as though she'd taken with her that moment on the river; she'd taken it and was living in it somewhere there on the place he'd sworn to leave forever. There's a girl in a blue dress, he'd call to the tourists going into town, keep your eyes open for her. And when they came back he'd ask if they'd seen her. When they came back, he interrogated them one by one. He stood in the middle of the boat barking at them, and they shrank from him, and lied. They lied that they'd seen her in the bar, they lied that they'd seen her at the hotel, where no one but his mother had lived for over forty years. They lied they'd seen her walking along the street. They lied they'd seen her among the ice, or the graves, and those were the lies he believed most, since he'd thought of her long before he knew her, or long before she even *was*, when he lay amidst the ice as a boy; and since she had, after all, come to bury something.

The group of them sort of huddled against each other before him. After he heard their lies he didn't even see them anymore. He kept looking ashore, at the town. He paced and waited, thirty minutes, an hour. Not a single one of the passengers worked up the courage to ask when they were going back. Two hours passed; it was nearly midnight. And then, like the man who must scream to himself, if in no place other than his own heart, as he hurls himself into the chasm beyond the cliff's edge, he leapt, though it was only inches, from the edge of the boat to Davenhall Island, and went to look for her.

17

He hadn't been on the island ten minutes before all the townspeople knew he was there. Even though it was midnight, when most of them were asleep, all it took was one witness, a man or woman reading by the window perhaps, who happened to glance out his window and see the sailor with the white hair striding down the street. At which point the man or woman in the window would have jumped from his or her chair and run into the back bedroom to wake the rest of the family with the news. Ten minutes and it was all over town. The general assumption was that the appearance, after so many years, of the boy with white hair, who grew up to spend his life sailing back and forth to the home he left and had surely grown insane in the process, could only be a harbinger. Something dreadful was inevitable, a storm moving upriver from the east; or the sinking of Davenhall Island altogether, after decades of its inhabitants honeycombing its innards with tombs they didn't fill; or herds of silver buffalo sweeping everything in their path: animals and birds and boats and tourist groups and lost asian tribes in a dying ghost town.

There's a girl in a blue dress, he said to Judy in the door of her tavern.

She was wiping the counter and picking up the furniture. Racking up the glasses, casually drying her hands on an apron. She came from behind the counter and crossed the room to him.

I'm looking for a girl in a blue dress, he said again, have you seen her?

She didn't say anything for a moment, as though still listening to sentences said between them that neither uttered; and then she turned from him just slightly, and brought her hand flying across his face.

He staggered a little, his eyes flared.

"You son of a bitch," she whispered, "your own mother might have died and you wouldn't budge off that God damned boat. All those years and you had no use for anything in this town, and now the thing that brings you back is a girl in a blue dress."

He swallowed hard but steeled himself: That's right, he told her.

She wiped her hands some more on her apron, though the hands were already dry and the apron was already wet. "I haven't seen any girl," she just said, "don't worry about it, there will be other girls." She added, "You should be careful, these are modern times. You should be careful." She almost laughed at him.

That isn't what this is, he just said. I wouldn't have come for that, if that was what this was. Then he turned and walked out of the bar.

Out in the street a gust almost blew him over. He pulled his faded blue coat around him and the wind ripped the last of the gold buttons off its stitches. Across mainstreet was the hotel where he was born and raised; he was startled to see a light in his mother's window, and the form of someone watching him. He only turned up his collar and headed toward the other end of the island. He strolled up mainstreet through the dust of the wind that was silver like razors; he went from door to door rattling them on their hinges to find them locked. He put his elbow to the windows and one by one knocked them in: this was the sound of Davenhall, the shriek of the wind and the blistering of windows, all up and down the street. The Chinese hadn't been wrong then to believe a storm had come to them from the river. Families huddled in their houses waiting for it to pass; finally the storm reached the ice, where it stood before the white and black machine that never stopped churning. In the dark, in no starlight at all, the blocks hurtled invisibly by, ejected into the night air; he heard them break but he believed it was only the echoes of bro-

ken windows, not even his broken windows but someone
else's in some other city, people all over the night searching
madly for those who transmitted the vague and unpersua-
sive frequency of destiny, not even this night but some
other night that came before, from which the sound of
breaking windows reached him only now like the light of
novae. Ice busting in the dirt. The storm turned north. He
left the ice machine and headed for the cemetery. To bury
something, he said to himself. At the cemetery the wind
was harder, because it faced the east of the river where the
other side could never quite be seen, but from which came
the red trains on the tracks high above the water. There
the trees were bare of obituaries, the graves silent. He stood
in the marsh that lay shadowstunned and bleeding up
worms between his feet, and faced the sky. He could not
call her name because he didn't know it. It isn't the time to
look for her, not at night, he said to himself; and yet only
in the dark would he have found the courage and desperation. Only in the dark would the frequency have been so
far beyond denial. It isn't the time, he said to himself, to
look for her body in the river, if she tried to escape by
swimming; or to look for the remains of a stray boat, if she
believed there was any other boat to take her back. But
there are no other boats, he said to himself. And he wasn't
ready yet to accept that she wasn't here.

There was only one other place to look, of course.

He wondered what he'd say. He practiced confessions in
his mind. He recalled all the confessions he'd made up as a
boy, all the confessions he'd put into the mouths of the
girls he met on the river. Those confessions didn't apply.
Those were confessions that begged never to be forgiven.
This was not a confession offered to or received from any
lover. This would be a confession to a woman with gray
hair who had borne him. She wasn't in the window anymore when he reached mainstreet again, but the light was
still on, the only one in the hotel: he had an overwhelming
premonition that he would mount the stairs of the hotel,

reach the room and find the door open, with the two of them, the girl and his mother, talking, waiting for him grimly. He understood that in fact the destiny of this girl in the blue dress had been to bring him back to face something, no doubt his own failure, from which he had formulated contempt not for himself, who deserved it, but his past and his home, which did not. He wasn't sure what else there might be to face unless it was the night he had left, and the echo, like the light of a nova, of the man he'd found dead at his mother's feet.

It had been an old man. Even old he'd still been a huge man, with red hair that had turned gold with the years, like the way leaves die.

Now the man who had white hair his whole life came in the hotel and, remembering hard, stumbled to the bottom of the stairs and found his way up to the next floor. He came down the hall to his mother's door. It wasn't open as he had foreseen, but it wasn't closed either, not entirely. He could push it open, and he did.

The girl with the blue dress was not there. His mother stood in the middle of the room, gazing long into her memories. She wasn't standing in exactly the same place she'd been fifteen years before, but it was close. And in much the same way as years before, there was the passage of probably five seconds before she turned away from her memories to look at him.

1 8

For several seconds, actually it seems to her like almost a minute, she knows he's there in the door. In a way she's been expecting him. She saw him in the street an hour ago as he rampaged among the windows. She doesn't know why he's here but she knows it's nothing small that could bring him back onto the island. And once on the island it was probably not possible that he wouldn't come here and see her now. So she's not surprised. But she waits a few moments before she turns to look at him. There's no recrimination in it.

He's shocked, she can tell, that she's become so old. What did you think, she says to herself, that time ticks to the clock of your memories? Her hair's as white now as his ever was. We look more like mother and son now, she says to herself, than we ever did.

It so happens that she's been thinking and remembering the same as he, remembering and thinking of that night. It so happens she hears the same echoes of the old man who came to die at her feet. Fifteen years later she hears his voice as though he's still here on the floor; she hears him talking at this very moment and so does her son who stands in the doorway in silence. The mother and son look at each other and together they listen to the voice of a man who hasn't been alive for fifteen years; neither mother nor son knows where the voice comes from now, and in fact both assume it's only a voice in their heads. Neither of them believes that the voice, recreated from the memory of what it might be saying to them if it was actually speaking at this moment, is now saying to each of them the same thing. Neither believes they hold the ghost of this long dead stranger in common.

You remember me, the voice can be heard saying. Well

maybe you don't, maybe you forgot me immediately after I left your sight as surely as I continued to remember you for the rest of my life. It changed the world, my seeing you. Literally it changed it but that's, you know, another story. Maybe it only changed *my* world. It only changed *my* Twentieth Century. Your world, your century, that's another story. It was in Vienna. You were in a window. You were only a girl then, I don't guess more than fifteen years old. The year was 1938, when we held the body of the long dead Twentieth Century in common.

1 9

My name is Banning Jainlight, the voice continues. The year is 1917: I am born. I remember it. I remember leaving her, the rush of it, my mother banning me from her, though it wasn't she who named me. That was my other mother. I had two.

I remember the long fall down such a short red passageway, as I fell I saw troops on the march, fields afire and black cannons in the sun, riots in the alleys of Russia and messiahs in the dunes of eastern deserts, and one fallen angel after another pulling himself up onto the face of a new hour. First one hand is visible then the second, nails grasping desperately for a hold of something, then the top of the head comes into sight, then the glistening brow, the harsh straining eyes, the grimacing mouth as he pulls himself up and finally hoists his body the rest of the way, lying there on the face of a new hour heaving for air. After the first, the rest come one by one, the fallen angels. They've come to change everything. Not just the countryside. They haven't come just to build a city or two. Cities can be built in any hour at all. They aren't here just to construct a canal or a bridge in the moonlight. They've come to change *everything*. They've come to change the very act of selfportraiture, disassembling it and then reconstructing it from some new vantage point of the soul, some corner of the soul's room that's been blocked eight thousand years by a chair we always thought we needed, a tablelamp we were always told was some heirloom too valuable to move, let alone give away. Out with the fucking chair. Out with the tablelamp that burned out long ago. *Everything*: they've come to disassemble and then reconstruct, from some blind spot in the middle of the room that's always obstructed by something no matter where you stand, the clock. A small nearsighted German with wild white hair, who cannot count the very numbers from which he writes his wild new poetry, just makes it over the top now, catching his breath.

That big redheaded American galoot fumbling his way up after him, that's me. When the German's finished, I'll just be getting started.

I see all this at the moment I'm coming out of my mother. I'm no sooner born than at the end of my rope. I pass out awhile and when I come to, a few things have been switched around on me and it's a while before I catch on.

It's 1917, and the clock is ticking.

20

It's 1925 and I'm eight. I live on my father's ranch in west Pennsylvania, near the Ohio border, in the nicest house I'll ever know, white and blue, sound and certain. But . . . doesn't this sound like I'm *visiting?* "I live on my father's ranch. . . ." The house faces south. My father's name is Philip; Jainlight's an English name. He's a burly little tyrant, a tyrant to the stable hands, the Indians worst of all. I never see kindness from him to anyone except once or twice when we go into town and he'll buy a little present for one of the women strolling up and down the walk, assuming Alice isn't there of course.

Alice is the woman he's married to. She's the woman I know as my mother, and if that *really* sounds like I'm visiting, you're starting to get the picture. I also have two older brothers, Oral and Henry. Oral's six years older and Henry's four. They act like my father and look like their mother. Oral treats the old men who tend to the horses worse than my father does, he probably believes they're our slaves. Henry might grow up to do something *really* evil like run for political office, if he were destined to grow up at all, which is something I'll take care of later on. He sweet-talks Alice and steals money from her. The fact is that even at eight I realize not only that he's stealing her money but that she knows it and likes it. Alice grew up in Pittsburgh and came to my father's house so she could fill it up with bric-a-brac from the Old World. She wears her hair in tight little vaguely purplish curls. Her once-darkness has been passed on to her two oldest sons, and Oral has on his mouth the small birthmark that Alice has a little higher on her cheek. The only thing I share with any of this family is my father's red hair.

I'm visiting, like I say. I'm a tourist. I don't know when I begin to realize this, I think at this point I still haven't realized it in full. I know of course that my brothers hate me, and my father's indifferent though no more or less so than to my brothers or my mother or anyone else except the women he sees in the city. Alice doesn't neglect me in terms of her obligations. When I'm sick she's there to take care of me, and she attends to my needs no less than to Oral's or Henry's. But she's cordial, you know? She's *hospitable*. A hospitable mother, like a concierge in a foreign country. I think she must have had some doubts of her own right from the beginning. But when does a kid figure his family isn't quite right? How old does he have to become, and how smart? I don't know yet that it's just me that's a tourist. I figure it's everybody.

21

I just know I'm doing something wrong, and it's about this time I'm beginning to have an idea what it is. I'm big. At eight I'm two years bigger than normal and getting bigger yet. In a couple of years I'll be bigger than my father, and in a couple of years after that I'll be bigger than either of my brothers. It's a bigness that's gross in this family, it calls to their attention how much at odds I am with them. My hands are big and my feet are big, I have long arms. I have this big face, this large open face, that leads people to the conclusion I'm a bit of an idiot. It's a bigness that conveys brutishness without any compensating intelligence. I mean, I come to understand all this later. Now I'm only eight. But I already sense that I'm not only at odds with the family but sometimes my own nature, and later I'll under-

stand the ways in which my own nature's at odds with itself.
When I lie in bed at night reading all the books from Alice's
library downstairs, I like to think it's the act of a small boy,
I trick myself into thinking this right up to the moment I
rip the book down the binding. It just happens, I'm lying
there reading and the bigness just comes out, the bigness
that the act of reading means to deny, it comes out in my
hands and there I am on my bed with half a book in each
hand, and pages flying around my head. Then Henry runs
downstairs to tell Alice I'm tearing up her books. Later I'll
come to read with the books propped against the bedpost,
untouched by me, at arm's length from an uncontrollable
bigness.

As it happens I'll make use of the bulk later. As it happens I'll learn to hide in it sometimes, move it others. I'll
use it to beat any fool to a near faretheewell, and for a few
minutes I'll have an especially good time doing it. And if I
appear stupid to some then I'll use that too, to beat them
as well, people who presume themselves pretty sharp and
presume they speak a language someone like me can't understand. Except I do understand, and by being the tourist
of their lives I become the spy of their secrets; you'll see
what I mean. Of course sometimes it helps to drive the
point home a little, drool at social events or occasionally
let one arm jerk wildly at my side for no reason at all.
People turn from these displays, and when they do I've
become so big and stupid as to be invisible.

At the age of eight I sit with my family through edgy
dinner conversations. Food drops into my father's gut like
paratroopers to French soil almost twenty years later, all of
which I can see at any moment I like from one of the nine
windows in my bedroom. At eight I'm not yet a lost cause,
I'm still trying to make a decent impression on life. Trying
and trying, and all they can do at the dinner table is look at
me as if to say, But where in God's name did this lug come
from? Alice and Oral and Henry. My father just tramps
along in the wake of his appetites, meat and potatoes

and beans, oblivious to us. As I'll come to learn, it's a way he has with all his appetites, the forbidden ones most particularly.

2 2

On Christmas Day in my tenth year the valley's all snow. I can see it from any one of my bedroom windows. This morning my brothers and I get up and go out to the barn with my father to check out the horses. The horses are the main business of my father's ranch, and these winters it's a lot of trouble to make certain we don't wake up every day to a lot of frozen horses. There doesn't seem much doubt to anyone at this time that Oral and Henry will grow up and take over the ranch after my father's gone, flip a coin for the house or give it to whichever of the two's been lucky enough to find a woman foolish enough to spend her life with him, stick Alice in some little cottage to be built on the other side of the stable, build another house for the brother who's left. That's the plan anyway. Don't know where I fit into it. As it happens one of them won't grow up at all, and there won't be any ranch house to take over for the one who does. On the Christmas Day of my tenth year we're still six Christmases away from all that.

The horses are all right and we come back to the house. I'm the last one in. The fact is I like the horses and like to spend time out there with them. Two or three I'm particularly fond of, a spotted one and a white and a butterscotch. But now I'm in the house which is warm and filled with the smell of the fire and food. In the kitchen is our cook, Minnie, who's been with the Jainlight household since before I

was born. She's from Virginia. She shows me what kindness she feels she can get away with, but she also regards
me with a confusion that's only another clue, among many
I can't understand, as to the truth of my presence and past.
Helping her is the Indian woman Gayla. Minnie tends to
send her out of the kitchen when I'm around. These Vir-
ginians don't like the idea of mixing up white and colored
before a boy's old enough to understand there's a difference. Gayla's fairly light, actually. She lives on the outskirts
of my father's land with some of the other Indians. It isn't
her real name, her real name is something unpronouncea-
ble. She grew up with an Indian mother and sister out in
Oklahoma, the white father having disappeared no later
than he first showed up, and she came to Pennsylvania
around the same time her sister named Rae married a white
newspaperman near Chicago. Like a lot of Indians or half-
breeds, Gayla could be any age at all.

As always when I go into the living room, the talk between my mother and my brothers seems to stop a little,
and then they go on as before, adjusting to the interjection
of my bigness into all their little coziness. The tree is
bright. It's green and silver. A fire roars in the hearth. I sort
of shove my way into the festivities. Sometimes I say something and usually Alice will ask me what I mean by it. I
could say the most routine thing and Alice acts like I'm
talking in runes. "Nice fire," I might say, and Alice's face
goes still and she finally answers, "Well Banning, I'm not
really sure what you intended by that remark." Actually,
it'll turn out to be a pretty funny remark at that. But all I
know at this moment is that I'm a kid who wants to be a
part of Christmas here and I can't seem to get in. Whatever
little breach of family bonds is left open for me to enter, I
don't fit through, and there I am outside, in the middle of
the living room. Henry has a little set he got for Christmas,
with a fort and men, and after a while when Oral gets bored
with it Henry relents out of need for another player: he's
Santa Ana with ten thousand troops and I'm a hundred

and fifty Texans defending the mission. I'm big enough
that I just reach across the battlefield and my arm wipes
out six or seven of Henry's battalions. "You jackass," he
shrieks, *"you're* supposed to die! *All* of you is supposed to
die!" Henry packs up the set and goes back to talking with
Oral and Alice. I head upstairs to my bedroom; on the way
I knock over this or that of Alice's bric-a-brac, reducing the
Old World to rubble. A chair or a tablelamp. "For God's
sake," Oral says scornfully. Henry shakes his head with
contempt. Alice sighs, deep and wounded. Out with the
fucking chair anyway, I say back, though not to them, or
to anyone who can hear me for years to come.

23

I get to the top of the stairs, the smoke of Christmas fire
and smell of food wafting up after me, and lumber down
the hall and crash through my bedroom door. I knock a
few more things over and sit in the dark of my bedroom
awhile. I don't remember if I cry. Well yes I do remember.
But I sit still awhile and soon I forget about it. I sit in the
middle of the room in the dark and look out the nine windows of my bedroom. Some I look through more than
others. Later I'll realize just how few windows all the other
rooms of the world have. I can't get over how only my
bedroom has just the right number of windows. It's possible
of course that I just can't take a hint. It's possible they've
put me in such a room with all these windows for a reason.
The better to hurl myself out one of them. But instead I
just take in everything I see from them. In one I see the
year of my birth and in one I see the year of my death,

though I see neither my birth nor my death precisely. In the seven windows in between I see the seventy or so years that are my time. Not my life but my time.

And I'm sitting there and I hear this sound. It's the sound of my time. I'd expect it to be a roar, like something up from the middle of the world, or I'd expect it to be the clatter of machinery. Or the cacophony of guys shouting, in southern fields or beerhalls or cadre meetings. Maybe the good taut yank of a rope snapping in Louisiana, or the soft wet smack of a head that falls from a German axe. The whispers of Russians selling each other out, or just that abysmal yawn of physical matter cracking like a nut, and everything around it falling in. That's what I'd expect this sound to be. And it isn't anything like that, wouldn't you know it. Nothing like that at all. It's this high vicious squeal, like a rodent would make, or a bat. And it comes from no place in the sky or the ground, no place outside; it's down under me. And I look around my feet but it isn't there, I pick up the chair and check and it isn't there. I can stand on the other side of the room and it's still under me, somewhere under the place in my belly where I was strung up to my mother before she bore me. It's a whistle in my bowels.

I write the first thing I've ever written tonight. I'm watching the Twentieth Century through my windows, though I have no way of knowing yet if it's my Twentieth Century or another, if the 1917 I see through one window or the 1928 through this window or the 1989 through that last window are the ones I know or have known or will know. So I open the windows and then I just see the snow, and I write a story about the white horse in the barn. The snow is blue in the moon and the drainage ditches my father built three years ago are gurgling a little in the light, the ice breaking up a little, pretty unusual for a Christmas night. Wonder where such a hot jungle blast might be coming from that it breaks up the ice and makes the ditches flow so that in the moon they're silver strings unraveling across the valley? I write a story about the white horse as it runs in the snow, which of course it wouldn't do. The snow comes down but the ditches keep on unraveling with a heat that insists upon itself, like blood that won't stop coursing through a body after the heart has ended pumping it; and in the white of the night's snowfall and the silver of the running drainage all that's to be seen of a white horse is the red of her eyes. It flits across the valley like fireflies. It burns in the snow until the horse sleeps, freezing where it stands.

24

It's the next year and I wake one morning to the thought of a woman I've never seen and cannot even remember five seconds later. The only thing that remembers her is in the middle of me, and it won't stop remembering until it spills its memory across the bedsheets. From this point onward I am erect like America. At the end of the year my cock is one of the few things in America that doesn't crash ground-ward without effort.

2 5

It's 1931 and I'm fourteen. My father's ranch is hurt by the Depression but not wiped out. Around us farms fail left and right, the ones financed by the banks. There's unrest in the valleys, the farmers and their hands seized by the malice of hopelessness. Every evening there's smoke in the hills, and sometimes looking from my window I think the hills are shifting across the horizon. And then I realize it's only that they're alive with desperate men, thousands of them. In the nights when their hands are filled with torches it's as though the world's on fire, but I'll come to see such fires the rest of my life. They're there in the streets of Vienna seven years from now, I can already see them. And the smoke I smell, and the blood in my fourteen-year-old nostrils, is from a fire to come two years from now, fire and blood by my own hands. These fires might seem different, hopeless fires and fires of my own liberation and fires of triumph in the streets of Vienna. But the hate of them is the same, and the heat's cruel and cold.

I lean out my window and breathe myself as full of it as my lungs can take.

My father puts rifles in the arms of the stablehands and the Indians. They'll fight if the hills come to the edge of the ranch. My father's happy enough to kill anything that sighs within earshot. It may or may not be he's killed things before. Given my own talents, I can guess.

The hills are hungry, and I don't doubt they'd kill every horse in the stable. Until nothing's left but the red of their eyes in the snow.

When the crisis ends my father goes into town to drink. Oral and Henry go along. I wake at about four in the morning to the sound of our motorcar pulling up the road, and Oral and Henry propping father under his arms and bring-

ing him in the house down below me. He moans in the
living room. Oral and Henry laugh about a girl they met in
a speakeasy. I don't get back to sleep until around dawn,
when Oral comes into my room and tells me to get started
in the stables.

26

I'm fifteen. In the mornings I lurch into the kitchen, with
the middle of me that carries its memories of dreamwomen
as hard as steel and big as a president's monument. The
family literally turns away from the sight in shock. Alice
has some sort of palpitations by the counter with the flour
canisters, and my brothers seethe in fury. Only my father
stares with perplexity, his mouth dropping slightly and for-
getting to chew. This is, for the rest of them, the most
terrifying manifestation of my size yet. It's almost more
than they can live with in the same house, I think.

27

Things I write now are also more than Alice can abide: she finds them in my bedroom. For someone in a state of nearly paralyzed mortification she manages to read every word. She takes the matter up with my father. They have a family council of sorts, my father and Alice and my two brothers. They analyze the situation. They speculate as to my psychology and morality and stability. The brothers lobby hard for an institutional solution, but my father settles for a whipping out in the barn and leaving me to sleep with the horses. "Try not to have intimate relations with any of them while you're out here," he says when he's done. His anger seems more personal than the others. "You're one to talk," I have the nerve to answer back, and he beats me some more.

It's 1933. A faultline runs through the epoch. Over here we've got Roosevelt, over there they've got this guy in Berlin. They've got this guy in Russia.

I'm sixteen. The things I see from the windows of my bedroom make less and less sense. Soon a new moment will come with a faultline of its own, and I'll step to the other side. And on that side it'll be a long time—perhaps not until the moment I die at the feet of an old woman in a little town on an island I cannot name—before I see anything so clearly again.

It's you I mean, of course, and it began that afternoon in Vienna when you were still a young girl. And no dream-woman I ever woke to, before or after, touched you. Nor did I, though it changed everything just to see you, no less than did the small German with wild white hair who wiped the clock clean of numbers altogether.

But that's later. This is tonight, in 1933, on my father's ranch. Or rather its outskirts, where the Indians live.

And tonight is the night.

28

Henry comes into my room and wakes me up. It's about eleven o'clock. The moon is whole and though I've pulled the curtains across all nine of my windows the moon's bright enough that they're like nine white patches on the walls. When I awake Henry's got his face about two inches from mine. "Hey soldier," he says. It takes me a few seconds to realize it's the middle of the night. "You awake?" he says. "How's the machine?" I sit up in the dark rubbing my face, still groggy. "What machine?" I say, and he says, "You know, the old monster."

"What's going on?" I say.

"How old are you Banning?" he says. He knows how old I am, or at least he has a general idea. I sit listening a moment, the rest of the house is quiet. Henry's being very friendly. His voice is big brotherly.

"What's going on," I say again.

"A lady, Banning," Henry answers, "a lady for Banning tonight." He pulls the blanket off the bed and throws me my pants off the dresser. "Come on."

I'm suspicious of his big brotherliness, and I'm also seduced by it. I've wanted it for a long time, longer than I've wanted to know a woman, though I've been wanting that pretty strongly for the last year or two. "Where are we going?" I say to him.

"We're going to see a lady friend, don't you want to see

a lady friend? See if that machine fits in something besides
your hand. You're going to be popular, little brother."

"But who is it?"

"Are you going to get dressed?" Slowly I start pulling on
my pants, there in the dark of the bedroom, nine white
patches swimming around me. "She's a friend of Oral's and
mine. Father's, too. Sort of the Jainlight men's all-around
friend."

"But why? Why's she a friend?"

Henry pauses and says, "We pay her to be a friend. I've
got the money right here in my pocket. You'll see." I don't
doubt he stole it from Alice like he always does. "Here's
your shirt," he says, pulling one out of the drawer, and
then he leaves the room. I grab my shoes and follow him,
not entirely sure about any of it, but unwilling to let escape
the prospect of manhood and brotherhood all in the same
night. He's at the bottom of the stairs when I'm at the top.
He looks up and puts his finger to his lips. A dim light
comes from the living room. Holding my shoes I move
down the stairs barefooted. In a chair in the living room
Alice sleeps with a comforter pulled up around her chin.
The tight little curls around her head begin to droop across
her brow. Henry approaches her, standing over her, then
looks over his shoulder at me and gestures to the back of
the house. I move through the kitchen as quickly as possible. I bang into the table and knock a pan from the stove,
catching it in midair.

Oral's waiting outside the back door. His hands are
shoved deep in his pockets, but actually it's a warm night.
Henry comes out the back door behind me and nods at
Oral, and Oral without saying a word signals us to follow
him. We head off with the valley before us bleached blue
from the full moon, and the fences of the ranch jag across
our view like white stitches on a wound. We make our way
past the barn and the stables and I can hear the horses
rustle and speak to the sound of our feet. None of us says
anything until I say, once we're past the stables, "Where

are we going?" and then we're quiet again since neither of
them answers me. Finally I say something like, "She does
it for money?" and then Oral says, "Will you keep quiet?"
and Henry says, "That's it, Banning, she does it for money.
Like I said." Then we go on some more until we're to the
outskirts of the ranch.

This is where the Indians live. There's not much left of
them at this point, one family that's made up of a mother
and father and two small kids and a grandfather, living in a
single hut; and in another hut an old woman whose man
used to work on the ranch before he died; and in the third
hut Gayla, the halfbreed kitchen help. It's Gayla's hut we
go to, in the dark. We're all looking around over our shoulders, though I'm not certain what it is we're looking for.
The moon splashes on the trees like milk. I don't know
what to make of it that Oral takes a screwdriver from his
pocket and snaps off the lock on Gayla's door. It takes
about as much force as opening a bottle. The two of them
burst into the hut and I hear some muffled sound from
inside. "Will you get in here," I hear Henry saying to me,
and I go in.

There's not much to see in the hut. The moon lights it
up clearly and I can see the Indian woman on a bed in the
corner. She's holding her arm across her eyes, maybe from
the light, but maybe from something else she doesn't want
to see, I don't know. "Close the door," Oral says, and then
he says it again. I close it a little ways, but leave it open
enough so I can see her. Oral's got her by the arms and
Henry's saying to me, "All right, soldier, all right," and he
keeps gesturing for me to come closer. I stand where I am.
"You can tear her clothes off if you want," I hear Henry
say. Gayla cries out. The other Indians in the other huts
must hear all this, but no one's running over to see what's
going on. It's easy to picture them huddling in their beds
waiting for the whole thing to be done. When I don't move
from where I stand, Henry tears her clothes off.

"I thought she does it for money," I say.

"It is for money," Henry insists, "it's just part of the game, doing it this way. It's just a kind of play, you know. Like one of those things you write all the time. Come on now. Get that monster of yours ready. We'll warm things up for you."

"Me first," I hear Oral command. Henry hesitates a moment and then obeys, taking Gayla by the arms while Oral takes her first. Oral's finished in about twenty seconds. He groans and rocks back on his feet, and then nods to Henry and holds her by the arms while Henry takes his turn. Henry takes a little longer. Gayla's stopped crying and in the shadow of Henry's body I don't see her face right now, and I'm thinking maybe it's a game at that. Henry finishes and collapses back for a moment, then gasps, "All right, little brother, all yours." But I can't quite move from where I'm standing, and after a moment Oral says to me, "Come on, I'm not going to hold her all night." Henry says, "We went to a lot of trouble on this for you, little brother. Don't let us down here." Slowly I take down my pants and approach the woman. I'm not quite ready. My body reflects the confusion of my head, neither up nor down. But I come up to her, exposed to her, and when I do her silence shatters, and she screams.

She screams. I think at first she's screaming at the size of me, and I feel humiliated and furious. For a moment part of me wants to hit her. And just as I'm thinking this, Henry says to me, "You can hit her if you want. She expects it," and that makes me stop. Because I know everything's wrong. When she screams she isn't looking at the middle of me, she's looking in my eyes. It's my face she's crying out at. And the scream isn't a physical one, it's from somewhere else in her, and the tears are running down her cheeks, and her fear is *tender*.

And that's when I know.

Don't ask me how I know. I don't know how. There's nothing in her face that would give me any idea, maybe a certain wideness around the eyes. Maybe a flatness of the nose. There's nothing about her that looks anything like me, as far as I can see, though if I could see further maybe there'd be something in the mouth. Maybe our hands would share the same lines, maybe our shoulders would slope the same way. Maybe her footsteps would fit exactly into mine, if mine were left in the winter snow. But she could fit so completely into me that I could never expect to know how I once fit so completely into her. Anyway, I know. I know at this moment.

And . . . things are jumbled now. They're slow and they're fast, and it's hard to tell what's happening between all of us in this dark hut, where what's happening in our heads and what's happening in our hands is the same. I'm not sure when Oral and Henry know that I know, exactly.

Big is the violence in me.

It has a sound, the slosh of Henry's brains when I take his head in my hands. I suppose in this last moment before his ears run with the pulp of membrane and blood he understands that I know. The scream from him, well, it's not much of a scream, really. A bit of a yelp. It cuts off mid-pain. If I were a bit more selfpossessed in this moment I'd prolong it a bit, to make sure he knows that I know. To make sure there's not a *misunderstanding*. I drop him from my hands and he crumples to the floor. Oral looks at the heap of Henry there in the moonlight and the expression in his eyes is very satisfying to me. He looks from Henry to me, his eyes wide as dollars, and he bolts for the door. I catch him long before he gets there. He's screaming so as to be heard clear across the valley, but the sound of it just can't travel fast enough to make any difference.

I'm a little more selfpossessed now. I take one of his hands in mine and it only takes a squeeze or two to shatter every bone in it. I'm a little more selfpossessed. "Don't mind me, Oral," I say, "I'm just a big stupid boy who's a sucker for a good joke. That's all this is, isn't it, just a good joke. A good joke for the big stupid boy." Oral's sputtering unintelligibly at what I've done to his hand. "I could do it to your neck too," I say to him, "and unless you think you might like that, you have to tell the big stupid boy all about it." I shake him by the neck long enough that he can begin to hear in his head the shiver of his spinal cord.

He tells me. He tells the big stupid boy all about it, and it's quite a good joke at that. Everyone was in on it except the big boy. Oral, of course, isn't making complete sense, Oral isn't telling the joke in an absolutely clear way. He mixes up the sequence a bit. But even a big stupid boy can figure it out, even I can put it together. The way I put it together, my father fathered two of us, so to speak. Maybe even the same night, for all I can tell from Oral's gibberish. Maybe the same night seventeen years ago he conceived a child with Alice, the way I put it together. At any rate he left the bed of his wife not having had nearly enough of a woman, and lit out for the Indian huts where he left his seed in Gayla as well; both women became pregnant. Both women carried their child in them within a mile of each other. For a while my father must have thought the joke was on him. Over and over he tried to send the Indian away, over and over she returned to the huts. Alice regarded Gayla's pregnancy as a sort of dreadful coincidence, maybe she thought the joke was on her. She held steadfast against acknowledging the truth of the matter even as anyone else could and did. Oral's struggling now to explain it, he's squirming in the balance of my wrath and curiosity. The way I put it together, both women gave birth within a mile and six hours of each other, with an orderly and almost precise clockwork that might have been the orderly and precise Nineteenth Century having one last good joke on the Twentieth. Alice's labor was tortured, her child dead. "Come on now Oral," I'm saying, "come on. I just *know* this is where it gets good." Oral spits and slobbers. Alice lies unconscious struggling for life. My father hits on the masterstroke by which he solves the problem of his bastard quarter-Indian child who's been born on this very same day and doing it in a fashion practically befitting a

white man. And it's damn shrewd of my father at that. For
such an unstable man, I mean. For such an unstable man
he somehow figured that the Indian woman who kept coming back every time he sent her away would let him take
the child and never say a word. He somehow figured that
if the wife he cheated lived long enough she would accept
the child in awful silent suspicion never voicing the slightest question that wanted no answer. I don't know how he
figured it, to be honest. So my father rides to the Indian
huts and takes Gayla's son, and returns with the baby to
the ranch and places it in the crib where another child has
died only hours before. "Who would have figured it, Oral?"
I say to him there in the dark of the hut with the sound of
my mother sobbing at my side. "But you're absolutely
right, it's a fine joke." He crumples to the floor like Henry
did, though life still moans from him.

The Indian woman has stopped sobbing but still holds
her face in her hands. Part of me still wants to hit her,
I want to make her tell me why she let him take me
from her. The idea I hate most is that she might have
actually thought it was better for me, to live in a white
and blue, sound and certain house, in a room with nine
windows. She might have thought it. I take the blanket
from the bed and put it around her. "I'll be back," I tell
her.

29

I tell it to her but maybe she doesn't hear me. I'm already halfway out the door, crossing the outskirts of the ranch with the moon white and huge above the blue hills. I'm driving the bigness of me across the stables toward the house in big strides, I'm not thinking at all. I'm not calculating anything, I'm just doing. They're sleeping in the house, they don't have any idea what's coming for them.

A big surprise, that's what.

I get to the back of the house, I damn near tear the door off the hinges. It isn't an act of fury, fury isn't part of it anymore. It's more deliberate than fury yet more instinctive than deliberation. I come into the kitchen and Minnie comes running in from the room off to the side where she sleeps. Even in the dark she takes one look at me and knows. The terror comes from her like a blast from a furnace. Even in the dim light of the moon I can see the whiteness of terror's blast.

"It's Minnie," I laugh, "it's Minnie from Old Virginie."

She dashes back into the house. I let her go, I can't be bothered with her. She's starting to yell through the silence of the house but it doesn't matter. It's only fair actually, it gives them a chance.

Alice is no longer in the living room chair wrapped in a comforter. By now she's retired upstairs. That's where I'm headed. At the top is my father, stumbling out of his bedroom. He's in the hall when I get to the top of the stairs. His tyranny doesn't allow him really to understand what's happening at this moment. He thinks it's something he can take care of with a rifle, or with a beating in the barn with the horses. "What the hell is this, in the middle of the night?" he says to me.

"Hello father," I say to him. I'm all the way up to him

before he has the sense to step backward. I catch him as he momentarily loses his footing. It takes only part of my strength to lift him from his place and throw him against the wall. It's a fucking nuisance that he doesn't wise up, I have to keep throwing him against walls. It's just absolutely necessary that he understands this, I can't feel good about it otherwise. Making him angry is useless to me and I have to keep throwing him against walls until the anger goes away. When the anger goes away he'll finally start to fear for something and when he finally starts to fear for something then he'll finally start to fear for everything, and then I can feel good about it. Alice is screaming in the bedroom doorway.

My father and I are in my bedroom doorway and I toss him into the middle of the room. I'm even working up a sweat at this point. "I got the joke," I say to him. It's useless. I don't think I'm going to make him fear for everything no matter how long or hard I try. Annoyed, I throw him one more time through the first of the nine windows, throw him out into the night and all the way to 1917. I have to be satisfied with the sound of his body hitting part of the roof below my window, the sound of its bounce as he tumbles onto the ground. It's hard to make out in the dark if he's alive. I have to settle for the odds that his back is broken, maybe in many places.

Alice is still screaming in her bedroom doorway which is between my father's bedroom and my own. Downstairs Minnie sounds hysterical. I go into the hall and now it's Alice I pick up and throw. She hits the wall pretty hard, her tight little purple curls all undone now. "I got the joke now," I tell her. "I got the joke, and isn't this the way I was supposed to act sooner or later? Sooner or later I was going to be too big to be anything but monstrous." Her whimper at the base of the wall is irritating, and her face is all snot and blood. "When you took me and named me, was it meant to be your blow against all of us? Did you think you were letting yourself in on the joke with a love that wasn't love and a trust that wasn't trust? Here's your monster." I pick her up gently this time, she screams at the touch. I set her on her bed. "Oral and Henry took me to fuck my own mother tonight," I say to her, "but the ones who wound up fucked were them. I killed Henry, mother." I'm still used to calling her that. She screams again when I tell her this and then starts wailing uncontrollably because she knows I'm not lying about it. "I killed him," I tell her, "and I'm sorry he's not alive so I can kill him again." Now I pick her up and put her over my shoulder and take her down the stairs; she's almost in shock now. Minnie's back in the kitchen wringing her hands; when she sees me with Alice on my back she flings herself out the back door and I can see her running through the moonlight. I drop Alice on the ground outside not far from where my father writhes on his back. I go back in the house and it takes me ten minutes to break up some furniture and build a good pile in the middle of the living room. I hunt up some heating oil from the side room where Minnie sleeps and some of the gasoline my father uses in his motorcar. I pour it all around the house until there's nothing left to pour.

The house goes up so fast I'm barely out the door in time. A white and blue, sound and certain light.

In the light of the fire and the light of the moon Alice just lies on the ground. Philip still writhes where he fell.

They've never seen such a light.

30

She isn't there when I get back for her. Maybe she didn't hear me when I told her I'd be back. But she isn't there at any rate. None of the Indians is there. Indians that have been living here longer than I've been alive have up and left everything, all the huts deserted. The pyre of Jainlight rises like Babel in the north. In the dead of morning the shouts of the whole countryside to the sight of it can be heard. The shouts and laughter, the applause to God.

God had nothing to do with it.

I walk on, the moonlight before me turned dappled by the new clouds. I leave the valley. I'm ashamed that I've succumbed to the monstrous nature of a monstrous body. I would like to leave that nature in the valley behind me. If I could leave my body with it, I would. Eight miles out of Pittsburgh I catch a train going east.

31

I'm sitting in this boxcar with four other guys there in the dark. We're not there very long because in the station at Pittsburgh men hired by the railroad go through all the cars and clear out the bums and hobos and vagabonds, which in 1933 must be about half the people in America. So as we're coming into Pittsburgh we have to jump from the train, and we can't wait until the train slows too much because guys with clubs will be right there on the outskirts looking for us. The trick is to get off the train when it's still far enough outside the city, then make our way to the other side of the city to catch the train coming out. This is assuming one doesn't wish to stay in Pittsburgh. I don't wish to stay in Pittsburgh. There's this other place I'm going and it's called New York City.

3 2

It takes me all day to get to the other side of Pittsburgh and wait with some other guys, hunkering down in the brush waiting for the train heading to Harrisburg, where I'll have to do this all over again. After Harrisburg I may be able to jump an express to Scranton, and after that another express that cuts across the top of New Jersey to my final destination. So about eight o'clock the train to Harrisburg comes by and about a dozen of us run for it like cats, desperate to catch it. The train's fast. I set my sights on a handle at the end of one of the cars and push my legs to their limits, it's all I can do to catch it in the dark. When I pull myself onto the side of the train the wind's tearing through me and I'm breathing the cold of the night into me so as to freeze my heart. I look back over my shoulder and there's still eight guys on the ground far behind us, eight who ran like I did but didn't have the legs to make it. I can see their dark forms in the fields watching me go. For about ten minutes I settle into a nook between cars and get my strength back. Then I have to crawl on top of the car and make my way like a spider, trying to get to what looks like an open box three or four cars down. I'm six-foot-four and two hundred thirty pounds and one good wind would blow me to Ohio.

In the boxcars are three other guys. They're not among the ones who were waiting with my group in the brush outside Pittsburgh. It's taken me twenty-four hours to learn that camaraderie among the dispossessed is the sort of nice idea that sixteen-year-olds believe in. Two days ago I was sixteen years old and I would have believed it too, but today I've killed my halfbrother with my own hands. I've studied in the college of mayhem and graduated when it had nothing left to teach me. These guys in boxcars, there are good ones and bad ones and no formula for figuring out which is which. Who knows what I have on me that one of these assholes wouldn't slit my throat for as soon as I fall asleep? My belt buckle, my shoes. My coat. One of them maybe has an attraction to one of my ears, or one of my fingers. I doze a bit and sure enough, I wake to some guy hovering over me with a blade. He's been on the other side of the car watching me in the dark, he doesn't see whether I'm big or little or what, slouched here against the wall as I am. He just sees I look like a kid, so here he is breathing in my face. I have *his* face in my grip quicker than he can consider his love of living. "The problem is," I explain to him in the dark, "you cut off one of my fingers, you got to take the other nine. I mean, you just have to. And if you take the other nine, it's just *imperative* you take the hands. And you take the hands—" and he's blinking at me now in utter black consternation, "—it's simply a *serious mistake* not to take the stumps. And when does it end then?" I've got his face so hard in my grip he can't answer, assuming he could think of one. "You just don't know the havoc, buddy. My hands are just filled with it these days." I push my body from the floor of the boxcar, catching my balance from the movement of the train, still holding onto him the whole time. His feet are dangling in the air for a moment and then I shotput him through the open door, and I and the other two guys can hear his scream in the night at least three or four seconds. Yeah, at least that. I don't know that it actually kills him though. On the next train outside Harrisburg I try to let people know what they're dealing with from the start, and I've drained my heart of havoc by the time we reach Manhattan, where my heart will need something stronger.

3 3

My first night in New York I spend on the streets huddled with a whole colony of men like me around a garbage can that burns in the middle of a block of West 34th over around Eighth Avenue. It isn't until daylight that I see the city's edifices black and wet like the watermark of a tide that rolled through in our sleep. At dawn the colony scatters a bit. I hunt down a roll of bread or a cup of soup off a line. Most of the day I'm hungry because I'm still learning everything, how you scout the lines early and maybe wait the whole night so you'll be far enough up front to get something the next morning. Then you wait the whole day for a bed in a flophouse. I hear about a pretty good one down around the Village, where the floors are clean and there's heat most of the night. It takes me a while to figure out where the Village is, though.

Then you learn where the trucks roll in at six in the morning and nab guys for work, guys who look like they're just desperate enough to work for almost nothing but not so broken they don't have the spirit for working at all. The pickup points change from week to week or maybe even day to day depending how fast the word gets out and how big the crowds become. A crowd of men angry to work, that's just plain unruly. But the whole city's unruly as far as I can tell, forty-eight hours of it tell me that. You keep looking around for who's in fucking *charge*, and there's just nobody like that at all. The cops just ride their horses back and forth through the park, up and down Fifth Avenue. Who the hell's angry on Fifth Avenue, that's what I want to know. Guys in black cars with machine guns roar by, laughing. All night is the sharp splash of guns, you can stand in the middle of Broadway and see their fire blossom like wild sunflowers in the dark. Roosevelt and LaGuardia are heroes but only in the way God's a hero: you know they're up there somewhere but you never figure they're ever actually going to do anything that has anything to do with a life as little as yours. Instead every street roils and churns with union men shouting at you from corners and telegram boys pouring out of Grand Central, running up and down 42nd calling out the names of people you'll never see, bringing wires with no words dated in years you can't remember, never delivering them to anyone until by the end of the day the gutters are filled with them, blank Western Union messages discarded by wandering lost telegram boys who wind up drinking beer in Coney Island. Those of us who don't get picked out for work in the mornings just hang around the streets watching the telegram boys or listening to the union guys or telling a joke to someone who just told it to us five minutes before, or sometimes someone will pull a radio out of the scrapheap somewhere and jimmy it so we can listen to the Yankees. When the weather gets warmer it isn't as bad. But you're tired of the street and the snarl of your stomach, and every day you have a choice between waiting all night for the soup or a job in the morning or all day for a bed that night in a flophouse, in which case if you're sleeping in the flophouse you're obviously not in line for the job or the soup. You make these choices all the time between what you feel the worst, hunger or fatigue or enough desperation to gamble on to-morrow holding some future.

34

I'm living like this a week and a half or so, it's hard to tell, when I start getting work. Let's say that in a crowd I stand out. The trucks pull in and the foremen are looking for big guys who can do some serious labor, and I'm made to order. For another three weeks I'm loading freezers in the packing companies downtown, where every thirty minutes they have to let you break because the cold robs your arms and fingers of feeling. This work goes from seven in the morning until nine at night. I can afford to buy food in a store and I could afford to buy a bed in a flophouse except all the beds are taken by the time I get off. I have the bright idea of just reserving a bed for a week with the money I'm saving but somehow it doesn't seem right, having a job *and* a meal *and* a bed all at once. Then the packing company lays a bunch of us off. I get another job delivering packages in the garment district, this lasts about eight days when the customers start complaining that I always look like some-one who's come to put the rub on them.

So I'm back hanging around the streets, this time for something like a month. The federal projects pass me over as someone who can get a job somewhere else because I'm big, and the foremen in the trucks start looking right through me when they're picking their crews in the morn-ing. It's funny. The only thing I can think of is that some-one my size just can't be counted on to submit to

everything there is to be submitted to these days, or maybe
it's that these days anything big is immediately on the
wrong side of things, at least down here in the street. I
guess I understand it. It's like this city itself that's hovering
over you everywhere you go and anytime you go there, but
only the part of it that exists at eyelevel below the watermark is the part of the city that's on your side. The rest of
it's your enemy, or dead to you. Sometimes I get the urge
to stand still and look up at this huge city hovering for what
seems miles above me, and wonder who the hell is really
up there on all those floors far away behind windows most
of us will never see through. I can't imagine the buildings
anything but empty up there, or maybe a stray soul wandering room to room wondering where everyone else went.
The whole top of the city isn't even here. It isn't even now.
It's another city from years ago, the image of its life only
now reaching us, the light of its extinction having taken
place sometime since, and which we can only now wait to
witness. Maybe that's the way the guys in trucks see me, as
a bigness that they know has died even though the vision
of its death is still busy traveling up through time to the
moment all of us, including me, can see it. I say bullshit. I
say they've got a long fucking time to wait.

3 5

Now it's the spring of 1934. And one day one of those
things happens, one of those small things that when it happens no one could possibly know will be important. I'm
standing around a newsstand up at 49th and Broadway, a
number of us are there trying to bum cigarettes off the

customers who just bought some. The man who runs the stand is Jerry. He isn't happy about us being around and he'll come out sometimes and shoo us like cats, and the boys just stand there with their hands in their pockets. I'm less interested in the cigarettes than the newspapers and magazines, but if I so much as touch one, Jerry goes berserk. So I stand reading the front page of the papers in the racks, actually I only get to read the top halves and am left to wonder at the bottom. The magazines I can only stare at, with these black and red and blue covers, amazing women in shredded clothes and gangsters whose faces are always shadowed with someone else's dying. I sometimes actually consider the luxury of buying one of these magazines for a dime or fifteen cents or whatever it's going for. But I never do. I just stand around with the others watching life there on the corner of 49th and Broadway, and most of it is life that's not so unlike me, but sometimes it's the life of theater people going by in taxis, actresses on their way to rehearsals in the day and patrons on their way to the shows at night, and financiers and office workers and men in suits in black cars.

The small thing that happens is one day someone comes running up to Jerry with news that his wife has had a stroke and been taken to the hospital. Jerry's frantic. "I'll watch things for you if you want, Jerry," I say, and maybe if he'd been thinking straight he'd have just closed up the stand and I'd have just wandered off to another corner, and the rest of my life would have been different, and the world and the Twentieth Century would have been different. But he isn't thinking straight and these are times when closing up work just for a day constitutes a sacrifice, and so my proposal that seemed nuts ten seconds ago is quickly evolving into a hopeful longshot. He breathes deeply and runs back into the stand and collects most of the money, leaves me some change and gives me a nod. Then he just runs off to his wife in the hospital without a word about when he'll be back or what to do if he doesn't come back. Maybe he's thinking it doesn't matter, the odds are I'm going to steal him blind anyway, and if he comes back later and anything of his life is still salvageable at all, he'll be lucky. As it happens he'll be luckier than even that. His wife will pull through and I don't have any plans at all to steal him blind, I don't even care much what he pays me, I just want to read one of those magazines and anything behind the top half of the first page of a newspaper, like this Philly paper I'm reading that has this story back around page eleven about how in Pennsylvania they're looking for this crazed kid who killed one brother, crippled the other, paralyzed the father, terrorized the mother and burned down the house. He sounds like one insane son of a bitch to me. Then I get to the part where they say his name and it's only then it occurs to me who they're talking about.

36

I'm working at the stand three days, never leaving but sleeping behind the counter, before Jerry comes back. He couldn't be more amazed to find me and the money still there. "How's the wife," I say, and he answers she's doing better but he's going to have to stay with her awhile. "So you want this job for a time?" he asks and I say all right. I have the job a couple of weeks and I don't mind it. Mostly I read the magazines.

One of the customers who rolls by in his Packard every day is John "Doggie" Hanks, who runs a big part of uptown Manhattan all the way to Harlem. He was a gangster up until a year ago when Prohibition ended and gangsters were either legalized out of business or frozen into legitimacy. Hanks is legitimate now more or less, or at least as legitimate as he can stand to be. He wears a nice suit and sits in the back seat of the car while someone else drives. In his early forties he has curly blond hair and a face shaved as smooth as a swimmer's legs except for the pock-marks around his temples. His driver has hair that stands up like a brush and a nose that points like a compass, except his brain tilts in the south direction as far as I can tell. "What happened to Jerry?" Hanks asks the first day, and I tell him his wife's sick. He gives me some money for her. "I hear Jerry didn't get it," he says, "and I'll come looking for you. You don't look so difficult to locate either." I give the money to Jerry the next time he comes by. As with a lot of people, Jerry's feelings about someone like Doggie Hanks tend to be a bit confused. He's too awe-struck and terrified to be purely grateful. "You tell Mr. Hanks," he instructs me very carefully, "that I say thank you very, very much. You got that?"

"Sure," I answer.

"Thank you very, *very*—"

"All right, all right." It's disgusting. Hanks comes by later that day. "Jerry says to tell you 'Thank you very, very much.' "

"OK," he says, taking his paper through the car window.

"You got the correct tone of that?" I ask. " 'Very, very much.' Solicitous as hell."

" 'Solicitous'?" Hanks looks at his driver. "Billy, the kid says 'solicitous.' "

"Yes sir, Mr. Hanks," says the driver with the beak.

"What do you think of it," says Hanks.

"It's somethin' all right," Billy says tersely.

Hanks laughs. He points at Billy and says to me, "Billy says it's somethin'. He's got a way with words just like you." He stops laughing after a bit. "How old are you?"

"Twenty," I say.

"Ha ha," says Hanks. He says to Billy, "He's got a way with numbers too, huh? Eighteen *maybe*." He waves, still

laughing, and they drive off. Every day after that, when he
comes to get his paper in the backseat of his car, he says to
me, "So how about a ten dollar word today," and I give
him one off the top of my head. This goes on for a week
and a half. Sometimes he'll say, "How old are we today?"
and I get a little tired of it. "Today I'm fucking retirement
age, Mr. Hanks," I say, "today I'm moving to Florida to
live with the grandkids." Hanks loves it. "Hear that, Billy?"
he laughs, and Billy says, "Punk's got a mouth if you ask
me, Mr. Hanks." Hanks just laughs more. "Billy's not too
happy with you," he explains, "I'd *never* let him smartass
me like that." Finally one day Hanks makes his offer. It's
the middle of the afternoon and he's just bought some
cigars. "I have a club on the upper west side," he tells me.
He gives me a card that reads *Top Dog*, and there's an
address. "I can use a doorman who's big as a damn wall
and smarter than he looks. You come tonight around seven
if you want it. Needless to say, you're twenty-one if you
take it. It's a step up from peddling cigars, huh?" He doesn't
wait for an answer, just gives me a small salute as though
to say it's understood I'll be there, and I have half a mind
not to show up because of it. But that's silly. I pick a guy
out from among the drifters hanging around the corner
like I was doing not too long ago and give him my job;
today I'm retirement age, like I said. I roll up an issue of
the pulp I'm reading called *Savage Nights* and stuff it in my
coat pocket.

37

Hanks' club, the Top Dog, takes up the second-to-the-top
floor of a brownstone on the West Sixties, between Colum-
bus and the park; the only floor above it comprises Hanks'
various offices. The club has heavy crushed velvet curtains
and an oak bar, European paintings and glass separating
the booths, chiseled in each corner with the design of a
rose. The women smoke from small ivory-and-silver cigarette holders and a guy in a dinner jacket begins playing
the piano in the corner around nine. The veranda stam-
mers with light. Sometimes standing before the windows
I'll remember when I could see the span of my life's time
from such windows. In these windows I don't see any such
thing. I see New York City.

38

Leona checks the coats at the Top Dog. She's dark and
dimpled, not one of the really beautiful women of the club
but not plain either. The first time I see her, which is about
five minutes after the first time I walk through the door, I
know I'll have her, I know she'll be my first woman. I may
have to work at it, but not that hard. She stares at me the
whole night.

This begins my career as the doorman for Doggie Hanks.
I wouldn't make too much of it, it'll only last about fourteen months and not once in that time do I see anything

particularly interesting. "Just how shady is this?" I ask him one night, and he says, "Prohibition's legal now, kid," a non sequitur but I know what he means. The clientele is a mix of the completely respectable and the faintly dubious, none necessarily any more suspicious than the clearly underage doorman. I'm never called upon to escort anyone out, though a couple of times Doggie does suggest I sort of shift my attention in the direction of someone who risks getting out of hand. I guess the mere sight of me is always enough, which is the way Doggie likes it. "And he's *smart* too," he'll say to this person or that. "So let's see him do something smart," the other person will say, and Doggie retorts, "He doesn't have to do anything smart. You can just take my word for it."

I have Leona my second week, one night after the club has closed. We're back among the coats that got left behind by people too inebriated to remember them. Because it's my first time I'm a little nervous, it's probably not the most impressive performance. Still, Leona screams like she's being impaled; when I begin to stop she croaks in my ear, "Don't you dare, don't you *dare*." She wants the light off but I have to leave it on because in the dark I see these things I don't want to see, the faces of Indian women, and I hear these things I don't want to hear, voices from the dark of a doorway; so the light stays on.

Leona wants me to go home with her afterhours but that isn't what I have in mind. For a month or two I sleep at the club on a couch in one of the offices upstairs until I get some money together for a room. I begin to do what I've been waiting to do. For a while I do it on a table in the cloakroom and later when I get my own room about seven blocks from the club, a room all of ten feet by twelve, with a bed and small dresser for my clothes and a table by the window, I do it there. Then I work up the courage to borrow the typewriter in Hanks' own office and in the early mornings around six or seven o'clock I teach myself how to use it, one slow finger at a time, until I've finished with what I've already written out by hand. When Doggie catches me in his office he's not very pleased about it; for the first time he scares me. Billy the driver happens to be there and is extremely amused. "Sorry," I can only say, "didn't mean anything." Hanks is smoking mad. "Didn't mean anything," I keep muttering, "sorry," over and over. Hanks nods to Billy. "Solicitous as hell," he says. Billy guffaws.

"What's this?" Hanks picks up my old beatup issue of *Savage Nights* next to the typewriter. He shakes his head. "Our fucking doorman's making with the *words*," he says to Billy, then he throws the magazine down and sighs deeply. "You want to use the machine it's OK, kid," he says, "but not in my office. You can take it down to the cloakroom where you've been boinking my check-in girl." I look at him surprised and he says, "Yeah I know about that, too. Look, don't get it into your head there are things it's better for me not to know about. There's *nothing* that it's better for me not to know about." He looks over his shoulder at Billy and turns back to me smiling. "When you're done with the machine, Billy will bring it back up for you." All the amusement goes right out of Billy's face. I want to laugh out loud.

Sometimes when I'm typing in the cloakroom Hanks sits out in the empty club in a booth with a girlfriend, or a business associate; then he comes by and sticks his head in. Or I'll finish up and while Billy's carrying the typewriter into the office, pale and fuming, I catch a glimpse through the door into Doggie's private washroom, and he's standing there with a razor in his hand and his face white with cream. As he shaves it smooth and rinses the razor he calls out to me and asks how the words are coming. Over the months I make up stories about some of the people who come into the club, once or twice I'm stupid enough to ask Hanks the wrong question as a bit of research. Like if he's killed many men. I never figured him for a somber man, but he answers somberly, "You're talking like a little kid

now. Who I've killed and whether I've killed isn't a joke."
I'm appalled by myself at this moment, but eight years from
now it will seem small potatoes, compared to the mortifi-
cations to come.

3 9

But then in 1942 I'll come to find myself oblivious to self-
mortification. I'll come to acknowledge it in principle even
as I never quite feel it. I don't guess in 1942 I'm aware of
anything except the room in Vienna where I ravish you
over and over while the most evil man who ever lived
watches us. I don't suppose anything ever really shakes me
until the night I watch my wife and child hurl themselves
to oblivion as some kind of price for saving you and me, a
woman they never knew and a man the depths of whose
soul they never felt the way they deserved. Both of us from
a pact which perhaps I chose, perhaps I didn't.

Damn the consequences of my acts, it's the consequences of my words I love and loathe. I wrap them like a
rope around a man's neck, or thread them like a string of
pearls up through the middle of a woman's womb.

I don't know whether I'm supposed to feel bad for Pennsylvania, I only know I don't. I cleared the decks of that
almost instantly, making room for the evil to come. I admit
it's a little appalling that it doesn't cross my mind hardly
ever. Maybe Henry deserved dying, maybe my father and
Alice and Oral deserved what they got too, but there's an
odd silence where my conscience should be wrestling with
it. It's like a man atomizing into nothingness hundreds of
thousands of men and women and children, maybe in a

little city somewhere, maybe Japan, maybe two little cities in Japan, maybe in the name of something righteous, maybe in the name of ending some larger barbarism, but then claiming that he *never* has a moment's doubt about it, he never loses a moment's sleep. Never in the dark does he see a face or hear a voice calling him. But then, that happens in *your* Twentieth Century. Not mine.

I've come now to see and hear things only when I fuck a woman in the dark or write words on a white page. It doesn't mean I stop feeling the havoc of my fingers. I write to the music of Henry's head sloshing when I broke it. My first story, there in the cloakroom at Doggie Hanks' Top Dog, is about a man who kills his woman on a New York City backway. He kills her at the story's beginning, but the story isn't about him, it's about her. She's telling the story and goes right on telling it after he's killed her, and goes on telling us how she longs for him still. When he sleeps at night she strips him on the bed, ties him to the bedrail with his shirt and makes love to him with her mouth. He wakes up and all he can see is that he's tied naked to his bed and bleeding. His thighs and belly are covered with blood and he cries out in terror at his dying. In fact he isn't dying at all. In fact the blood isn't his but hers, she's still bleeding from the top of her head where he bashed it in. But he can't see her at all, he only sees the blood that he assumes is his own; and the sight of it, the image of what he believes is his own death, as well as the mysterious inexplicable climax he comes to from a sucking he cannot fathom, literally stops his heart. I also manage to work in some social observations of life in the streets of Manhattan.

I work in dread of every word I write. It leaves me abysmal and burdened rather than released. When I lie down to sleep I have to put the papers away, where I can't reach or see them. When I finish I don't wait a minute with it, but take it right down to the offices of the magazine, so as to have it out of my life.

40

The magazine buys the story for forty dollars. That's the long and short of it, actually there's a great deal of fussing and hesitating and general screwing around that goes on several weeks. First they don't believe I'm really writing stories, because I don't look like someone who writes stories, then they don't believe I wrote this particular story, then they're trying to figure out what to do with a story like this. This then is the second career which comes of standing around Jerry's newsstand on the afternoon Jerry's wife had a stroke; and the first career, as Doggie Hanks' doorman, provides me the resources with which to pursue the second. The second will lead to the third, which will take me away from my country for more than thirty years. But that's almost two years away: it's now early 1935. I'm writing for the pulps. The stories are a cut above average and my rate goes up from forty dollars to fifty, but the secret of success is writing *lots* of stories; I don't have the energy. Also, I don't know anything. What do I know? I know how to destroy the manifestations of my youth in a single night. Out of it I write stories I can barely stand to hold in my hands, after which I travel for days inside my own black hour.

41

I make a fateful and entirely conscious decision right at the beginning. This decision is to put across the top of my stories the name Banning Jainlight. I know that this has got to catch up with me, I can read the papers. The Philly papers have run a couple things, and Philadelphia just isn't that far away. They've heard of Banning Jainlight there. Maybe I'm just not willing to be a tourist anymore. Maybe I'm not visiting anymore. The name goes where I go, bad or good. Maybe I keep it in defiance of Oral and Henry in that hut, Alice and my father thrashing on the ground beyond the licks of the flaming house, maybe I keep it to defy my mother who disappeared into the night, when she should have disappeared sixteen years before and taken me with her. Then I wouldn't have been Banning Jainlight at all.

Sooner or later someone's going to come. Little man, big man, whoever. I remember them already, actually. They're still about twenty months into the future but I already remember them coming out of the night, down the street: "You know someone named Jainlight?" they say to me out of the dark. Little man. Big man. I turn and run. I hear their footsteps running after me, rounding the last corner of 1936.

But now in the spring of 1935 after I've been working for Doggie almost a year, I'm at the club one night early before the crowd has come in. Not much is going on, Doggie's just strolling up the aisles and Billy's with him, and Billy's thinking very hard, hard enough to practically launch his head from his shoulders. When they're close to me Billy says out of the blue, but so that Hanks will hear it, "So: Jainlight." Just like that. First time he's ever used my name, and I know it's come to mean something to him.

I'm leaning in the door reading a paper. News all over the front about Germans. I don't even look at Billy.

Billy's eating a toothpick and talking around it. "Heard they're looking for someone named Jainlight in the Pittsburgh area: that's what I heard. A big redhead kid about six foot somethin'. Went on a rampage one night wiped out his whole friggin' family." He gazes off for a moment even though there's nothing of interest in his line of vision except a bourbon glass on the bar that's empty anyway. Doggie looks at him in confusion and then at me.

I look up from my paper now. "The news is fascinating these days," I say, "take these fucking Germans for instance. I was under the impression we taught them what's what around the time I was being born. Anyway, I can barely tear my attention away from it."

"A big redhead kid named Banning Jainlight," says Billy.

"Banning Jainlight is my alias," I say, "must have been the *real* Banning Jainlight you heard about."

Billy turns his gaze in my direction; now he appears a bit befuddled. "The real Banning Jainlight?"

Doggie's looking at me, then at Billy. "You heard him," he says to Billy, "the real Banning Jainlight. In parts of Pennsylvania there are probably several."

"I know sixteen or seventeen myself," I say.

Billy can't believe it. He looks at Hanks and then at me and scowls; his nostrils actually begin to flare.

"Say, why don't you take a walk," Hanks says, putting his hand on Billy's shoulder. Then he turns and pulls me by the arm toward the cloakroom. All the way I'm looking over my shoulder at Billy and Billy's looking over his shoulder at me.

Leona's been waiting in the cloakroom to ambush me, she has my coat halfway off my body before she sees the boss. She flushes and tries to sputter something ridiculous. "Give us a few minutes, OK, sugar?" Doggie says. When she scampers out he takes a long time looking at me. We're in the dark and about all we see of each other are our eyes.

For a moment I think I'm going to see fear, for a moment I actually think he's going to be afraid of me. I guess he sees something too. "The whole family?" he finally says.

I don't want to sound like I'm justifying anything. "I think," I'm whispering, "I think we might more accurately say part of the family."

"Oh," says Doggie. In the dark I see him nodding. "Only part." He nods.

Over and over in my hands I'm rolling a picture of the chancellor of Germany. "My mother wasn't even my mother," I blurt.

"OK," he finally says, and now I definitely think he's a little afraid. He doesn't entirely comprehend but he's managing his doubts into shapes he can live with. He turns around and, leaving me there, walks out, and I wait awhile in the dark of the cloakroom thinking about everything. Leona comes in and throws her arms around my neck, I shrug her off. I go out into the club, I want to find Billy and say, I'm your Banning Jainlight and always will be; but he isn't there.

42

I don't stay at the Top Dog much longer. I leave for several reasons, not because of Billy, I wouldn't give him the satisfaction, but Leona's becoming a nuisance, she's always around, and a couple of times when I wind up spending some time with other girls, a waitress in a luncheonette over on Seventh Avenue and another of the girls at the club, it causes problems. Doggie doesn't like it either. But the main reason I leave is that this third career comes along. The editor at the magazine tells me about it rather confidentially one afternoon. He says it involves writing books and when I say I can't come up with a whole book, he says he thinks I might actually be pretty good at these kinds of books, given the stuff they have to cut out of my stories. A whole book of that kind of thing, that's what they want, he tells me. I'm still a little thickheaded about what he's driving at. "Books," he says, "they don't put out on the shelves, books you have to ask for and they pull them out from under the counter." Now I know what he's driving at but I still can't quite see it, and then he tells me the pay starts at a dollar a page and is guaranteed to go up if they like what I'm doing.

Who "they" are remains a little ambiguous at first. At the outset they're nameless dealers dealing for other dealers dealing for . . . who knows. Some of the stuff is sold to anyone who walks in and asks for it and some of it is commissioned by private collectors. I figure I know even less about this particular area than I do gangsters. But I come to learn that the less I know the better. I just sit at the typewriter laughing my head off. That's when I know I have something going.

I guess that's why I do it. To write something I don't dread. I set myself a schedule, every morning squeezing another cup out of the coffee grounds that have been sitting on the bookshelf the last month and then knocking out three pages about whatever or whoever was in my head all night, reducing every nightmare and misunderstood impulse to something I can laugh at. Three pages every morning of someone fucking Molly or Amanda, this morning it's a gangster who's having her and tomorrow it's a Prussian sergeant, the morning after tomorrow a cannibal chieftain. Next week it's a man from Mars and the week after that it's somebody dead. After lunch I labor on whatever I happen to be doing for the pulps, and then I have to take my mood out into the city and walk it off, have dinner, stand outside the dancehalls and jazz clubs listening to what's inside.

Sometimes I'll see Leona on her night off, other times it might be someone else. The sheer heft of me either attracts them or sends them running for cover. It weeds out the squeamish. If nothing happens with someone it doesn't matter, I go back to my room and write a couple more pages, at this rate it takes a month to finish a book and then I set off to deliver it to a man in a backroom at Charles and Bleecker in the West Village.

43

This continues about six months. During this time I deliver four thin books, each interrupted by a general haggling over the money. The man in the backroom at Charles and Bleecker is small and pudgy, with eyeglasses so strong they seem to disassemble his whole face; he regards me as an oaf. He acts like it's impossible to believe I'm writing these books, and he's always giving me messages to deliver to my "employer," for whom he assumes I'm an errand boy of some sort. "*I'm* my employer," I explain; he ignores it. "My employer," I tell him one day, "says to tell you a dollar a page doesn't cut it anymore. My employer is making three dollars a page writing for the crime magazines."

"A dollar's a very good rate," the man answers, quietly and insistently.

"It won't do," I say. Ultimately my employer and I eliminate the middleman altogether, because it turns out my employer isn't me after all. It's a guy named Kronehelm, I notice because his business card gets clipped to one of my manuscripts as soon as I bring it in. This means the Charles and Bleecker man with the disassembling eyeglasses is selling the manuscripts to a private client who, for whatever quirk will explain it, has developed a partiality to *my* work in particular. I've got a good idea Mr. Kronehelm and I can come to an arrangement both of us prefer to the present one.

44

Make that *Herr* Kronehelm. He lives in a flat in Gramercy Park, and that's the listing on his box. The whole hall seems to vibrate when I go up the stairs, and when Herr Kronehelm opens the door he seems to shrink before me, cowering. He's a middleaged man with flesh so thin and translucent it barely covers anything. The vague blue innards of his head hint at themselves like the meat in a Chinese dumpling. He's actually not that small but he walks and acts that way and speaks that way. He's dressed in a red bathrobe and keeps his cigarette in a holder, and it doesn't smell like American tobacco. We go into his flat which is very spacious and well furnished and would probably be very impressive if someone cleaned it now and then or pulled the curtains back from the windows once a month. Kronehelm sits on a sofa and gestures next to him, but I settle for a chair nearby, some little European piece that creaks with the burden of me. Kronehelm winces.

We get down to business. On the telephone I've already identified myself as the author of *Maiden Voyage, Tunnel of Love* and several other notable works of contemporary literature. He's having a hard time, I can tell, matching me with these efforts. A fog seems to fill the space between us, across which I've been hurling words for some months

now, only to be received and transformed by Herr Kronehelm on the other side. The fog's now quickly lifting. I
have to subject myself to a discursive quiz on my oeuvre
before he's willing to believe my manuscripts and I go together. "You must be a man of some wide experience?"
Herr Kronehelm asks; his accent is Austrian and heavy.
"But how many years are you anyway?"

I'm tired of being asked how old I am. I dispense with
my usual smart answer and just ignore the question.
"Look, Herr Kronehelm," I begin, leaning forward in the
little creaking chair. I explain the situation without tipping
my hand too much, I'm trying to get a fix on his situation
first. He's surprisingly open about it, allowing that he buys
the work from the man at Charles and Bleecker for six
dollars a page. When I hint at how little of that has been
coming my direction, he isn't especially indignant about it,
but after a while he starts to see what I'm getting at. He
starts to see that if I deliver the manuscripts directly to him,
he can pay me three and a half dollars a page, which is
better for both of us. Kronehelm weighs the pros and cons
of this. It's a good business move on the face of it but he
worries that it'll get him in trouble with the man at Charles
and Bleecker as well as, I guess, whatever other characters
he's dealing with in this matter. But then another aspect of
the situation occurs to him, one of great appeal.

"This way," he says, "we can *specialize* the work, one
might say."

"What?"

"This way," he says, "we might *customize*, so to speak."

So to speak, one might say . . . he means he wants me
to tailor the stories to him and his tastes. And for a moment
I almost think I'm not going to laugh about it anymore, for
a moment I almost think I'm going to feel the dread again.
I almost feel it knowing that somehow I've locked into the
preferences and passions of this man who, the more and
more I watch him, appears as a blotch of human tissue that
still hasn't completely formed, with an unfinished cranium

and a cigarette holder in his unfinished mouth. I almost think I'm going to feel it . . . but there's not a chance. No chance at all. I'm just going to laugh harder. I'm going to feel better than I've ever felt. I'm going to feel better than the night in my mother's hut, I'm going to feel better than the time I threw the bum out of the door of the railroad car. I'm going to have the time of my fucking life. I may not be able to write a syllable, convulsed as I'll be with the mirth of it all. I'm going to be in fucking stitches. "Why that's *fine*, Herr Kronehelm," I say, "that's jake. We'll specialize it. We'll customize it."

Kronehelm's almost a little taken aback by my zeal. "Not that I would presume, please understand," he interjects, "not that I would presume how to tell an artist." He winces again like he did at the chair when I sat in it. "My English."

"Don't worry about it," I assure him, "everything's understood." All that's left are the details. We even arrange an advance of a hundred dollars, just for the sake of inspiration. Herr Kronehelm suggests we share a drink to seal the deal, but I beg off insisting that inspiration is rising to the boiling point at this very moment and I've got to be home when it spills over. I'm not halfway down the stairs before I'm splitting a gut over it. Molly and Herr Kronehelm, Amanda and Herr Kronehelm, Molly and Amanda and Herr Kronehelm. We'll dress him up in a little uniform, with a little sword and some medals; he'll be ecstatic. He'll come all over himself just from the feel of the black leather boots on his feet and the little pointed hat on his fetus-dumpling head. There won't be anything left of him for Molly and Amanda, he'll be so spent with excitement. They'll have to work him over just to get a little blurt of him. Don't worry Molly, don't worry Amanda; I'll make it up to you. We'll leave him passed out on the floor and it'll be just the three of us.

4 5

1935–36. I laugh a year and a half. I rise in New York to just below the eyelevel of the city; I believe my past is past. I move amidst the present at large and at liberty. Moans of murder from the Spanish prairies, sobs of love from the King of England: I ford these sounds like a river. I'm building obsessions for my Austrian mentor, word by word, specialized and customized, blond and strawberry-nippled and voluptuous; I laugh so hard people in the streets stop to stare at my window. After a couple of months Herr Kronehelm presses into my hand six hundred dollars and disappears for months. I keep working and laughing. He reappears suddenly one day with no explanation, accepting his specialized obsessions in silence. I walk the streets with my hand over my mouth: everyone who sees me wants to know what's so damned *funny*. In his room where the curtains never part Kronehelm withers gratefully before cruel delicious Molly. Two more months pass and he advances me more money and disappears another four months, reappearing to take from me more of my comedies. Leona and I have a final irrevocable fight, she cries outside my door and splatters abuse across the air like vandalism. Molly and Amanda come and go like they're told. It's not as though they're slaves, they just have better things to do. They're professionals.

On his second return some things about Herr Kronehelm's secret trips come to reveal themselves. It seems he's established a market for my work in Austria and Germany. He takes the work with him, has it translated and then copied, so that he may keep one and sell the other. It's not any sort of mass production, part of the appeal is the work's rare exclusivity. No doubt I'm portrayed to his European clients as one of America's most sensational authors. I have long flowing black hair and wear a cape, I am the secret passion of Claudette Colbert. I'm tubercular and perhaps an opium addict. Anyway I'm sure not a six-foot-four farm-boy with a big goofy face. Kronehelm now wants me to feed the pages to him five at a time, which has me crossing town to Gramercy Park every other day. My rate, however, rises to four dollars, almost unheard of in this business.

Keep it so wonderfully American, he advises me. Molly in the company of gangsters and cowboys and tycoons.

It's the end of 1936. It's the end of many things. I don't quite know it yet, but my head has just begun to bob above the watermark after all. If only I were a foot shorter. It coincides with recent discussions between me and the Austrian over our general residency. He wearies of shipping little bundles of five or six pages to the translator in Vienna, more than that he just wearies of New York. He proposes we relocate the business to homesoil. I don't even know where Austria is: in Switzerland or some place. "Austria is in nothing," Kronehelm explains with frustration, "it is only in Austria." He's resolute about returning. I suggest that nothing has to change, I can continue to work here and ship it on to him in Vienna, from where he can wire back our agreed-upon sum. He doesn't think this is very satisfactory. I shrug and leave him with his dissatisfaction.

Truth be told, it's the laughing that I weary of. I'm re-telling the old stories, I'm retelling other people's stories with the things they left out. The girls are beginning to bitch at me in my sleep, we've lost the yearning for each other. We're too familiar with forbidden things. But I haven't any idea what to do instead of laugh. The laughing's a habit by which I clear my throat. I'm tired as well of the dread of the pulp stories, and I do less and less of them. Months pass since the last one, and finally one day I go into the magazine not to deliver anything but to get some money owed me from a previous piece. The editor has some news for me.

"Couple of guys were here looking for you," he says. He seems agitated.

"What couple guys?" I say.

He shrugs, disingenuously. After a moment he says, "It was yesterday." The twenty-four hours since haven't calmed him down. "They saw your name in one of the old issues. Or someone else saw it, they didn't look like big readers." He laughs nervously.

"Did they say what they wanted?"

"I don't think," he answers slowly, "it was a family visit," which is a little funny, I guess, because it turns out in a way that's exactly what it is.

"What did you tell them?"

"I had to tell them something," he says, "so I did the best—"

"What did you tell them?"

"That you worked at John Hanks' Top Dog." He pauses to see how I take it, to see if I'm going to break his neck. When I don't react he seizes the opportunity to spit out a rationale. "Well I figured you weren't working there anymore and it was better than giving them your address and if I didn't tell them something or if I tried to tell them something untrue they would have found out and come back and—"

"And broken your neck," I nod. But he's right, after all. It's my situation and he isn't responsible for it. "You owe me some money on the last piece," I say, "we agreed on fifty and your accounting office coughed up forty." He's happy to pay me the ten, he'd probably pay me a hundred right now if I asked for it. "If they come back," I say on my way out, "you don't know anything else. Remember? And you sure haven't seen me recently."

"Goodbye, Banning," he says, almost inaudibly.

46

I'm walking across town. I think about taking the train or a cab but the fact is, well, there's this havoc in my feet, this havoc's back in my heart again. All in the course of twenty-four, forty-eight, seventy-two hours everything's begun to change, in the way things do: Kronehelm's leaving, and someone's looking for me; and I have to adjust to the havoc of the times. But I haven't figured yet if the havoc of the times and the havoc in me are the same.

I'm thinking as fast as I can, as I make my way across town.

It's dark by the time I get to my street. The streetlights are on and from the windows I smell food, I hear the radios and people talking around their kitchen tables. Nobody's out on the street except two guys hanging around the front of my building.

Little man, big man.

I barely register them at first, but as I come down the long street I realize they're not moving, they're waiting, and I start to slow down. I start to slow down and then they're looking at me, and I've almost come to a stop in the middle of the street, with no sound but the sloshing of the gutters, the radios and voices seeming to die away, and then their steps coming back to me out of the night. They stop where they are and wait for me to make a move, and it's when I don't that the small one says, "You know some-one named Jainlight?"

All my life. We're inseparable.

And as fast as I'm thinking, it can barely keep up with as fast as I'm moving. I'm running wildly, and they're right behind my wildness, for one block after another. I'm fran-tically trying to think of somewhere I can lose them, maybe the park, if I can run that far and fast. It's hard to measure how far and fast they'll stay behind me, dogging me to the end. And then this makes me think of something else, and I don't especially like the idea but it's the only thing that comes to mind, and I need a favor now.

Seven blocks away from my place I reach the brown-stone and head for the top, taking the stairs instead of the lift. Little man big man have no choice but to follow, if they take the lift I'll lose them. I get up to the club and the doorman who got my job actually isn't sure he remembers me or not; Doggie doesn't brag to the customers about how smart this one is. The two men show up right behind me and I just bull my way in. The doorman yells something and then he's got the other two to deal with. The bigger of them is almost my size.

The commotion attracts a lot of attention. I don't like this ruckus because I know Hanks won't like it, I don't like it that I've run straight to him like a kid who got into trouble the first time he left home, when he thought he was so smart and on top of everything. At first I don't see Hanks, only Billy and I'm not interested in smart repartee with Billy right now. Then Doggie comes to us out of the smoke from the ivory and silver cigarette holder of the blonde next to him. Other people standing around the club are wondering what it's all about, and as I figured the boss isn't happy. "What's up kid," he says. He's looking at me and at the two guys over my shoulder. "I was on my way over," I pant, "then these two get on my tail and won't step off." I point to the little man and the big man, all three of us breathing hard. It's obvious we've been running.

"So you thought you'd bring them here with you," Hanks says. He's annoyed. "You used to dress better when you worked for me, kid," he says, fingering my shirt; in the light of the bar big circles of sweat underline my arms. The little man's pouring it off his face while the bigger one makes sounds through his nose. "You can't," asks Hanks, "take care of a couple of jackasses like these?" Billy's going through their jackets now, and I get lucky: he comes up with a gun on the smaller one. This immediately makes my situation look more legitimately desperate. Still, it never occurred to me they had guns. I don't know why I ran. Hanks is right, I dealt with characters before when I was riding the rails from Pittsburgh, but this time I ran without giving it a second thought.

It was that no stranger has ever called me by my name before.

I find myself studying the big guy. Meanwhile the little one's talking. He introduces himself as Johnson and the big one as Blaine. Johnson has a red bushy mustache and a pocketwatch that hangs from a chain. They're local investigators hired by an out-of-state client to find and take me back. "What's the matter with you," Hanks says to them, "can't you see this is just a kid? 'Take him back.' Where's there to take him back to?" And Johnson says home. "You got the wrong guy," says Doggie, "I've known this kid forever."

"The fact is," Johnson says, shifting his feet, "the fact is this man is Banning Jainlight from outside Pittsburgh, Pennsylvania, where he left three years ago."

Hanks slaps his hands together. "Well there's your error," he says, almost jubilantly. "This kid isn't Banning Jainlight, Banning Jainlight is only his *alias.*" Now he slaps me on the back at the joke. "It's a common mistake though," he reassures Johnson. I'm still studying the big guy Blaine, and behind him I catch a glimpse of Leona, who disappears back into the coats. I feel badly for her, because I know now that this Johnson and Blaine must have come after talking to my editor at the magazine, and Leona tipped them. At first I assumed it was Billy, he's standing by the bar with another toothpick in his mouth. But it takes all of three seconds to see Leona lost in her hate for me and for herself; for the first time, at this moment, she understands we'll never be together again, and for the first time I understand what it means to her. And now the big guy Blaine happens to turn his head and look over his shoulder to see what I'm looking at, and when he turns back there's no expression on his face at all. The mere sight of him and his blank face makes the havoc in me go all crazy, moving around to every part of me until it settles somewhere in my mouth.

Johnson's steady and composed, given the hostile circumstances. "We're not here to share a moment of humor with you, Mr. Hanks," he says, "one way or another Mr. Jainlight will be going back to his father in Pennsylvania. We can take him back privately or we can go to the police and have him arrested and extradicted."

"Maybe his father should come get him himself," Hanks says.

"Mr. Philip Jainlight doesn't move around a great deal these days," Johnson answers, his eyes on mine. Next to him Blaine never speaks. His face never moves, a big passionless lug, his feet planted squarely and his arms hanging at his sides. In his midthirties or so, his hair's already thinning and his face has little patches of broken blood; he might have had his last drink a week ago and the smell of Jim Beam still rises from him like heat. "Look," Johnson is still talking, and he moves his eyes from mine to Hanks', "folks have been looking for this boy three years now. He's a big boy. Pretty hard not to notice a boy this big for three years. For a boy this big to get along three years he'd have to have a lot of luck, a very big city to get lost in, and some big help keeping under wraps. I'd say anyone giving him that kind of help, well, in the eyes of the law, that kind of person's called an accessory." His eyes are steady on Hanks'.

"Is that right," Hanks snarls back. He's lost patience with the entire episode. "Go get your extradition papers," he snaps, "you're out of your territory here," and Johnson snaps back, "Out of our territory? Where do you think this is," looking at the club around him, "Mexico?" Hanks then turns to the big one standing behind Johnson and says,

"You. Why don't you talk to your partner here. *Clarify* things."

"No use talking to him," I start saying, and everyone turns to me as though to say, Who are you and what business of this is yours? But the havoc's running down my chin: "No use talking to him at all. It's obvious who's the brains of this operation and *he's* not it." Blaine just stands motionless and expressionless with his arms dangling at his sides; not a spasm of tension runs through him. "He's the muscle of the operation and that's all he is. He's one of those characters who can't take two steps in life without tumbling into it and knocking it the fuck over. Look at him. Does he even understand what the fuck I'm saying?" Hanks and Johnson are watching me like I've gone crazy, they look at the havoc like it's the flow of a strange black fluid from some crack in my head. I've now crossed the space between me and this Blaine and I'm standing toe to toe with him; he may be an inch shorter than I but no more, he's the only person I've ever known who measures up to me. I loathe the bigness of him, the big brainlessness of him; I loathe the grotesque outsizedness of him. "You fucking stupid jackass," I hiss in his face, "big man, big man. Why don't you say anything? No use talking to you, anyone can see that." Hanks is grabbing at my arm and I shake him off, and everyone around us is stunned. "Use it," I say to the big man, and who knows if anyone understands what I mean, let alone him; but I mean the violence: *Big is the violence in you*, "use it." He doesn't even quiver, his eyes dead and dull. Hanks grips me by the arm and literally pulls me back from Blaine's face, and he has a look that's alarmed and shaken. Johnson has the same look. Billy's dumbfounded, and all the rest of them: well fuck all the rest of them. You too Leona, I want to scream across the room. I'm all havoc now.

"Go upstairs," Doggie just says, somewhere between a whisper and a croak.

Some time later I'm upstairs in his office and he comes in. I'm looking out his windows at the city trying to see the things I once saw. "You've got to get out of here," he says the moment he walks in. He says it calmly and insistently, without panic. I won't be back, I tell him. He says, "I don't mean the club, I mean you've got to get out of the city, you've got to get out of the country. You could go to Canada but those guys will follow you to Canada. Better South America."

South America? What will I do in South America?

"I can't see you again, kid," he says. He pulls from his desk a wad of cash and peels me out five hundred dollars, just like that. I don't want it, I tell him, but he shakes his head. "This is business," he says, "this is five hundred dollars that says I don't see you again." He pauses. "Killing blood, you don't shake that. Killing a stranger, killing your enemy, that you shake *maybe*. But not blood."

My blood *was* strange, my blood *was* the enemy.

"Maybe it was, maybe it wasn't," he says, "I'm not passing judgment. Maybe your father is one son of a bitch, I don't say he isn't. All the more reason you're not going to shake it, not without putting lots of places between you and the more the better. So here's some funds, and here's one more ride. Billy?" Billy comes in the door. He doesn't even look at me. "You're going to give the kid a ride," Hanks says to him, "no funny stuff. Anywhere in New York City he wants to go, train station, the docks. *No funny stuff.*" Billy doesn't do or say anything for a moment until he understands the boss expects an answer, and then he nods. I turn from the window to look at Hanks; the office seems dark and distant. My ears pound with time and momentousness. I ask if I can make a phone call.

When Kronehelm answers I say it's time to relocate the business to homesoil after all. When I put down the phone and look up, Doggie's nowhere to be seen. It's just Billy leaning in the door waiting. No funny stuff, Doggie said, but Billy's laughing just the same, all the way to Gramercy Park in the middle of the night.

47

The next forty-eight hours are spent with Herr Kronehelm plotting my escape from America. He's been taken by surprise at the new change in plans, and is still two weeks away from getting his own affairs in order before he can leave. I've made it clear that I can't and won't wait two weeks. In my head I have a whole scenario in which Johnson and Blaine show up sooner or later. My clothes in my apartment, my typewriter, my books and the money I stashed there the past year, all that's lost now since I don't dare take a chance going back there or sending anyone else. The five hundred bucks I didn't want to take from Doggie Hanks I'm very happy to have, on further reflection, though it also feels something like a disgrace. Of course I don't mention it at all to Kronehelm, rather I hit him up for an advance.

During the day Kronehelm's arranging things with various people. He gets me passage on a cargo ship that's disembarking tomorrow morning at dawn. His connections in Europe will have a visa waiting for me in Cherbourg when the ship arrives in about five weeks. From there I'll get a train to Paris, from Paris a train to Vienna probably by way of Munich. Kronehelm's translator will be waiting for me there; not long after that Kronehelm himself will arrive. It sounds like he's got everything figured out. I suppose he believes I'll be under tight rein, there in a strange city in a strange country. It'll be just like right now, the two of us—well, I guess the three of us with the translator—sitting in a cozy apartment in Vienna where all the curtains are closed, shuffling around in bathrobes and creating the literature of love, gangsters and America. In the meantime here in New York City I peer through the curtains to the street below; there's a jeweler's shop, a diner, a little flower shop up at the corner of Third Avenue. No Johnson and no Blaine. In these forty-eight hours, the winter that's hung back for almost a month arrives suddenly. Like a cat with a bird it takes autumn in its teeth and squeals with it, thrashes it against the ground until nothing's left of it but blood and feathers. One miserable wind disperses the rest. A few hours later the windows form ice.

I have another eighteen hours of lying low.

Finally the time comes. It's five in the morning, still the dead of dark, and Kronehelm rises from his bed to phone a cab. He gives me the name of the cargo ship's captain, and then some money, most of it in Austrian schillings. I wait by the window watching for the cab that turns off Third Avenue and slows to a stop. There's nothing I have with me except the clothes I'm wearing and the money in my pocket; Kronehelm stands in the dim light of the tablelamp clutching his robe around him. He looks stricken by the possibility of betrayal. Part of me would like to leave that look on his face, but the other part says to him, "See you in Vienna." He's reassured because he wants to be. I shake my head a little and I'm gone from him.

I get down to the street and in the cab. I'm looking over my shoulder all the time, up and down the street but not taking a lot of time about it. I have my eyes peeled for the little man and the big man. In the cab I take a good look at the driver, I don't know him. He looks back and says hello or something. If he hadn't looked back, if he hadn't said anything or said it funny, I'd have waited till he got to around Park Avenue and then I'd have jumped from the cab and gotten another one. As it is, I don't tell him right away where we're going, just the general direction downtown. I leave myself as much time as I can to get out if I have to, and get to the harbor without anyone but me and Kronehelm and the captain knowing where I'm ending up.

We cross the Brooklyn Bridge to the Brooklyn Pier. It's five forty-five, with the ship scheduled to leave in fifteen minutes. The dock's cold and hard and an old warehouse to my left has crusted with ice during the night, ice hangs from the doors and the roof. At the end of the dock is the ship, it weaves in the sea. On deck someone's standing, the captain maybe but more probably one of the hands. I pay the cabbie and he pulls away and I pull my coat up around me, and I move to the plank at the end of this time I am in. I'm about ninety seconds from the plank when Johnson and Blaine come around the corner of the warehouse.

I guess I feel both furious and relieved to see them. I don't think I would have believed my own life if I hadn't seen them again, I would have always thought they were going to turn up no matter where I was. And at this moment as they emerge from the warehouse I don't have the slightest impulse to run from them as before; I'm even thinking maybe I'll take them, or give it a good try. But then, you know, they spoil it, I mean with the gun and everything. And though I know, or at least I think I know, and they know I know that my father wants me back alive, I also have to figure that under no circumstances can they allow me to leave the country, never to be seen or found again, that's just not going to be acceptable. If that means crippling or killing me, they'll do that, I guess. I guess they will. And now I want the havoc, I could use it; but it isn't there. Now I'm just trying to calculate my way onto that ship sometime in the next five minutes, because I don't think the captain or anyone else on it is going to risk so much as a patch of time or flesh waiting for me to resolve my difficulties with the little man and the big man. When the hand comes up with the gun, I lurch to my left for the warehouse, into the nearest door.

The warehouse is nothing but crates stacked to the ceiling and rows of space between them. In my head I'm trying to figure how to lose them among the crates and then get to the ship. I hear one of them behind me. They'd just be waiting at the plank to cut me off if they were willing to risk losing me somewhere in New York City again, so I guess they intend to take me here; time's against me. I know I'm not going to make it, it's obvious I'm not. But the funny thing is I can see myself running up that plank; I'm already five minutes into the future, running up the plank and diving onto the ship. And for a split second I'm almost serene with this, and now I just follow this moment to come, follow it through the crates of the dark warehouse like following a string. This split second ends when I hear the shot and feel it by my face.

I've never heard or felt a gunshot this close. Not in all the time I was working for one of the city's biggest gangsters. But then maybe that's the measure of a good gangster, the measure of control. The sound of the shot is cold like the snap of a whip, even sharper in the cold air. But the smell has heat and it's that heat that turns everything inside me, as though I'm going to be sick and have a bowel movement at the same moment, everything in me is at flashpoint, about to explode out both ends of me. To call it fear is to trivialize it. If one smells the flesh burning when the bullet hasn't even entered it, what's the smell when it has? I'm crashing among the crates now and I don't see that five-minute future anymore, I can't get the image of it in my eyes no matter how hard I look. The cold warehouse fills with echoes. I can't tell which are mine, I can't even tell which way I want to be going. I can't tell who or what's before or behind me.

And then he's there. He just puts his hand out and I run into it, and I'm sprawling across the ground. He stands over me, his dull dead expressionless face in my face, inches from it; I can smell the bourbon from his pores and count the broken veins of his nose.

Everything in my head ends. I look over for a moment and can see the boat and the plank, can see the hands getting ready to pull the plank on board. The sun's coming up now, its light is blue in the cold but gold on the sea. It's all only ten seconds or so from me, I almost made it. I'm at the other end of the warehouse, me and Blaine. The only thing I can think of now is everything I said to him two nights ago. He's thinking the same thing, and maybe he remembers better than I do.

He has my head in his hands, as though to do to it what I did to Henry's. He's thinking about his own joke, the one that's been on *him* his whole life I guess, like the one that was on me when I was a boy on a farm. In the distance I hear Johnson calling. I hear them beginning to pull the plank. I hear the whistle of the boat and guys yelling instructions to each other. I hear gulls on the water. I'm waiting to hear the big man with my head in his hands tell me he got the joke, and tell me here's the monster everyone always said he was, here it is, and then there'll be a slosh inside my head and that's all. I'm thinking for a moment, still scheming for a moment, how far away Johnson is and how if I were to cry out now, maybe Johnson would get here and stop Blaine from killing me; but that seems like a long shot. I can't imagine getting much sound out of my head before Blaine would cave in its walls.

Blaine takes his hands from me. He says, "Go on."

For a moment, for several moments in fact, I don't understand exactly what he's telling me.

"Go . . . *on*," he says, and looks at the boat, and back at me.

It's a plan, is all I can think. He can't explain killing me with his bare hands but they can explain shooting me to keep me from getting on board the boat.

Johnson's still calling. Blaine looks over his shoulder in the direction of Johnson's voice, and turns back to me and nothing in his expression, as ever, has changed.

I go.

I scramble to my feet and run. I wave to the hands on deck, the plank slides back to the ground. I wait to hear the shot. I wait to smell the heat that will send everything in me exploding out. But all I hear are the gulls and the whistle, and the crash of my feet up the wet icy plank. I dive onto the ship. I lay there some minutes, the deck freezing up into my back, foreigners standing around laughing down at me. When I pull myself up to peer over the railing, we've already started to move. The land's sliding through my hands on the rail, and the new violated water's hissing in my face.

Johnson's on the dock already getting smaller. I can barely hear him over the sound of the water and the engines of the boat churning beneath me. He's stamping his foot, any second he's going to throw his hat on the ground and jump on it. Blaine stands behind him in the doorway of the warehouse; his hands are in his pockets and he's not really looking anywhere at all. I stand there on the side of the ship wanting him to look my way once, wanting just to catch his eye before he's out of sight and it's too late.

But I won't catch his eye, he won't look my way. I won't get that last chance to say something to him, he's going to have the last word. It's part of the price I pay that he will have the last word. He's just a lug anyway, anyone can tell that. Not the brains of the operation.

We leave the harbor, the city lasts another hour of my life. The sea lasts a month and a half. In that time the year turns. My life to come will see it turn many times, before I see this city and this hour again.

48

A visa waits for me in Cherbourg as planned. As planned I take the train to Paris and there spend four freezing bewildered days. I don't feel any rush to get to Vienna, at this point all these places sound the same to me: places for a tourist. "A hell of a time to be going *there*," people say to me. I don't know what they're talking about. "Anyway," advises a guy I meet in the American Express, "at least go by way of Zurich. Not Munich." Is there a difference? I ask. "Yeah," he answers, "one of them has Germans."

The train to Vienna by way of Zurich has no heat. I'm in a car with three Spanish girls who live in Vienna and spend Christmas in Paris with one of the girl's families; they're exiles at least until the civil war ends. Their families have enough money that the three girls can afford to live and look like bohemians. They speak every language within a thousand miles except English. I can't make up my mind if I prefer their company or not, it's just less room to sprawl. But when the cold really settles in around one in the morning, no one's sprawling anyway. I doze fitfully, waking on and off into the night to find, around an hour before dawn, two of them huddled against me in their sleep.

In Zurich we stop long enough to get off the train fifteen minutes and have some coffee in the station. The daylight is thin like a sword. By the time it pulls out for Vienna the train's full and two more people have gotten the last seats in our cabin. One's an Austrian woman in her middle forties, a gray hat stabbed imperiously in her hair, who has little use for me and none for the wild Spanish girls. She doesn't say anything for half the trip until we get to Linz. "This," she explains in precise though accented English, nodding out the window, "is the city of the Leader's child-

hood." I accept this information respectfully, since I have
no idea who the leader of Austria is. Of course she isn't
talking about the leader of Austria. Not yet anyway.

The other person in our cabin is an American about my
age who waited all night in the station, having just come in
from Toulouse. Later he'll recount his futile search for
Toulouse's mythical jazz clubs. Carl's about five and a half
feet tall. He tries to sleep and I gaze resentfully at his feet
that keep getting in the way of mine. Every once in a while
he opens his eyes to peer out the window at the white
Bavarian valleys that keep rolling out beneath us; every
once in a while the train jerks to a halt so that someone
can clear the snow off the tracks. The fires of the little
houses burn in the hills like the red eyes of a white horse
on my father's ranch. It's only when the Austrian woman
in the gray hat makes her comment about Linz that he sits
straight up, blinking at us in confusion.

"Where are we?" he wants to know.

"Linz," I say. Actually this is the first moment I understand he's an American.

"Linz?" he repeats, baffled. He peers around at the Spanish girls and the Austrian woman and then back at me.
"Isn't this train going to Italy?"

"Vienna."

"Vienna!" Something about him sags. He turns to the
Austrian woman and speaks to her in German; she confirms the bad news. He slumps into his seat, disgusted but,
more than that, shaken. He planned to go to Italy where
the winter would be milder; there's a wire with some money
waiting for him. In the meantime he's spent his last money
on the wrong train. But it's more than that, I just don't see
it yet. I haven't gotten to the point yet where I see from the
window of my train, or any window, the time to come. I
don't see the Jews on their hands and knees cleaning the
cracks of the Kärntnerstrasse with toothbrushes while Austrian society ladies kick them with pointed yellow shoes and
spit on the finished spots. Actually, not only do I not see

this before it happens, I don't see it so well as it happens.
Like a lot of people I guess. But Carl, crumpled into his
seat at this moment on the train, sees it already. His mistake already seems so vast that he must ask himself whether
he's really done it on purpose.

"Supposed to be a nice place, Vienna," I shrug.

We don't arrive until nearly dusk, a five hour trip pro-
longed to ten by winter. For only thirty or forty minutes a
silver and red sun reveals itself to our backs, and the snow
of the steppes glitters in the Balkan twilight that first nibbles, then swallows whole our train and the entrails of track
it leaves behind us. The sky smells of ash and animals, it
swims behind itself like a black lake behind the gray ice that
freezes over it. The Spanish girls stand in the aisle of the
train leaning out the windows; the Austrian woman doesn't
so much as quiver in her place. Rumbling into the Westbahnhof we pass the city in a fog, a thousand balconies
clutching at their windows like old severed hands. Mongo-
lian domes swoop nightward. Gypsy flutes blow from the
watery halls of the Wien-Fluss and as the train curses to a
halt we're overcome by the hordes who've been waiting for
us, Asian beggars and Aryan elite, Greek tailors and Mil-
anese bankers and mountain nomads, a jangle of life like
I've never seen. In no time I've lost sight of Carl and the
Spanish girls; at some point on the platform of the station
I look back to see only the Austrian woman in the door of
our car, picking her way among the rabble. Outside the
station I catch a trolley to the outskirts of the Inner City
where I'm left in the vicious shadows of the Rathaus, reading Kronehelm's address by the light of the sparks from the
trolley's departure.

49

All night I wander the Ring of the Inner City looking for the address Kronehelm's given me. The streets are hard with ice and in the waning hours as it begins to snow the squares scurry with people in red capes. The Ring's circular passages fill with the orange lights of taxis and the yellow windows of carriages that gasp along at the clip of the horses pulling them. A caravan passes me through the archways of the Hofburg and the passengers gaze at the way I affront the grandeur of their obelisks. Two in the morning I'm shuddering beneath a footbridge. The naked vines of dead autumn ivy snap at my eyes. By three I've found an open door on the east side of St. Stephen's; at the core of the cathedral sleeps an encampment of bums and cripples and vagabonds. We all stumble out at dawn. When I see Vienna in the cold sun, the buildings white and chiseled, I understand how the city laughs in its rituals of humiliation and how this lot of riffraff accepts their state of prostration with gratitude. They'd prefer to bleed into their own seats or piss into their own mouths before wringing so much as a drop on the snowy gown of bridal Vienna. The gutters of the Danube run silverpure while the beggars eat their own scum.

I wind up on the river's edge of the Ringstrasse. In the east, at the very stitching of history where Europe is sutured to Asia, the ferris wheel of the Praterstern spins empty in the wind. The rattle of its cages is brittle beneath the bellow of Hungary. My destination turns out to be a small sidestreet off the main boulevard below the canal, a block away from the Ring. In the window of Kronehelm's address sits a guy probably not much older than I at a desk, I can see him writing in a ledger as I cross the street. His face is a bloodless pallor; he looks up from his ledger and, when he sees me, waves. Nothing in his face changes, he waves at me like I've been walking up this street to this building every morning for years. I've never seen him in my life but he waves, he's waiting for me, just sitting there at this ledger patiently filling it in until I show up. There's no doubt in his mind who I am. When I get to the door he's come downstairs to open it. He doesn't smile and his handshake is perfunctory. Herr Jainlight, he calls me; his name is Petyr. He introduces himself as my translator, though he looks to me more like an accountant. We go upstairs to an apartment that might as well have been flown in from Gramercy Park, where the curtains have all been drawn except for the window where Petyr's been watching for me.

Petyr and I don't have much to say. I'm cold through and through, disgusted with everything. I want to eat and sleep, or maybe sleep and eat, and only after I've folded myself into a hot bath half my size. The morning's passed before I'm finally warm, and when I sleep I dream that I'm cold, I dream that I'm walking in Vienna's circles. When I wake I have the sense it's night, though with the curtains drawn in my room there's no way to be sure. But a light is on by my bed, and I've turned over and over about eight times before I notice Petyr's sitting there looking at me, from the chair in the room's corner. He has his hands folded in his lap and it looks utterly unnatural. In the same way he sat in his window waiting seven weeks for me to show up, he now sits waiting for me to wake up. "It's an honor to be your translator," he finally says when he's sure I'm conscious enough to understand him. His English is good.

I sit up in the bed and make some polite retort about the honor of being translated, and wonder what in the world I'm talking about. Petyr just nods, his pale face never cracks for a moment, and then he taps something on the desk; squinting into the dark I do believe I see a typewriter. I do believe I see a stack of paper, and several black pens lined up like muskets for the cavalry. "Everything's ready for you," he says. That's swell, I tell him, and lie back down to go to sleep: We'll get to it in no time. April, say. I doze off for a bit, maybe twenty minutes or so, and when I wake again he hasn't moved, he's still sitting there. "Yes," he says, "it's all ready for you," in a voice no louder than the snow on the roof, and only when I don't jump up and run across the room and start typing does he finally add, "But I suppose you'd like some time to rest from your travels." Now I have to sit up and take a good long look at this character. Finally I just cancel the light by the bed and leave him there in the dark. I never hear him move, so it's a relief to find him gone in the morning.

It must be that Petyr looks like an accountant only because he is one. Not only does he translate what I write but handles the business end of it as well. Over the next week, watching him at his desk by the window, it's impossible to tell whether he's diddling Amanda or decimals; his face never changes. I can't imagine what my writing must read like as interpreted by this manager of numbers, though it's possible he's perfect for the job, leaving the passion to me and claiming only precision for himself. What a team, Petyr and Amanda and Molly and I.

Kronehelm wired a week ago to say he'll be here in four or five days. There's a fairly unveiled hint that I'm expected to make up for lost time. The clients in Vienna and Munich and Berlin wait with great anticipation for my new adventures. In the first week I find it impossible to get much done, though thinking about the Spanish girls on the train from Paris opens up a couple of inspiring possibilities. Petyr's disappointed though. The clients don't want Spanish girls from Paris, he reminds me, they want Americana—gangsters and Indians. He tells me Client X has a particular penchant for Aztec mysticism, so I cook up some stories involving conquistadors. Client X isn't to be underestimated, a very big shot in the German government. Neither Petyr nor Kronehelm says much about him but it doesn't take long to figure out they're scared to death. One afternoon I overhear Kronehelm make some reference to "the little cripple," and there's a moment of silence that's palpable even in the next room; both he and Petyr hold their breaths as they ponder the recklessness of the remark and wait for the consequences of its indiscretion, as though any second German police are going to come through the windows.

This goes on a month or two. In a quarter of this time I reach a breaking point. I can't stand to stay in the flat and I can't bear the idea of facing either Vienna or its winter again. I'm fucking cooked, that's all, stuck here stewing in my juices. Petyr's such an unsettling little worm that the day Kronehelm arrives I'm almost happy to see him slither in with his trunks and crates and immediately pull the curtains even tighter so not the thinnest slice of dank gray European light can come through. Kronehelm throws his arms around me and begins to cry with joy; I guess he figured I'd never actually show up. After a few more days I know something's got to give, what with three freaks waddling from one dark room to the next publishing obscene books for the private collections of deformed midgets in Berlin five hundred kilometers away. You just know that kind of enterprise is going to have one or two pressure points somewhere. When I've been in Vienna eight weeks, spring begins to slip into the city like a refugee, and I, also like a refugee, am looking to slip away.

51

March 1937. The snow melts and the ice breaks in the gutters, and people hustle up and down the Kärntner-strasse from one coffeehouse to the next, painters set up their easels around St. Stephen's with little fires to keep the colors from hardening in the chill. Every once in a while a palette gets too close to a flame and you can hear little pops of ignition and hue all over the square. There's the smell of sugar, cologne, cabbage. The Hofburg rises at the middle of the Ringstrasse like a mountain range that's ripped itself loose from the ocean bottom and floated to the surface; through the streets wild dogs run in herds. Political bombings set off peals of giddiness among the cafe crowd. Phony military guys in high black boots and brown uniforms march back and forth between the fountains.

I try to write in the mornings before Kronehelm wakes. Petyr seems never to sleep at all and almost any time I look up, he's sitting on the other side of the room watching me. Both of them literally sit and wait for me to deliver another chapter. I can't take much more of it, I keep telling myself they need me more than I need them. Petyr translates faster than I can write and Kronehelm's off to Deutschland with it and back before I've figured out another escapade. Lately there's been someone coming by the flat to pick up the material; he wears a long gray coat and his face is pasty-white like Petyr's and scarred by acne. He's surly and officious and thinks he's quite an important fellow running back and forth as errand boy for this Client X. Kronehelm always collapses at the man's feet and grovels an hour or two. The emissary's a little surprised to meet me and I don't blame him, I don't much look like the dashing figure who tweaks the libidos of the high and mighty in the Chancellery. Between us Kronehelm, Petyr and I have maybe enough worldly experience to fill the closing hours of a slow night in Salzburg. We must look like frauds which, of course, we are. Anyway the flunky in the gray coat takes the new stuff and, as he's leaving, gives the German salute, which both Kronehelm and Petyr return with shitlicking haste. I just look at the three of them standing there with their arms in the air and I start to laugh and can't stop. I can't help it. I laugh like the night I set my father's house on fire, it's that funny. The errand boy gets so mad his head looks like a tomato that's going to pop, and I think Kronehelm's going to start sobbing in terror any second. "Say, I didn't mean anything," I try to assure them, "sure, you go right ahead if you like. Look here," and I start at it, walking around the room shooting my arm out here and there, then collapsing on the furniture laughing, then jumping back up and saluting some more. I throw the windows open and salute the whole fucking city. It's the only good afternoon I've had since I got here.

When I leave a few minutes later, Kronehelm's in quite a state. Petyr's running back and forth with hot tea or something, any moment he's going to start measuring Kronehelm's pulse and peering under his eyelids. I'm in too upbeat a mood to let this nonsense undo it, and I just walk out the door leaving the two of them in each other's care. It's a fine afternoon and I decide to take a walk over to the Volksgarten and then cut up through the palace over to the Karlsplatz, see who's being burned in effigy this afternoon or beaten to a mush before the general bloodlust of the Fräuleins in the coffeehouses. Sure enough it turns out the episode with the errand boy from Berlin is only an omen of better luck to come, because I'm walking along the outer wall of the Hofburg when I hear someone shouting from across the street. Galoot! he's calling, and I look over and there in the doorway of the Cafe Central is Carl. I haven't seen him since the night I arrived in Vienna. There he is now waving at me and then I hear a pounding on the window of the cafe and look over, and there are two of the Spanish girls waving as well. I cross the street and Carl and I shake hands, we go into the Central and the Spanish girls jump up and embrace me. Actually I don't remember us ever being that friendly but it turns out they have grateful recollections of huddling against me in the cold of that train. I'm almost speechless with happiness to see the lot of them, to know someone in this city besides the two loonies I've been living with. I spend the rest of the afternoon sitting beneath the arched ceiling of the Central with Carl and the Spanish girls and the rest of the clientele, revolutionaries and journalists and Italian tourists, and waiters running up and down the wide marble stairs in their white jackets.

Carl, it turns out, is still not happy about being in Vienna, but I gather that at least one of the girls has taken him under her wing in more ways than one, and so it isn't the worst situation he's ever been in. He's still trying to get his money from American Express so that he can get to Italy. The two of us sit at the table opening all the sugar cubes while the waiter ignores us. With his command of foreign languages Carl negotiates the conversations. Without going into a long story I explain to the three of them my own insane arrangement with Kronehelm and Petyr. "For God's sake, come live with us," Carl says, just like that, and then he turns to the girls and lays it out for them in Spanish and German, and they agree that living with them is the sensible solution. I don't even want to ask if they really have the room for me because I don't care; I don't want to know what their place is like or whatever reasons there might be I shouldn't go. The only question in my mind is how I'm going to break the news to Kronehelm without him putting a gun in his mouth and painting the walls of his flat with the slush of his brains.

I decide I need to spell it out for him this very night. Carl and the girls come with me and wait out in the street while I go upstairs and wake up Kronehelm, who's retired early. "Say, mein Herr," I start talking as soon as I see his eyes flicker, "I've reached a business decision here, I'm leaving," and he's still rubbing his face getting himself oriented, looking at me, saying to himself, What's happening? "I'm taking a powder residencewise, I think it's best," and now he's shaking his head as though to clear it out, "but I'll be in touch with you very soon because we're still partners, partner," and now he's finally starting to get it, "I just don't think this is a good idea my being here, it, uh, well it ebbs the creative flow you know, it uh, well, let's just say," and he's shaking his head but I bull my way through, "let's just say that if I stayed here another night, another minute, I'd probably, you know, kill you. Probably. Because you drive me fucking crazy. But the business, that's still on, I mean I've got the goods and you've got the market, so let's not worry about it, I'll probably write even bigger and better, look at it that way," and now, as I feared, he's starting to clutch at my clothes. No no no no, he's starting, first quite low and calm really, just No no no no, and then when I take his hands and try to pry them finger by finger from my coat he just starts screaming. He's raving about Client X this and Client X that, and I realize that given the little party we had with the German flunky this afternoon and all that saluting we did together, this is probably not timed absolutely the best it could be, but there's no going back now, if I stay Kronehelm and Petyr will be up all night plotting strategy how to keep me. They'll bind me to the damn typewriter, glue my fingers to the keys. So I'm going now. Client X, Client X, Kronehelm keeps choking; he's holding my ankles and letting me drag him across the floor as I walk to the door. It's appalling. Then he's slipped out of his bathrobe and I'm dragging him across the floor naked. This old man with half-finished flesh like the tissue of a fetus, sliding across the floor on my ankles. Petyr stands in one of the doorways staring at us. Finally I just kick him loose; he shudders there at my feet and, as though to mercykill something that's just been delivered up between birth and stillbirth, I raise my foot over his head and am ready to bring it down. And Petyr, without a sound, screams. He screams without a sound, his whole body's racked with it, though nothing comes out. The white of his pallor has turned blue. I bring the foot down but not on Kronehelm and just lean into the doorway breathing hard; none of us moves until finally I say, "I'll send word in a couple of days," to Petyr, and then stumble out into my life.

52

I move into the Spanish girls' flat and stay awhile. In almost no time it takes on an utter familiarity—books and empty wine bottles in the corner and wooden chairs that are broken and old family photos on the wall, and pictures of Greta Garbo and Louise Brooks, revolutionary tracts under the table and antique clocks stuck at five minutes before two, a small fish tank beneath a window. The Spanish girls live the free life. A whole entourage of people constantly pass through, conversationalists and exlovers on leave from psychiatric wards, philosophers on the make and female Dutch photographers who shoot nude selfportraits, bartenders from Brussels and a plumber who brings a bottle of French champagne every time he fixes the hot water because he wants to make a celebration of it and listen to Bessie Smith records. They all jabber away at the same time and eat roast rabbit, doze off for an hour and wake up midsentence finishing the conversation they began before others coopted it, have violent quarrels and rearrange their lives before my eyes. They tend to have a lot of cockeyed ideas if you ask me. Absolutely everyone smokes and the ash of their cigarettes always grows to about three inches long before it falls to the floor at which point they grind it into the carpet. The world is their ashtray, and soon I notice that the city itself has begun to take on a dinge since I got here, until even the sky is the color of cold cinders.

Most of them consider themselves Trotskyite bandits of a sort who get by through various means. Each day the three Spanish girls leave me careful instructions about cops, tax collectors and utility inspectors who come knocking at the door to inquire about forged papers, back taxes and the meters that have been jammed to keep the bills down. The flat is something of a way station for lots of shady characters, in whose ranks I suppose I must be included. The guy who was here before I arrived was a homosexual who placed an advertisement in a Viennese homosexual newspaper a couple of months ago. The advertisement has appeared since his departure and I now get many letters, wires, secret codes and even personal interviews on the other side of the door. Sultry male voices whisper Guten Tag or deliver rasping promises or sobbing accusations. Thierry? they call. Thierry no longer lives here, I answer. There's silence and then they either disappear or make their pitch anyway. Bitte, bitte, they moan, and scratch at the door. In other words, these people are all slightly cracked. I'm regarded as a naif and puritan because I don't fuck every casual acquaintance three seconds after they blow through the doorway. I suppose I might be less inhibited if the population of the place wasn't on the scale of India. They know I'm a writer but not the exact nature of what I write; they'd probably be amused but who can be sure. As proletarian rebels go they're a highly refined lot. They eat the best, drink the best, buy expensive objets d'art and wouldn't be caught dead riding the streetcars. There's nothing quite as screwy as a bunch of revolutionaries zipping around Vienna in taxis, unless of course it's Kronehelm and Petyr goosestepping around the suite with dirty books in their arms.

After a week I send a note to Petyr to meet me at the northeastern corner of the Karlsplatz at four o'clock on a Friday afternoon. I have some new work to deliver: Don't, I tell him, bring Kronehelm. On Friday afternoon Petyr brings Kronehelm. Kronehelm wears a huge coat that overwhelms him, a hat and dark glasses; in such a defined and dramatic costume his person looks less formed than ever. It's also the first time I've seen him outside and I swear I can see the sun setting right through him. He's whimpering before I'm even close. "Oh Banning, please," he's saying, and then gurgles a little unformed sob, "please." Petyr glowers with hate, at me for abandoning his mentor, and at his mentor for caring. "Stop blubbering," I snap, "if you don't, I'll leave at this moment and you'll never, *ever* see me again." Kronehelm holds his face in his hands, I push the work into Petyr's arms. "We're still in business," I continue, though I can't bring myself to be soothing about it, I'm so fed up with them. What else, after all, am I going to do? I'm stuck, I'm not going back to America, and nothing else here is going to pay off like this; lately it's all I can do to write anything. "I'll send word in a week when I have more," I say, and turn on my heels and walk away quickly. I have this horror that any minute I'm going to feel an unformed man clutching at my ankles again, I'm going to drag him naked across the Karlsplatz. I keep walking and don't look back until I've turned at least four corners. Then I double back to the Cafe Central where I sit until ten at night with pen and paper waiting for Amanda and Molly. They never show.

53

Amanda and Molly and I become just friends. They stand me up routinely, they have dangerous adventures they never tell me about. Our relationship is strained, they're no longer at my beck and call when I need them. I don't laugh anymore with them, though Kronehelm hardly seems to notice. Client X's satisfaction supersedes all other considerations. Living with the Spanish girls in their crazy flat with all the crazy people coming and going doesn't help either; Amanda and Molly don't care for their company. By now it's the summer of 1937. The news from Spain casts a pall. I have some money saved from what I've written and sold to Kronehelm over the last six months, and decide to take a room of my own. When I ask Carl to go in on it with me he only seems vexed, he knows he has to leave soon; as a Jew, it doesn't make sense for him to stay any longer. He keeps asking if he should leave and I keep lying, but I'm at the point I can't lie any more. He's managed to get some of the money from Italy, and when he's ready to go, if he needs it, I'll give him the rest. There's a bombing every other day now somewhere in the city. People in the cafes wager as to the day and hour the current chancellor of the country goes the way of his predecessor, who had his head blown off in his office three summers ago by the blackboot boys. If that happens the Germans will come, which seems fine with the Viennese; they practically start fondling themselves at the thought of it. For me the bombing has ceased to be such a jolly business. Let's say it's a distraction. From a political standpoint I couldn't care less; for all I care the Viennese can blow themselves off the planet. But it scares away the girls, you know, the ones who might replace Amanda and Molly. I look for a quiet place a quarter of an hour by trolley from the Inner City and find one on a street

with a long name that translates roughly as "storm of dogs."
It's a small single room with a toilet down the hall and a
couple of large windows that open onto the street three
floors below me. Here, alone and celibate on Dog Storm
Street, I hear the girls knock on my door, sometimes
they're waiting for me when I come home. I don't see them
so well at first, but after a while they come closer. I know
nothing of their backgrounds and don't want to know.
They are Lauren and Jeanine, Janet and Catherine and
Leigh. They do whatever I want which is the way I like it
—none of this willfulness I got from Amanda and Molly. A
whole new crew, I break them in my way, right from the
start, not repeating the mistakes of the past. Outside my
windows are the vagabonds of Vienna. They're not much
interested in Lauren or Catherine, but since the first dawn
I stumbled out of St. Stephen's with them, they seem to be
everywhere; one can escape the bombs but not the vagabonds. Vagabonds and beggars and cripples run, hobble,
crawl and roll amok in Vienna. Every amputee, every blind
tramp, every mutilated visage is a citizen of the world and
they've all beaten a path to the city of the fucking good life;
it's a rich disgusting joke. You can't miss a single spasm or
tic in the glare of the bombs, you can find them basking
and warming their deformities in the glow of Vienna's ton-
iest society spots. The whole damned city's overrun with
them, and the best any one of them can hope for is that
the next person who kicks him wears a soft shoe. I look out
my window and see them everywhere; they're well mobi-
lized, women in rags and waifs without eyes and men who
have nothing to show for their lives but the puddle they're
sitting in, guys in boxes, the Ring littered from one end to
the other with the wayward, the unsheltered, the stinking.
They've mapped out the territory, they've cut off all means
of retreat. They lie in wait to ambush me. I know I'd never
have the nerve to ask anyone for a schilling, such shamelessness demands more backbone than I've got; I'm sure I'd
steal something before I begged someone for a break. Beg-

ging for a break is too profound a step toward one's own humanity, I can't walk that far. I recognize this and these people know I recognize it and now they're after me. Now every time I leave my room, I must look both ways to make sure someone isn't coming toward me on little wheels. I know one morning I'll walk out into Dog Storm Street and there they'll be, an army of human wrecks at my feet. There are only two things that will resolve this, of course. One is time. Live here long enough and one learns how to stop the bleeding. I'm happy to say the process is already beginning to work. I'm happy to say I'm becoming better and better at passing more and more vagabonds without feeling anything at all. Oh, sometimes in a weak moment I'll muster up an expression of sympathy for a particularly hopeless excuse of a human being; but a good night with Catherine or Lauren will fortify the meanness in me, and if it doesn't bring out a real strong throaty horselaugh, like I haven't had in a while now, then it's at least good for a chuckle or two. I can throw open the windows and give out a good chortle for the palsied little boy who's sleeping in the garbage around the corner from the fruit stand. The other thing that resolves my contest with the cripples, as I walk along the Danube and the dreamlike quays of night and gangrene, is the realization that once, among these very vagabonds in this very city, roamed the most evil man in the world. Twenty-five years ago he wandered these streets with these vagabonds and beggars and cripples and fed on the slime of his own evil, sitting in the Karlsplatz drawing pathetic little pictures of the cathedral. And the world, feeding on the slime of its evil, knew a kindred spirit when it saw one; now he throws athletic galas in Berlin and builds himself cities, and plots the new millennium. He's the evil that doesn't devour the child in one gulp but first licks its hand like a puppy, then nibbles at it as it shudders into shock. Then the world licks the blood from *his* hand. Soon he'll come back to the vagabonds, maybe next year or next month or next week; he'll come back to look at his youth, and he'll eat it. His blackboot boys have already begun the work, they're going through the streets and pummeling the youth of their leader into grit and gutter-meal, so that not one trace of the original moment that bore him and all his evil is left to be seen. When I see the vagabonds of Vienna I see two men in each of them: one is the Leader, and the other is me. Every day I walk the streets of Vienna with one consort or another, Catherine or Lauren, whichever one suits me at the particular moment, thinking about the things we will do when we get home, and invariably I stumble onto one scene or another when the blackboot boys are having at it with some poor ruin of a human being who is irrefutable evidence of another beast loosed and rapturous in God's universe other than the one who intends to rule the world from the shit-hole that calls itself Germany, and it's one such afternoon, not far from the corner of the Ringstrasse where I came my first night in Vienna, and it's one such melee, when they're beating an old Jew outside a candleshop, that I happen to look up and, in a window above the street, watching me, I see you.

54

You remember me. This is, after all, the moment that razors the Twentieth Century down its middle, this simple afternoon you're leaning out your window, all of fifteen years old I'd say, while below you men are scuffling in one of history's countless shards. Now there come along some comrades of this poor pillaged soul, a platoon of bums, and for the first time I see something like resistance in this city

to the blackboot boys, a vagabond war. As though it's a
battle for your benefit, you there in the window, as though
history scrambles and brutalizes and bleeds for the face of
you. I cannot recollect your beauty. I recollect the memory
of your beauty, which we both know is not the same, because my memory made you beautiful. Whether those vagabonds think you're beautiful too is impossible for me to
guess; they never cared so much for Catherine or Lauren,
who are more beautiful. Much more beautiful. Come to
think of it, you may be plain as sand. Your long hair a
tarnished panic of fool's-gold yellow, your eyes a banal
mud brown. There may not be a single curve of your jaw
that's anything more than ordinary. You say nothing to the
scene before you, but your face says everything, the contempt for the blackbooters not simply because they're bul-
lies but because they presume to hold history as their own,
they act like it's tied to the post with a collar around its
neck. The vagabonds have no history, they don't even
know history. It doesn't intimidate them in the least. And
when you look up and raise your eyes across the street, and
mine meet them, we follow each other's look as I make my
way past the shard of history; and you say you don't remember. I don't believe you. Fifty years later I don't believe you. Seeing you haunts and binds me, and I don't
believe this defiant maybe-not-beautiful moment that ra-
zored the century lengthwise was utterly gone from you
before your century had passed another five minutes.

They're banging around in the street, the window of the
candleshop explodes and wax tumbles over the sill, when a
stone someone's hurled strikes you. A moment follows in
which everything almost seems to stop, and in that moment the beggars pull the old Jew from the tumult and
haul him down the street. The blackboot boys are happy to
pretend they've won the skirmish, throwing more stones in
the beggars' wake, not far or hard enough to bring them
back for more; the boys don't want more. For a minute
they stand around and mark their victory with general

commentary about Jews and Germany. In the window you turn as soon as the rock hits you, you raise one hand to your face. In the moment you turn I'm almost sure I can see your blood, I can see the corner of your mouth where the stone opened your flesh. We don't see each other anymore, our mutual stare is lost in the wound, washed away with the blood of it; maybe the moment's washed away too. You turn and without looking back once—if only you had looked once—you disappear from the window and shut it closed. The boys are singing and carrying on, and I'd stay there on the street until they've left, waiting for you to come back from washing your wound to stand in the window again, or to come to the door and open it, and if not I'd go to the door and knock; I'd wait, but I'm the only one left in the street with the blackbooters who are in a frenzy now, walking around swinging their fists and singing, and far up the street, slowing to a standstill, who should I see but Carl. There he is. He stops, I see him, and I wait for him to see me, and then I turn my back and walk away, and I know he's done the same.

5 5

Tonight I return to my room and it's empty. Lauren and Jeanine, Catherine and Janet and Leigh are gone. They understand I no longer want them here; I can't stand the light. I can't stand the dark, something drunker than blood courses through me. I'm caught between the sheets of the bed; the light of bombings and parades blots the night outside my window. When it fades I sleep an hour, when I wake I sit up in bed in the dark of the room, and find that the gray Hungarian moon has dropped from the sky over the river, has moved through the circular streets of the city, up the banks of the Wien-Fluss to Dog Storm Street, and dangles now in my window like burst mutant fruit from the low limb of a tree. From some place I can't see the moon casts a shadow on the left corner of my room and there in the shadow opens a door, and there in the door you are. We're children. I'm twenty. Your breasts are fifteen, your legs twenty-five, your eyes and vulva ageless, neither old nor born. You're already becoming what I remember rather than what you are. You step from the doorway of the shadow of the moon, your face only a quarter in light, and I see grow from your womb curling out the tuft of your hair a long wet vine; it precedes you, an umbilical thistle. It grows before you across the floor between us, it winds up the side of the bed. It wraps itself around my feet and up my leg, it coils around my waist and binds my erection. Dog Storm Street creaks with blue carriages, I hear the hooves of white donkeys; lakeless swans slap dead against the walls of houses. The window runs with the juice of the moon, I smell the musk of the steppes beyond the eastern hills. At the end of the long wet vine that winds from the center of you and seizes me is a black flower that grows new petals as soon as it sheds them. In a matter of moments the bed's covered with black petals, I peel them off my thighs sticky and damp. I know you're a virgin. I didn't expect anything else. I didn't expect you to come to the bed like this and prostrate your pink body across the wet black of the crumbling flower. I can already hear, fifty years from now on your Chinese island, every word of your lies. Every word. I hear them above the songs in slavic belfries, you can fill your mouth with the black flower but nothing stifles the deceit of your denial of me. The flower never stops growing. When I grab you by your wrists and shake you into looking at me, it's as though I've taken a live wire: I'm stunned with your cold voltage. I want to let go but I can't, it takes your own fingers to pry mine loose; you

smile as you do it. I wake later and the bed's soaked with
the dew of the black flower. The vine's withdrawn back into
you, only its marks are left on my legs. You've gone back
into the door of the gray Hungarian moon and closed it
behind you. I sleep again and when I wake the wet of you
has coated me. On the desk in the sunlight are these pages
that document you were here.

5 6

I sell you to them. As though I've put chains around your
feet and led you by a rope down the Kärntnerstrasse, I sell
you, for the usual amount. I guess Petyr's finally convinced
Kronehelm not to come along to the rendezvous; the translator waits at the appointed time and place alone. They
don't know what they have in you. You're worth more than
any of them can pay; at the next appointment Petyr even
complains. "Herr Kronehelm," he announces coolly, "says
to tell you your last chapter won't do. It's much too . . ."
he looking for the word, ". . . elusive."

"If it isn't satisfactory," I answer, "then you should find
yourself another partner." I take my money and leave.

The other day I went to find your street again. There on
the edge of the Ring not far from the street where I lived
seven weeks. I walked up one road and down the other,
looking for the candleshop. I scoured maps, I questioned
residents of the neighborhood. I mean, it's not such a big
neighborhood. It doesn't have so many streets, and there
are only so many candleshops. But I couldn't find the candleshop, and I didn't find your street. And I wonder if I'm
really leading you by a rope, chained and enslaved, or if

I'm the gateway through which you've escaped to other places, as though through a shadow's door.

But you come back to me every night. Wherever else it is you go, you come to me and when we're through with the night I sell it. By the high price they pay me, I know I love you.

5 7

When the summer's over, Carl finally leaves. His affair with the Spanish girl hasn't gone so well lately, and I've been urging him to go anyway. The city's become dangerous for him. Italy doesn't make a lot of sense anymore either, so he takes a night train back to Paris. No way the fucking Germans are going to take over Paris, right? The Spanish girl and I see him off at the Westbahnhof, and I shake hands and then I watch his train disappear.

. The Spanish girl is somber. She's invited to a dinner hosted by a rich Scot the other Spanish girl's been seeing, and her escort with all the languages has just vanished on a train in the distance. In lousy English she pleads that I come along, if only awhile. I don't know if I owe it to Carl, I certainly don't imagine I owe it to her. From the windows of the station the city is ignited by the scatter of fire and glass as though chandeliers have plunged to the streets below them.

We take a taxi to a neighborhood behind the museums of the Burg Ring. Anyone with a house in this part of town has a few extra schillings jangling in his pocket. We go upstairs in this house where there are already four or five other people, all of them young and rich and attractive. I

don't think one of them is Austrian; most are German.
From the window I can see the dark dollopped trees of the
Volksgarten rustling against the light that lingers in the
west. Standing in the doorway is a guy in old disheveled
clothes with a three-day stubble on his face drinking
Scotch from the bottle, and I think to myself that one of
the vagabonds has somehow wandered up; I wonder if the
German guests will start thrashing him. He's the only one
who looks almost as bad as I. Turns out he owns the place.

One Spanish girl is moping about Carl, whom she's insisted half the summer she doesn't love anyway, and the
other Spanish girl is plotting marriage with this derelict in
the doorway. Everyone's on their way out to dinner and
the girls say why don't I come along. I don't have any
money and I don't fit in with the crowd at all, but we all
pile into a couple of taxis and are on our way. We arrive at
an apartment we could have walked to in six minutes, and
take a lift up to a suite that would shame Doggie Hanks'
joint back in New York, an Eighteenth Century apartment
facing the Inner City. The hostess is a beautiful young girl
who appears to have sprained her wrist and wears it in a
fashionable little sling resting below her breast. She greets
everyone in a very cordial fashion until she comes to me,
whom she regards rather peculiarly. It's explained to her
delicately that I'm an American.

My only recourse is to saunter over to the bar and drink
something. Then I walk over to the hors d'oeuvres and wolf
down about half the table. This is exactly the kind of behavior that's expected of me. I'm regarded by the other
guests, who now number twenty or thirty, with fascination;
they all think I'm a direct descendant of Geronimo. Standing at the table is a plump little English girl who appears to
be about four feet tall. She's squeezed all of herself into
about six inches of clothes, and she has a tiny little waist
from which the rest of her bubbles out. It's not unappeal-
ing. Her hair is a blaze of red redder than mine, and she
has freckles. "Big appetite," she observes, watching me. I

stroll through the suite checking out the rooms and opening windows and emptying other people's drinks, and finally the party decides to move again and everyone loads into half a dozen taxis and we caravan off down the Ringstrasse. We come to a dark alley near the Hofburg where the taxis can't go and get out and march to a dark street near the center of the Inner City where all the strippers and streetwalkers live. The building looks like a warehouse. It doesn't have a single window, and only a single door. The door opens and somebody in the shadows says this or that, and then we go inside.

We're now in the sleekest nightclub in Vienna, maybe in the world for all I've seen of nightclubs. It makes the Top Dog look dull, everything's a deep blue that's very popular with people who can afford not to look at themselves. One of the Germans tells me it's the most exclusive private club in Europe. I order a double bourbon on ice with no water. It occurs to me what money I have isn't going to go very far here. The menus have no prices. But I figure I'm a guest, right? The Spanish girls are seated across the table from me with the Scottish bloke who's tastefully discarded his bottle by now; we get to talking and he's not a bad guy, actually, though his accent's incomprehensible. There's a beautiful Dutch blonde on my right and the voluptuous freckled little English redhead on my left, and we're all talking and everything seems jake, and the people at the table now assume that if I can talk and dress and act this way and lumber around in polite society as though I don't give a fuck about anything at all, then I certainly must be the wealthiest person in the room. They've decided I'm from some frontier in America with cotton or oil, a shrewd fellow who neatly sidestepped the Crash like a croquet ball. They've concluded I'm absolutely stinking with money and probably a regular patron here and a couple of them ask what I recommend as far as the cuisine goes. I point out this or that, whatever part of the menu my finger happens to be on, and I give them a knowledgeable wink as I do so.

Pretty soon I'm ordering the wine and cheese, I'm calling out to waiters for another bottle of Chateau Whatever 1896, and everyone's having a splendid time. These Yanks may not look like much, they're saying to each other, but they have style. The Spanish girls are ignoring it completely, jabbering on and on about the Scot and Carl who with luck is about to Switzerland by now, and the only one who watches me intently and doesn't look like she's fooled for a minute is the little English pudding at my side, who seems to be having the best time of all. Her knowledgeable winks are for me.

The evening progresses, so to speak. We have a fine meal but I'm careful not to act too impressed. I tactfully but pointedly disparage the pureed carrots and look a little bored with the brandy mousse. The only thing I wonder about are the other guests in the club. Lots of men. Women with our party to be sure, but the rest of the clientele divides up into male couples, all seated at intimate tables. As I sit there listening to the voices from these other tables, I'm sure I recognize some of them. Soon I'm sure I recognize all of them. I realize I've talked to every one of these voices on the other side of the door in the Spanish girls' flat where I was living not so long ago. I decide to pay no attention to this and before I know it the meal's finished and I'm enjoying a cognac and talking with the Dutch blonde when some German two seats down from me begins to catch my attention; he's rattling off numbers and figures and various divisions, and I look over and realize he has the *bill*. The Spanish girls want to investigate the dancehall downstairs and I interject that this sounds like an excellent idea and let's do it *jetzt*. We get down to the dancehall and the Spanish girls disappear, and I'm hanging around biding my time until all the figuring over the bill is finished upstairs, when this guy comes up and asks me to dance. Excuse me? I say and he repeats the question and I'm shaking my head, Uh nein, nein, es tut mir leid, when some other guy comes up and he wants to dance too. Soon there are these two guys arguing over who's going to dance with me. As fast as I can, I run back upstairs and back to the table only to find they're just getting around to shelling out the schillings, so I beat it back downstairs where the two guys are still squabbling; moreover the more these guys talk the more familiar their voices become until I'm certain that at least one of them stood haranguing me outside my door a few months back. If I say too much now they're going to discover I am in fact Thierry, elusive object of desire who places advertisements in newspapers as a vicious tease. I get back upstairs pronto and ease my way back into my seat at the table where everything seems to be settled. The money's already on the tray with the bill and nobody's too concerned with it or looking around saying where's that cheap stinking-rich American who hasn't paid up. The coast seems clear to me. I sit down and let the conversation wash over me like the waves of the Mediterranean, when the German two seats down who's been tallying the score passes the tray to me and says, cool as ice, "I'm certain you would not wish to leave again without paying for yourself or the lady."

Myself or the lady? I don't know which lady he means, unless it's one of the Spanish girls. It's one thing to call me a freeloader, which of course I absolutely am, another thing to saddle me with responsibility for the lady. He shouldn't have said that, actually; it was a bad move. He had me shamed until he came up with that lady bit. "Don't worry about it, Wilfried," I say, and get up out of the chair for the full effect, "don't you have something better to concern yourself with? Aren't there a couple of old Jews wandering around outside you and the boys can beat up, a crippled old gypsy woman you can lay out and fill up with rancid brown German cum?" The room seems to have gotten quiet, and I like it. I feel perfectly fine at this particular moment, I should have done this long ago. I'm almost certain at this moment I'm going to kill someone again; it seems like much too long since I last did it. This asshole's perfect. He's every little piece of German shit I've seen in the last eight months rolled into one, I'd crush him and grow a plant from him if the little white worms of his fecal matter didn't make it impossible. The color of his face is just like the white of little worms, I see their little heads wiggling in his soulless pisscoated eyes. "Tell you what, Heinzly," I say, "send the damned bill to your minister of propaganda, the little one with the foot that looks like horsemeat. See, he's a *client* of mine. He works for me. Tell him I said to write you a nice big tip for licking every shithole in Wien where I've set my ass in the last eight months after blowing your pathetic soul-curdling goodlife right out the end of it. He'll be glad to, that boy jumps when I say to," snapping my fingers. "He may write *your* propaganda but I'm the guy who writes *his*. He reads it with one hand while he pops his wang with the other until your fucking Berlin drips with it." Now the little white worms in his eyes are practically dancing on their tails, and while I refuse to tear my own eyes from his, I'm vaguely aware of the other men in the room around me beginning to stand; I gather they're all Germans too. Also, by now they're *certain* I'm Thierry, mysterious messenger of passion who's led all of them to their respective moments of unfulfillment, which makes them even less happy about me.

"Now listen here," I hear someone behind me, and without even turning I can tell it's the English redhead, though for a moment it's not certain which of us she's talking to, if not both of us. Turns out it's him. She comes up alongside me into my peripheral vision and says, "This gentleman is my guest, I thought I could count on this evening to show him what Viennese hospitality's all about, my mistake obviously. Nothing wrong with the Viennese I suppose that one or two less *foreigners* wouldn't take care of," and she's directing it at the German and he blanches, even though it's completely crazy since she and I are a lot more foreign than he is. By now he regrets having brought up the whole thing, by now he wishes he'd just reached into his billfold and paid the God damn bill. I haven't the slightest idea what the English girl's up to except that she's taken command of the situation, a nightclub full of excitable men, and though a few seconds ago my murdering this German seemed an enthusiastic inevitability, while she talks I start figuring that if she can get me out of this, so much the better. She steps right up to me, and without looking at me once, still staring the others down, she keeps talking while she reaches into the pocket of my coat lining. "As I see it you owe all of us an apology," she says to the German, "but if you offered it we'd then be in the position of having to accept it, assuming we have more social grace than you deserve." Out of my pocket she pulls a wad of schillings, pounds, Swiss francs, French francs, Italian lire, German marks, more money than I've seen or held in my life. It's an amazing sleight of hand, and I probably look as stunned as everyone else. "Your lot may fancy itself fit to rule the world," she says, "but you're not fit to dine in public, so why don't you just leave bloody civilized behavior to the bloody rest of us, all right?" and she casts the wad of money on the table like something she's blown her nose with; half of it flies all over the room. No one has the shamelessness to pick it up, and no one makes a sound. She has me by the hand and, not too quickly, utterly self-possessed, leads me out of the club. The silence roars at our backs when, at the door, she whispers, "Let's go, big boy. The trouble here is even bigger than you are."

5 8

We get outside and she breaks for the Ringstrasse, pulling me behind her. We catch a cab and head for a section of town on the other side of the Wien-Fluss from Dog Storm Street; in the cab I'm breathing hard and feeling myself all pumped up. She's looking out the window and then she's looking at me from out of the dark of the backseat of the cab; we get to her place and she gets out. The door's still open for me to climb out so I do. She pays the driver and off he goes; if I had plans to take the cab back to my flat, she clearly has other ideas. She hasn't said a word in all this, she understands exactly what she wants, and what she wants is exactly what's going to happen. She unlocks the door and we go up to her flat.

It's a nice enough flat. In the light she unpins part of her hair, which is even redder and longer than it's looked all night. "My name's Megan," she says, and begins to prepare tea. We'll have little shortbreads too, I guess. "Banning Jainlight," I tell her. "Make yourself at home, Banning Jainlight," she says. She has a lovely little beestung mouth but other than that and the blizzard of freckles there's nothing special about her face. From what I've seen so far nothing's unnerved her in the least about the evening, she acts as though she manages her way through episodes like this all the time. She's twenty-four years old and, more than once in our short lifetime together, the four years difference will feel profound.

We sit on a little sofa in the corner of the flat, something she finds cozy and I find like trying to cram myself into a doll's house. We talk about this and that, the woman's pulled me out of a tough spot; it would be rude of me just to get up and leave, wouldn't it? Her father runs some sort of shipping empire out of London or something. I gather he owns half the boats on water these days, though in no way is she making a big thing of it. Somehow she's totally in charge without seeming the least bit overbearing. I tell her I'm a writer but I suppose it's clear I don't want to go into it, what I write or for whom I write. She doesn't press the matter at all, she'll toss a line out if I want to bite, and if I don't she reels it back in empty. "And what am I going to do with you now, Banning Jainlight?" she says.

"Do with me?" I say.

It's not my fault, it's seduction pure and simple. She's brilliant at it, always giving just what I can handle at the moment, in fact giving just a little less than I can handle if you want to know the truth. I . . . I never forget you, though. I always have you in my mind, when she's got her hands in my hair and her full little mouth on my face, you're still there, though I've never seen your face so well in the shadows, and some time's passed now since I saw you there in that window. My brain grasps for an image of you, and all it retrieves is your pink body in the black petals on my bed; and I try to hold that when she unbuttons her clothes. Her breasts float up enormous and white, I must look completely stunned because she laughs. "Now come on," she jokes, "I just know they're not too much for you." And in that instant it's all I can see, whatever else I want to see, whatever else the mind's eye searches for; I'm lying back in this ridiculous little sofa and soon she's straddling me and rocking back and forth. I'm so far up in her I can feel the tip of me tickling the underside of her heart. "Oh love love love love," she moans.

And when I come into her, it's then of course you come over me. You and I know it's infidelity. There in the little sofa with her slumped over me I can hold grief and torment at bay only so long; when I feel her asleep I move her, pick her up and put her in her bed. She whispers in her red hair; I like her. I haven't even begun to know what she's worth. Ten weeks from now I'll marry her, though at this moment it doesn't remotely occur to me I'll even see her again. I escape in anonymity. I return to Dog Storm Street, when I come into my room I'm sure you can smell her on me. The first thing I do when you come to me is trace with my finger your face so that never again will it defy my reach. Your banal mud brown eyes and your dirty blond hair, and in the corner of your mouth, for the first time it's clear to me, the scar where you were struck by the rock that first day I saw you. It's small and white, and sparkles like a diamond in your tooth. I open you beneath me and expect your reproach, but you're happy. You already know that the seed left in the folds of a little English redhead has sanctioned that love in a way you would never choose: I would rather, you say when the window blows violently open, be your adulteress than your wife, it makes me fuck you ferociously. I would rather, you say as the window bangs open and shut, hold the part of your love that's clandestine and damned, it's what you created me for.

I deny it completely, my lie to you.

"Is there someone else?" Megan asks me later. Not at all, I answer, my lie to her.

59

Yesterday I went to meet Petyr at our designated rendez-vous point and he wasn't there. I sent Kronehelm a message that I would be at the same place in the Karlsplatz the same hour today, but no one was there either. We're left to our own devices, you and I, emancipated and gateless.

Tonight I sit down to my desk in the gray light of the moon; a car turns the corner of Dog Storm Street and pulls to the door downstairs. I can hear the bell ring several times and, peering over the sill, I see a box of long yellow light that appears in the road when the door opens. There's some discussion, and the door closes; there are steps on the stairs. I turn in my chair just as the shadow of someone's feet obstructs the glint beneath my own door; I wait for the knock. It's one of the few occasions when I expect nothing.

The knock comes again and I get up and open the door, standing in the dark of my room. "Mr. Jainlight?" a man says. I hold my hand to my eyes to block the light, so as to make him out. I notice immediately the "mister" rather than the usual "herr." He says, "My name is Holtz. May I speak with you a moment?" and only then do I detect the German accent. He doesn't barge in like most of the Germans in Vienna these days, he actually waits for an invitation. I back away and hold open the door.

He doesn't ask me to turn on a light, and I'd as soon proceed on my terms; my terms include sitting in the dark. He doesn't take a chair until I push one toward him. Then he takes off his long coat and I see the uniform. I assume he's a big shot. Not a field marshal but something fairly impressive. "Colonel," he smiles in the dark, to the question I haven't asked. I peer over the windowsill, the car's still there and I assume someone's in it. I assume someone's standing at the door, too, though I can't see. "However," he says, "plain Holtz will do." This is the most cordial damned German I've ever met. So far I haven't said a word to him.

"What's up?"

"I've come from Berlin," he says, "I've come from Berlin to see you."

"Hardly worth the fuss," I tell him.

"That's a matter of opinion," he answers, "you underestimate yourself. You're an author of real note in my country, sir," he says, "your work has a significant following. I think you're aware of that. Do you want me to come right to the point?"

"It's of no concern to me one way or the other. Will it shorten the conversation?"

"I'll come right to the point," he says. He's in his late thirties, early forties, but he speaks to me without condescension. I keep looking at the car outside. "Please don't be concerned about the soldiers outside," he says, "no one's here to arrest you."

"Why should I be concerned? This isn't Germany."

"Well, that's certainly true for the moment," he answers, and he finally sounds like a German. On the other hand, he sounds like a lot of Austrians these days too. He's blank-looking, handsome in a way that has no distinction; his hair's thinning a little in front. He lights a cigarette. Maybe as much for the light in the dark as for the cigarette. "For some months you've been doing work for an individual by the name of Kronehelm," he says now, "who's been placing the work with someone very, very powerful in the Chancellery. I believe you know this person as X, or Client X." He waits for me to say something and when I don't he continues. "The situation's changed a bit on our end, though not on your end in any way except for the better, as you'll see. To put it directly, Herr Kronehelm is no longer the intermediary in these transactions. Do you follow?"

"What's to follow? You've eliminated the middleman."

"What do you think of that?"

"I'm not happy about it."

"Are you close to Kronehelm?"

"He's a slug, actually, but that has nothing to do with it."

"What bothers you about it?"

"Who knows? Who knows what bothers me these days and why? I've eliminated middlemen before, Kronehelm and I eliminated our own middleman as a matter of fact. But cutting out Kronehelm, well, it isn't square, he had the contacts, he created the market and brought me to Vienna."

"You just keep underestimating yourself, Mr. Jainlight,"

Holtz answers. He's looking for an ashtray so as not to drop the ash of his cigarette on the floor; I push a coffee cup toward him. "Thank you. You see, we'll pay you what we were paying Herr Kronehelm. If it will mitigate your sense of loyalty let me just say that from our standpoint it was you who created the market, and that what Kronehelm was paying you was a fraction of what he was making off you."

"Well, I guess the market developed . . . a more impressive clientele."

Holtz just sits in the dark. He finally says, "You can't even begin to know, sir."

I say, "Maybe and maybe not."

"Did Herr Kronehelm ever explain to you exactly who Client X was?"

"Has Client X died? It's not on the radio if he did."

"No, he hasn't died," Holtz says, lighting another cigarette. I get up from my chair and open the window for some air. Leaning out I can see there's someone by the door downstairs as I figured. When I sit back down the colonel says, "But you're not working for Client X now."

I laugh, "I never figured I was. I figured he was working for me."

After a moment Holtz laughs too. "Let's say," he continues, "you have a new client. All right? Let's call him Client Z."

"Z? Maybe you ought to discuss this with X. Before the secret police show up and discuss it with you. Are you trying to cut yourself in on some action, is that it? Maybe X doesn't like this new arrangement. Maybe X doesn't like Client Z so much either."

"Client X," Holtz answers calmly, "understands the arrangement perfectly. Client X," he adds, "serves at the pleasure of Client Z."

In this first moment, when he says it, I'm not sure I understand. Something in the back of my mind must understand, I guess, because for the first moment, and then the second, and then the third, I don't say anything at all. And then I can only repeat it: "Client X," as much to myself as to him, "serves at the pleasure of Client Z?"

"That's right," Holtz answers, in the same calm way he first said it. He reaches over and takes the coffee cup and puts out the second cigarette. He'll sit and wait all night for me to say something, before he says another word.

"And Client Z," I finally ask him, "at whose pleasure does he serve?"

Holtz hands me back the coffee cup, full of ashes. "Client Z," he answers, rising from his chair, "serves at the pleasure of history."

6 0

I don't believe him.

6 1

And in that moment I'm blinded by the gray Hungarian moon moving toward me up the Wien-Fluss and I forget everything. I notice I'm sitting there with the lights off, and I think to myself, Why are the lights off? I notice the window that I opened for some air and I think, Who opened the window? I notice the other man in the room who moves from his chair to his coat without saying anything and I think, There's someone else here?

"I don't believe you," I think I finally say to him when he's in the doorway.

Opening the door he tells me, "But it doesn't matter, sir. It may be better that you don't believe me. Let's say, if you wish, that I haven't told you anything new at all. Let's say, if you wish, that nothing I've said in these last moments means anything. All that matters is the work, after all. A client is a client."

He leaves me in the dark, where I thought I was on my own terms.

6 2

Nothing he's said means anything. At the pleasure of history? We all serve at the pleasure of history. It doesn't concern me; all that matters is the work. I'm an American; a client is a client.

The window remains open; the car below leaves. I'm left alone. Comes the moon to my street.

63

"There may be someone new now," I finally say it, "a new client." You hoist yourself up onto me. "A new friend." You take my face in your hands and move it till it's caught in the web of what you see and know. I keep trying to look away. Don't you think I understand this, you laugh, don't you think I understand everything? "Don't laugh," I insist. You lunge at my mouth with yours.

If he serves at the pleasure of history, you answer, then history serves at the pleasure of us.

64

You and I together. A day passes, two, a week passes since Holtz came. I leave the flat only to walk three doors down the street for a meal. I keep thinking, Someone's going to miss me. I keep thinking, There's a rendezvous I've failed to keep. But there's no one who misses me, there's no one for me to meet. Every contact with my life up until this week has been broken, all the moments that have sailed behind the present in a single line scatter to new winds. The common compass spins wildly to no north. Somewhere far away is the moment I stand on the corner at Jerry's newsstand and covet the pulps on his rack. Further is the moment Henry stands at my bedside and wakes me to follow him and Oral out to the Indian shacks. I don't know if I actually see these moments or if the glare of the sea on which the present moment sails plays tricks on my eyes. Now we wait for the new client, the new friend. I guess I already know he won't simply buy you like the others. I guess I already know you're not simply to be sold to him like the others. At the end of the week I've decided a client is just a client, or did I decide that before? I decided before but this time I make myself half-believe it. That's it. I'd breathe a sigh of relief except that to breathe anything at all connotes life, and the life I've carried almost twenty-one years in me has now scattered to another wind as well. An entirely different kind of ghost lives in me now, you and it together.

6 5

Five weeks pass. It's autumn in Vienna, frayed and hushed. I go to see her. I wait for her to come home, plump little anglosaxon dumpling bouncy and wild. It's dusk, she unlocks the door and I come up behind her. The shadow overwhelms her; she turns where she stands and drops the key. I retrieve it. "Hello," I tell her. She's breathing heavily and in the light her face is as red as her hair. It might be she's going to say to me, How are you? or, You just left me that night, or Go away. Instead she says, "I'm pregnant," and no sooner has she said it than she bitterly resents the desperation it betrays. I won't insult either of us by pretending to wonder if it's mine. "I'll marry you," I say, and am horrified by the way it sounds: "Marry me," is the way I rephrase it. She laughs shortly in the doorway, still bitter, then just smiles to herself, melancholy, and for a moment she's only going to take the key, put it in the lock, open the door and shut herself away from me. In the next moment she's sprung at me, to the place where I've backed away from her so I don't loom so large, and she's pounding me, beating my chest with her fists, wailing furiously. On the other side of the street people stop to look; I'm holding her by the wrists and she begins kicking and I pull her to me to make her stop. She sobs into my shirt. "Megan," I whisper, "Megan. It's for me." I whisper, "It's for me I'm asking it. I know you don't need pity from me. It's for me because . . . everything's gone wrong lately. This is my conscience throwing me a line, this is one little bit of decency in the middle of. . . . There are many things I can't explain. Just let me have this little normal decent thing that tells me not everything I do is corrupt." We stand in the street several minutes and finally go up to her apartment. I stay with her on into the night, and leave about eleven. In her sleep I promise I'll return by dawn. Under the moon of madness I cross a bridge at the Wien-Fluss; thirty-five years from now I step onto the old man's ferry and he sails me to your island. There's a moment, between the island and the boathouse on the shore, when neither's in sight.

Winter comes like Gramercy Park, irrational and overnight. I strain to remember the winter of Gramercy Park, three or four winters ago I keep thinking, until I remember it was only last year. Megan and I marry nearly as suddenly. There's a last moment flurry of activity by the shipbuilder and Megan's mother to thwart things; the mother hurries to Vienna to approve. She's aghast at the sight of me. I think all the more highly of her for it. "Oh Mama, go bloody *home* then," Megan tells her. When they threaten to cut off her money she only says, "You ought to have done it years ago." The wedding takes place on a Saturday morning before a vaguely denominational minister who's nearly as little as Megan; I'm Gulliver in matrimony, yet barely large enough for the occasion. Megan wears a peach dress with a small veil. She's sweet and the awe she shows in her eyes is humbling. When we leave the wind rips the veil from her head and hurries it over the rooftops where it passes out of sight beyond a post office spire. We take a new flat upstairs from where she's been living, somewhat smaller actually except that it has an extra room. A stairway leads from right outside our door up to the top of the building where another door's unlocked by the same key that unlocks ours. At night we fall asleep to the roar of rallies in the hills. People talk of nothing but Germany, and by the end of winter the government calls an election in which Austrians will decide whether to be Austrians. Only Austrians would need an election to know such a thing. Only Germans would be enraged by the temerity of it, or would call it temerity. I pull Megan's voluptuous little body close to my head and place my ear to the core of her, where I hear redemption growing inside her. When her water breaks in seven months I'll let it splash on my head as baptism. We both know it's a girl and have named her Courtney. "Oh big boy," Megan whispers in my hair, "love me just a little." I hold her hard. I've kept the place on Dog Storm Street, I go there each twilight. To work, I tell her. Discreetly, fearfully, she doesn't ask where or what. My part of the bargain is that when she opens her eyes in the morning, she'll find me next to her.

67

I work through the winter. Once a week the car pulls up
the street and stops at my building, and someone comes
to my door with an envelope of money in exchange
for a folder of finished pages. I've had to protest being
paid in Deutschemarks. The middleman's been eliminated,
though sometimes I wonder if Petyr's been eliminated as
well; someone's translating the work after all. I can picture
him as he sits before the pages incensed with Kronehelm's
betrayal; what white rage is he bringing to these scenes?
He's sabotaging me with politically incorrect interpreta-
tions of the way I love you. We're in his hands, the temp-
tation must drive him crazy, restrained only by the
possibility that another translator could discover his deceit
at any moment.

It's early March when Holtz comes again.

I know it's something extraordinary because it's not the
night the car usually comes; I think it's a Wednesday. I
hear the car outside and sit waiting for the knock on the
door; I just reach over and turn off the light on the desk
and wait. Finally he opens the door himself and steps into
the dark room. He stands for a moment waiting for me to
say something. "Mr. Jainlight," he finally breaks the silence. "I apologize for disturbing your work." I finally turn
in my chair. He closes the door behind him; I've already
opened the window. He comes in and takes the same chair
he sat in the last time. He's as composed and cordial as the
last time. "How does it go for you," he asks, the first of
several questions I won't answer. He notices that the room
is cold, and touches the radiator. "They don't give you
much heat here," he says, "I'll attend to that. It must be
difficult to work when your hands are cold."

"Lots of things are difficult when your hands are cold."

He nods. "I hope the arrangement's been satisfactory so far," he says, "if there's anything that—"

"I don't like being paid in Deutschemarks."

"Would you rather American dollars? It's no problem."

"Austrian schillings are fine."

He waves it away. "Whatever." He rubs his hands together; he's kept on his long coat this time and now fumbles inside it for his cigarettes. "I want you to know, Mr. Jainlight," he begins, "I've been instructed to convey to you the great enthusiasm our client has for your recent work." He shakes his head emphatically. "Very delighted about what you've done. Deeply moved. As an artist himself, our client is in a position to understand its worth."

"Horseshit."

"He wants you to know, it's important to him that—"

"Why are you here?"

Finally he finds his cigarettes. In the cold of the room he has difficulty lighting one; he keeps looking at the window, wishing it were closed, but not, I think, for the weather. "I believe," he says, "the work has taken a new turn over the last six months." He motions with his cigarette.

"Why are you here."

"Well, Mr. Jainlight." He keeps looking at the window. "I'm here to talk about that work, to offer some of the client's comments, from one artist to another so to speak. Specifically, I'm here to talk about her."

"Her?"

"It's nothing of import," he says dismissively, shaking his head, having just traveled all the way from Berlin to say it, "very small details, a few adjustments to reinforce the client's boundless enthusiasm for what you've done. Of course we could make the changes on our end, if it came to it, or if you wanted to proceed that way, but . . . but my sense . . . well, I couldn't in all conscience tamper with an artist's vision without—"

"This is all complete horseshit."

"The eyes, for instance," Holtz says. "The eyes should

be blue, not brown. The hair. The hair's to be a bit more golden. Like spun sunlight, perhaps."

"Spun sunlight?"

"Whatever." He sits puffing on his cigarette.

"Why don't you just find another person who will do the work the way the client prefers it."

After a moment Holtz says quietly, "No, sir."

"Maybe this is a case of mistaken identity. Maybe we're not talking about the same girl."

"No, sir," he says, "we're talking about the same girl." He licks his lips, I can see him do it in the dark. He looks at the window once more and says, "The only girl he ever loved," and gets up from the chair and walks to the window and closes it. It's not the weather. He goes to the door and opens it, and says something to the guard outside who goes downstairs. He closes the door and returns to the chair, and turns it so that he's straddling it with his arms rested on the back.

He takes a long puff on his cigarette and then puts it out in the same coffee cup he used three months ago. "The only girl he ever loved, Mr. Jainlight," he says again. I unnerve him when I don't say anything, but he's getting used to it. "Now, what I'm about to tell you, well, I suppose it's something of a secret to those whose memories are short. Which, fortunately, in the case of the client, happens to be most everyone. But the fact is that ten years ago it wasn't such a secret at all. It was rather well known in the party, and in Munich, where the affair took place."

I think I know now why he closed the window. I think I know now why he sent the guard away.

"Her name was Geli Raubal," he goes on, "she was a singer from Vienna, and his niece. He met her when, frankly, his political fortunes were at their lowest. The party had just gotten thrashed in the elections, and who's to say that if things had been going better, he might not have been so . . . turned. Who's to say. What's unmistakable is that he fell in love with her, and in fact a year after their meeting she began living with him. The exact nature of this affair was . . ." He stops. "That is to say . . . well, whether their love of the heart was expressed with physical love, no one knows. That she would or could not relent to his particular wishes in this regard may have been what strained the affair. I should perhaps say, for the purposes of your work, that . . ." In the winter light of the night I can see the gleam of his brow. "I understand," he begins again slowly, "that Z's wishes in the regard of physical love may have been rather specific and . . . a bit sophisticated, for a girl who, at twenty, was half his age. Do you see what I'm saying?"

"No."

"Well," he continues, "the long and short of it is that after three years they had difficulties. By this time the Depression had come, of course, and politically he was very much on the ascent. The pinnacle was barely eighteen months away. But the course of their affair did not follow that of his other successes, and there were, on her part, affairs with other men. The client's own bodyguard even. She also wanted to return to Vienna. One afternoon they argued, and the next morning she was found with a bullet through her chest. The coroner ruled it a suicide."

"Not usually where people shoot themselves, in the chest."

Holtz shrugs. "Perhaps she meant to deliver a shot that wasn't fatal." He stands from the chair and paces. "I know what you're suggesting, of course. Others suggested the same. And again, who's to say. Perhaps he shot her. Perhaps he had her shot. Perhaps political supporters had her shot because they were afraid she would become a scandal and humiliate him. Perhaps political opponents had her shot to untrack him. Who knows. At any rate, untracked he certainly became, of that there's no doubt. For a time his right-hand people stayed with him every hour because they actually believed," and he can't even fathom saying it, but he does, "because they believed he might well try to finish himself off. He was that devastated. It was months before he found his vision again. He never really found his passion for a woman again, though he keeps the company of women." He stops before the window and begins to tap on the glass, absently. "It has, until so very recently, left a space in him."

There's a pause as though I'm supposed to respond to all this.

The snow falls slightly from the upper sill at his tapping. "But now, you see," he says, "she's back." He turns to look at me.

The havoc of my hands has long since become the havoc of my dreams. "She's back?"

"You see how the situation has developed."

Either I don't understand at first, or I do and am too stunned to realize it. "It's preposterous," is all I can finally answer.

"Eyes of blue," he says. "Hair of spun sunlight."

"This is a mistake. Mistaken identity."

"Then it's you who makes the mistake." He opens the window now, wider and colder than it was before.

"I won't change anything about her."

"The small scar on her mouth, that won't do either, of course."

"I won't change anything."

"It's no matter," he says easily, "we can take care of things on our end."

"Go ahead and try. She'll defy you as she defies me."

"There's another thing," he says at the door. "We would like you to come to Berlin. It would be easier for all of us if you worked there. Berlin is quite the most exciting place in the world now. It's the center of our century."

"The center of our century," I answer him, "is right here," and I take hold of my crotch. "Take me to Berlin and I won't write a punctuation mark." I cannot hide the hopelessness. "I have a wife in Vienna," I tell him, almost pleading, "we're going to have a child." It's dreadful how this news doesn't surprise him.

"Then if you won't come to the client," he smiles in the doorway, "the client will have to come to you," and he's gone.

6 8

The client came today.

His troops marched down the Ring. The Austrians canceled the election and conceded the issue: they will be Germans. All the parks were filled with New Germans. From my flat with Megan I heard the fall of the soldiers' feet like the gunfire of steady executions; as I walked to the Inner City the thunder of it grew. Half a mile away I could feel the earth shake from it. Traffic came to a stop, the newsstands were emptied of papers, the beerhalls and cafes emptied of people who flooded the Volksgarten, the Burggarten, to watch his troops pour into the Ring from all the boulevards leading into the city. Against the blue and silver sky the mean granite sliver of the Rathaus stood like a frozen white flame from which you could hear the whimper of someone burning. At the top of the steps of one of the Hofburg buildings I could see nothing but soldiers for as far as the Ring curved; around me men were hoarse with liquor and adrenaline. Women lined the porticos of the theaters, pressed against the stone walls along the street. Some dark shiny ecstasy rushed out from the middle of them at the sight of him; when they moved from the walls they left round wet spots behind them. Sometimes they fainted and crumpled to the ground, and all along the road women were lying in the street while on the walls above their heads were the wet exclamations of subjugation. In the empty alleys of the Inner City herds of dogs met up with each other, all of Old Vienna left to them. Not a vagabond or gypsy or Jew to be seen. A thousand front pages floated down from the cathedral towers.

The client was in a reviewing stand on the other side of the Burg Ring. I couldn't see him as clearly as I wanted. He appeared slightly paunchy, with scrawny forearms, but I couldn't see the eyes, where they say the power lies. Someone next to me said, He's a god, and everyone murmured assent. I laughed. They turned and looked at me and I laughed again, slapping my leg. Everyone watched me with hate and horror.

Well I'm the one who's resurrected your god's greatest obsession, I said to them. So what sort of god does that make me?

I'm back on Dog Storm Street now.

Revelry and fury in the city. The night passes, we spend it quietly. You suck me toward midnight, into the new day, but nothing comes. I watch the ceiling and run my fingers through your hair, it's nearly time to return home when the car arrives. I didn't expect it so soon, his first night here.

A soldier waits for me at the door. He orders me to follow him, and I guess I have to; we're in Germany now. We go downstairs, the landlady's peering from a black crack in the door. I'll have to tell Holtz to talk to her so she doesn't evict me. I get in the car waiting outside and soon we're at the Ring just a few blocks from the Opera. I'm taken through a side door of the Hotel Imperial and up through a side lift. We probably go something like fourteen or fifteen levels until we're near the top. The door of the lift opens and the same German soldier who came to get me waits for me to step out.

The hallway's dark. A small light at the end reveals a

sitting room, the double doors of the suite are closed. I decide I'll wait here in one of the chairs on the other side of the room.

After twenty minutes the door opens and someone's back is to me. He's giving the German salute, beyond him the room is only dimly lit. There are voices, the German of Germans, harder than the German of Austrians, at least until today. I have confidence the New Germans will find the requisite measure of brutality inside themselves somewhere.

The man in the door turns and it's Holtz.

He closes the door behind him and walks with quiet care across the sitting room; he extends his hand to me. We've never shaken hands and on Dog Storm Street I would ignore it, but here it seems a good thing to do. Now the door opens again and several other German officers come out. At first they ignore us completely, but then they look again, and they look at each other as they walk down the hall. Way down the hall they're still looking over their shoulders at me.

"Hello, Banning," Holtz is saying. Along with the handshake it's also the first time he's called me this; I call him colonel. "Sorry to bring you here in the middle of the night," Holtz says; he's practically whispering. "The client would like to meet you," he says, very carefully and pointedly; and I can see in his face what's unspoken, he's saying, We're both sitting on dynamite here. You can treat *me* like manure, he's saying, but this is the client. I just nod and he nods and we both stand here nodding at each other. I say something like he must be busy, maybe we can do this another time; and then the fear passes to a realization, and then rage: I never wanted to have to *know* this. It wasn't supposed to be like this, he was never supposed to be anything more than an unseen unheard client, Client Z. He was never supposed to have a name or face, particularly not this name or face; I don't want to have to live with it.

"It's impossible," I suddenly blurt out.

Holtz is holding me by the arm. He can barely get his hand around my arm, and he's a good half-foot shorter than I, but he's got my arm in a clamp and I can see now he's shitless terrified, just out of his mind with terror. He'd like nothing better than for this to have never come to pass. "Don't move, don't speak," Holtz rasps, "when you wake up tomorrow you can pretend it was all a dream if you like. But right now. . . ." He looks at the door. "I have to go back in. Sit and wait and don't try to leave, the guards will stop you anyway."

Holtz disappears back into the room and I sit and wait like I've been told. I'm not sure of the time but it must be around two in the morning, perhaps later. It seems to me I'm waiting the rest of the night, though later I realize it's only about an hour and a half. More officers come in and out of the suite. Most of them are looking at me when they do, it's difficult to know whether they watch me in mystery or informed fascination. I must assume it's the former, though the next several years will give way to the latter. Then the traffic ceases altogether and I'm left sitting in the dark. Holtz does not reappear for a long time. Not a single sound comes from behind the door; for all I know whoever's in that suite has slipped out through another exit. The daybreak may come and I'll be shot as an intruder, I muse without anger. I study the room awhile. Baroque tapestries hang from the walls, scenes of Metternich and Mozart, one Hapsburg or another being enthroned or entombed. It's warmer here than at either of my flats, and I sink further into the chair, suspended and patient.

Holtz finally comes out, once again opening and closing the door as though not to wake someone. He does it so tentatively the door doesn't really catch behind him. He comes over and I stand up; he looks relieved. "I'm sorry," he says crisply, quietly, "it can't be tonight. The . . . the client is leaving Vienna." But he just got here, I think to myself. "He'll be back in a week or so, there's going to be a new election. Perhaps then." Perhaps not, he adds without saying it. His face sags from the tension. I just nod all right. Behind us the door that didn't quite catch closed drifts partly open.

For just a moment I look and, in the faint light of the suite beyond the door, the client looks back.

He's standing over a desk, both hands flat on the desk as he leans over the papers scattered before him. To one side is a half-finished plate of food; it looks like it may have been sitting there all night, eaten from erratically. On a couch behind him I can barely see a blond woman, pretty in a very ordinary way; she's curled up asleep, or partly asleep. Maybe she's waited for him to come to bed, maybe she's been waiting for a sign it matters to him whether she goes ahead to bed or not. When I look through the door he looks up from his papers, his hair falling in his face; he looks first at the affront of the open door, and then at Holtz, and then at me. At each stage of this small act his face slowly changes; at the sight of me he goes white. His mouth falls slightly open. In his eyes is no power at all. When we look into each other's eyes, his beg to be conquered in the way he's conquered this very city on this very day; there's the fear and hope that I'm as merciless as he. I can imagine that he's sat behind this door all evening picking at his food and glancing distractedly at his papers, wondering what he would say to me; when the nerve finally failed him, he couldn't go through with it. My anonymity to him is no less compelling than his to me: this has all been a mistake.

Holtz follows my line of vision, turns to peer over his shoulder at the open door. He blanches. He races to the door and, muttering profusely through it, closes it. Z never turns away from me, nor I from him, until the door shuts us off from each other for thirty years to come. In thirty years, when I'm an old man and he's an ancient living in a basement in Italy, I'll wonder if he remembers this moment, or if he remembers ever seeing me at all.

Holtz walks me to the lift and sees me off without a word.

He's still standing at the door when it slides closed; he has a funny look on his face. The car's waiting for me, and I let it take me back to Dog Storm Street. I have a pact with Megan to be there in the morning, but I don't want the Germans to know where she lives, and I'm not finished at the other flat besides. You didn't finish me earlier this evening and now I'm ready for you. I have to unbutton my fly on the way up the stairs, I'm that urgent; I can only hope the landlady isn't watching.

You're putting on lipstick when I come in. You stand naked at the sink, studying your mouth in the mirror. What did he say? you ask, and I answer, He begged us. You touch yourself reflexively, unaware you've even done it.

At the window something's coming out of me, it doesn't sound so much like laughter except that you begin to giggle, so it must be laughter. I seem to be shaking with this sound, there in the window; it fills the room and runs out the window. Down on the street by the corner is a man smoking a cigarette; I notice he's looking up at my room. I think he may have been there when I drove up in the car; I believe he's a German tail. Not one of the New Germans born today but an Original German. Even now he pretends to be casual but the sound that comes from me moves up the street toward him, and he lights another cigarette nervously and discards it quickly, pulling his coat up around his neck. A woman in the belfry across the way opens her window in alarm. Other windows open up and down the street; it's still an hour before daybreak. The sound keeps coming and if it's laughter it's of a different virus, not like when I used to laugh in the windows of New York with the other girls. The landlady downstairs in her room is making noise. You sit on the bed giggling your lipstick into a smear, and then laughing louder the more I laugh.

The level of it rises in the city. Doormen posted outside the pensiones leave their places, chairs tip over in the gutters. Midway through it people are erecting barricades outside their doors and boarding up their windows, I can hear the fall of hammers and the searing of steel down the block. The landlady's hurling herself furiously from wall to wall in the room below, lights come on in one window after another all over the neighborhood until the laughter obliterates them one by one in turn. A woman with an open shirt moves into the streetlamp below, her mouth streaked with butter; the doormen are replaced with other doormen, keys jangle from their belts large and white like bones on a ring. In the window I take off my clothes. I don't even need to call you to me, you know to come. You stand against me embracing me from the back, we can barely hold each other in the mutual convulsion. The sound of me dies and only the convulsion's left, but the sound of you never stops. Reaching around in front you seize me with your hand; the sound in me's dead: Don't laugh, I say. You take me in your hand and still laugh; with your other hand you reach around and hold all of me; you laugh into my back. You can barely get your thin pink arms around me. Don't laugh, I say. The more I say it, the more you laugh; the more you laugh, the wilder you caress and thrash me. My love explodes in the snow on the sill. Just don't laugh anymore, I groan in the window, sinking to the floor beneath it. With your hair you tie yourself to the bed and begin to sing.

69

Redemption comes to me in my daughter.

Courtney's born in the summer of 1938. She's no sooner out of the womb than her head looks to be on fire, all blood and red hair. Megan insists she gets the hair from both of us, but I know it's from her. She's one big brilliant freckle, her skin hums of innocence. Her big eyes grip wisdom from some primal gene that has leapfrogged her father; I can hold her in a single hand. I can run up and down the stairs with her poised in this hand over my head, I can dangle her from the rooftop of our apartment building and she only laughs at my joke. I'm the funniest man in the world to her, I was born to be her clown. My heart's soaked with her until it tears like tissue just to look at her.

What does it say about this universe that such a thing comes to someone who deserves it so little.

I'm leaving you.

It isn't your fault that Megan gave me such a thing as Courtney. I don't deny that even in the throes of this redemption, the dark doesn't kiss me. There's enough love somewhere to love both you and my kid, the love dangles like a single rope from the mouth of a well, open beneath the sun and sky, to the well's pit, wet and black and hot; it's the same rope. But I have to try and be good. I struggle to warrant this moment that I shot into the middle of my child's mother, and from which the child of that moment is now given back to me. The light of a star that exploded months ago, and has now arrived to stay.

Don't come here anymore.

I've sent word to the landlady on Dog Storm Street that we won't be needing the flat.

70

The summer passes. We have no money, Megan's parents having cut off her stipend in retaliation. The arrival of the granddaughter may yet alter this course, but for the moment we live off what Megan's saved, and what little I've saved from the work that I no longer do. I stay home with the child while Megan looks for work; it's unconventional but I can't be walking around the streets of the city in broad daylight, Holtz and the boys are out looking for me. I wish we could get out of Vienna but if we tried I'd be arrested. Megan asks no questions. She's happy to have all of me even on mysterious terms. She's taken to theft; she shoplifts food, silverware, furniture, books. She comes home with dressers, beds, sofas. I hear the sound of the day's crime in the stairwell, and go down the stairs to find a table or trunk perched on the back of her four-foot-eleven frame. Our apartment is lavishly furnished by the finest shops in Vienna. She made the decision to resort to a life of crime easily enough, but the Anschluss didn't hurt. She's not stealing from Austrians after all, but Germans now. Think of it as a political act, she explains; but I won't demean it that way. I seem to spend most of my days washing clothes, dragging them up to the top of the roof where I've strung a line. From up there I can see the Westbahnhof less than a mile away; I scheme all the time, to no avail.

Go away.

Sometimes I'll see someone watching me from a window across the street, and I think it's a spy. A spy for them, a spy for you.

The Czechoslovakians will be Germans soon, too, all of us touched to Germanlife by the god who loves you.

Courtney lives on my shoulders. It's the only place high and right enough for her, every other place too close to the

ground. On the rooftops now, to the witness of spies, I toss
her into the sky, she laughs and laughs. She folds her little
hands, each the size of my eyes, across my face and chal-
lenges me to live in the black world of her creation. I cry
out in mock alarm and she laughs some more. When I hear
her I clutch her to my chest and keep her tight to me; I see
something. I clutch her so as to make her part of my bigness, which will protect her. I see something horrible. It
glints sharply across my vision and then vanishes. She protests the chest and demands the bird's-eye view from my
back. For just a moment I refuse her and hold her anyway;
something in me, at the sight of something I cannot or will
not keep in my mind's eye, drops away, as though what's
below my waist is only a dream, and I'm really a tree rooted
to a void.

71

One night at the end of summer I wake in the early hours
of the morning. I have the sense that something's on the
rooftop waiting; lying there next to Megan I try to dismiss
the feeling. I turn to Megan and, in her sleep, I take her.
But while my back's to the ceiling, and while I'm inside
her, I can't get over the feeling of something trapped on
the roof above me. I finally withdraw from her still hard. I
get out of bed; sleepily she calls for me. It's nothing, I say
to her; I turn in the moonlight so she can't see I'm still
hard. I walk out of the bedroom, I walk past Courtney's
cradle. I open the door and step out onto the stairs naked;
I open the door leading up to the rooftop. My erection
hasn't passed and I climb the stairs until, at the top step, I

stop and listen; I can hear something on the roof. I step
out onto the roof now. Vienna's glazed with light; the roof
is white and angular; a wave of familiarity rushes over me.
I feel that soon I'll drown in this wave, sinking to some
bottom, drifting in the wake of some tide; and I can barely
wait for it, it can't happen soon enough. I climb over the
peaks of the rooftop; it seems to me, drowned and frozen,
I might splinter against an empty pier. In the corner of an
alcove on the roof is a bird, the sound I've heard. I reach
for it and then there's another sound, and I turn. You step
from behind the building's steeple, coy and distant. I deserve it, I guess. I deserve it for sending you away. I guess
you've been sleeping here on the roof above the bed in the
room below where I've been with my wife: I have a wife, I
say, I have a daughter. "I never wanted to be your wife,"
you answer, "I never wanted to be your daughter." You
come toward me and stop at the chimney that rises between us; you writhe before me bent over the chimney.
The dark center of you opens to me. "Call me wife if you
want," you whisper, "call me daughter." I can barely
breathe until I'm inside you; somewhere before us Vienna
winks and groans in a haze. "Call me anything you like."
Oh Geli, I say into your hair spun like sunlight. I take you
by the hips and pull you closer; your gasp slithers to the
ground below. Oh Geli, I say it again, to your eyes of blue.
I clasp your breasts, my hands run to your neck and shoulders. My fingers touch your face; at the corner of your
mouth is a scar. Semen swims out of me in confusion. But
where, I can only moan, touching the scar, did you get
this?

72

This morning I return to Dog Storm Street. Megan watches with anguish; she's still in the window when I look up from the street. I won't try to explain it. At my old flat there are Germans waiting; a soldier sees me and fumbles quickly with his telephone. Another emerges from the doorway with a gun, looking for the first. I suppose they have orders to arrest me on sight. I suppose they have orders not, under any circumstances, to cause me harm. They approach and I knock one of them down. Shoot me, I laugh at them. They can only wait until Holtz shows up. I go on upstairs; there's someone else living in my flat, a fat New German. I open the door and he jumps up off the bed, I take his things and throw them out the window onto the street. I salute him, Heil, I salute the soldiers below. The landlady runs upstairs and when she sees me her eyes grow wide and she begins to shriek; I salute her too. Holtz arrives in almost no time, he gets to the top of the stairs as I'm throwing the fat New German down them. He reassures the landlady and coaxes her down the stairs; he turns to me and says, Banning, such a spectacle. He's furious with me but he doesn't want me to leave again. We have an agreement, he says, smooth and disappointed. Tell him, I say, that I'm fucking her. Tell him I fuck her all the time, and she sings for me from the bed, tied by her hair. I fuck her many ways, tell him that. Tell him, I'm saying to Holtz, my face inches from his, tell him I ravish her over and over. For a moment Holtz says nothing, only smiles slightly. But Banning, finally comes the response, he's counting on it.

7 3

1939. Love rages. It cries out from you, seething and red; I come back for more and more. These German nights we sit at the bottom of the well joined and impulsed, in the mornings I climb up the rope of my love to the light, where my child waits. Megan grows sadder. Her parents resume the stipend, inspired by the grandchild, and she gives up her life of crime; but the days are still, disquieting. Austrian papers scream of "the Polish provocation," Swiss papers tell it differently. In September the British declare war and Megan's sorrow spreads like her hair on the pillow behind her head. All touch is lost with her nation and people: We're at war, I say to you. The happy delirium on your face at this news is unmistakable, you coo for defilement. "Is he watching?" you mutter beneath me; I look for his form in the shadows of the room. The heat inside you detonates me. By the end of the year people in the street are certain the war will be a short one. When Holtz visits I can tell he isn't so sure; he's dazed that events have gone this far. Many more Germans soon, Danes, Belgians, Dutch. One afternoon in the autumn of 1939 I'm standing in the Volksgarten with my little girl, now almost one and a half years old; she teeters precariously on her little legs; and as we're watching the Viennese strolling in the unnerved hours I gaze around and I'm in a boat. The boat is on water with a thousand other small boats around us, a city floats in a lagoon behind us, the Adriatic Sea glistens to the east of us. A fisherman at the other end of the boat watches me knowingly. Everything in me aches; I'm old. I have a beard. It's thirty years from now, and lying in the bottom of the boat, wrapped in a brown cloak, is a very old man, white thin hair and dead eyes, gazing up at me. It's not a vision I'm having, or a dream. I feel the boat rocking

as surely as anything I've ever felt. I look at the old man
trying to remember who he is, because I know I've seen
him; and then I have this distant memory of thirty years
before, when I caught his eye for several seconds through
the hotel doorway.

74

1940. Come here. There are still a hundred things for me
to do to you. Paris has fallen, I was there once. I met a
friend from there, or was it there he was going when we
said goodbye? What was his name? We shook hands on the
platform at a station: No way they're going to take over
Paris, I said; and then he was gone. In the window above
Dog Storm Street a procession of planes sails black like the
years before my birth. I hear you panting beneath me.
Your hair's tousled in the wind through the window. This
is Paris, Geli. There's smoke from Montmartre and bright
wet lipstick on the Vendome column.

   Holtz is troubled. I'm watched by Germans all the time,
I try to shake them when I leave the flat to return to my
family. Perhaps he worries I'll vanish again, perhaps it's
something else. Lately he comes to my room and sits in the
dark for hours rambling about something he calls Barbarossa; it takes you and me away from each other. I see you
tapping your foot impatiently waiting for him to leave, I
watch you touching yourself and tasting it. Holtz won't tell
me about it at first. "One of the client's lifelong dreams,"
he only hints grandly. Some piece of distinctly audacious
treachery, I guess.

"But. . . ." Holtz says.

But?

Lighting cigarettes all night, putting them out. Rising from his chair, pacing the room, sitting again. "The client's *distracted*," Holtz says. Distracted? I laugh. Holtz hates it when I laugh. You're distracting him, Geli. From one of his lifelong dreams. "Banning," he says, and in this moment I know something's wrong, "Banning." I stop laughing and listen to him. "You have to understand what I'm trying to tell you," he continues, "it's *deadly*. The affair's become *political*. He doesn't concentrate the way he used to. Barbarossa's critical to the war, its timing is absolutely pinpoint." He's pacing again. "If it doesn't take place in the spring, if it's delayed too long, then we must wait another spring. Worse if he decides not to wait at all, and presses forward too late. . . ." He stops, turning to me. "They removed her nine years ago when she became a problem for him. They'll remove her again."

Remove her? I blink at him in the dark. "What does it mean," I say, "they'll remove her?"

"It means," he says, leaning across our bed, "they'll remove me. It means they'll remove you."

"Then fire me," I laugh. "Or rather, I'll fire you."

Holtz gestures in the night. "But you see," he starts again, "you see, there are those," and immediately I know he's included with them, "there are those who think Barbarossa's a potential disaster. A potential catastrophe. Who would like to see him forget about it altogether, before he pushes history farther than it can be pushed." And now he's rambling again, talking to himself or someone else. "Napoleon tried to push history that far, and history pushed back." Holtz is a nervous wreck. "For some of us," he says, "she's the woman who will save the country. She's the woman who will save him from himself."

"I'll think of something especially good for tomorrow night," I offer.

He narrows his eyes. He'd advise or threaten me at this moment if he could think of anything that would do either one. I thought he'd never leave, you say when he's gone. Courtney, freckletot. Even you could not redeem this.

75

1941. Barbarossa's called off. When Holtz tells me, I can see he thinks it's a good thing for Germany but maybe not so good for him. There's relief and wrath in Berlin, eye to eye across the political barricades; Holtz runs low, crossfire flashing above his head. Fifteen years the client's dreamed of making Russia German; now cronies despair at his wandering nights. I've saved Russia, I laugh to you, I've saved the world. You squeeze me in your palm, fondle me. "What a very good boy you are then," you answer. We celebrate. Your legs shine like your eyes. Guys hack tubercular on the stairs outside, there are sounds in the woodwork and the sink pipes rumble like the streets. Russian whispers rise to a wail from the Danube. "Is he here?" you ask, and when I look, sure enough, he is. I guess I never believed he'd come. I know you said it all along; I guess you were right. Do you want him? You look up at him; he rustles in the corner, shrinking away into the dark: "He's rather a puny one, isn't he?" Yes. I've seen him before: he isn't much. "Is he as big as you?" Of course not, I laugh. What a question. I push myself into you; he holds the corner of the wall so hard I can see the blood fall from his fingers. Geli, Geli. "Oh my God, my God, my God, my God," you're nearly screaming it. To me, though; not him.

76

March 1942. I've saved Russia but doomed England. The invasion of the island began today, the German frenzy that's been building Russiaward now unleashed across the Channel. Japan that was once tempted to strike in the Pacific now becomes attentive to the British colonies in Asia. America that was being gradually drawn into the war only months ago is now forced to wait for England's fate. Megan twists painfully in the silence from home, phone communication impossible. Sometimes I feel I have this clarity, sometimes I think I see it all rather lucidly. I look around my flat on Dog Storm Street and there's no one there at all, I tell myself. In the streets of the city people anticipate news of surrender any moment; there are also uneasy rumors of conspiracies in the Chancellery. Something's happening, people tell me. I have to restrain myself from explaining: He's gone, you see, they can't find him. I have to hold myself back from telling them, He isn't in the Chancellery anymore, he's here in Vienna; he lives in my flat. He stands in the corner and watches me with the woman both of us love.

Sometimes I'm sure I view it all without obstruction, the Twentieth Century sighted from my window. Today, with news coming in over the radio, I saw it for instance: I looked out my window onto the street, the same street, the same buildings I always see, the windows that stare back at my own; and it was different. The moment was a different moment, of a different now. What I saw from my window was the other Twentieth Century rolling on by my own, like the other branch of a river that's been forked by an island long and narrow and knifelike: the same river but flowing by different shorelines and banks. This was the river of the Twentieth Century that was forked at that very moment I saw you in the window of your house across from the candleshop, when the melee was taking place before you in the street; this Twentieth Century I saw from my own window today was the one in which I never saw you at all. In which I never saw you and never wrote of you, and your invention never came to the attention of special clients. In which no evil mind was ever distracted by the reincarnation of a past obsession, no Barbarossas were suspended and therefore evil came to rule the world; or else such suspended invasions were the catastrophe Holtz predicted, and evil therefore collapsed altogether. I longed for this century, seeing it from my window, because I was absolved in it of some of my monstrousness; but I also knew such a version of the Twentieth Century was utterly counterfeit. That neither the rule of evil nor its collapse could be anything but an aberration in such a century, because this is the century in which another German, small with wild white hair, has written away with his new wild poetry every Absolute; in which the black clock of the century is stripped of hands and numbers. A time in which there's no measure of time that God understands: in such a time memories mean nothing but the fever that invents them: before such memories and beyond such clocks, good views evil in the same way as the man on a passing train who stands still to himself but soars to the eyes of the passing countryside. It just couldn't have been, that's all. It's nice to think so, to think evil remains collapsible. But I saw you in that window and the true Twentieth Century found itself, and abandoned the lie it might have chosen to live if you hadn't been there.

There's a camp west of here at Mauthausen on the lovely shores of the Danube. I can see the smoke from the rooftop where I hang Courtney's washed clothes. I remember his name now: Carl. Every day trains come from Switzerland with escaped Jews, the Swiss sending them reliably back.

Holtz has a plan tonight. In the four and a half years

since he first came to this flat he's aged twenty, continental cordiality falling away from his face in chunks. His eyes are debauched by terror, his flesh yellow. His hair drops out in tufts, cigarettes are killing him. There are rumors in the street. "Kill her," he says. What? "Kill her." I won't, I answer. If you want, I'll stop. Get me and my family passage out of the country, and I'll just quit. "And where will you take passage to?" he asks in a deathly croak. "Where are you beyond his reach except perhaps America? You can't go back to America." He looks at me. "We know about you and America." He's sitting on the edge of the bed; his eyes don't quite focus. "The translator's under house arrest," he finally says, "every new chapter is now delivered under armed guard. This is what it's come to. Z waits pacing in his suite." I saw a blond woman there that night in the hotel four years ago, I say. "She's nothing to him," Holtz answers, "she's not the one he cares about. It's the one you've brought to him he cares about. Kill her." Neither of us speaks for several minutes and finally I just say to him, Let the translator do it, but I won't. He nods as though he knew all along, that even if I had agreed, nothing can now be turned back. For the first time I feel a little badly for him, he's in way over his head. Me too probably. Look out that window, I say to him; and we both sit in the dark looking out the window onto the empty street. I want to show him the other century, when none of this happens, and when all he has to think about is his place in the kingdom or the death of his country. I don't think he can see it, though.

77

You and I distant. Lately we argue; I suppose we're arguing about him. He just sits in the corner. It isn't that we're bored, the three of us. Rather the math of our evil is constrained by the math of our bodies. I find myself missing my little daughter, and America. I return to Megan sooner and sooner each night; she sinks drowsily deeper and deeper into her sadness. She no longer looks at me when I get home. I pull her to me and lie that there will always be an England.

78

August 1942. England falls. The invasion has been a savage four months and has cost the Germans, but this is the end. London, Manchester, Birmingham, Edinburgh are all gone, only the seaport of Glasgow holds out besieged. The news comes over the radio this evening as I hold you by your ankles and feed on you, you bursting at my lips rapid-fire. The Germans, knowing what it will be, have not jammed the broadcast but rather pick it up from London and send it out to all Europe; it's the prime minister. "We survive bombs," he says, "we may survive tanks. We survive the blade, and bullets. We survive history of a thousand years, the caprices of political tempests. But defeat, that we choose not to survive. It finishes, countrymen. I'm sorry. If the damnation of an eternity for whatever follies

I've committed would spare my nation this, I would with gratitude be so damned. As it is, damnation is insistent with no exchange for it. God save the King. God save the Empire." There's a moment of black quiet and then a muffled pop; the weight of him can be heard thudding against the microphone. The ooze of him can be heard this thousand miles. In that black quiet perhaps he snickered to know that where he once thought lay the century's conscience there's only a oneliner, a vaudeville smirk. I leave you to your spasms. When you ask, "Why are you going?" I answer, To Megan; I have to. "Don't leave," you say. Don't leave, he calls from the corner. You bastard, I answer him. Halfway down the stairs you ask me one last time.

79

In the mere moments since the broadcast the streets have filled with people, shouting and cheering and embracing that the war in Europe is over. Some wonder out loud whether the Germans will now declare war on America. I run the whole way to Megan and Courtney, dodging revelers and honking cars, civil guards posted on the corners who are hailed as though they just got back from England in the last five minutes. On the quays of the Wien-Fluss small victory parades are taking place spontaneously. From Megan's street I can see the light in our flat, it seems a silent light in the middle of the din.

I run up the stairs, every flight. At the top the door stands ajar and I know something's wrong.

All the lights are on, everything's in its place. I go from room to room; I don't call her name but say it normally, just to confirm to myself it won't be answered: Megan. It isn't answered. There's no sign of Courtney.

I'm thinking, It's such a hot night, and there's much ruckus in the street; they went out. I think it but I know it isn't so. I sit in the flat ten, fifteen, twenty minutes that ache in their passage. I look up finally to see one of the neighbors in the doorway, an old man from the flat below. He darts away. By the time I've chased him downstairs he's got his room closed and locked; I bang on the door for him to open. I'm shaking it by the knob and about to rip it off the wall when the neighbor across the hall protests.

"What's happened to my family," I say.

"Soldiers," she says.

I go back down into the street. People are running up and down the sidewalks swilling beer and shouting. On the other side is a man I know is a spy. I've never seen him before but I know because he looks like every other spy who's tailed me over the last five years. I walk across the street to him. Like all these other very subtle spies he looks away from me as though he doesn't notice me at all; when I get right up to him he's still pretending he doesn't see me. I hold him by the waist and lift him over my head and hang him on one of the streetlamps. I slap him and tell him, "Get Holtz." Some other people gather around in the throes of their jubilation; they've decided this must be political in the way everything is now. "Get Holtz," I say again, and no one likes my accent much. Maybe one of them wants to hit me in the head with a shovel, maybe another would as soon shoot me. "Leave him be!" the spy is screaming at them; I guess I must be the most invulnerable man in the world at this moment.

I take him off the streetlamp and put him on the ground. "I'll be across the street," I say. I return to the flat.

Holtz is there in about forty minutes. He looks terrible. Things don't improve when he sees me. He comes into the flat, I'm sitting in the same place I've been since I got here; he looks around the flat and knows what's happened.

Something in me sinks to see him as surprised as I am. I understand now that he's not in control of the situation. "They're gone," I say from where I sit.

He doesn't say anything at first; for a man whose country has just taken over the English empire, he doesn't appear enthusiastic. "Banning," is all he can muster. It was a poor precedent, ever allowing him to call me that. I've set another precedent tonight: the lights are on. "Banning." He shrugs pathetically.

"Tell them," I say, "tell them I want to make the swap tonight."

He looks utterly befuddled. "The swap?"

"That, or I'll kill him. Tell them. I won't wait."

He's still doing his befuddled act. "What are you talking about?"

I shake my head. "I won't wait. Z for my family, in an hour."

"Z?" It's a good act, I give him credit. "Banning, you've . . . You're disturbed at this moment, I think." He says it slowly, as though gingerly handling a grenade where the pin is loose. "Z's in Berlin, Banning. Berlin. We've conquered England this evening."

He doesn't understand the true situation. *I* understand the true situation. "No point you and I discussing this, let's take matters up with the big boys. Whoever's in Vienna now that can handle it." I get up from my seat. "I'll be at the other flat. You tell them we swap tonight, that I won't wait." I walk by him, our shoulders clash. Out in the street the spy's waiting by the same lamp; he steps back at the sight of me. He looks up at the lighted window. "Back to the other flat," I advise him. After a moment he nods.

80

When I return to Dog Storm Street you're gone.

It isn't that you've taken all your things and left, because you had no things, really. A stick of lip rouge, you must have thrown that away. Perhaps you took a coat of mine and now you walk in the streets with it wrapped around your shoulders.

He's still in the corner. If I move toward him he just pulls back. "Haven't you heard," I tell him, "your war's over." I sit in my chair and wait. "Keep your shirt on."

After an hour and a half I think I hear the car amidst all the other racket down below. Then I know I hear the door, but doors after all have been opening and closing all night now. There's no mistaking the steps on the stairs, though; Holtz's knock is rude and impatient.

He doesn't wait for me to get the door, which is all right since I have no intention of getting it anyway. But when he turns on the light, he isn't Holtz.

Soldiers in the doorway raise their guns.

"You don't want to hurt me," I explain to them, "your boy here wouldn't like it." I gesture at the corner where he's been so many nights now, and it's empty.

Sometimes I have this clarity, sometimes I see it all rather lucidly. On the way to the hotel people are pounding on top of the car; the Germans in the car accelerate and people in the street leap out of their way. It remains to be seen to what extent the Austrians will share the fruits of victory. We get to the Hotel Imperial where I'm taken through the side entrance I was taken four years ago. We go up the lift and get off at a floor near the top of the building. The soldiers lead me into a suite.

I have this clarity, this lucidity. Right now the only thing I remember that seems real is a Christmas Day I tended to

the horses in my father's stable. Now I'm at the far end of
this suite and a huge window with a small footrest at the
other end opens over Old Vienna, St. Stephen's lodged in
the night like a dagger. The window's open, the August
heat's overwhelming. There's another door in the other
wall, several sofas and chairs, and a desk. Seated in the
sofas and chairs are three or four military officers of an
unusual rank, given affairs in England tonight, and behind
the desk is a small dark man at least seven years older than
the pictures of him in the papers. Once he was a client of
mine. Once he worked for me. He limps around to my side
of the desk.

He stops half the room away from me; he doesn't want
to get so close because standing next to me will only em-
phasize how little he is. He raises one finger and, his black
eyes tiny and still like dead insects, says only, "It's not jealousy." He keeps holding up the one finger to make the
point. It's several moments before he lowers his hand and
paces staggeringly to and fro, thinking. He stops and says,
"Permit me to introduce you," and then names off the
generals, and adds, "Of course you know Colonel Holtz."
He indicates behind me and I turn to see Holtz sitting in a
chair. For a moment Holtz looks a bit odd, and then, transfixed, I see his blue fingers, and his eyes that never move
or blink, and his mouth that's open for the flies. Less than
an inch over his right eye is a black hole; the ink of his
brains cries down his forehead to his nose. There's a titter-
ing behind me from the other generals, although not from
X, who regards Holtz almost squeamishly.

"It's not jealousy," X says again, emphatically. "I admit
she had great appeal to me. But," he says, on the other side
of the desk, leaning into it, "what I felt for her can never
match the way I love him. If she made him happy, no one
would have been happier than I. Even having her myself
could not have made me happier." He pauses. "Do you
understand?" I don't answer and he doesn't care. He goes
to the window and stares out over the city. "Look," he

exclaims with some enthusiasm, "isn't that the big wheel," pointing toward the Praterstern. He's talking to the generals now. "I took my children on the wheel . . . last year, I believe. Last year or the year before. Some were too small but the ones who were a little older found delight in it." Limping back toward me, he smiles, "Children. My wife and I just had our sixth." He stops; he's become braver about being closer, almost as though he now taunts the way I'm so much larger and more helpless. "Daughters," he smiles.

The city raves up from beneath us; I can't sit or quite stand. I feel sick.

"I learned long ago," he's saying, through the hiss of blood in my head, "that his will is an inviolate thing. One doesn't toy with it." The generals are making an effort not to let their attention wander; they move in their chairs. There's a sound behind me, and the others look; I think Holtz has slipped where he's propped. I can't bring myself to check. X doesn't notice at all. "I'm ashamed to say," he goes on, "that I learned this the hard way, almost twenty years ago, when as a very intemperate young man I made an effort to oppose him in the party on a particular issue. It says something about the magnitude of the man that he embraced me in his victory and my defeat. Do you know what the issue was, Herr Jainlight?"

"No," I finally say. I barely have the voice for it, but I'll answer anything he asks now.

"Russia, Herr Jainlight," he says. I'm too confused to know exactly what it means, but I nod. He shrugs. "What to do with her," he's saying, "which is to say, what to do with you." He moves around to his seat and sits; his head doesn't even rise above the back of the chair. He rubs his face with his hands. I'm looking at the window, the generals, the soldiers at the door.

"I'll go away," I whisper. Tentatively, afraid to even say their name, I add, "My family and I."

"No no no no, Herr Jainlight," he answers, with great

annoyance that such a foolish thing could even be pro-
posed. "That's no solution at all. How would I explain it to
him? 'We let them go'? And where will you go, where is
left? Do you really want to go to Russia? He'd have you
sent back here. America?" He shakes his head. "Nor,
frankly, can I shoot you." He shakes his finger at me, "You
should appreciate that someone else probably would. But
you know, Germany rules half the world today for one
reason more than any other. And that is that we seized
control of people's myths. The myths they believed meant
one thing, we persuaded them they meant something different. And the problem with shooting a myth is that it
freezes its meaning in death."

"I'll change the myth."

He's utterly annoyed with my lack of sophistication; he
literally throws up his hands. "Mein Herr, don't you suppose we've thought of that?" He says furiously, "Do you
suppose the idea here is to *trick* him? Do you suppose I'm
another one of these traitors who conspire against him? I
can show you motion pictures of the traitors we've hanged
from butcher's hooks with the wire from pianos, I'd wrap
the cord around my own forsaken throat before I betrayed
him! Do you suppose," he demands, struggling for control,
"that this is *your* myth? It's not *your* myth, Herr Jainlight,
you didn't create it. It's *his* myth. It's slept somewhere in
his dreams every night of the eleven years since she died,
it's slept in the dreams of our history, our time." He falls
back into the chair. "You tripped into it while you were
stumbling in the dark like the overgrown American oaf you
are, you woke it. You keep waking it. I can't shoot you, I
can't send you away. I have to break your legs, your arms,
your tongue, not literally—my God it's a new gloryday,
when barbarism is of a newer and more glorious sort as well
—I mean I have to break the legs and arms, the tongue,
that walk and reach and talk in the place where his myth
lives. I have to make you the saddest man alive. A dead
man caught in the body of a living one."

If you take the hands, it's simply a serious mistake not to take the stumps. And when does it end then? "Just do it to *me*," I whisper. "Whatever it is, please do it to *me*."

He's silent long enough I believe he hasn't heard me. "Russia, that was the issue," he finally says. "Almost twenty years ago he argued that we would have to take Russia. I thought it was . . . a mistake. He was right, I was wrong. But now we don't have Russia, his inviolate will violated. Now instead we have this uneasy alliance on our eastern border, which it may be too late to do anything about. We would rule not only Europe but Asia at this moment, perhaps with Japan . . . perhaps without. The American solution would be self-evident." He says, "Of course I won't do it to *you* mein Herr, you just haven't been *listening*." Drumming his fingers on the desktop for a moment, he turns to the guard by the door and gives a signal. The door opens and after a moment the soldier brings into the room my wife and child.

I can't say anything. Megan looks at me stunned, the color has run even from the freckles. Courtney has the insolent courage of four-year-old girls; she keeps looking up at the soldier waiting for him to explain himself. Megan pulls her into her skirt. I would abandon all of my moments before or after this if I could only remove the two of them from this one. But it's too late for that now. One's no longer young when he understands some things are irrevocable. The little crippled man hobbles over to Megan and Courtney; he doesn't look at Megan but only Courtney; he rubs his hand in her hair. He turns his back on them and the soldier rips Courtney from her mother. He pushes her onto the footrest before the window and then up onto the windowsill. Megan wails with horror. "Daughters," X mumbles to himself, shaking his head. Courtney on the windowsill turns and looks at me, and we hold between us the moments I dangled her from rooftops, all the high places she lived and owned. The soldier pushes, and she steps out.

All my moments, if only to cut this one out of time. It seems to hold in place. In it, Megan, four-foot-eleven, takes, in the last moment I'll ever know her, command in a room full of Germans not entirely unlike the way she commanded the first night I knew her. She tears herself from any attempt to stop her and leaps through the window before the moment is out; and with what's left of this part of time, she spins Courtney in midair and pulls her to her chest. There's no question, you know, of retrieving her. There's no question of rescue. Megan knows this, everyone knows it. It's only so the freckletot will not take the long ride down all by herself. It's only so that however extended this moment will be after only a brief four years of them, it won't be so utterly lonely, out there in the black Vienna night, with all that night beneath her little feet. In the last bit of this moment Megan turns and looks at us with defiance. The moment joins itself to every other one I will know, all the ones I cry out in my head to exchange. I carry it everywhere, Megan clutching our daughter to her and the two of them seeming to hang there in the window.

Then they're gone. Then the next moment there's nothing in the window but the still Vienna night.

You should have taken the stumps.

He buckles somewhere between my hands. . . . Someone's hitting me with something, the soldiers with their guns I guess; I'm sure it's rather amusing, X croaking out from between my fingers, Don't shoot him, don't shoot; and then, when the life starts to dribble out of his eyes, he says, Well, yes, shoot him. The soldiers are a little confused. After they've hit me in the head with the butts of their guns enough times, the blood runs into X's hair, eyes. After a while I don't see anything anymore.

Actually, they did take the stumps. Actually, they took everything. Or did I just hand it all over, long ago?

8 1

1943.

8 2

1944.

8 3

1945. I can see the smoke.

8 4

1946.

85

1947. I come to the place one afternoon while walking, I lose track much better when I walk, I've walked every day now for a long time, the place is there on the sidewalk before me, and though there isn't a single sign that it happened here I know immediately even though I haven't been conscious of where I'm going, and I step back looking around me and realize I'm in front of the hotel and that high above me one of those windows is the window. I look at the place on the sidewalk and begin to smash myself against the stone of the hotel and strike at the sharp edges of the edifice with my wrists that I might open up some vein and pour the blood of my impure mongrel mother over the city that it will be fouled in some way that fouls him in turn, that fouls the humiliation he inflicted on this city by which he meant to glorify his squalid vagabond womanless youth and to make meaningless the way the city beckoned her away from him sixteen years ago. Soon there's blood all over. They come and stop me soon. Five or six of them pull me down, before they do I'll ring the Ring with the black blood of the Indian who bore me, twisting bloody wet in the grasp of them, my guardians who appear from nowhere to protect me from myself, and who will always be with me for as long as he lives, his moment joined to mine.

86

I lose track much better when I walk.

It's 1948. Springtime, I guess.

The war goes on. Dead soldiers come back from Mexico and are sealed up in the walls of the Hofburg. Z's final revenge against the city he loves and loathes; he'd rather fill up Vienna with them than the deserts of Occupied Yucatan. The rigor mortis has set in on all of them, their bodies frozen in strange shapes. The walls of Old Vienna protrude with dead elbows, dead knees that jut out from the new cement.

Z speaks to the continent over radio on a weekly basis. Most of the time it's obvious the tape is an old speech from ten years ago, his voice stronger and clearer. When the news is a bit more momentous they try to get by with a new speech. His words slur and his voice breaks, sentences wander off to no resolution. The rumors from Berlin never stop. The military seems to have taken control of things, many of the top party people have vanished. Though there has never been an official announcement, X is apparently dead. I like to think I killed him. I don't remember that night well enough to be sure, and if I analyze it I admit it seems unlikely they would have let me do it, but who knows. All those generals standing around there looking at each other saying, Why not? Sure. Maybe it makes sense after all.

I don't write anymore, which is exactly what X had in mind, of course. But others have something different in mind, and they still keep me on Dog Storm Street where this toady or that regularly visits. Sometimes they cajole me, sometimes they rant. They know I would not mind their torture. They know I would not mind dying. I'm sure they'd consider just doing away with me if it didn't threaten the decrepit passion by which Z still mesmerizes Greater Germany. With the guerrillas in the hills and insurrection in the cities they can't afford it. It doesn't matter to me in the least what they do. Every two weeks an envelope is brought to my door; I'm paid in Deutschemarks.

The alliance is no better than ever. Rumor even has it that it was the Russians who smuggled the Bomb to America as Z was preparing to use it. Courtney would be ten now.

I am . . . thirty-one? Megan would be thirty-five.

Today I find your street.

After eleven years during which I looked for it often, only for it to have seemingly disappeared off the face of the earth, today I chance upon it as though walking up to my front door. The exact same candleshop is across the street, people go in and out even now. The shutters of the window where I saw you are pulled closed, and after I've stood there watching a quarter of an hour, I cross the street and knock on the door. When no one answers I open the door and walk up the stairs to the next level. At your room I pause for a moment, and walk in.

The flat is vacant. Requisite furniture; no sign of residence except the sound in the bathroom off to the right. I walk around the bed to the bathroom door; for a moment I almost believe I see someone. I almost believe there's a reflection of someone in the mirror. But the only thing I find is the water running in the sink.

"Geli?"

In the answering silence I lift the window and push open the shutters. From this place I see the street as you saw it that day except there are no blackboot boys. They're running banks now, or in jail, most of them.

"Mein Herr?" someone says behind me. I turn and an older woman is in the doorway. "Have you come to look at the apartment?"

"Has it been vacant long?" I ask.

"Only a few days," she answers. "It's not difficult these

days to find a renter, especially in the Inner City. I already have several people who've made inquiries." She adds, "But I can take your name if the others change their minds."

I look around. "Who lived here?"

"My husband's brother actually, he died several weeks ago."

"Do you have many apartments like this?"

"Yes," she answers, "but none is vacant presently."

"Have you owned the building a long time?"

"Twenty years," she says, "we bought it, my husband and I, the year before the Depression. Lucky on our part."

"Eleven years ago a girl lived here. Probably with her family. She had hair like spun sunlight." I stop. "I mean, dark blond. Blue eyes." I stop again. "I mean brown."

"I think you must be referring to the Russians," she answers coolly.

"The Russians?"

"He was a refugee who left Russia and spent some time in Africa. Then he came to Vienna. He had a daughter, there was no wife."

"Yes, perhaps that's who I mean."

She says firmly, "They were finally sent back."

"Back?"

"About five years ago. When the new treaty was signed. The Russians wanted them back."

"No," I answer after a moment, "somehow I don't think she's in Russia."

"I hope you weren't attached to them." She explains, "They were enemies of the state after all."

"Were they?"

"I'm sure they must have been. They wouldn't have been sent back after all if they weren't enemies of—"

"I'm sure you're right." I take a last look from the window; she watches me suspiciously.

"What is your name, mein Herr," she says, the good citizen.

"Banning Jainlight."

"What sort of name is that?" She's holding her hands together now.

"It's an English name."

"The English are Germans now."

"I understand."

"It's a German name now."

"No. It will never be a German name." I step past her. I turn to her. "I could have this flat, you know." I start down the stairs and at the top she gives me the German farewell, hailing his name and saluting. "To hell with the son of a bitch," I just answer, but I feel no pleasure from her gasp of shock. I feel no pleasure in the way she'll try to report me only to find the authorities will take no action at all. I close the door quietly behind me.

I forgot to ask if you were beautiful. I forgot to ask if she ever heard you sing.

I walk through the winding streets of the Inner City. The walls bulge with the mortified joints of fallen warriors. The black and red twisted cross of the new empire faces out from the banners that hang on every building and fly from every steeple. Most of the flags are worn, shredding. The empire becomes dilapidated. A new elevated train under construction two years ago has stopped in midair. Guards are everywhere, on every corner, but at night there are the shots of rebel groups hiding in the basements and towers. I cross the canal and walk to the amusements of the Prater-stern.

The park is only partly filled today with families and couples and German soldiers on leave. German officers walk with city girls and cut in front of all the lines for the rides. There's a funhouse with anti-American slogans painted over by anti-Berlin slogans; in some of the booths one throws a ball or shoots a gun at the face of an American president I don't recognize. A small cinema shows footage from the Mexican Front. I buy a ticket for the ferris wheel, then on second thought go back and buy a whole roll of tickets. I get in one of the cages with several other people and the wheel begins to turn. It takes about ten minutes to go completely around, and at the bottom when the others get off I give the guy another ticket. He demands that I go through the line again. I refuse. He certainly isn't the one who's going to move me from where I'm sitting in the cage; he calls an officer to report me. The officer means business when he arrives; I think he's even going to draw his gun. I quietly tell him my name is Banning Jainlight and he should speak to his superior if there's a problem. He doesn't need to speak to his superior. He gazes at me a moment and nods slightly; he castigates the man running the wheel. I hand the man the whole roll of tickets: I'd like the cage to myself if you don't mind, I say to him. Flushed and angry he closes the gate. I rise into the sky that darkens. I forgot to ask if you were beautiful. I forgot to ask if she ever heard you sing. From the critical point of a fever when it either breaks or consumes you, Vienna is displayed from my feet to the west. It lies blasted by dusk and dwindling with the Danube; the palaces of the Hapsburgs rise from the edges of the Ring in fields of wind and granite. A flight of black-hooded bicyclers crosses a bridge in the south. Every window of the city stares back at me bugeyed and untold. If I turn on this wheel long enough and often enough, fast enough and forever enough, it may yet catapult me beyond my moment and yours, into the century that flows on the other side of the island, a white hot blur shot into the round woman moon.

8 7

Three years later, the rising moon slips out of Banning Jainlight's Twentieth Century into the other. It flies high above the river where another large man is sleeping in a small wooden shack that stands on four wooden pillars over the water. There isn't much in the shack but the bed, a table with a chair, an old oil lamp that still burbles fire, a small iron stove with only crumbs of dead coal. It must be past midnight. The river's silent but for the boat which now approaches the shack, not a ferry but a rowboat; the man in the rowboat has left his ferry docked behind him in the dark. The man invests his oars with righteous stealth. In his lap sits gasoline and rags, flaming love. The large man in the shack sleeps through the sound of his demise sailing to him through the water. If the large man were to wake at this moment and make his way to the door of the river-house and out onto the small landing, if he were to lean over the rail of the landing and, in the pearlshattered shine of the white moon, look into the water, it isn't even certain he would see the boat anyway, more likely he would gaze again on the afternoon that precedes him, when he stood in this place and looked into the water and saw her. Saw first her face as though it was just floating down there under the water; but it wasn't floating, he could see her coming toward him. And just as she came up to him from out of the river, he leaned over and reached his arms to her; from out of the water she shot up. His hands caught hers and pulled her the rest of the way. He almost stumbled as he pulled her into his arms. Now he sleeps with this memory; it's only the sound of memory if he hears in his sleep the sound of the boat coming. He won't wake until the moon has lifted out of the doorway altogether, until he doesn't even know there is a moon. Then he'll smell the smoke, and wonder where all the fire came from.

Fifty-six years later, after the century has long since run out of numbers but only begins to understand it's doomed never to die, the man whose hair has been white since the day he was born comes home for the last time. As he did many years before, on the night he exiled himself to sail between home and escape every day again and again, and as he did three years before, on the night he came to find the girl named Kara in the blue dress, he climbs the stairs of the hotel where he lived as a child. He's lost track of how long he's looked for the girl in the blue dress. He accepts that he's lost track of more than just this. Climbing the stairs, the man is neither old nor young now. He doesn't hear the voices of other men and their stories anymore. He would settle to hear his mother's voice as it was when he was small and she read the stories that held no interest for either of them but for the sound of her reading them. Here at the top of the stairs he expects now to find the dark he was born from, which drained his hair of color. He knows the Chinese of the town are waiting to hear her call out her own name before she goes; they have a tree all ready for her. The street outside the hotel fills with Chinese and they begin to shuffle into the building downstairs, where the doors barely hang from their hinges and the windows are empty of glass, and no one else, including a manager, lives anymore. Fifty-six years the white woman has lived in the hotel, most of those years its only tenant. Like scavengers the Chinese wait to pick over not the woman's possessions, which are worthless, but the eyes, ears, fingers attached to the mystery of who she was. He has other plans. Over my own dead body perhaps, he tells himself: but not hers. At the top of the stairs in the hallway her door stands open; for a moment he's about to call out Mother, that she might hear him from her bed as he turns the door's corner. Instead he calls her by her name; turning the door's corner there's a split second when he sees her white hair on the pillow and believes it's his own. "Dania?" he asks.

In the final months of the year 1917, a man on a horse chases a train thirty kilometers outside St. Petersburg. The steam of the engine is silver in the night, black against the moon, and the train reliably eludes him like the hour that's always an hour away. Behind him revolutionaries spur their own horses in pursuit. His ears are filled with their inevitability; it sounds with every passing moment as though they've nearly overcome him. Yet he's already chosen to defy that inevitability they claim for themselves; he means to ride into history as the agent of chaos, believing that if history has a will at all, it's owned by no man for more than the moment it takes to change it forever. Remembering this, he rides harder. Remembering this, he frees himself from the inevitability of their pursuit and from the way the train eludes him. He lashes his horse and screams into its mane, he reaches down to the saddlebag to confirm that what it holds is securely fastened, and he rides out of his hour and crosses it to the one that's always an hour away. The horse rears at the track. The Russian leaps to the second from the last car of the train and mutters a prayer to the abandoned animal already disappearing behind him. The man scrambles into the car's doorway clutching the saddlebag around him as the wind batters him at his back. For a while he just sits in the door watching the mounted revolutionary guards that have chased him from just outside the city: If they *are* the forces of history, he thinks to himself, gasping for air, they'll catch the fucking train too. He's trying to figure out where to stash the contents of the saddlebag should this occur. But soon it's clear this will not occur, soon he sees them disappearing in the night as his horse did. Over the roar of the train he might almost hear their gunshots; he's almost arrogant enough to laugh, but not quite. After a while he picks himself up and makes his way down the aisle of the

dark thundering train. He finds an empty cabin and holding the saddlebag to his chest lays himself out on the seat
to sleep. He keeps one hand in the bag where he holds a
gun. He dozes awhile, the blond Russian, and wonders if
he'll shoot anyone this evening. It's in the early hours of
the morning that the door of the cabin slides open
abruptly, and he lurches upright and nearly showers the
doorway with lead; only a moment saves the woman who
stands there. She's dark in the dark, perhaps slavic or mediterranean. She's moved from another cabin of another
car. She looks at the expression on his face, the expression
that immediately precedes the decision to hold his fire,
though that expression gives no indication of reprieve. She
looks at the saddlebag where his hand disappears; she intuitively knows her death waits there for that once in a
lifetime command. When the command doesn't come she
accepts this as gracefully as if it had. She breathes deeply
and takes a place on the seat across from him. He's
watched her only half a minute before somewhere in his
loins rises the first smoke that, six years later, is to become
his daughter.

By the time Dania had lived with her family fourteen years
in the middle of the Pnduul Crater, she could no longer
discount the possibility that the rim of the crater was moving. Its livid ridge turned slowly but distinctly around her,
traveling to the right as the black clouds above raced to the
left like Dobermans. During the year, she and her father,
mother and young brother would migrate with the other

European exiles of the colony, following the rim of the crater to higher and lower ground depending on the rain and heat; the southern curve, where the trees stood and several wells had been dug, was best. The dusk lay low in the branches of the trees like the foliage of a thousand black trunks. In the middle of autumn she walked through the avenues of the forest while the white leaves fell from above her as though the dusk itself was dying. She lay on the ground and covered herself with the leaves and when her little brother came looking for her she leapt out in an explosion of brittle white, laughing at his little terror all the way back to the gray tents that stood invisible against the ash of the Pnduul. For days afterward her body wore against her will small bits of the white leaves as evidence of the young secret savagery inside her into which she had every intention to grow. She marked the seasons by this savagery.

It wasn't until a number of years later, running alone through the nightstreets of New York, the frantic large lumbering sound of her lover behind her, that in the middle of her fear she questioned the exile of her childhood. From Paris and Madrid and Brussels, writers and geologists and dull bureaucrats had left their homes and come to the colony when one intrigue or another was about to catch up with them. There was a young doctor from Berlin who arrived in her thirteenth year. It took her about a day and a half to fall in love with him. He was in his late twenties with black hair like her mother's and blue eyes; what crime brought him to the East Sudan was unclear. It was possible he was a missionary who'd come to live with the savages: I'm a savage too, she insisted to him. The doctor watched her with genuine longing but kept his distance. He wants to be respectable to me, she thought disgustedly, like an uncle or older brother. His name was Reimes. Good day Dr. Reimes, she said when they passed, the word doctor spat out in acidic irony. She despised the fact he was such a gentleman. On a train in Russia years before, her mother had decided in the course of an evening to go with her father to Africa; it was the thing about her mother the girl came to remember most vividly, as though she'd been there herself, and admire most fervently, as though her mother had never done anything else so remarkable.

She came to understand that her father's flight to the Sudan had to do with the blueprint he kept rolled in an old saddlebag that no one else ever knew. She saw it one night when they were living on the western curve of the crater as the face of the crater revolved beneath them. Her father laid it out on the table under the lamp that swung from the top of the tent; five or ten minutes she stood in the shadows watching the light sway back and forth across his hair the gold of which had become distinctly wan over the recent years. He was intent enough studying the blueprint that even when she took a step from the shadows it was a moment before he noticed, and he was more violently startled than she'd ever seen him. "Is it a map?" she said to him. He sagged a bit and smiled. Yes, he said, it's a kind of map. She stepped forward a little closer and looking at the blueprint more closely asked, "Is it a house?" Yes, he answered, it's a kind of house. On the blueprint she could see the general living area, a dining area, the bedrooms and the toilet. There was an attic and basement. There were two passages that ran secretly in the walls from the downstairs entryway to one of the upstairs bedrooms, and from the basement straight up to the attic somehow without passing any of the floors in between. Overlaying the blueprint were several other sheets, fine and nearly transparent, with other lines, but years later when she examined the plan more carefully she could never get the lines of one overlay to correspond with those of the other, or with those of the original blueprint. She began to understand it wasn't quite a house at all. I said it was a *kind* of house, he explained without explaining, I said it was a *kind* of map. "Is it," she asked on this particular night when she saw the blueprint for the first time, "where we're going to someday live?" Her father's face, now lined in a way she'd never seen short of the light of the lamp swaying from the top of the tent, broke into a sad smile and answered, But we live there already, my girl.

She was rare color against the toneless chalk of the crater, a tawny blot snatched from the genes of her father's younger years. All the other people of the colony were the white and gray of Europeans or the black of her mother's hair or her brother's or Reimes from Germany, or the deep gray of African flesh, the natives venturing into the crater only when the religious dictates of the moon allowed it since they believed the Pnduul was in fact a patch of the moon that had fallen to earth and therefore not to be trespassed casually. Against the bleached whirling rim of the crater anyone could see her dance. Her father brought her when she was six to a Frenchman with aristocratic pretensions who taught ballet in Paris before becoming ensnared in whatever particular disgrace brought him here. The Frenchman considered the Russian and his dirty little girl to be beneath him. "She moves around so damn much," the Russian said, "see if she can dance," as though the one was the logical extension of the other.

Well it's impossible clearly, the Frenchman said to himself an hour later, as little Dania postured around the stick he perched between two stones out in the middle of the plain. She has no balance, look there! He wanted to laugh out loud. He could hardly wait to show the presumptuous father. The silt of the crater blew over them in the afternoon, sometimes so dense the girl was only gold flint in the white air. The Frenchman peered over his shoulder to see if the father was watching in the distance. Good, he thought, she'll fall over any moment and he'll see for himself. She did not fall over. The wind that whipped the rim of the crater rose and fell; even in the wind she didn't topple. I don't understand, the Frenchman said to himself, it's clear she has no balance, look at the way she teeters in relationship to the ground. But the girl wasn't moving in relationship to the ground, she moved in relationship to the moment. From each moment in which she was destined to topple she danced away. She had no particular grace, she had no rhythm anyone would identify as such. She didn't move or dance like any little kid the Frenchman had seen. He fumed. It enraged him, the impertinence of her not falling.

Meanwhile the little blond girl was squinting at the Frenchman through the dust. He's waiting for me to fall over, she said to herself. Occasionally, just to make him a little crazy, she'd wobble in a particularly precarious fashion before pulling herself back from the future. "What did I tell you?" the Russian said to the Frenchman. "She's going to be beautiful too, anyone can see that." The ballet teacher would have considered it small consolation to know that while the girl might be destined to dance, she was not destined to be beautiful, if there was such a thing as destiny.

After the young German doctor came to the colony she danced for him, dirty auric in the white crater. Out of the corner of her eye she could see him standing off in the trees watching her against his will. She found him one night in her father's tent when no one else was there. "Are you lost," she said, and he whirled to the sound of her voice behind him, "did you wander off by mistake?" In the dark of the tent she thought she could summon up the beauty she didn't have; if there'd been room she'd have danced him into submission. It was too dark to see if he blushed.

He put his hand out to her and pulled it back; she could almost hear him thinking, My God, she barely bleeds yet. "It's blood enough," she muttered in the dark, "in the jungle it doesn't take so much blood." He began crashing wildly around the tent where not long before she'd found her father reading his blue map. "So what kind of doctor is it," she taunted him as he finally bumbled his way out, "who's afraid of the sight of blood?" After a moment she stood there alone. Or is it just *my* blood, she asked herself, lamenting her plainness.

After twenty years of exile in the Sudan, Dania's father decided it was time to take his family back to Europe. To the alarm of his wife, he made arrangements in Vienna. "Vienna's right under their noses!" she cried, to which he answered, "Exactly right." He reasoned they wouldn't be looking for him right under their noses. "Paris or London they'd expect, why, they'd nab us off the streets the first week we arrived." After twenty years of wanting to leave Africa, Dania's mother now dreaded the escape. "Vienna, Vienna," she whispered to herself over and over. But Dania's father proceeded with the plans, which would take them up out of the jungle through Egypt, from where they would sail to Italy.

For the last five years the colony migrated the rim, Dania saw a cave in the northwestern pocket of the crater. It stood at the top of a small slope that funneled out into the crater's dish, and the fourth year she and her brother made their way to the cave and stooped in its mouth, out of which came an inexplicable blast of arctic cold. They gaped into the black of the cave waiting for a light from some other end. Even then she swore she heard the rumbling of hooves. The boy and girl ran down the slope sliding part of the way and then scrambled up the rocks to the plateau where the colony was camped. Nothing came out of the cave that year. Nearly twelve months later, the crater having turned its full circle, they saw the cave again on a mild African winter day when the light on the edge of the earth was tarnished the color of her hair. They hadn't even reached the crater's bottom when the buffalo flooded out the lightless doorway. They came in a hundred herds, all together. She would have thought the whole Sudan heard and felt them. Their hair was short and glowed a strange silver; all the more curious was that even from the distance of the cliffs some twelve feet above, even in their relentless rampage across the hot desert, Dania could plainly see on their hides the white patches of unmelted snow. She had never seen snow. When the children returned to the tents they were dismayed to find that no one else in the colony heard or felt the buffalo. Her father went with them out to the cliffs to see for himself but not even the clouds of the silver stampede were left.

It's not long after this, as her family spends its last days in the Pnduul back on the southern rim by the trees, that Dania wakes one night hearing and feeling the buffalo. They're nearly here, she says to herself in horror. She jumps from her bed and stands in the opening of the tent; in the camp, everyone sleeps. If I wake them for no reason I'll appear ridiculous, she considers to herself, and looks back into the tent at her sleeping little brother. She wants him to wake now and hear and feel the buffalo too. She keeps peering out into the flat night and walks past the dead campfires to the tent of her mother and father where she stops because she can hear them inside. What a time for love, she thinks to herself. She's only turned back to her own tent for a moment when there's a sound like the earth splitting. She spins to the abyss of the crater only to see the night suddenly bled of color. The buffalo come so quickly there isn't time for anyone to scream; they flash silver in the night. Dania's paralyzed with the choice of running to her parents or her brother or the trees for safety. The animals rip through the camp pitilessly, tearing through the tents and emerging with the gray canvases sheathing them like ghosts. The sound and smell of them overwhelm her; on all sides of her are the gutted flapping tents hurled into the air. When the buffalo have disappeared as quickly as they came, the tents float down from the sky like parachutes. She's appalled by the way everything, the running buffalo and the descending gray tents, seems to have happened around her as though to deny she's a part of it. There isn't any sound at all now. In shock she stumbles over to where her own tent had been. Several feet from it she finds either her brother's bedding or her own, she can't be sure which. The bodies of other people lay in the dirt as though they never woke, only the contortions of their sleep and the way their mouths are open tell her it's not sleep at all. She finds the body of the French ballet teacher. Twenty feet from him she finds her little brother. She kneels over him and begs him to be alive, she beats him furiously for his deadness. Only when she begins to cry does a sound rise collectively from the trampled village like the sound of birds when they fall to earth, manic and mournful, not a sound of the throat but beneath the heart, life not immolated but made a vicious sizzle. She's still beating her little brother for his deadness when her father's hands pull her from the small body. The two of them stagger through the camp together. Vienna, Vienna, her mother cried when she was on top of her father, as though to love the Vienna right up out of him; seconds later the buffalo came through the tent and dragged her into the campfire embers. The stunned fading life of her trickles out in whispers of Vienna as Dr. Reimes tries frantically to keep the life in her, to no avail. Dania's mother and brother are buried with the other members of the devastated colony the next day below an African rain, a score of natives witnessing the funeral somberly from atop the crater's rim. Afterwards Dania runs into the trees hurling herself from trunk to trunk to knock the last of the white leaves to the ground. She buries herself in the leaves and lies silently as though to affect death itself, while her father wanders the groves calling her name.

91

Lying here in this particular burial, she is at once in three separate moments. She's lying beneath the leaves of the Sudanese forest, she's lying in her bed in Vienna, she's lying in the bottom of a rowboat on the shores of Davenhall Island. She's not asleep or dreaming, she's perfectly wakefully aware and conscious. She remembers. She remembers last night the shorthaired silver buffalo, she remembers this afternoon the riot in the street outside her window, she remembers running to the beach in the early hours of morning to see the small wooden shack burning on its pillars over the river. In each of these moments she's waiting for a lover. She's waiting for the man she loved in the jungle, Dr. Reimes. She's waiting for the man she loved in the city, a dancer by the name of Joaquin Young. She's waiting on the island for the man who's always loved her across time and space. The rain beats down on the African leaves, on the Austrian rooftop, on the tarpaulin that shields the boat. It's the same rain in three different moments, all of which she lives in at once. Her head pounds. It aches with the thunder of buffalo from the night before.

It aches from the stone that struck her in the window this afternoon. It aches from the guilt and confusion of a woman old before she's thirty, in the chinatown on the other side of the river Rubicon that has no other side. She can't stand it anymore and sits up in her bed. Outside her window she watches the lights of Vienna. Her father snores like an old man in the other room. She feels the side of her face, thinking the swollen pain is what's awakened her. Had she not turned from the stone when she did, it would have struck her in the mouth and broken the flesh; she might have lost a tooth or even scarred her lip. She would have at least bled. She's thinking these things, believing they're what have awakened her, when she realizes these are not the things that have awakened her, she realizes it's something else. She realizes someone is here in the room. She looks for him in the dark, she'd call to him if she knew what to call. She doesn't believe she's imagining it, she can practically see him. He's big. He's very big. He makes her shiver with the way he looms. He's not any lover she would have expected. She cannot decide whether to rebel against the anonymity of this first lover or revel in it. She isn't sure she's ready for him. He tears into her. She hasn't even had time to grab tight the knobs of the bedposts, she's gasping from the presence of him up inside her before she completely understands what's happening. He fucks her till she's ripe with him; holding onto the bedposts she never gets the chance to touch his face, so that she might know what he looks like. In the morning when she wakes she would almost believe she's dreamed it except for the way she's torn and the way her thighs are crusted with her blood and the glue of him. She'll wash herself before her father awakes. In her Viennese bed among the dishevelment she's amazed to find the white leaves of the Pnduul Crater, as though she grew them herself in uterine savagery.

9 2

They'd lived in Vienna a month, in an apartment building on the edge of the Inner City across from a candleshop, when Dania found a job. Her father, devastated in spirit by the loss of his family, and without resources, attempted only feebly and uselessly to stop her. Dania was now fifteen. She knew four languages fluently and her command of two others was fair; in the jungle over the years all the languages of the colony had woven into something like one. While her first job at the dance school on the other side of the Karlsplatz was menial, her linguistic skills soon landed her an office postion. After six or seven months she summoned the nerve to audition before the school's entrance committee. The committee was embarrassed by her. It was also a source of some exhilarated satisfaction that the Russians, who'd once produced the greatest dancers in the world, were now spitting out grubby little refugees like this one. One of the young dancers of the school was a man in his early twenties by the name of Joaquin Young. Young was a star pupil who taught one or two classes during the school year; the Italian son of an English father and given a Spanish name, the boy had come to the school from Rome eight years before as a prodigy. The school doted on him. They beseeched him to accept Austrian citizenship; he declined though for reasons that had nothing to do with anything as politically prophetic as the fact that only a year hence Austria would no longer exist. It was rather because of the obstinacy and disgust Young felt for the way the school supposed it might use him, when it was clear to Young that it was he who would use the school. In the same way he became legendary for having declined just eight months before a position with the Vienna Ballet, Young made it clear that while he may have passed the ballet's audition, it failed his. He didn't want to dance as he would have if he had been born a hundred years before.

When Joaquin Young watched Dania dance he understood, though he might not have identified it in this way, how she danced against history. She danced against it in the way her father crossed its irrevocable hour on horseback twenty years before in pursuit of the train that would take him out of Russia, in possession of the blueprint that the forces of history wanted so badly. She danced her moments so as to own them for herself. He understood that if she was as bad as the instructors and professors on the committee claimed, then there were a hundred misturns, missteps and misgestures she would have made that she did not. By intuition she didn't strive to control her body but to risk losing control every place she took that body, every place in her own psyche that thundered with gleaming buffalo. "But there's no structure to her form," one of them argued, or perhaps he said there was no form to her structure. Young laughed, "She's inventing her own structures, can't you see?" He detested the way they supposed that the structures they didn't recognize weren't structures at all. This argument raged as the blond girl stood there in the middle of the floor with her head bowed, arms folded in determination, seething; raged as though she wasn't there at all. Young was overruled, but the committee was unnerved. Days afterward people were still talking in the halls about Dania dancing. What now? he said, the first thing he spoke to her, since he hadn't actually spoken to her in the audition. I go back to translating letters in the main office, I imagine, she answered, to which he replied, Then your imagination's limited. Yours, she said back, has danced away with you. That night she returned to the floor where she'd danced for them and pondered the meaning of her own steps.

They didn't speak again until some months later, when Young caught up with her in the street to tell her he was

leaving Vienna. It seemed to her she'd spent enough time
pining for young Dr. Reimes back in the jungle and that
there was no call now to pine for Joaquin Young. Three
weeks after he'd gone she got a letter from Amsterdam. He
asked her to come to him. This was the plan all along, she
considered, to make me come to him; he didn't, after all,
take me with him. He didn't say three weeks ago in the
street, Come with me. He said goodbye so that he could
write three weeks later, Come to me. She put the letter
under her pillow and went to the window where she was
still thinking about it as the scuffle broke out in the street
below her. I'll go to him, she decided almost defiantly only
a moment before she turned away and the stone grazed her
face. The next day she still had a large bruise there beneath
her eye; she was barely aware of it, conscious only of the
way she was enflamed between her legs from the lover who
had come that night. "My God," croaked her father at the
sight of her face. She told him about the fight in the street
the day before.

Her father didn't seem so much now like the dashing
rider who outraced history outside St. Petersburg back before she was born. He lowered his eyes and when he began
to cry, she began to cry. "Oh father," she ran to him,
holding his hand. I've cost my family everything, he said. I
had it in my head that coming to Vienna was shrewd and
look what it's cost. It's my mother he means, she thought.
He means that if he hadn't said Vienna she wouldn't have
been on top of him that night, going Vienna Vienna over
and over as though to draw the doom of it right up out of
him into her. She would have been below him as usual and
he'd have sheltered her from the silver buffalo. "I
thought," he said bitterly now, "we'd live under the very
nose of history. Rather we've jumped into its mouth. And
for what?" It was then he drew closed the shutters as
though all Vienna was looking in on them, and pulled up
one of the floorboards and lifted out in a cloud of African
dust the old saddlebag and took from the bag the old blue-

print and unrolled it across the table. For a moment he only stood there above the open blue map and shuddered, hacking African dust in his lungs. She held him by the shoulders until the attack ended. In the following silence he ran his hand across the print, lost in thought until she finally asked, "What is it, father?" At first he didn't seem to hear.

"It's the map of the Twentieth Century," he finally answered. He began poring over the blueprint. "There's a secret room I can't find." He shook his head in consternation. "I've looked a long time," he said, "it's here somewhere." He flipped through the overlays, he ran his finger along all the lines. "It's not in the passages or the halls, the likeliest places," he said, raising the tracing finger emphatically, "not in the bedrooms. I would have thought maybe the bedrooms. I would have thought maybe the attic. The basement," he rubbed his chin with his hand, "well, the basement doesn't make sense. Where can a secret room lead from the basement? A secret room from the attic might at least go outside." Outside the Twentieth Century? she thought, terrified for him. "But what's in the secret room," she said gently, and after a moment he only answered, "The conscience." She slowly ran her own hand over the forehead of her old father, wiped from him the dust from the crater which he wore in the same way she secretly wore the leaves of its forest. Tenderly she gazed upon her father's madness. For twenty years, she told herself, he's believed this is the floorplan of the Twentieth Century, with a hidden room that is its conscience. She wondered if those who had pursued him were as mad, or whether anyone had ever really pursued him at all.

Take it with you when you go to Amsterdam, he said, and she gave a start; she hadn't said anything to him of Amsterdam. I didn't mean to read the letter, girl, he said quietly, I was making up the room while you were at the school today. If he'd seen the blood and white leaves of the sheets as well, he said nothing; he would not be the sort of father, now that he'd lost everyone else, to so abhor his daughter's womanhood simply because he always wanted her for himself. I won't take it, she answered, because I'll be back. He didn't believe her. I'll be back, she said, and we'll find the secret room together. We'll find it and I'll dance there, if there's space for a dance.

93

On the night before she arrived in Amsterdam the lover came again. It was her second night on the train, past one in the morning; they'd just pulled out of Paris. Her father begged her not to go by way of Munich and so the trip had taken nearly a day longer than it might have otherwise. She'd just returned from the dining car where she had a sandwich and some wine, sitting alone at a table as the bottle bounced nervously on the cloth to the clatter of the tracks. The wine left little red droplets on the cloth before her. The old bartender sat beneath one thin light reading a newspaper; he offered it to her when he finished and she took it. The train passed several villages where men swung lanterns from the station platforms. She finally rose from the table and returned to her car; a mother and daughter who'd been in her compartment were no longer there and she had the cabin to herself. She stood in the aisle of the empty train snaking through Europe at two-thirty in the morning and the cold air through the open window blew against the part of her face that was slightly yellow from the fading bruise. A lantern clamped to the wall of the train jiggled wildly. When her face was cold she returned to her seat and lay there some time underneath the newspaper before she slept.

Because she slept, she'd say to herself, while it was happening, It's a dream. But she never really believed that, not from the first moment when she found herself startled to attention by the realization that, as in her room in Vienna, someone was there in the compartment. It was dark but not that dark; she saw the looming form of him above her. "What are you doing here?" she actually said; he stopped for a moment, as though he might try and explain. Then she heard a sound like something ripped, and understood the fabric of the dress had torn around her thighs; she heard another rip and flinched. She sat upright as though to hold him off. The buttons of her dress scattered across the floor; she scrambled to her feet only to realize in the cold air that came through the windows of the aisle outside her cabin door that he'd pulled everything off her. Her bare body fell against the window. The heat of it sent the cold of the glass running down the wall. She had one foot on the floor and the other knee on the seat, and held her arms to her breasts; perhaps she believed something might yet be protected. Take your arms away from your breasts, he said to her. She rose to him in the frosted glow of the compartment. The definition of his eyes bled into two sightless blazes of glass through which she could see the night beyond him. Through his glass eyes she could see the passing small fences and blue silos and little houses in the distance with lights; when the lids of his eyes fell shut she felt the top of her legs glisten. He put his mouth there and held her ankles to the red velvet seat; she flailed at the seat in the cold of the moonlight. He pulled her down and she clutched the armrest as she'd clutched the bedposts; amidst the thump of the train she felt him enter her. She kept expecting him to dim and die with some rush of light. It was like waking in the night to find some part of her numb, feeling as though she didn't have an arm or leg, and waiting for the feeling to come back slowly in a warm throb. She let go of the armrest. The newspaper rustled beneath her chest. When she pounded at the glass he took her hands in his. He flooded the center of her and she screamed into the seat, opening up to him again.

When she woke she guessed she'd slept a quarter of an hour. She was still folded across the red velvet seat in the dark; she could smell him running out of her, and his sweat on her back. She untwisted herself and burned anew. The train was somewhere in Belgium. She slowly dressed and went down to the end of the car to use the bathroom and wash her legs; she slumped against the toilet gasping. Back outside she stood staring out the window. Dutch rivers fled across her vision. After some time the train came to a station; it was possible she was now in Holland. She took her one small bag and left the train, walking across the dissipated light of the platform. She walked through the station and out into a small Flemish village. She walked down the one road and within minutes she was out by the tall grass where the little houseboats could be seen bobbing on the river. A windmill stood against the night. She turned to look over her shoulder once and then walked out through the grass under the moon; she heard the train pulling out and for ten minutes she walked slowly amidst the grass toward the river, listening to the train disappear toward Amsterdam. The clouds tumbled above her. She whistled a song she'd heard some of the other women sing in the office at the school. At the end of the tall grass she could see a wooden fence that ran along the river; over to the south were the houses of the village, dark but for a single light each one burned for a stranger lost on a hot night in Holland. She pulled her torn dress closer to her when she looked over her shoulder again. For a moment she had the sinking feeling there was no one there at all, but she reassured herself. The small boats were drifting on the river a few meters before her; unlike the village houses they burned no lights. The smell of the grass and the water

mixed with the smell of him and she liked it. At the fence
her feet sank into water. She continued watching out over
the river even when he came up behind her; she didn't turn
to him. Her ragged dress blew around her. As he separated
her, she leaned her body over the rail of the fence; her hair
fell into her face and brushed the tall grass. He reached in
front of her and held her breasts. She moaned into the
grass, her ragged dress caught on the fence; her hair was
tousled in the wind. He was talking to her and she wanted
him to be quiet. She didn't move from the fence while he
had her, she only brushed her hair away. The sails of the
windmill were full, drifting on the field of grass a few meters from them. She didn't move until she simply couldn't
stand the sound of him anymore, and the things he said to
her. "You bastard," she finally turned to him furiously,
spitting in his face, "my eyes are brown not blue, and that's
not my name."

94

She found him living on a houseboat in Amsterdam one
canal north of the Dam Rak. He was surprised to see her,
as was the woman with the flurry of black hair who
emerged from the boat's cabin with him. Joaquin stood on
deck silently buttoning his shirt as Dania waited on the
edge of the canal; he was trying to decide if he was happy
to see her this soon, or happy to see her at all. Perhaps
what he loved was the act of calling her to him, rather than
the act of her coming. He spoke in broken Dutch to the
blackhaired girl who climbed off the boat and brushed past
her new rival as though rivalry meant nothing to her. Joa-

quin didn't explain the girl to Dania and Dania didn't ask him to. They went and had dinner in a restaurant. All around them was nothing but talk of Germany and all the Germans who were trying to get out. It bored him. He was nothing like in his letter to her; she now felt young beside him. He explained he was going to start his own dance company: It'll be, he offered, for those who want to dance as you do, willfully and enraged. What are we enraged at? she asked, and he looked at her dumbfounded and blank.

In the hungry light of the houseboat he could see the fiery ravishment of her legs and belly; he could smell the other man, and her devourment of him. They'd walked through the streets halfdrunk back to the boat but now the moment sobered him enough that when the boat weaved with the water he couldn't quite weave with it, pliant. But I believed you'd never been had, he said in almost a cry; when you knew me, she replied coolly, I hadn't. The boat rocked and he toppled into her; he regarded the proximity aghast. He flew back from her. Don't tell me your other girlfriends have all been virgins, she said. He neither denied nor affirmed it; he wasn't angry so much as wounded. Sex abandoned him. If she touched him it only seemed to make matters worse. They slept unconsummated and the next day she put her things together to go. Don't go, he said; after a moment he said, No, go. He walked with her to the train station. Inside she felt dead, she wanted only to be on the train as soon as possible in a cabin that was all hers in the bright light of day, so that she could cry. Halfway to the station anger finally came to him; when he pushed her he was like a child, she even laughed, though nothing about it was funny. She just walked on and didn't look back to see if he was standing there watching her go. She read her ticket in the station as though on it was written: None of these men is worth the impulse of a true heart. Beyond Joaquin Young and Dr. Reimes, she wasn't sure whom she meant.

Two days later in Vienna her father, older by the minute, staggered into the flat with a loaf of bread to find, astonishingly, his daughter returned. She was tottering in the middle of the room with a bottle of vodka. What is it? he asked, rather than, When did you return? She answered drunkenly, I'm plain. I'll never waste the time regretting it again, that I'm plain, I'm going to get it all out of my system tonight. I'm plain, I'm plain. Girl, he said, how many men already love you? None, she answered. That's not true, her father said, I didn't ask how many love you perfectly or well, or nobly or without selfishness. I asked how many love you at all; I know myself of at least two. All right then, she said. Two. She thought about it a moment. All right then, she said: three. She thought again. Four. She sat down hard with the vodka and her father came and took it from her. He set it on the dresser. He put the bread on the table, he bent over to look into her eyes and make them smile. But looking at her closely, his own eyes narrowed. With a finger he touched her lips. But girl, he asked with a frown, where did you get this scar? She sat in the vodka daze for a moment before making her fragile way to the bathroom where she gazed into the mirror; there, as her father had done, she raised her fingers to a small white scar at the corner of her mouth where there'd never been one before. It shone in the light of the bathroom like a diamond in her tooth. But I never bled, she thought to herself in confusion. It's my heart, she called to her father, the words it doesn't know catch in the cracks of my face, I wear the words I can't spit free. Not until later, after she'd slept some hours, did she wake in bed with the question that the receding tide of vodka left beached on her brain. "Four?"

95

A year later they were living in a country that no longer was. For a year after that he lived with the fear the Germans would seize his daughter in all her mother's slavic heat and send her to the camps with the other slavs and gypsies and Jews. If anyone asked he claimed for her the purest Russian bloodlines, a strategy that might have held faint possibilities of survival until still another year passed and against the expectations of the world Germany and Russia signed an alliance. Dania quit the school, no longer trusting those she worked with. She and her father remained in the flat most of the time, believing that if they were caught the Germans would return the exiles to the homeland that hounded them. Her father despaired that they hadn't remained in Africa, he despaired that Dania hadn't remained in Amsterdam. Dania believed the Russians weren't after them at all. She believed no one had spent a quarter of a century trying to find the floorplan of the Twentieth Century. Over this time her lover came to her like clockwork and she became only vaguely aware he was there at all; sometimes he brought a friend. She came to sleep through their visits, the dawn's semen the only manifestation of the night's memory. Sometimes the lover and his friend were already there when she came to bed, waiting for her, sometimes they acted as though they lived there. On those nights she would take him: she was Lilith to history, coming to history on the night he feels most abandoned and alone. She'd straddle him and let his years erupt into her. On these occasions she told herself that if there indeed was a floorplan to the Twentieth Century with a secret room, then it was not a room in which the conscience dwelled but rather this room here, hidden in the capital of a country that no longer was, where she fucked history and owned him. That was when she scoured the room on her hands and knees looking for the secret way out of the century marked on her father's blueprint. She looked beneath the bed and behind the bed's headboard, she pried loose the tiles of the bathroom floor and ran her fingers over the walls. She moved pictures this way and that, as though they were secret controls.

On the first summer night of the year 1941, her father prepared to leave the flat. He'd made many daring journeys in his life, crossing thousands of kilometers over three continents; this journey, the most daring, would take him across town. For three years the old Russian and his daughter had survived the Germans, and for two years the alliance. He knew the landlady had many times considered reporting them; he could see by the way she looked at him. That she hadn't done it yet only meant she feared making trouble for herself. Now, the course of the war convinced him he could no longer count on her timidity; little did he know that within forty-eight hours Germany would invade Russia in an operation called Barbarossa and everything would change. He didn't tell Dania he was leaving the flat or about the arrangements he'd made to have the blueprint smuggled to England and then America. He slipped out in the middle of the night while she slept. He made his way into the core of the Inner City and then cut up through the alleys that ran behind the Hofburg Palace. He felt fortunate that the evening was so mild; yet halfway to his destination he was already exhausted. He remembered how the horse he had ridden across the steppes of St. Petersburg had pushed itself beyond endurance to cross that hour that defied crossing between his past and his future, between the history that was determined and the history that could be undone by a single man if he chose to undo it. As he turned a corner behind the palace, not far from the Cafe Central, history chose to undo him back.

She'd been lying in her bed finishing with her lover when she heard her father leave. She threw back the sheets, threw on her clothes and ran from the room; down the moonlit streets of Vienna the hot seed ran from her and left its trail. It didn't take any time to catch sight of her father; she kept her distance all the way through the city until that final corner where she watched him die. At first, from where she stood, since she could only see him and not the other one, she didn't understand the gunshot was a gunshot, and only after she saw her father hurled backward by the force of the shot did she understand that what her father reached for in the old saddlebag was the gun with which he'd almost shot her mother on a train twenty-four years before. The gun, as old as the saddlebag if not the man, jammed and didn't fire. He lay there in the street. All the windows above remained conspicuously empty. She only faltered a moment at the sight of her father shot down, and then continued walking toward the body. The blood was black in the moonlight. It was then she saw come into view the other man with his own gun smoking in his hand; her father's gun lay a meter and a half from his dead open fingers. She focused on nothing but that gun; the other man was going through the saddlebag and found the blueprint. In the moonlight he unrolled it and studied it, excited. She walked up to her father's gun and picked it up; only then did he glance up at her. His face was stricken by the sight of her; she suspected he'd longed for her after all, watching her dance as a bit of dirty gold in the pale ash of the Pnduul Crater. She held the gun up to him. "And here I thought you were afraid of the sight of blood," she said. His eyes were as brilliant as ever.

He stood up with the blueprint. A streetlamp burned above him and at the end of the street the night opened up behind him. He looked very sad, not so much, she guessed, at killing her father but that she should know it was he. For her part she was as cool as the wind off the Danube. The rage she felt at her father's murdered body was held far at bay for this moment; for this moment she regarded events with as little humanity as her humanity would allow. She kept switching the gun from hand to hand. "It doesn't work, Dania," Reimes finally choked, "it's an old gun. I didn't want to shoot him, if he hadn't reached for the gun I wouldn't have—"

"Don't lie to me," she said. "The idea was always to kill him, we both know it."

"What do you know about it," he said angrily, "be a young girl awhile longer before you presume to know the things young girls can't know." He watched her switch the gun from hand to hand. "I'm sorry," he said, softening, "it was my political role." For the Russians or Germans? she began to ask, but it didn't matter. He thought for a moment and added hastily, "It doesn't mean I didn't want you, you know." He saw the look forming on her face when he said this and, misunderstanding it, went on. "When you found me that night in the tent, it's true I was looking for this," he gestured with the blueprint, "but it's also true that on another such night I would have looked for you. You can believe that."

"Is that what you think," she said, "I'm angry that it was the map you wanted and not me? We stand here over the body of my father you just murdered and that's what you think?" Rage wasn't so far at bay now.

"Dania." He pointed with the hand holding the blueprint, at her hand that held the gun. "It's an old gun, Dania." Coaxing her. "It's broken. It doesn't work. It's *out of date.*"

"Oh?" she said, and blew a hole right through him.

She heard the plop of something several feet behind him, his insides flying out the back of him onto the round cobblestones of the street. His look became befuddled, as though he was still listening to the sound of her gun much as she had listened to the sound of his, which lay with the saddlebag beside her father's legs; as though he was still figuring out the sound for himself, not willing to take the gun's word for it. Then he looked down. He could see the hole in him but not quite so clearly as she saw it; she could see through him the Vienna night at the end of the street, as though a part of the black sky and the stars it held were lodged there in the middle of him. He had the night for a stomach. It was like when she'd been on a train to Amsterdam and looked into the open eyes of the lover she otherwise couldn't see, and saw in those clear blazes the small fences and silos and houses passing her by. Reimes staggered in the street a moment; he said over and over, "I feel . . . I feel . . ." and could never quite finish it. Behind him his insides on the street began to lose their form and dissolve. Reimes turned a moment to the window of a shop; in the reflection of the window he could see in the middle of him the reflection of another window of another shop behind him. "I feel . . ." He pitched forward. The shatter of the window was much louder than that of the gun with which she'd killed him. She dropped the gun, walked briskly to his body; the rage was a good deal nearer now. She unclasped the blueprint from his hand which now stuck wedged to a piece of glass. I must get this from his hand, she told herself methodically, and away from here before it comes; it was the rage that was coming. She took the map and was going to turn once and look at her father, and thought better of it. She walked determinedly but not hurriedly away from there, toward the end of the street where the night without a country had shone to her moments before beneath the heart of the first man she loved.

9 6

The lovers didn't come much anymore; there was no trace
of them in the mornings. Over the next few years Dania
moved many places in the city, sometimes she took up with
men who sheltered her, other times a friend from the
school where she'd worked protected her. It may have been
that police and spies were pursuing her; she was never sure.
When the war turned against Germany, the soldiers in the
streets became much less vigilant. Everyone in the city
sensed the approaching end. By the closing months of 1944
the bombs fell regularly. Bridges on the Danube and the
Wien-Fluss lay in rubble. The besieged Viennese came to
be familiar, as others had, with the airborne shriek of
death. One afternoon Dania pulled a small child from a
black abandoned carriage just as the wind of an explosion
hurled both of them into a building archway; when she
looked back the carriage was gone. There was only the
smoking mass of meat and wood, and a wheel that rolled
down the road. All winter the people of the city warmed
their hands over the ashes of their lives. When the Russians
marched in the following April, Dania became yet another
sort of refugee, yet another sort of unvanquished. Two
weeks after that the war was over.

She was now a twenty-two-year-old woman. She returned to the apartment where she'd lived with her father,
and with another woman she took the same flat. Like the
other Viennese, the landlady now spoke harshly of the
Germans and hailed the occupation of her city by the Russians, French, British and Americans; the apartment happened to be in a British zone, to Dania's good fortune.
Nonetheless she was careful where she walked during the
day, since the zones weren't marked and, unless one had
memorized their borders, she could suddenly find herself

where she didn't want to be, which in Dania's case was the Russian section of town. At night the Russians sent secret patrols into the British and French sections, sometimes even into the American sections, snatching people up; thus Dania didn't go out at night at all. She spent three years trying to get out of Vienna and Austria. Only when she had a letter from Joaquin Young in London offering her a position in the new dance company he'd begun there, was she able to obtain the official papers. By then she was living alone, the other woman having married a soldier from Indiana who took her back with him. Dania packed up her few possessions and sent them on to England; she didn't consider in the least loving Joaquin, rather what she loved was her escape from the murder and heartbreak of where she'd lived eleven years. On the last day, standing in the empty apartment gazing around her, she didn't even think of it as a place of lovers; she thought of it as the last place her father lived. In the empty unlit flat she held her hands to her face and sobbed huge desolate sobs. Dania, she finally said, stopping herself. She went into the bathroom and ran the water in the sink and washed her face. She was too intent on washing away the tears to have ever heard the door open, had the door opened.

She was almost sure she heard, however, someone call a name, a name she might have remembered hearing once in the tall Dutch grass before the shadow of a windmill; but not her name.

When she went back out into the apartment, the shutters of the window stood wide open. For a moment, there in the window, she almost believed she saw someone.

But there's no one there. She collects quickly her papers of transit and takes her small bag and walks out of the flat as though on her way to the market or a stroll through the Volksgarten. She runs into the landlady on the way down; the older woman averts her eyes. "Mein Fräulein," she simply says. Dania thinks to reproach the woman for all the treachery she's considered over the years: but there's a difference, she tells herself, between what's considered and what's acted. "Auf wiedersehen," she replies instead and continues on her way. She walks through the winding streets of the Inner City. The walls lie in piles of crushed stone and people stand in food lines; the Union Jack flies from the windows. At the train station she waits with all the other people trying to get out of Vienna and finally presents her papers to the officer in charge; when he's stamped and returned them to her, and only when she's located her train on the proper track and understands she's really going, does she turn to see the city from the windows of the Westbahnhof and, overwhelmed, vanish for a moment from sight. I think she's gone off somewhere to be alone, I can't be sure. There are views that remain hidden, there are times one cries unseen.

She wasn't to be in London more than ten months. The city in its victory was indistinguishable in its destruction from Vienna in its defeat. Joaquin Young greeted her arrival with the same astonishment he'd shown the afternoon she appeared in Amsterdam; he'd written the letter without any idea it would even reach her. More than this she was quite grown up, the years between fifteen and twenty-five even more profound than his between twenty-two and thirty-two. She was chagrined to find herself still excited by him. She'd thought that the night she blew a hole through Dr. Reimes she exiled herself from the caprices of attraction in the same way she'd been exiled from so much of life. "I've no consideration in the least of loving you," she told him; in a more insolent moment he would have laughed at her. Eleven years however he'd lived with the impotence of his one night with her on the houseboat, and the mark of her other lovers.

Between this time that she arrived in London and the morning ten months later that the Joaquin Young Dance Company sailed for New York, she met another dancer named Paul and thus slept with a man for the first time since the end of the war. Paul was innocent and fragile in the way Young was arrogant and scheming, a dark French boy two years younger than she. They walked along the collapsed tunnels of the underground and slept with their hands full of shillings next to a heater that had to be fed coins every twenty minutes. Because Joaquin didn't think Paul warranted competition, he was somehow all the more incensed by Dania's affair with him; Paul may have been half the charismatic figure Joaquin was but it could be presumed that with a woman at night his body was at least adequate to the task, and that his heart was true enough neither to see nor care about the traces of other men on her. "Then don't love me," Joaquin told Dania, "with or without consideration. Just dance the way I watched you dance before." With this declaration, and fully intending to win her back whether she wanted it or not, he wrote a dance especially for her.

98

She danced and men died. They died across New York City, sometimes in penthouses and sometimes in bachelor's flats where the beds lowered from the walls. They died as strangers in their middle years, grown comfortably into nerveless resignation, men who might never have thought her beautiful on the street but would be transfixed by her dance, if they ever saw her dance. They didn't have to see her dance. Just the fact that she danced was, somewhere in the middle of a turn, enough to send them miles away slumping to the floor as though from a poison in their wine that was this moment hissing its way into their bowels and blood. They lay in large purple circles on their rugs. Empty goblets rolled listlessly around their heads. She left a trail of middleyeared strangers in large purple circles though she didn't know it, not until the investigator told her in the middle of the fog of Davenhall Island, where neither the destination nor the point of departure could be seen.

This was two years after she'd been in America, this time when she danced. This was two years after she forgot the lover who'd always followed her. This was two years during which she came to realize that having survived the war and having freed herself of jungles of exile and cities for fugitives, the lover was following her again. She could feel the cast of his shadow in a way she never had before, even when he'd taken her; it was a large shadow. By then there was trouble with Joaquin and Paul. Sometimes she convinced herself she wasn't really certain who the shadows belonged to anymore. One night she left the theater where the company danced, and stopped for a sandwich at the corner of Bleecker and Seventh; there for the first time in two years she felt the shadow. It began walking after her down Seventh toward Houston where she thought she

might more easily find a cab that would take her back uptown; she adjusted her pace. She dropped the rest of her
sandwich a block later. She peered around to see if there
was anyone who could help her, if it came to that. She
knew as soon as she ducked into the old vacant building
that it was a mistake: Not much chance of catching a cab
here, she thought ruefully. Rushing through the building
and up the stairs, she cornered herself further and further
until she ran out of corners. It was on an upper floor of the
building, where glassless windows watched out on the city,
that she turned another corner and remembered for a split
second that her father once turned a corner like this and
never another. At that moment someone stepped out of
the dark there on the vacant floor and spoke to her, an
eerie and lost hello. For the only time in her life she fainted
deadaway. When she woke it was in the early hours of the
morning under a very bright streetlight, on a bench way up
on Riverside Drive not so far from where she lived. The
strange coat of an unknown man was wrapped around her.
It was a large coat.

Like a coat too large to be grown into, the savagery she'd
once aspired to in the Sudan jungle seemed too large as
well, and she could never make it fit. This was difficult for
her to understand since after all she had shot a man down
in the streets of Vienna. For a while she spent time uptown
with some of the gangs that appeared on the last dark
streets untouched by the afterglow of a war that had vanquished in a very complete and absolute way complete and
absolute evil. She'd ride up and down the urban island on
the back of a motorcycle with a kid who gave her a mangy
tabby cat she called Dog for the way it fetched things and
followed constantly at her heels. But this wasn't savagery
enough. She drank too much. The vodka bottles piled up
in the corner of her apartment where she sat beneath her
skylight trying to remember the Russian folksongs her father sang in the jungle. But this wasn't anything near truly
savage, and moreover she despised the phony romanticism

of it in the way she despised the phony romanticism of artists. "Oh Dania, what is this?" she whispered to herself with irritation, when she found herself crying alone one night for no reason she could identify, "this isn't about not being beautiful. This isn't about not being loved." Another vodka bottle for the corner. She and Dog slept curled together in the vodka stupor, as she was coming to do more and more nights. In the skylight above her, the city became a psychetecture complete with men who followed her, whom she only occasionally sensed, and men who died when she danced, whom she would have repudiated had she sensed them at all. The horizon filled with the vision of a Japanese sunflower that blossomed five years before and only now came into view. Before the flash of this flower, in the moment it lit up her corridors, she considered that the savage century was unleashed not by the act of standing in a Vienna window, but by the act of being seen there.

Soon after, she left the dance company. Matters with the two men in her life had become impossible. Joaquin calculated constantly, though he had many other women at the same time; she thought to herself, He's more tormented by his past sexual defeat than any genuine passion, a hundred other successes with all the others will never compensate for his failure with me. Paul was tormented by genuine passion and almost more unbearable for it; his adoration became oppressive. When he worshipped even the most flawed inch of her, that small flawed territory at the corner of her mouth where the scar grew whiter with the years, her affection for him surrendered to claustrophobia. "And what about this finger," she asked him, "this one that pulled the trigger one night in Vienna, do you adore it as well?" For this adoration Joaquin threw Paul out of the company, which was petty even for Joaquin. She wearied of the havoc she wreaked. Employing the confidence of a girlfriend in the company named Ingrid, Dania gave up her apartment and moved herself and Dog into Ingrid's place; she went to work for a bookstore in the Village. In this way she dropped out of the lives of both Joaquin and Paul as though through a trapdoor. After some time she would telephone Paul, conscientious about his fragility. He begged to see her. She refused, relented, it was a mistake, refused, refused, relented, it was another mistake, refused. She had no idea what her life was supposed to be and feared that it wasn't necessarily supposed to be anything. There were times she'd watch the theater until everyone had left, then go through the back since she still had the key and up to the studio on the twelfth floor where the dancers would rehearse in the mornings and afternoons. One entire wall was a window that looked out on Manhattan, the opposite wall was lined with mirrors. Alone, before a hundred scarred dancers, she'd dance the dance written only for her.

She left the bookstore one twilight and by the time she reached the corner a block away, she was looking over her shoulder again. It quickly became dark. Occasionally she'd slow her pace, then stop and look back; stepping into the street she waved down a cab. From the backseat she watched out the window for him, but there was nobody. She had the cabbie drive around a few minutes before taking her back to Ingrid's street. "Pull over here," she said at the end of the block; she paid him and got out. If there was someone behind her she didn't want him to know exactly where she was living. She got halfway to Ingrid's building when she stopped: for the first time she heard his steps. Not in all the years had she actually heard the steps. She'd felt his love, sometimes in Vienna she'd worn his love and felt it run from her; but she hadn't heard his steps like this. She headed not for her building but a hotel across the street; on the first floor was a coffee shop. She went inside. She stopped long enough to look behind her. She gazed around; the coffee shop was empty. Beyond the coffee shop was a bar; the bar was empty. She made her way through the room. On the other side of the room she heard the sound of the outer door opening; turning, she waited for someone to appear in the dim light of the bar or the coffee shop. "Joaquin?" she called. There was no answer. The lobby of the hotel was small and empty; no one was behind the front desk and the mail boxes behind the desk were all small and empty too. Crossing the lobby she moved several steps up the stairs.

This is the wrong way, she thought to herself. This is the wrong thing to do. This is like the night I went into the old vacant building on Seventh Avenue and there was someone there and I fainted. She took herself to task, once again, for fainting. But now she was on a set of stairs again, at an irrevocable step, stopping to watch and listen in the direction from which she'd come. There was the pause of dead silence before she heard his footsteps again. She hurried further up the dark stairs. She reached the first floor and moved down the pitch black hall, groping desperately along the wall for a light switch. By the end of the hall, where there was nowhere else to go, she still hadn't found it; she turned. In the dim light from downstairs he was only a silhouette at the end of the hall. "Joaquin," she said. "Paul," she said. She didn't really suppose it was Joaquin or Paul, the silhouette was too big to be Joaquin or Paul. "It's over between us," she said in the dark, "the war's over, Vienna's over. What are you doing here?" She grabbed the knob of the door nearest to her and rattled it; locked and merciless, it wouldn't open. She turned back to him and waited; for a moment there in the dark nothing happened; then he turned on the light she'd tried so hard to find.

99

"Are you all right?" he said.

He was older than she'd expected; she wasn't sure he was what she'd expected at all. He didn't come any closer to her, waiting instead. "Were you following me?" she finally said. Her voice broke.

He turned and looked behind him, stepped back and gazed down the stairs. His arms hung at his sides. "There's no one," he said, as though it took him several moments to assess the emptiness of the stairs. Everything about him was a bit slow, she decided. He turned back to her in the hall and she took a step away.

"Please don't come closer," she said.

"There's no one," he said again. He reached into his pocket and pulled from it a key. "It's my room," he said, pointing to the door she'd tried to open. He could see she didn't believe him. "Here, try it." He tossed her the key. She hesitantly took the key and, watching him the whole time, put it in the lock of the door and turned it. The door swung open. He stepped toward the door and again she took a step behind her; she was caught at the end of the hall. He raised his hand: "Watch." Astonished, she watched the big man lower himself onto the floor of the hall face down with his hands stretched above his head. He was now speaking in a muffled voice into the carpet of the hall. "See," he explained, "I'm on the floor. See? You can walk past. You can see my hands. If I try anything you can run back and lock yourself in my room and call the police maybe." While this preposterous scene was taking place she was indeed making her way past him. "See, I'm on the floor here," he was saying as she got to the other end of the hall where the stairs were. She looked down the stairs into the darkness, trying to listen for the footsteps. "Are you by the stairs now?" he called out from the floor, his mouth in the carpet. After a moment he said, "You can wait in my room a bit if you're afraid to go. You can lock the room and I'll go down the stairs and look to see if there's anyone there. See, I'm right here on the floor of the hallway."

She didn't want to go back down into the dark yet. She walked back toward his room; in the door she turned to watch him lying there. She decided he was a bit dim. She turned on the light; the room was undistinguished, a quaint blue paper on the wall, a small desk by the window that looked directly across to Ingrid's flat except that her flat was several floors higher. "You don't have to lie on the floor," she said finally.

After ten or twelve seconds he slowly and clumsily got up off the floor. He walked into his room and for a moment seemed unsure what to do next; he sat down at the desk. He got back up and turned another chair for the woman to sit, then returned to the desk. He didn't take off his coat or do anything that had the appearance of making himself at home; if his speech and manner had been any more of a monotone she might have regarded him as frightening. She sat in the chair he'd turned, looking past him out the window to the building across the street. Neither of them said anything at all for a moment. The big man pointed to the phone on the desk. "You can make a call."

"No, I'll just stay a bit. Actually," she thought for a moment, and then finished, "I live just across the street with Ingrid." He turned and looked through the window at the building across the street. "I don't want him to know where I live." She paused. "Maybe he already knows."

"Does he always follow you?" the big man said.

"Yes. It seems to have happened every day for a long time now, on my way to and from work."

"Maybe you should call the police."

She looked around the room for a clock but couldn't find

one. In the light from the street she saw the red blotches of broken blood in his face, she could smell the liquor. "I'm going to go."

"Would you like me to walk with you across the street?" he said.

"No." For a moment she stayed where she was; then she slowly stood, always with her eye on him. At the open door she said, "It isn't necessary. Thank you, though."

"You're welcome."

"Perhaps you wouldn't mind . . ."

"OK."

"Perhaps you wouldn't mind," she finished, "watching from the window, as I cross the street. You can watch to see that I get across the street all right."

"OK."

"Can you do that? Can you just watch me?"

He hadn't moved from his place in the dark; his hands were flat on his legs before him. "Yes, I can do that," he said. Downstairs, in front of the hotel, she stepped from the door and looked up and down the street; then she walked, arms folded with determination, to the other side. At the door of Ingrid's building she turned and looked up to Blaine's lighted window. Then she turned back to the door and disappeared into the building, and in the window across the street the curtain fell back before his silhouette.

1 0 0

Blaine didn't actually live in this particular hotel room; he'd taken it only some time after the client first hired him to follow and watch Dania, and when Dania then moved in with Ingrid from her place uptown near where Blaine left her on Riverside Drive wrapped in his coat one night. That was the night he no longer worked for the client, that was the night the client's case became a different sort of case. The client had said that night that none of what happened made sense since Dania wasn't beautiful, but it was pretty obvious to Blaine that she was the most beautiful woman he'd ever seen. He'd seen her dance many times. He discovered that every time she danced something terrible happened, something terrible to slow aging men like himself. He didn't understand what the dance meant, the only dancing he'd ever seen before was the kind in clubs and movies. No more than Joaquin Young, who was smarter and more sophisticated than Blaine, was Blaine able to consciously understand how she danced to the resurrection of his memories and certain possibilities precluded forever; he hadn't begun to be even more than dimly aware that there *were* possibilities until long after he'd allowed them to slip away. Blaine was caught to the moment of Dania like the strand of her hair to the wet red of her mouth when the dance finished. He'd been devastated by that first inkling which everyone eventually knows, that there are things which are irrevocable. This moment is the one when one either saves his spirit or watches it die in tandem with his body.

The morning after he'd followed her to the door of his own room, he followed her to work. She was about to turn when he raised his hand and waved; she was relieved to see him. She no longer had the sense of someone following her. When she told him she was a dancer he said the only dancers he knew were in clubs and movies. I don't dance anymore, she told him. Why, he still wondered, there on the sidewalk outside her bookstore eight hours later, his hands in his coat pockets that were secretly stuffed with newspaper clippings. I used to dance this one dance, she tried to explain in Washington Square, as she moved from the shadow of one tree to the shadow of the next, circling Blaine as he remained in place, his hands in his pockets now black with ink; sometimes he could see her speaking and sometimes he could only hear her. She tried to explain in a way that she understood herself, let alone him. This dance was written especially for me. She paused and went on. There was something dangerous about it; it was written for something dangerous in me. She paused; he couldn't see her now; and went on. And, uh, I knew it was dangerous, and I loved it. She stepped from the shadow of the tree into one of the lights of the square. She turned to Blaine and he could see her beautiful face more clearly than he'd ever seen it. But then I stopped loving it, she said returning to something of a circle again: it hurt too many people. And when I finished with the dance, I finished with all dances.

I finished with all the dances, she says to herself in the dark, behind the door of Ingrid's building as she listens to Blaine walk away. She's been saying it to herself since Washington Square, in the silence of their return home; and now she knows she doesn't believe it. Now she knows the danger of it still lures her, the depraved druglike thrill of it beckons her on the other side of resolve, and she hasn't gotten three steps up the stairs toward Ingrid's flat before she's turned and, peering surreptitiously out the door, loosed herself back into the night and the street. She looks toward Blaine's window to make certain he doesn't see her; it's still dark, he hasn't gotten up to the room yet. She walks down the street and turns toward the direction of the theater. Halfway there she hears all their footsteps, not one lover or two but a legion of them. When she comes to the theater she goes around the back and walks up the twelve flights; by the eighth she's pulling the dress off over her head. By the time she's in the dark studio before the long window that looks out over Manhattan she's nude, absolutely alone in the single light that shines from the ceiling. As she begins to dance she's unaware of Joaquin and Paul; Joaquin and Paul are unaware of each other there, and barely aware of her. They're mostly aware of their own danger, which they allow themselves to believe, as most men do, has something to do with her. In their approach to her they're frozen in a way that suggests they're moving in relation to each other; only when they recognize that relationship, however, does it lapse into something hostile. If she's aware of the presence of either of them, she's displayed no recognition; perhaps she loves not being aware of them in the way she loved being loved by a lover she never saw. It's as though no one could conceivably be worthy of this moment or this danger; circling her own reflection in the mirror she can barely see the forms of Joaquin and Paul in confrontation with each other against the night and the city beyond the window, until they simply take off from her dance, grappling. The shatter of the window cuts off midchord. She stops and for a stunned moment considers that men who were there a moment ago are gone now: there's nothing in the window but the still Manhattan night rushing in at her.

Blaine did not need to turn on the light in his room to see the clippings. Sitting at the desk, he pulled them from his pockets with his dark grubby fingers and laid them out before him; he'd studied them so many times that now he knew which was which by their shapes. If he turned on the switch and was faced with them in the bald light, he would once again begin to feel the guilt, and then he'd certainly want a drink, and he'd tried hard for some time now not to have a drink. And at this moment he might well have succumbed to his desire for a drink, even in the dark, had he not looked out the window just as Dania was walking up the street. By the time Blaine got down to the street she was already gone. He walked around the neighborhood a quarter of an hour and when he didn't see her the only place he could think of was where he'd seen her so many times before. In front of the theater he watched the studio window high above him, waiting as discreetly as he knew how until she came back down. He had certainly never seen anything in his life before like the two men who launched themselves out into the night in a spray of glass. Oddly, in their fall, they regained the balletic composure they'd abandoned when interlocked with each other; but Blaine didn't know much about that. There was no sound as they fell, they didn't even cry out. In Blaine's mind perhaps, but only in his mind, was the echo of the glass breaking. He followed them down with his gaze, he watched the way the two men danced down. There was silence for several moments and after they hit there was only the small sound from twelve floors above him, and it took some time for him to recognize it.

She doesn't look at the window. She kneels on the floor wondering, in the middle of the strange sound that comes from her, what in the turning of the black clock has made her play this role. She finally rises. Walking away from the window, she still doesn't look, in the same way she didn't look at either her father in the street or Reimes in the glass of his own window nearly ten years before; she doesn't look at herself in the mirror, she doesn't need to look to see the woman who couldn't resist dancing one last time. She doesn't take the elevator down. She walks the twelve flights figuring that around the sixth she'll pull her dress back over her head and around the third she'll begin to hear the sirens. She hasn't a clue how to explain it. As it happens she's all the way to the bottom before the sirens come, and they're so far away there's no telling which atrocity in the city they're answering. She opens the back door of the theater and steps across its threshold to find the tide that's come in, that rolls into Manhattan in our sleep, leaving the edifices dark and wet and its watermark high above our heads. She dives into the street and the roots of civilization drift past her black cold glide.

1 0 1

The client had sat in Blaine's office striped by the gold slits of twilight that came through the blinds. He was nearing sixty with the kind of paunchiness that had only now begun to show in his face; at first appearance he seemed groomed and well dressed. After a while, though, Blaine noticed the dapper clothes had frayed at the corners of the collar on his coat; it wasn't a new suit. Blaine didn't have much imagination and was just smart enough to know he wasn't very smart, but he was observant after years of training himself to be, so he saw that about the client, the way he was frayed. Had Blaine more imagination he might have seen the way the man's story was frayed too. The client explained that someone had been following his girlfriend eighteen months and now he wanted Blaine to keep an eye on her and if necessary protect her. For a man in a frayed suit he set a fair amount of money on Blaine's desk. He didn't give his name but Blaine didn't question that, nor did he question whether eighteen months wasn't rather a long time for someone to be followed by someone else without anything coming of it. Blaine didn't involve himself with the subtle complications of a case, he didn't feel possessed by an investigator's compulsion to know the truth of something. He took the money and did the job, as long as he believed he could live with it. This was the nature of being in business for himself. He'd been in business for himself since he and his partner split up over a case Blaine couldn't remember anymore; sometimes he'd run into someone who'd mention it and Blaine just got uncomfortable. He always wanted to say, Well then, tell me all about it, will you, because it's just entirely slipped my mind. But that didn't seem like it would sound so intelligent. All he remembered was spending the rest of the 1930s and the war in the corner of a bar down on West 59th called the Unforeseen where the name curled out of the wall above the door. Once Blaine was walking at four in the morning through Times Square, it was deserted, all that was left was the long peach-colored veil of a bridal gown floating down the middle of the intersection until a stray car roared through catching it on its fender, and the smell of someone's sour liquor overwhelmed him, he became sick there on the curb, made himself walk several more blocks to get away from this smell of drunks but couldn't, went back to where he lived, the smell was still there, got his big lug body in the hot shower and the smell rose in the steam of the water and he realized he was oozing it. He was oozing the smell of the Unforeseen. So he opened up an office for business. It was piddling business, without bravado or anger, anger having become buried so long in him that the very name anger eluded the confounded emotion it finally became; he never bothered trying to explain to himself why he was and always would be small time. He stopped drinking awhile. Ninety-nine nights of a hundred were alone, the hundredth spent with some woman or another who wanted to know if he wore a badge or trenchcoat, if he picked locks. After the war the nitty-gritty cases got nittier and grittier in weirder ways for some reason; there were nitty-gritty ones back when he first began but they still resembled something like normal sins then, normal people breaking normal commandments, not ones God never thought of.

For instance, in this particular case involving this particular client, the dancer wasn't really the client's girlfriend at all; she hadn't even laid eyes on him. The client was the one who'd been following her for eighteen months, the client who hired Blaine to follow the dancer because she was being followed. This doesn't make the slightest bit of sense to me, Blaine thought to himself standing there in the old dark vacant building that final night while the client held the unconscious body of a fainted dancer in one arm and the gun in the other hand. The client kept looking at the woman's face in the dark and then far up into the ceiling, anguished by the way a man who's had a great deal of what he wanted in life can arrive at a point when the only thing he wants lies right there in his arms and yet remains somehow untouchable: God, she's not even beautiful, Blaine heard him say there in the dark. What happened to me, the client said, how did everything change? You see the way she dances? he said to Blaine. Blaine answered, Yeah, I've seen. The client said, I was one of those guys who only a few years back ran the world, wasn't it only a few years back? The next day the papers said he once ran a club on the Upper West Side; Blaine might have even been there once. Say, do I know you from way back, did we once meet long ago? Blaine asked only seconds before the shot, before the smell in the dark, the only smell stronger than that of the booze Blaine drank a world ago, the smell of brains and gunfire. He pried the unconscious girl from the dead man's arms, carried her out onto Seventh Avenue and Houston, hailed the cab and directed it up the shores of the Hudson.

Then the client's case became a different sort of case, it became a case of middleyeared strangers in purple circles on the rug. Blaine had discovered it the morning after the third night he watched her dance from his seat in the back row of the auditorium for which the client always left him a ticket at the box office. It was in the papers, the unexplained death of an auditor in his bachelor's flat where the bed lowered from the wall; the next time she danced there

was a piece the next morning about a rich man in his pent-
house. The more Blaine investigated the more he found
men dying every time she danced; they had the signs of
being poisoned right down to the wine glasses in their
hands, and that odd look poison leaves in the eyes. No
poison was actually found. Blaine investigated the dancer,
her boyfriend, the company director. He wasn't interesting
enough in his thinking to suppose there was any explanation that wasn't literal, yet he was obsessed enough as his
client had been to know intuitively that no literal explanation applied. He might have come to a point where he even
accepted her power to dance men to death, except for one
night when on his way to the theater to see her for the
eighth or ninth time he was thinking about who it would
be tonight, which guy out there was at this moment un-
corking the bottle to let it breathe, and he realized that
even if he knew who it was going to be, even if he was the
best and smartest investigator in the world and had the
opportunity to jump in a cab and make his way across town
to save the man's life, even if he could walk to the other
side of the street to put a dime in the telephone and call
the man, he would not. He would not because it might
mean he would miss one minute of watching her. This
understanding unraveled him. He dreaded the next day's
paper. When he finally opened the paper and found the
story, he read it as one who had foreseen it and could have
stopped it, and didn't. It so happened it was just around
this time that Dania, in the middle of her troubles with
Joaquin and Paul, left the company. Blaine stopped reading the paper. He hung around the theater for a glimpse of
her he wouldn't get until, after some time had passed,
Dania returned late one night when the theater was vacant
so she could dance alone in the studio up on the twelfth
floor. In the meantime Blaine began to drink again, living
at the Unforeseen, not going to the office so much. Business piddled to nothing.

Blaine stopped drinking and went into business for the

last time when he moved into the hotel across the street from her. On the night he watched Joaquin and Paul launch themselves out into space from the window of the studio, he ran around to the back of the building only in time to find the door standing wide open and the woman gone. He got in a cab and was on his way to Ingrid's apartment as the sirens were passing him up the street. Neither Dania nor Ingrid was at the flat; Blaine broke in. He looked around awhile waiting for Dania to show up; a mangy tabby cat followed at his heels from room to room. After half an hour had passed he returned to his hotel across the street; he had no reason to think Dania might not return, since none of her things seemed to be gone. He sat at his desk facing the building across the street and spent the rest of the night pondering the only interesting thing he'd found in the women's flat, a blue map. Over the course of the passing hours his imagination took a rare flight into a time when he and the young woman lived together in the house that was diagrammed on this map. He filled the house with furniture, the study he lined with wood shelves, old books, maybe he would try to read the books, pieces of music, an old clock. Here he put a window. Outside was a dark barren landscape with rare patches of green, somewhere on the coast of Nova Scotia. Blaine sat in the middle of the study in a large burgundy chair which matched the color of the wine in the decanter on the table. A piano sat by the window. Somewhere in the doorway she stepped naked from a bath; with a glass in his hand he looked her way, and took a drink. Blaine rolled up the map at dawn. He went down to the coffee shop and ate at a table that looked out onto the street, and when he finished he went back up to the room and returned to the desk. He waited until evening when he went back down to the coffee shop; he didn't stop at the bar. He ate again and took with him several lidded Styrofoam cups of coffee for the evening. By now of course he was exhausted, not having slept in over thirty-six hours. A woman returned to the building who he believed might be Ingrid. After several minutes he called a number he had read off the telephone in her apartment and written on the other side of the map of the house where he and Dania would someday live. When Ingrid answered he asked for Dania, and when she said Dania wasn't there and asked who was calling, Blaine hung up. After about twenty minutes a car pulled in front of the building; two men got out of the car. It was immediately clear to Blaine they were police officers. They went in the building for about forty-five minutes and then came out and left.

Blaine sat in the room three weeks waiting for Dania. Because he sometimes fell asleep, he could never be certain he hadn't missed a clandestine return. Nevertheless he was reluctantly beginning to conclude that Dania wasn't coming back. He'd gambled that she wouldn't leave without her things, but now, going from train station to bus terminal in Manhattan, he saw what he'd lost in the wager; no attendant or ticket taker remembered anyone from three weeks before. He sat in his room some time and considered calling his former partner, Johnson; he wished he could recall why they'd broken up their partnership. He assumed it was something he'd done wrong. He sat in the room another day or two and then went back over to Ingrid's flat where he once again broke in. He went over all the apartment. By now Dania's clothes had been packed in a box and the drawer where her personal effects had been kept was in disarray. By the telephone, among a week's worth of messages, her name was nowhere to be seen; there was, however, a word which caught Blaine's attention, scrawled on the third sheet of the notepad. The word was blueprint. When Ingrid came home that night she found a big man who smelled of long-drunk liquor sitting in her apartment with Dog on his lap; she'd barely begun to cry out in alarm when he said, You can tell her I have the blueprint. Two nights later the telephone in Blaine's hotel room rang. Yes? said Blaine. Ingrid said, She called and I told her. Yes? said Blaine. Ingrid said, She cursed and hung up. But— Yes? said Blaine. But the operator, Ingrid said, had a record of where the call was placed. It was collect, after all.

Blaine went to his office with the blueprint and took some money from the safe in his washroom and rented a car that was built before the war and set out across the country. He was all the way to Ohio before he remembered he'd left the blueprint sitting on the desk in his office. I'm a big stupid man, he thought to himself, I've left on the desk in my office the very map of the house she and I are to live in together. When he got to the town from where Dania had called Ingrid, she wasn't there, but the memories of the people who worked in the bus station were better, and touched by more recent experience. Blaine continued driving west. Much of the country was now just roads and swimming pools waiting for the unbuilt houses that would go with them. There are a hundred blueprints, maybe thousands, to go with all the houses that haven't been built, he told himself. We'll find another just as good, her and me. The skeletons of new unfinished parkways towered above postwar America, pocked with all the blue abandoned swimming pools that shimmered before him every time he drove over a hill. From every small town where she'd been, he sent a blank white postcard back to Manhattan, addressed to himself. He sent the last postcard, a year after he began, from a town called Samson farther west than he'd believed one could go without arriving east, on the other side of a river that seemed to have no end. In Samson a tourist told him about an island twenty miles away called Davenhall.

1 0 2

Blaine stood on the dock waiting for the ferry that drifted toward him out of the fog on the river. The dark young Greek, with the long blue coat and bright gold buttons, didn't much like the looks of him. You some sort of gangster or something? the boatman asked. No, Blaine answered. You from the city? said the boatman. Which city, said Blaine after a moment, I've come from a lot of cities. I've come looking for a woman. The ferry started back across the river. Maybe, said the boatman, you mean a woman you've been following a long time. That's right, the big man answered dully. He stood on the edge of the boat with his hands on the rail looking out into the fog. Young Zeno was small next to Blaine. Halfway out into the fog Blaine couldn't see either the shore of the river or the island. Is it far? he asked finally.

Feeling wily, Zeno said, Why yes, that's it, it's far. It's quite far. It's quite a trip, actually, over to the island. The big man didn't seem completely bright to him. Now it might be better, the young boatman went on, that we either go on back, or I drop you off at the house there until the fog lifts. He pointed north to where Blaine could see in the fog the outline of a shack that stood on four wooden pillars over the water. There's a stove in there and a bed. I can bring you some food over from the shore later on. When the fog lifts you're just that much closer to the island, if you don't want to go back to the mainland, that is.

Tell you the truth, Zeno added, I haven't seen any woman like you're talking about. Not at all. It's probably quite a waste of your time, this whole thing.

I'll look for myself, said Blaine. He studied the fog for some sign of the island. OK, said Blaine, I'll wait at the house.

It wasn't much of a house. When Zeno left him on the landing and disappeared with the boat, all that was left of the world was the gray of the fog and the river; it was more like a small room in the middle of time, hidden and undiagrammed. Inside was the bed, a stove that had only a stick or two of wood and several chunks of coal, a table and chair, an oil lamp. Blaine lit the lamp and sat on the bed with his hands on the tops of his legs. After an hour he got back up and went out on the landing of the shack to see if the fog had lifted or the boatman was returning.

Several more hours passed; soon it would be dark. Blaine realized now that he was a prisoner in the middle of the river waiting for someone to come to him out of the fog. In the same way he didn't move from his desk in the New York hotel room across the street from where Dania had lived, he didn't move now from his place on the landing. He stood listening to the water, and then he leaned over the rail to look far down into the river below its surface. Below the surface of the river, Dania swam in her black cold glide past the roots of civilization. She could see him up there, looking down. She rose through the water to him, she shot from the water and found his big pawlike hands there waiting to pull her up. When he pulled her up out of the water he almost fell back with her; and there he stood holding her a long while, sometimes daring to look down at the wet hair that lay against her face and the simple salmon-colored dress that clung to her body. Her face was set against his chest and she was shivering. He held her and stood absolutely still with her in his arms as though to move at all would lose her; he knew at this moment they wouldn't live together in a house built from any blue map. As he held her closer to him than he ever had before or would again, he knew the lost despair the client felt his final night when he held her and knew she would never be his, would always be, in his hands, untouchable. Finally she shivered so badly he had to take her into the house and wrap the blanket from the bed around her. Then he sat in the chair as she slumped on the bed with teeth chattering. "The man with the boat didn't come back like he said," Blaine told her. "He left me here. He wants me to die."

"I'm sure he doesn't," she said. After a moment she explained, "He was protecting me."

"He loves you too," Blaine nodded, understanding.

"Why are you here?"

"I came to bring the map of the house," Blaine said.

"Thank you."

"I got to Ohio," he said, "and remembered I left it in New York."

For a moment she appeared very annoyed. Then she smiled and laughed. "Oh." She said, "How did you find me?"

"Hunches."

"Oh," she laughed again.

"I don't get many good hunches," he said.

She just continued laughing. "You turned out to be the strangest one of all, didn't you," she finally said. "Of all the strange men."

"I watched you every night," he said, "every night you danced. Don't know much about dancers except—"

"In clubs and movies."

"I was only someone who knows about the things people do that they're not supposed to and that they've always done anyway. Just people's secrets," he said. "Sometimes in the middle of a secret you don't know what. You just don't know what anymore. I saw you dance and there was something secret about it."

She pulled the blanket closer. He saw she was thinking about something else now; he was going to say something about all the men, and couldn't decide. "What's your name?" she said.

"Blaine." He said, "All the men."

"The men?"

"Who died when you danced." Not just those two, he thought watching her, because he knew she was thinking of the two who fell from the sky through the window. "The others. In the papers."

"What others?" she asked, still thinking. "There were others?" she said after a moment. She began to cry then. He turned away from her when she began to cry because he didn't want to soften.

"Every time you danced," he said.

"Don't you know," she finally said when she'd stopped crying, "how long I waited for someone to come accuse me of something? I got tired of being men's dreams. I got tired of being Paul's, I got tired of being Joaquin's. I was tired of being yours when I didn't even know I was yours. I never meant to be anyone's dream but my own. If I dance someone's dream does it have to be my dream too?" She stopped shivering; the blanket fell from her, along with something else she'd held much longer. "It was your dream." She stood up from the bed and ran her hands over her face. She pushed back her wet hair. "I may have danced but you watched me."

Blaine was confused. He watched her walk back out toward the landing ready to plunge into the cold river again and swim back toward the island. "My dream?" he said in some consternation.

She said to him from the landing, "I'll tell Zeno to come pick you up. It may not be till morning, though." She nodded toward the fog. "Unless you want to swim to town."

Blaine was still trying to understand. "But—"

"Don't you see," she said with some exasperation, "it could just as easily have had nothing to do with me. It could just as easily have had everything to do with you." She looked toward the water once and then back at him. "You thought someone was dying every time I danced. But maybe that wasn't it at all," she said. "Maybe," she said, before disappearing, "someone was dying every time you watched me dance."

He lunged toward the landing not with any thought of pulling her back from the river, but rather to convince himself, to provide himself with the evidence of his own eyes, that she'd been there at all; a ripple on the surface of the water would do. He still wasn't sure when he turned back into the house, even though he could clearly see the ripples and even, he believed, her form disappearing into the black depths of the river. Even though the air of the shack was still heavy with her presence and the sound of what she said. That he wasn't sure, however, perhaps said more about him than her, as she'd implied: if men insisted on seeing her flesh and blood as the apparition of the promises they once made to each other and then betrayed, that final betrayal was theirs, not hers. He slept that night in the house on the river, slept rather well, actually. Somewhere in the final moments of this life, even as a dim slow man whose good heart was never sophisticated enough to understand the Twentieth Century sins that God never thought of, he understood something; and what she'd said to him remained the last words on his mind. "I know," he said to himself simply, opening his eyes; and he might have grasped what he knew and held it and looked at it had he not been distracted by the fire. He sat up in bed and gazed at the house on fire around and above him. And then he didn't know anymore. He would have liked to know it again but there wasn't the time. "It doesn't matter now," he said at last, before the secret room in which he'd always lived burned to a size much smaller than a man.

103

At dawn, she could see the smoke. She saw it from the end
of mainstreet with the other people of the town; by then
the fire burning out over the river was dead and done. All
night she'd slept through the sounds of people running
down the street to the edge of the island to watch the shack
burning; she tossed and turned in her hotel bed and her
dreams filled with the fraught rumble below her window.
When she saw the smoke she ran down to the shore and
pushed a vacant boat out toward the black remnants of the
shack as the Chinese tried to pull her back. Two police
cutters drifted at the scene; there wasn't much left to in-
spect. Dania sat in the boat in the fog watching awhile, she
waited for the police to pull her aboard one of the cutters
and ask her questions. They'd ask her if she knew him,
they'd produce witnesses. But that didn't happen. After a
while she lay in the bottom of the boat and fell asleep; when
she woke she heard the rain on the tarpaulin pulled over
the boat. It wasn't until later that day or sometime the next
when she saw the dark young Greek ferryman and the way
his eyes wouldn't meet hers that she remembered what she
told him the first day she came to the island. Take me to a
place, she said, he can't follow me. Zeno, lovestruck,
started his boat. "God, what have you done?" she whispered to him now. He looked around him with furtive guilt;
he was about to speak when she stopped him. "Please don't
say that you did it for me," she begged, and turned back to
town.

What's the matter with all of them, she said to herself
that night thinking of Reimes and Joaquin and Paul and
Zeno and Blaine, do they imagine I'm beautiful, or ever
was? Please, she prayed in the dark, don't let them find
a body. Please don't let them find a trace of him, out

there in the river. Let the last sign of him have been the smoke.

She paid up her hotel bill for a month and stayed another. For a while she worked for the man who ran the tavern across the street. When she'd been on the island a year, a child-swollen Mexican girl stumbled into the tavern one evening and in her wan frantic face was left only a single impulse of life by which she might bear a baby girl. No man was with her nor did she have any reason to be on the island except that she'd come to the most secret place she could find to have what was intended to be a secret child. The child was born several hours later. The mother died by morning. By afternoon the Chinese had a spare eucalyptus pruned and prepared for her. Singlehandedly Dania held them off as the woman's body lay wrapped in a quilt with the dust of mainstreet rising around it into the red light of the sun falling past the river. "Her name was Consuelo Garcia," Dania told them. You're making it up, they said. "She told me herself only moments before she passed away," Dania answered, Consuelo Garcia's baby in her arms. Years later when the baby, who Dania named Judy after a girl she saw in a movie once, grew to understand the story of her birth, she never knew whether Dania had invented the mother's name or not. Dania buried the young mother out behind the ice machine and stood guard several days to satisfy herself the body wouldn't be unearthed. We're not barbarians, you know, one Chinese woman told her. As a small girl on the island Judy sometimes took trips across the river with Zeno, who called her Little Greek. You're only confusing her, Dania might have said to him, if she'd ever spoken to him again after the night he set Blaine on fire.

After she'd lived in the hotel for many years, alone and untouched, the lover came back to her one night. They were older now, the two of them, and their love was older. She woke to find him sitting by her bed holding her hand, stroking her wrist; the next time she found she had her head on his chest. She reached up in the dark and lay her fingers against his face. In this way he appeared over time and sometimes she simply talked to him, telling him everything that had happened to her while he sat in the chair next to the bed. Their carnality retreated not by virtue of age or indifference but by the nature of what it had once been, limitless and inexhaustible; they wouldn't trivialize it now by the shame of their consciences or the rote of their bodies. You don't have to speak, she told him, it was always beautiful that you didn't. He answered, I always said the wrong thing anyway. I got the color of your eyes wrong, I said the wrong name. Any name, she said, would have been wrong. She meant the presumption of naming it at all, what they did together. Our love owned only a face, it owned its own strange body that flowered from the middle into male and female; history served at its pleasure. One night, when she slept, the lover brought the friend; by now the friend was very old. While she slept, the lover, understanding it was time to give something back to the history they'd defied, left something of the friend inside her. There was no trace of this transaction in the morning; no semen leaked from her, no tissues ached with remorse. All she felt was a little dizzy.

The dizziness went on for two weeks. She was now nearly fifty years old. Something is wrong with me, she told Judy one afternoon; and Judy, now eighteen, took off the afternoon shift from the mainstreet tavern she would herself inherit seven years hence, to accompany across the river on Zeno's ferry the woman who'd fought to save her mother from being perched in the trees by the people of the town. To Zeno's devastated sorrow, Dania still wouldn't speak to him. At the other side the woman and the girl got the bus to Samson. The woman, just short of half a century, considered that in her life she'd come farther than her father only to choose exile after all, without any map of a geographic or temporal residence; on the bus to Samson she looked at the hands that had shot men and buried women and delivered children, she looked at the feet that had cast spells and shocked conventions, and felt the only scar that would allow her touch, the one at her mouth, given there by the same hand, though she didn't really know this, that now tickled and left queasy the base of her womb. The bus rolled down the highway, the Twentieth Century slowly passed in those increments it chose to surrender. In Samson the woman and girl sat together in the doctor's office and waited the duration of another small piece of the century until the moment the doctor examined her and revealed, to the astonishment of all three of them, that she was pregnant.

104

I have given her a child.

This is the beginning of my revenge. For many years I had no reason to believe revenge was possible. I didn't imagine I'd have the opportunity for it, or if I did that there was a revenge commensurate and fitting. For many years I had no reason to believe I was worthy of exacting revenge from anyone but myself. I only know revenge insists upon itself and that now the opportunity for it is in my hands. My wife and daughter who died twenty-five years ago cannot be denied, my own unworthiness and guilt notwithstanding. This revenge will light up his ancient eyes with loss and grief. I can't sleep at night, the prospect so thrills me. I'm sure he's not yet so old his eyes can't cry anymore, or that he's so beyond the beat of life his heart can't break. There's just enough life left in him as to still hold the most

terrible sorrow of a lifetime. Alone in my small room beneath the sea, seized by my revenge, I shake my fists with
a mean fevered joy.

105

My memories are willfully winged, capricious in flight. I
lived in this room a long time before I knew where I was.
For a large part of the last twenty years I own no memory.
Sometimes I'm afraid to speak my own name, I'm afraid I'll
hear nothing. I don't remember when I began to write for
them again or why. For years I refused and then one day I
was here at my small table writing. By then she was far
away and it took a long time to call her back. I don't know
where she went all that time, or what she did. I hadn't seen
her since that night she called to me from the top of the
stairs in our room on Dog Storm Street. When she returned she hadn't changed at all, I'm sure. I don't see her
so clearly anymore but I'm sure she hasn't aged a day.
Though we've forgotten many things we used to do, we
remember we were in love, the three of us. Assuming as I
do when I feel the hair on my face, assuming as I do when
I wake in the morning and find my feet grown arthritic and
stiff, that I'm now more than fifty years old, then the year
is at least 1967. The waves of the sea rock the room, they
hum in the walls. I hear fishermen far away. I insist sometimes that I be allowed to see daylight. I only want to see
and breathe it. It's been just in the last several years I've
come to understand I'm imprisoned in a sinking city in
Italy. Except for my guards, I seem to be the only person

living here; the city's empty. The Germans have camou-
flaged it from the air, covering all the city's passages and
canals so that now it's just one great maze with a blue roof.
So as to fool the enemy. One big mazed boat that never
disembarks. I tell my guards I insist on seeing the daylight,
and they take me past empty bridges and houses and empty
piazzas to a tower where I have five minutes to look out at
the city's massive blue tarpaulin which has been made to
appear as if it's the sea. It's at this moment that it occurs to
me I'm not the only person living in this city after all, it's
at this moment it occurs to me he's here too. After five
minutes in the tower they say, That's enough.

Until that moment in the tower it never occurred to me he
might still be alive. I left that possibility behind in Vienna
when they moved me; I have no certainty when that was, I
have no recollection when or how it happened. The Germans continue to broadcast his speeches but I thought he'd
only become a myth the world couldn't allow to die. Sometimes I see the broadcasts on the small TV smuggled in by
the fishermen who live out on the islands. There's always a
picture of him from when he was much younger, with his
voice speaking over it. I'm not sure how they've worked the
voice. I suppose they've taken the old speeches and spliced
them together into new speeches and cleaned up the
sound. In my room I continue to write of her but I never
thought I was still writing for him. I assumed someone else
had fallen in love with her; she's seduced so many. I write
each day, and each night someone comes to take what I've

done, not unlike the way Holtz did long ago. Our passion has become mechanical in the way of most passion, I build it like a house. No one's ever been so good at it. I build my own house that defies architecture, I've compelled the landscape of history to readjust to my visions. I've done it from a blind spot where no one sees me yet my presence cannot go unacknowledged. The guard comes and whether there are ten pages or one, a sentence or a word, he takes the work; no one comments or changes or complains. I assume this is meant to go on until I die, since there seems no chance the seduced will ever be sated.

107

Down here in my room I don't get much on the TV, and the fishermen claim there's nothing on it to believe anyway. To hear the German commentators tell it, Germany's on the verge of winning the war. Germany's been on the verge of winning the war about twenty years now. Sometimes I get a signal from an American pirate station in Africa, broadcast into Germany until the Germans find a way to jam it; the Americans insist the tide is turning. The war is as endless as the century. Not long ago I received a transmission that seemed to come from nowhere at all. A man in a sea diver suit was floating in a black sea, a lifeline attached to him from some point unseen. Spheres floated around him and the sea diver just continued to hover there for some time. In the visor of his helmet was the reflection of an immense light that came from something unimaginable; beyond that his face was dark and blank. I imagined the man was myself. The beauty of his image was that anyone could imagine the sea diver was himself, in this transmission that came from nowhere at all. The later broadcasts out of Africa and Germany said nothing of this transmission, and none of the fishermen know anything about it either. When I think about the sea diver, I remember a river of gone time that once forked in two.

108

Giorgio is the fisherman who brought me the television. He's fair like many northern Italians, and his very round face beams red like the twilight sun. He literally came up through my floor, in a tunnel the Germans don't know about. The tunnel leads out to the edge of the city emerging on a deserted piazza that faces the lagoon. Apparently there are hundreds of these tunnels the Germans don't know. The fishermen laugh at the Germans. The idea of the Germans ruling the world is preposterous to them, since the fishermen come and go in the lagoon as they choose, to the Germans' general befuddlement. Giorgio and the others warmed up to me when they learned I'm an American. I can't tell them what I'm doing here, and I won't allow them to believe I'm a political prisoner; it would be more hypocritical than I could stand. Through this tunnel Giorgio and his friends have brought me food and televisions and company. They could easily take me out with them to the islands, there'd be nothing to it. I protest that the Germans would be sure to find me, and that Giorgio and his friends would suffer the consequences. I argue that the Germans would only move me somewhere else in the city where there'd be no tunnel coming up through the floor and I'd never see Giorgio and the fishermen again. Giorgio disagrees heatedly but also accepts my argument as some kind of inarguable sign of my nobility. It's almost unbearable to let him attribute such a fine quality to me. I'm a man the Twentieth Century can't redeem, I try to explain to him. The truth is that if I were to escape I wouldn't know how to live free of her. Later, it's the revenge that keeps me here. Still, I can't resist the opportunity to go out with Giorgio and the fishermen on their boat, and at night sometimes I lower my old arthritic hugeness into the floor and follow them out to the deserted piazza where we sail the lagoon for thirty minutes, round and round in the black water under the stupid wandering searchlights of the Germans who never see anything. I sit on the front of the boat. There the amber lights of a hundred piers circling the lagoon surround me; I listen to the mosquitoes and the wind, and for a moment again own no memory. After a while we return to the room and that night in my sleep I'm laid out on the wet bow of the lagoon itself, in a place where memory owns me. I wake in the dark, a sailor marooned on his own life.

109

I don't intend to try and redeem my infidelity. I haven't come to redeem anything. Rather I ride history like a wild horse that's pursued redemption into a century where redemption is replaced by revenge. I knew two women, I'm sorry I was so weak as to need them both. I understand that if I hadn't betrayed her for my wife, then my wife may not have had to pay betrayal's price, clutching in her arms against the Vienna night the child of redemption's and infidelity's liaison. I would only add one thing now. I say it not for the sake of what one thinks of me, I say it for them, I say it because it's so. I'd only add that while perhaps, in the eyes of infidelity, what I had with one was supposed to render counterfeit what I had with the other, in fact what I had with each was true unto itself. I don't expect anyone to despise me less for this. I don't expect anyone to regard my fingers as less marked by blood. Though the century disgraces the words innocence and honor, I won't do so by supposing those words could ever apply to me. My daughter, alive today, would be thirty years old, with a hundred undiminished sins of her own.

110

This is where I've lived years and years, then, in this little room with no windows and the hum of the sea in its walls. I think after a while everyone's come to forget what it is I'm here for. The guards aren't particularly friendly or attentive, but neither are they unreasonably harsh. They don't pay much attention to me one way or the other, and in the last year they've begun wandering off at times without locking my door behind them. At first I took it as a sign of their contempt for me, that I was so harmless as to warrant such casual surveillance. They didn't imagine I'd have the nerve to open the door and just walk out. But now I'm fairly certain that, well, they did imagine it, they in fact presumed it. Now I'm fairly certain in retrospect that everything which has happened they've meant to happen. The first couple of times, the guards caught up with me right

way, since I don't move so quickly these days; I hadn't even
gotten down the hall and around the corner. But eight
months ago, by accident or intention, they didn't. I pushed
open my door one afternoon and stepped into the hall and
shuffled down the other direction from where I'd gone before. I expected to shuffle right into one guard or another.
Now I realize that the guards caught up with me those first
couple of times because I was just going in the wrong direction. I moved down the hall now, it became darker. After
five minutes I found a hallway where lanterns burned in
the hollows of the walls. I felt overwhelmed not so much
by the exertion of the walk as the thick air of the corridors.
I came out into another hallway of blue light; I looked up
to the city's tarpaulin above me. Any minute I figured one
of the guards would be retrieving me; I even stopped awhile
to wait for him. I never figured on getting this far. I had no
interest in getting this far, I'd been out of my room ten
minutes now. Then I heard a voice in German, and only
after I'd stood there leaning against the hallway wall awhile,
listening to the foreign words, did they not seem so foreign;
my own German was proficient enough to finally recognize
that I was listening to a translation of the very words I'd
written this morning. I followed the voice. Up half a flight
of stairs, after the blue corridor led back into a black one
like my own, I came to the room where the old man and
the younger one were living.

111

Their room isn't much larger than my own, and no less spare. But it's high enough to have a window near the top; water seeps in around the window's edges and its smell is occasionally obnoxious. While nothing can really be seen from the window, it still lets in light. I envy their light. They don't seem to notice it. For a long time I began coming to their room regularly; the two of them always sat in the same place, the old man at the table in the middle, slumped in his chair and staring straight ahead as the other read to him. The old man always wears the same black suit. He's around eighty, his hair's thin and white. The mustache is so white and scraggly it's hardly there at all. I don't think he recognizes me; he's only actually seen me once before, after all. I didn't recognize him until after I saw the picture. Like all old people he's surrounded by his mementos, as with all old Germans I assumed at first they were the mementos of his Germanness. Pictures of him in his uniform, leading armies, posturing with statesmen, shouting at the people who worshipped him. Only after a while did I realize this wasn't just another old German with pictures of his god, this was the god with pictures of himself. But it was the other picture that told me, the only picture that wasn't of him. It stood alone on a small table by his cot, a dead brown flower crumbling from the photo's heavy brass frame. At first I didn't understand that it was her. At first it was just a picture of a girl I'd never seen before. But then I saw the inscription, and her name, and I remembered perfectly: I remembered perfectly that this was her: Yes, I told myself, this is exactly what she looks like. I remember exactly the eyes of blue and the hair of spun sunlight. When I picked up the photo that first time in their room, to look closely for something in the corner of her mouth, he became alarmed. As with all helpless old men he no longer could find the words for alarm, the alarm was all in his eyes. And then I realized. I put the picture down. It's you, I said to him.

1 1 2

It's you, the younger one repeated to me. He wore a dark gray coat, like me he was in his middle years. He was thin and soft, except his eyes, which watched me with hate. Like the old man he seemed attached to where he sat, as though nothing of him was alive beneath his neck; he was made forceful, for the first time in his life, by his hatred. He had a presence the old man seemed to have transferred to him long ago. In Petyr's eyes at this moment was exactly the power I'd always heard was the client's, in Petyr's eyes at this moment was the power to rule Germany. At this moment he was struggling to some point rational enough for killing me, some point not so distant from his hate that he would lose its strength but distant enough for calculating the schematic of murder. In the same way the client had mourned Geli and his kingdom all these years, in the same way I'd mourned Megan and Courtney and my conscience, Petyr had mourned Kronehelm, I suppose. He'd been translating a long time. He'd translated always with the same precision; if he'd ever subverted or deformed the translations there wouldn't now be in his eyes the force of this livid hatred, rather I'd see his guilt and deceit. All this was happening the first time I stumbled on them in their little room; we all watched each other with hate and fear and amazement. Though my feet were growing gradually but surely lame, my hands were still capable of the good old things; I could break Petyr in his wormful wrath, and then throttle the old man. I could speak Megan's name as I did so, I could speak Courtney's. I could speak all their names, from Warsaw to London, from Treblinka to Mauthausen. And yet I knew that even if I could kill the old man for that long, before the soldiers burst in and shot me down, that even if I could kill him long enough to speak the names of the six million, or ten or twelve, or however many flesh markers he lay down in the pages of time to gauge his evil, in the end there'd only be one little old throttled life to pay for it. That wasn't revenge enough. If I could find my way into this room every night for another thirty years and kill him little by little each night, it was still just the small miserable life of an old senile memoryless man to whom his own evil no longer meant anything even if I snarled the name of every victim into his wrinkled little face. What's the revenge of killing a man who's forgotten his own evil? I left the two of them that first time, I turned my back on Petyr's eyes in the same way the soldiers show contempt for my own harmlessness. I came back several nights later, and then every night after that. It's crossed my mind that someone meant this to happen; it's crossed my mind that if I were to kill Z, soldiers might not burst in at all. Rather they might be watching it all from somewhere secret. Rather they might let me kill him as they may have allowed me to kill X that night in the Hotel Imperial. Still, each night I considered it. Each night my hands felt fit for it. Petyr's hate, seething and never acted upon, came to bore me. Before my hate came to bore Z, in the depths of whatever fog he now lived, I'd find a revenge to catch his attention.

113

So there were the three of us, the hellgod of history, his dreamwriter and his translator, aging crippled and insane and unseen in a damp Italian basement. What came to repulse me most was how time made the client's evil so feeble and therefore shredded the illusion that his evil was inhuman. It was utterly human. I saw the humanity the day the doctor came and changed Z's clothes and cleaned him from his fouling himself. His fouling himself was specific to his oldness, but not to his evil. His shit stank, but it stank human, not evil. In the way time and age broke him down, it broke down his vicious godliness, his distinct monstrousness. He lived in abject fear of both of us, Petyr and me. He lived with the pain of his slipping life and approaching confusion. He was afraid and sore enough of life that it was all the more reason not to kill him. I'd hit him sometimes, though. I couldn't stop myself. I hit him to test the situation, to see if whoever watched us in secret sent in the troops to stop me. His blood stank too, enervated and toxic. When I hit him, Petyr forgot himself for a moment and smiled. Go on, I said to Petyr, nodding at the old man, take a shot. Petyr did, in his impotent fashion. When the old man's face burst with blood and his confused pitiful cry at the blows, Petyr shrank back, but not I think from having struck the ruler of the world. Rather I think from having allied himself with me; he hated me all the more then for having seduced him. As time passed Z became more rank to see and smell. I tried hard to believe it was the smell of his soul rising up through the body, but his fragility denied this pretense. I didn't understand how history would bear this evidence of humanity, or how anyone could ever believe in redemption again, since the protest of history had so long been that all men were redeemable.

This was a man who could not be redeemed. In my memory of what had been, I was now more him than he was. So here were two men, incontrovertibly human in their foulness, who in all their humanity could not be redeemed. History, clutching to redemption, might insist we were monsters, but the god has human shit in his shorts when the doctor comes to change him. The doctor says nothing, however, of Z's swollen face, where I hit him. He says nothing of the blood. This is how I've come to realize Z is mine to do with as I choose. The followers cannot bring themselves to kill their god, they'll let his own god do it for them.

1 1 4

For months, revenge commensurate and fitting eluded me. I lay thwarted in the dark. Then last night it came to me, on my bed. I woke to it with clarity; for a moment I couldn't believe it. I mustered my strength to raise myself and get to the desk. It took thirty seconds to do it; I didn't precede it with an act of pleasure. I wouldn't give him the satisfaction of pleasure even if his eighty-year-old body was capable of knowing it. I'd never given him the pleasure of her before, after all, other than his witness from the corner of our room on Dog Storm Street. Because I'm the god's god, no act of pleasure is necessary: I can touch the egg of her without a penis or its pollen. I can touch the egg of her with my pen, with a sentence: Life is committed at the core of her, I write, nine months short of creation.

1 1 5

When they come the next day for the work, I inform them I intend to deliver it personally. The guards make a token display of disbelief, claiming such a thing's impossible, though my door's been unlocked eight months now. Then I have nothing to give you today, I answer. There's a conference and one of the guards leaves to discuss the matter with an unknown authority; he returns after several moments. He explains I'll be escorted under guard to Z's room.

1 1 6

I won't chance subversion on Petyr's part. I'm present when he translates the single sentence to the client. Immediately Petyr knows something is up. He translates the sentence precisely. It's impossible at first to know if the old man understands. "Do you understand?" I ask him, in German. Petyr protests. "You can't speak to him this way," he says in English, "I'm the only one who speaks to him. You speak to him through me." I ask Z again if he understands. "It's a child," I tell him, "wonderful news." Petyr protests again, loudly, in German. The old man looks back and forth from Petyr to me in confusion; I keep trying to talk and Petyr gets louder and louder. Now I turn from the client and answer Petyr in English. "Please," I say to him, "he's confused. The guards will hear you, and it'll be worse for all of us." Petyr answers, "Worse for you, you mean," and I say, "Certainly not. Certainly it's clear how superfluous you are in this matter. I'll have them take you away if you don't be quiet." He glares at me hot and silent. We just sit there watching each other for a minute before I turn back to Z. Z is still rattled, frightened by the way this afternoon is unlike other afternoons. "It's your child," I tell him now. Petyr still glares at me, bursting with outrage, but saying nothing. "Do you understand?" I ask the old man. "Your child and Geli's. The child you were always meant to have. She's quite beside herself with joy. She's honored to carry your glorious germ in her. Someday you'll take this son—and I can tell you with complete confidence that it'll surely be a son—and groom him to rule the world after you. In such a way, the idea of a world after you becomes bearable, doesn't it?" When he hears this, the old man's face begins to shine with a small radiant smile. The ancient eyes light up exactly as I supposed they might, and I can already well imagine the dark shattered desolation they'll show when I finish my revenge nine months from now. He begins to consider, even in his dim fog, how beautiful the child will be, beautiful like his mother; and life that seemed rather purposeless now finds a final way to matter. He's linked to immortality forever, linked in flesh and not just the world's memory. It's at the same time evidence of both his godness and humanness. Dim and fogged as he is, he begins to cry a little; I could beat him if I wanted and he'd still be happy for what I've given him this afternoon. After a while he moves from his chair for the first time I've ever seen him do it, and lowers himself on his cot in emotional exhaustion. In his old strangled language he cries out to her with thanks. In his sleep he's calm and ecstatic at the same time, and I can only hope that, in all his peace and excitement, he doesn't die on me before I'm done with him.

1 1 7

I allow several days to pass in which I don't leave my room.
The guards are perplexed and even distressed by this. At
night I can hear him, from far away, howling like a lonely
dog. When I finally go to see him, his eyes beseech me. In
the days that have passed since I first saw him, doubts as to
the joyous news have begun to grow in his head. I put them
to rest. Day after day Petyr reads to him while I sit listening
to make sure nothing's amiss in the translations. Petyr
fumes, caught as he is. Z has actually begun to open up
and talk a little, in his crazy fashion, small words here and
there, a phrase or two of the future. Plans to take his boy
up to his retreat in the Bavarian Alps, where everything as
far as anyone can see is under his rule. That sort of thing.
I feel immense satisfaction to see the past and its memories
flood back into his face, to have him remember bit by bit
who he is and what he's done. It's as though the past and
its memory grow in his head in symbiosis with his future
and child growing in her, until the two grow to the present
that emerges from between her legs. He flourishes as time
passes, he occasionally even does respectable imitations of
what he used to be, giving forth with this ridiculous state-
ment or that about things of which he never knew anything. We joke together sometimes in the way a grownup
jokes with a child or plays with a pet, dangling a string
before its claws. In such a way I dangle before him the
heartbeats and kicks of the life inside her, and like a small
animal he frantically reaches for what I dangle until I
snatch it away, laughing. Petyr has sunk so far into the
force of his hate for me that his eyes have almost become
dull with it, the power frustrated into seething languish.
The weeks pass and then the months. The days I spend
with the client and our translator, the nights I sail with

Giorgio in the lagoon; soon, I tell Giorgio, I'll go with you
to the islands. You come, Giorgio says, they'll never find
you.

118

At night I go on a secret mission inside her. I voyage up
her canals, wander her passages searching for a place to
build what she'll give birth to months from now. I find a
fertile plain on the banks of her womb and begin to work.
I don't have much time for what has to be accomplished.
I've brought my materials with me. I cast the mold, I make
the mortar. I dig a pit there on the beach inside her, trans-
form the whole belly of her into a cauldron. There I make
the very ooze of the thing that's to be born. I concoct it
from a hundred things. I concoct it from the hush of those
who vanished into the fog on his orders, without a cry or
remnant left behind for those who would wonder where
they went. I concoct it from the mealy red ice left beneath
those shot face down in the snow. I concoct it from the
terrified squeal of children transformed abruptly into gunfire, which transforms in turn to the bright afternoon still-
ness. I concoct it from the gypsies in the ghettos and the
Jews naked in the pits. I've given to the mortar those he
starved, that from the pulp of their bones this thing I make
can stand. I've given to the mortar those he gassed, that
from the small pockets of gas left in their flesh this thing I
make might quiver and lurch. I've given to the mortar
those he burned, that from the unbearable odor of their
ash this thing I make might be smelled from any place in
paradise. I grind into it the teeth he pulled from their

heads, the genitals he ripped from their loins, the eyes he
left open when he killed them so that he could always assure himself he had indeed killed them. I concoct the garbage of evil, of which he is father, and which he's fathered
without the passion and sex of a man. Often I break down.
Often the fumes of it stop me in my place. And when I've
given to the mortar all of these, and have watched them
disappear into the swirl of the cauldron's awful whirlpool,
I finally give to it Megan, I give to it little Courtney falling
through Vienna space. After a while I think, I can no
longer do this. But I can do this. I can do this for that day
not long from now when he comes to see his son and I
present him with this thing I've built inside her, and he
reaches his fingers tremulously to feel the child's silky skin
and instead touches hard scales, and moves to stare into
his son's blue eyes and instead sees a thousand black eyes
the size of pins, and presses to his old chest the soft innocent hair and instead is stung by the twitching antennae. I
can do this, Megan; I can do this, Courtney; for that moment when the old face of the god gazes on what his god-
seed has spawned, not something grown from an embryo
or fetus or even, godlike, from a star, but rather from larva.
At that moment he'll either kill it or it will kill him, or he'll
drop it to the floor in horror where it will come crawling to
him on a hundred legs, twitching at him for love. Let him
love it if he can. Let him hold it in his arms like the mothers
and fathers who clutched for the last time the children he
tore away from them. Let him name it with a Christian
sound, and parade it in his cathedral of a thousand years.

119

Dania doesn't know what grows in her, as she crosses Davenhall's mainstreet to her hotel room. She only knows it isn't of her, that something's being made inside her that's not of her tissue and soul. Several times, over at the tavern where she's still trying to work, the nausea and pain inside her is so startling it nearly stops her heart. At first she assumes it's because she's almost fifty years old, after all. She's never had a baby before and therefore has no real reason to suppose her experience is uncommon. But now some months have passed and she understands, instinctively, that something in her means to be formed and born of a will that isn't her own. In the middle of mainstreet, not far from where she once guarded the body of Consuelo Garcia, she says, No. No, she says; the lover of all these years, who came to me unseen when he chose, will not have this victory. What's in me is mine, and though I might have chosen never to have it in me at all, I won't relinquish anything else anymore. All the men, she tells herself, and all their history, may have believed I was theirs to manifest whatever nightmare they needed to hurl free of themselves; perhaps they all believed that this presumption extended even to this thing in my belly. No; again no; no again and again and again. No. She gets to her room and lies down, and feels her belly and the movement in it. Conscious only of the sunlight through the trees beyond her window, she prepares to fight.

120

The snow comes. I wake one morning to its muffled din. It falls on the city's tarpaulin, lightly and soundlessly except that the city's emptiness transforms even the fall of snow into an echo. I have to argue with the authorities several days in order to get some heat in my room's radiator. What about the old man? I ask the guards. At first they don't answer, then one of them tells me, The Leader has heat. When I see the client that afternoon, the room is cold but neither he nor Petyr seem to notice; it's like the light through their covered window. I'm rubbing my hands together but the two of them sit the way they always do, still and sullen in the room's center. All the old man cares about is news of the child. Oh don't you concern yourself with that, I assure him, that's all taken care of. Things are proceeding just fine on that score. I suppose I don't need to worry about Z dying from cold; he's flared with life. He lives for his son. Petyr doesn't even look at me anymore. Perhaps he's busy staring into the face of his own end, approaching now from not so far away with its hand outstretched. The echoes continue for a couple of weeks and when the snow stops and the sun shines down on the ice melting into the tarpaulin, the corridors and piazzas of the empty blue city fill with weird rainbows. Out of the misty colors fly flocks of birds that have been trapped under the city's ceiling for years; they're old and their wings flutter heavily in the wet air. Now the echoes I hear are the birds trying futilely to batter their way out.

121

I work day and night. The shores of her womb are lit with fiery torches. Sometimes I fall asleep in the middle of what I'm doing, wake to find the sludge cooling in my hands, waiting to be fed to the larva. At times the whole universe of her hurls itself into upheaval, in rebellion. The larva grows. I can already see the thing moving, ready to live. In the day, when I go to see the old man and Petyr, I can't quite get the black of the work off my hands; yet it seems that only I can smell it. Winter passes into spring, which passes into early summer. Giorgio comes up through my floor with food, I'm ashamed to take it with my black fingers.

122

The old man pulled quite a good one on Petyr today. I still shake my head thinking about it; Petyr just misjudged the situation, that's all. He just couldn't keep his head, his rage got the better of him. We were sitting in their room, Petyr reading to the old man who sat in his chair holding the brass frame with her picture and the dead brown flower in it. Petyr couldn't go on with the reading. Convulsed and shaking, he looked up and said to the client, "My Leader, this is a lie." The old man didn't seem to have heard, and Petyr said it again, "This is a lie, my Leader," and then he looked at me. He's going about it all wrong, I thought to

myself calmly, taking me on this way. But then he doesn't
have the imagination for going about it any other way.
Now we both looked at the old man, who still seemed en-
tranced by the picture he held, until he slowly raised his
head to look at the translator. "This is a lie," Petyr said
firmly, having gotten his attention, "this is a sadistic joke.
Do you see? This big stupid man is playing a joke on you.
He likes jokes," and that was true, actually, I always had
rather liked a good joke. I remember a good one a long
time ago; my father told a good one about *his* son. The old
man just blinked at Petyr, still holding her picture in both
hands. "There is no child, my Leader," Petyr shook his
head, tears in his eyes, "you're not going to be a father. I'm
sorry." The old man just kept blinking at him, and Petyr
just kept on saying it over and over, There's no child,
you're not going to be a father, it's a stupid joke, and the
more he spoke the more upset he became as though he was
going to cry any moment, while Z just sat there blinking at
him, appearing not to register anything he heard. And
then, faster than I would have believed possible, the old
man brought her picture up over his head and crashed its
heavy brass frame down onto Petyr. Petyr dropped to the
floor without a groan or shudder; every bit of life just flew
out of him with the blow of the picture, and there he lay
looking up at me, a slight discoloration on his forehead
from the brass of the frame, before the blood streamed out
into his hair and face and the shattered glass of the picture
frame and the picture itself, which lay in Petyr's head.
There was her face with a hole in it lying in his. Little
shavings of brown dead flower drifted in the air. I thought
I was going to choke from laughing so hard. The guards
came in then and looked at Petyr in amazed horror; the old
man just sat in his chair, looking at her torn picture. I
didn't bother trying to explain to them how an eighty-year-
old man could kill someone with that kind of force; if they
didn't know that about him by now, they didn't know anything. "I believe the Leader has no further use for this

gentleman's services," I said. The guards looked at the old man and looked at me; one of them snapped his fingers at the others and they dragged poor Petyr out. I looked at the old man when they'd gone, trying to keep a straight face. But I laughed some more and slapped him on the back. "Something to tell your children about," I suggested. After a while he smiled back.

1 2 3

With Petyr gone, I now translate the work to the client myself. The authorities wanted to bring in a new translator but they've relented to my insistence otherwise. I'm not willing to chance a third party at this point. My German is crude compared to Petyr's and lacks Petyr's exactitude, but it's sufficient enough. Soon I find myself writing in German, which I've never done in the thirty years since I left America. By writing in German I find I now write in something close to his own voice. I write in his words, I write in the grunts of the beast which are there beneath everything he says.

124

Two weeks after Petyr's death they've tried to move me in with the old man. That they waited this long reflects less the etiquette of a decent interval than the fact they were too stupid to think of it sooner. It doesn't matter; I refused. The two of us living and sleeping in different places is the only psychological semblance left to me of being separate from him. In a catacombed sinking city empty except for soldiers and the two of us, I won't have the two of us now living within the same hundred square feet; the city would corrode outward from the disease of it. I'll sit with the old fucker in the day and build his child by night, but I need some place and time to be alone with the smell of my befouled hands. Besides, Giorgio comes up through the floor of this room, and at the moments I can barely live with myself, I still go out that way too.

125

On my approach, I'm surprised at how dark it's become. I stream farther into her, looking for the light of her beach; I can only discern the outline of the thing that fills her. Even I didn't expect it would become this consuming. The larva's now so large as to block out everything, and my way to the cove of her womb is obstructed by it. For a moment I regret everything. For a moment I forget the smell from which I've made this thing inside her is the smell of his evil, rather I confuse it with my own infidelity. Until I make myself remember Megan and Courtney, there's a moment when I forget my resolve to sacrifice whatever redemption might be left in the world for their revenge; and my memory is owned by the nights in Vienna I loved you. I turn back and desperately retreat. Someone calls out: is it he or I? "Geli."

Dania screams. She sits upright in her bed which is soaked with sweat. Across the street she can hear the voices of the tourists in the tavern; she looks at the clock. It's past midnight. She can't be sure at this moment what it is that's made her cry out, it could have been any one of a number of things. It could have been the convulsion, only one of many, of whatever's inside her; she presses her hands to her stomach. It could have been the dream, only one of many, of giving birth to a monster; she shakes her head clear of its image. She suspects, however, it's neither of these that's made her scream: she believes it was the voice calling her by the name she will not accept. She stumbles from the bed to throw up yet again, long past the time for throwing up; this is now her eighth month. I'm not fighting hard enough, she fears; she would reach down into herself if she could, and struggle with it hand to hand, and make it her own. Her will wanders desperately looking for a weapon.

126

This evening the old man comes to my room on the way back from the tower. We went to the tower this afternoon together. The guards escorted us through the winding streets and over the bridges; it was a long walk that tired Z profoundly. At the top of the tower he wheezed the whole time. I convinced the authorities it was a good idea; as the momentous occasion nears, I want him worn down. After a five minute dose of the sea and sky, we started back and had to stop in an empty cafe so he could rest. He speaks sometimes but I don't understand what he says. When he talks to the soldiers they don't seem to understand either. Yes my Leader this, yes my Leader that, that's all the soldiers say to him in return. He holds no majesty for them at all; the kind of hysteria he inspired thirty years ago, there's none of that. On the way back, when we come to my room, I surprise myself and suggest to the guards that he rest there for an hour or two. I heard there's going to be a broadcast tonight, it seems a good idea to have him see it. For the momentous occasion I want him to be good and full of himself. So we go into my room and I sit on the bed and set him on the chair where I write, because I don't want him falling asleep on me. I close the door and wait for the guards to drift away, or maybe doze themselves; then I pull out the TV. I turn it on and wait for the broadcast; any minute I expect we'll see his face and hear some reassembled speech he gave a long time ago. I hope to fill him with his own glory in the way the photos in his room fill him with glory, but he only sits staring at the TV mute and uncognizant. The broadcast comes on, the picture of him from very young days, when everyone thought he was quite impressive, quite the thing; and he begins to speak; and then it goes blank again. And then, out of nowhere as has happened before, there's that man in the sea diver suit, except this time he isn't just floating under the sea. This time he seems to be walking across the bottom of the sea; a strange vessel sits in the background. There, on the bottom of the sea, he plants an American flag. This is what your war's come to, I say to the old man, armies claiming victory on the bottom of the sea. They're out there right now, at this moment, on the bottom of the Adriatic, planting flags and little plaques. Z stares at the scene in stupefaction. I turn off the TV and hide it away, and the guards take him back to his room.

127

I go with Giorgio and his friends out to their island tonight. It takes about an hour to cross the lagoon. I'm in a state like that of the air before rain. The people of the island welcome me like a member of their family who's returned home after half a lifetime. No ceiling covers the island, we walk along the streets under the stars and the lights of windows. The little houses are composed and tidy and painted with exuberant colors. Giorgio explains that the Germans have tried to cover the island, as well as the other surrounding islands, to no avail. The islanders sabotage their efforts, and when the Germans come to arrest them they only find a village as empty as the city I live in. It occurs to me when I hear this that perhaps my city isn't empty at all, it's only that its people, like the people of this island, will not be vanquished by those arrogant enough to presume history has dictated their triumph. To live with the people of this island is to be in a place and time where

there's no war at all; it isn't as though the people pretend
there isn't a war, but rather it is that the war is truly insignificant to them. The Germans who rule them are objects
of ridicule and mirth. The fishermen take me to a restaurant where the food and wine are already waiting. There's
another fisherman, a small man about half my size, with a
golden tenor, whose name is also Giorgio, and after I've
gone around to all of them and they've thrown their arms
around me in welcome, it seems half of them are named
Giorgio. There are also ten or twelve Brunos. The women
are all named Maria. Maybe they were named something
else before I began with the wine but after an hour they
become Maria, warm and voluptuous and without a trace
of mystery. After a while when we begin to eat the fish, the
fishermen begin to sing gondolier songs celebrating the
day's catch. They sing about the lonely life on the water
and the age of the city. They sing, Give me your kisses of
fire. I can't stand the beauty of it. I hold close into my lap
my black hands that smell of the night's work, but the
Maria next to me wrests my hands away from me and
brings them to her mouth. I'm appalled that her lips should
kiss them, but she won't let me draw my hands back. When
I begin to cry none of them asks me what it is I cry for; my
rain has begun. I've lived so far from life this true I'd forgotten its power. One song after another the fishermen
sing, there in the small restaurant swept by the open wind
of the Adriatic. The fishermen invite me to live with them
on the island and never go back to the hidden sinking city.
If I want to leave the lagoon forever, they tell me, I can do
that too. They've been free so long I don't think they understand how impossible it would be, that even if I wanted
to go there'd be no way. The Germans, I try to tell them,
they'd catch you too, and arrest you for helping me. How
could you expect to elude them? The fishermen laugh and
pour me some more wine and pour themselves some more
wine and that's when they explain about the regatta. They
explain about the regatta and how there will be a thousand

boats on the lagoon at once: How, says one Giorgio or another, are the Germans supposed to check a thousand boats? One or two, or ten or twelve perhaps, but not a thousand. After the wine is gone all of us stagger down to the dock and head back for the city; I lay on the bow of Giorgio's boat flushed with the wine and the songs I've heard that seem to come out of the sea as though it's filled with singing sea divers. Give me your kisses of fire. And it's then, as though in response to their songs, I hear her first cry, the first strangled sound of her labor.

1 2 8

Dania has arranged a signal with Judy, who's working at the tavern across mainstreet, that when the time arrives the pregnant woman will wave her lantern before the window and Judy will come immediately. Now pain slashes though her spasmodic and incandescent, and Dania reels across the room. It's all she can do to get herself on the bed and not pitch herself through the window to the ground below. She cannot believe that it can actually start in this pain; if this pain is only the beginning, what will the birth be like? Her fear is boundless. She fears of course not only the pain but the vision of what will come out of her. She heaves on the bed and the lantern she tried to swing from her window rolls on the floor; she hopes its glass doesn't break and set the place on fire. Already something in her is strangely wrong: the contractions are already only moments apart. She screams once, then again; Judy, who's already in the street because she saw the weird weaving light on the walls of Dania's room, now bolts into the hotel

and up the stairs. She's up the stairs and into the room as
Dania feels herself rip from the middle, opening up to un-
loose what's inside her; she opens like the night before me.
On the bow of the boat I'm sobered by the sound and pain
of her. The night's gleaming and luminous next to the
fuliginous larva gushing out from her. The Twentieth Century is being born from her in a wash of steaming evil. Z's
spawn will eat its way out of her, dragging from its hind
legs the afterbirth of twelve million faces that felt its father's misery. It will make its way out of her and up through
the cracks of a blue city, scampering down the hallways to
Z's room, dreading the light. It will find its way up Z's arm,
onto his chest, and wake him from his sleep, its thousand
black eyes staring into his. The afterbirth trails behind. We
dock at the pier and I run through the tunnel of the piazza
as quickly as my crippled old feet will take me. It's inconceivable to me I might miss it, it's inconceivable that
Megan and Courtney and I might not be there to see it. I
want to witness the first tip of the first black antenna that
emerges from her, feeling its way out. In a moment I'm up
from beneath the floor of my room. There's a roar in my
ears, the roar of myself bellowing madly, or perhaps it's
her. It's inconceivable I might not be there to look into the
thing's features and see *him*, incontrovertibly him, the outline of the father in the face of the fathered thing. She
screams, and in the pit of this scream, as what's being born
travels into the light of the world, because she's stripped of
any other weapon, finding neither the rage that killed Dr.
Reimes in retribution for her father nor the resolution that
swept her through the river of Davenhall Island to be sufficient for the fight, she's left with only a single choice; and
that is to love it. Whatever comes from her, in all its monstrousness, she can only love it. It's such a pitiful weapon.
Later, she'll wonder if there really was such a weapon.
Later, she'll wonder if it really lay there inconspicuous and
unthreatening on the barren floor of a small secret room.
Later she'll think it's only a theoretical love, and she'll won-

der if loving it so deeply was ever really possible. But for the moment it's not only possible but inescapable, one measly love. It doesn't seem nearly pure enough, or perfect or holy enough, it isn't love untainted. It's love marked, wounded, suffered and doubted and denied by the humanity that attends it. It's nothing before such a huge evil. But in the pit of this last scream it's all there is, and she bends down and picks it up, and clutches it, a used broken little weapon, with a lifetime of blanks to one live cartridge, if there's even one. The noise of the weapon is flat and whispered. Somewhere in the sounds of her own scream and the noise of her own love she's vaguely aware of Judy by her side. In the noise of her love she begins to expel the thing from her; in the noise of her love the thing seems, for a moment, to stop in confusion in its exodus from her. If she's to unleash a swarm of them, she vows, if she's to fill the room with them, then it will be with her love's noise, flat and whispered and pathetic. The century, in confusion, stops in its own time. Caught inside her, it devours its own time, which is to say it devours itself, and then begins to grow again from its inside out. Evil thunders past it like a river. Dania calls for Judy to take whatever it is being born from her. Give it to me, whatever it is, however monstrous, raise it to my breast. And Judy does this. And Dania feels her womb released of it, and feels that to which she's given birth lying there on her chest, in her arms, and the sticky slime of the way it feels convinces her it's a monster indeed, until she clears her vision and looks at him, to see a son quite human, drenched in afterbirth and blood, the only sign of a birth this extraordinary not to manifest itself for some weeks, when the hair on his small head will grow drained of all color.

1 2 9

When I see that she's not given birth to what I made inside her, I'm aghast. It's unthinkable that one small act of will has defied the soul of a century bent on finding its true dark literal form. When I see she's given birth to a child I think to myself, Then I must kill this child. What she's defied in the act of birth will not deny me my revenge; in killing the child I'll kill the father in turn, who will die from the grief of it. I know grief. Uncertain as the mysteries of birth may be to me, there's nothing mysterious to me about grief. I take my pen in my hand and make myself remember what I need to remember in order to do it. It isn't hard to remember. I look at the child, look for the ways in which the child is like the father; and though the child in truth is more like his mother, there's enough of the father. There's plenty enough, plenty of the father and plenty of what I remember.

1 3 0

I'll kill him; I mean to kill him; I've killed enough things to kill one more. The baby's head fits right in the palm of my hand. Right in the palm. My fingers curl over his little skull. One small pop of his little skull, I'm black enough for that. It's not such a difficult thing, given all the revenge that will come of it.

131

I mean to kill him; give me a moment. I promise, Megan. I promise, Courtney. Just a moment. The child, he really doesn't look so much like her. Quite a bit like his father, quite a bit like me. Much easier to do it, then. I mean to.

132

I mean to: I'm beyond the reach of mercy, assuming there was ever mercy in me. I can do it.

133

I can: I'm sure of it.

134

I cannot.

135

I drop the pen. My face falls to my empty hands. I'm weak; my heart gasps with light. Give me your kisses of fire. I'm miserable in my failures.

136

Three days later, Giorgio comes up through the floor of my room. I'm lying on my bed, my hands at my sides stale with my failure to avenge things irrefutably heinous. I lie on my bed considering all our fatherhoods. Giorgio calls me from across the room, his head poking up out of the ground. Listen my friend, he says, the regatta's tomorrow. If you want to go, you must come with me now. I move myself with great effort to sit up, and place my feet heavily on the floor. There's only one thing, I tell him. Of course, says Giorgio. Someone, I tell him, is coming with us.

137

Giorgio waits in my room while I make my way down the hall. The guards are sleeping. One peers up at me half-consciously, grumbling. I'm going to see the old man, I tell him. Disgruntled, the guard says, All right. He's talking in his sleep. Perhaps I'll stay with him tonight, I tell him, or bring him back here. The guard nods and readjusts himself, and the other guard sleeping close by protests the volume of our discussion. I move down the hall and across the larger open hallway that divides my part of the city from the client's. Some of the lanterns in the hollows of the walls are burned out. At his room I find him sitting in the dark in his same chair, neither asleep nor awake. When I speak to him he responds with an incoherent mumble; he holds the pages I've written for him in his arms, presses them to himself. He begins to talk with some excitement; he originally thought he'd name the child August, after his only childhood friend. But recently he's begun to lean toward Petyr. I lift him by his arms; he's confused, but then everything confuses him. This isn't going to work, I'm thinking, they're watching me. But I bring him with me out into the hallway and we slowly head back to my room, the white pages curled in his fists.

138

One by one I blow out the lanterns that still burn, casting his hallway into pitch black. The blue hall that divides his from mine is now the dark deep blue of night; when we reach its mouth there's a sudden pandemonium of wings, the old feeble birds of the city panicked and thunderous. The old man's eyes fly around maniacally at this. We get to my hallway, a dim gold from the last lanterns burning; I blow them out too. The guards stir and groan in disorientation, and then settle back to sleep. I push open the door of my room. Giorgio's there waiting. For a moment I fear Giorgio will recognize him. He'll recognize him and hate me, and they'll all hate me, all the Giorgios and Brunos and Marias who treated me as though I belonged among them. They'll hate me as they have a right to hate me: this is what I'm thinking there in the doorway of my room. What will the discovery of my deceit do to their village and life, I'm thinking, how will anything ever be the same for them again. In this moment, standing in the doorway of my room, I believe I've made a terrible mistake, I believe that once again I've corrupted something, when I should simply have said to Giorgio's offer of escape, Leave me. But Giorgio looks at Z and sees only what in fact Z is, only an old man; and the fisherman helps me set him on the bed where he can rest. Giorgio has brought a brown cloak for me but we wrap it around Z. He's very old, Giorgio says, it could be a difficult trip for him. But I understand, he adds, that you cannot possibly leave him. We'll do our best. I nod humbly. We'll get you another cloak out on the boat, Giorgio says. After the old man has rested a few minutes Giorgio says, with great apology in his voice, It's important we leave right now. I nod again, silently, and we lift the old man up, and Giorgio lowers himself into the tunnel. The old man goes next, and then I follow.

1 3 9

By now they know we've gone. By this morning, when they came to my room and then his, they knew we'd disappeared. Perhaps they've scoured the city for us, perhaps they've searched the room to find the tunnel. At any rate we've left the city, on the afternoon the fishermen's regatta takes place. With the spray of the lagoon now in my face, I gaze around from my place in the boat, and there are around me several boats, and then I see tens of them, and then hundreds. The city with the blue roof floats in the lagoon behind us. The Adriatic glistens to the east of us. Overhead swirl the German helicopters, I keep glancing up at them. Don't look at them, Giorgio calls to me through his fixed smile from the other end of the boat. Any moment he's going to understand about the old man. Sooner or later the word will be out, a manhunt will be underway, underway at this very moment by the helicopters above us. The fishermen were right. There are too many boats for the Germans; the lagoon's filled with them. I'm overwhelmed by the sight of them. I hunch down in the boat, and at my feet, lying in the boat's bottom, wrapped in the brown cloak, Z shivers from the cold of the sea, befuddled by the very blueness of a sky that's bluer than any blue ceiling. I look up from the old man to Giorgio, who smiles. I look around at all the other Giorgios sailing on all sides of me. The boats dazzle the lagoon with colored flags that fly from their masts; the white of the swept water erupts in the air. I can't bring myself to look back at the blue city again, I expect it to have sunk altogether now that we've gone, that if I look back once more there'll be only a huge silver bubble rising from beneath the sea. I'm a little queasy from the boat and the panic. The end of the regatta and the Italian mainland are in sight. On the mainland they'll certainly capture us; I'm thinking how I've used all the Giorgios and Brunos to smuggle out of exile the most evil man in the world. With the mainland just moments away, and with the sight of German soldiers lining the shore, Giorgio now says to me, When we reach the shore we won't have time to say goodbye. So goodbye now. Goodbye, I say to him. I look around at the fishermen on the other boats, and the colors of the regatta flags; they're all looking back at me, even fishermen I've never seen, fishermen who seem to have come out of nowhere, out of unseen islands. They're all smiling goodbye.

140

Z and I are not arrested at the mainland. I pull the old man up from the boat's bottom and we climb out, trying to lose ourselves among the hundreds of Italians milling around under the eyes of the Germans on the ridge of the banks. The old man and I are wearing brown cloaks and hoods like two monks, one small and shriveled and the other over-sized and lame; we're surrounded by fishermen, the same ones who smiled at me from their boats, who now take no notice of us at all. Everyone begins to head into the town on the mainland. Z and I travel with them, soldiers watch us as we pass. At the mainland station I pull from my cloak a wad of the Eurodeutsch currency Giorgio's put there for us; it takes most of it to buy two tickets for the train. The station's swarming with German soldiers. The whole thing seems ridiculous, it's obvious we'll be arrested any moment. We climb onto the train heading for Milan and, beyond Milan, the territories that were formerly France. The train's packed. Someone gives up a seat for the old man; I set him there with his train ticket sticking out of his coat pocket underneath the cloak. In his hands he still holds pathetically the last pages I wrote before leaving the sinking city, the ink on them having long since run in wet indecipherable streaks. I take my own place out in the car's aisle. After thirty minutes there's a shudder beneath our feet and the station, with its platforms full of German soldiers, begins to drift past us. In another thirty minutes the lagoon is far behind us. Halfway to Milan a conductor wanders up the car and punches our tickets without a second look or thought.

In Milan we don't get off the train. I find a window seat for the old man. He's dazed, stupid with silence; he stares straight ahead. From the window of the train I buy some bread and wine from one of the passing food vendors. After a little less than an hour we pull out again. At the border they'll take us, I know that. I have my eye out at all times for the officials. No one carries passports anymore within Greater Germany but at the territories someone will no doubt want to see our identification. Occasionally one soldier or another comes through the car looking us over. Two hours outside Milan, the train's full again, and the conductor and a train official and two guards come down the aisle. With them is also a German lieutenant; the passengers watch him with fear. Everything's routine until our cabin, where the conductor asks Z for his identification. Z sits in stunned incomprehension. The lieutenant with the conductor and train official and two guards is considering me rather closely. The conductor and official begin to berate the old man; then the lieutenant says to me, Are you with this old man? There's no reason for him to assume I am, since Z is sitting in the car and I'm standing in the aisle. No one has told him, as far as I know, that I'm with the old man. After a moment I say, Yes, I'm with the old man. The conductor and the official turn to me and ask me for my papers, and after another moment I tell them I don't have my papers. He doesn't have his either, I say, nodding at my client. The conductor and the official take great indignant satisfaction in this news and the guards seem about to arrest me, when the lieutenant raises his hand and says to me, Where did you get on this train? Thinking about it, I'm prepared to say Milan, but instead I decide to astonish him with the truth. He nods at this, looks at the old man, looks back at me. Then he signals the conductor, train official and guards to move on to the next cabin. Dumbfounded, they compose themselves and comply. The five of them pass by me; I'm a bit dumbfounded myself. I'm trying to study the face of the German lieutenant for an answer, but he never looks my way again.

141

In Nice, I use the rest of Giorgio's money to get us a small room in the back of a kitchen run by Original Germans. The room's on the upper floor; it's bare and shabby but we have our own stairway leading down to an alley. In the mornings for breakfast there's bread and coffee; I have to feed him. I constantly ask him if he needs to go to the toilet since I don't want to change him or clean him. Sometimes we walk along a street that leads to the beach, where the cafes are filled with Original Germans attended to by New

Germans who used to be French. The vineyards in the hills sixty kilometers from here were scorched years ago in order to build the camps, and the French say that there's been this smell in the air ever since. One tastes it in the food and wine. I don't know what we're doing here except that I'm compelled by something, I guess I've been compelled since I stopped writing in the blue sinking city. We've been released, the two of us, by the birth: there's nothing more for me to write, there's nothing more for him to read. We're left to flee what I wrote and he read. Quickly I've run out of money and have asked the German who runs the kitchen if I can work off the fare of our room. I'm sure in other circumstances, when rooms in Nice have been at a premium, he'd have thrown us out, but the fact is no one likes the way the wine tastes anymore, the taste of the camps, the taste of vineyards scorched twenty years ago. The German is a short man with curly gray hair and a bushy mustache. He figures he might as well get something out of the room, so he hires me but only on the condition the old man works too. The old man can't go to the bathroom by himself, I tell the German, what do you expect him to do around here? He can wipe off tables, the German answers, it's the easiest thing in the world, to run a wet rag over a table. He asks us if we're original or new. I'm new, I tell him. He considers this and asks, The old man? He's original? Yes, I almost answer, the original Original, but I remember this isn't really so. Austrian, I tell the German. The German puts me to work washing dishes and Z stands in a soiled apron staring at tabletops with the brown water of a dirty rag running down his fingers. The German screams at him and the tourists eating their lunch laugh until the old man loses control of himself, which makes the German rail all the more. Fucking Austrian, he shouts. I take the old man upstairs and change him and lay him on the bed. You're going to get us thrown out, I tell him. He clutches my arm from the side of his bed ask-

ing, And my son is well? He says it as though he means
me.

We live in the room above the German kitchen through
the following winter. The city doesn't go untouched by
war; there are American submarines off the coast, and
sometimes everyone's put on alert. The Germans, not so
entirely in control of matters, have problems with looters,
and there's a mass escape from one of the camps north of
here. A number of the prisoners are picked up outside of
town. On my days off from washing dishes I take the old
man with me down to the beach where he sits on a low wall
that runs around the bay. The palms and the Mediterranean sky are gray with silt like an African crater. I walk
along the water, every once in a while gazing over my
shoulder to make sure the old man's still there on the wall.
This one particular time I see him stumbling across the
rocks toward the water in his usual trance; I have to catch
him so he doesn't walk right into the ocean. "Come on," I
tell him, taking him by the arm and leading him back across
the rocks. Who knows what it is he thinks he sees out there
in the ocean? "Just sit here," I say, putting him down on
the wall again, "what did you think was out there, Russia?
Do you think we're in Berlin, with the crowds ecstatically
crying your name? No one's ecstatically crying your name
anymore, so just sit down here." He sits; his feet don't even
touch the ground. His eyes and nose run with the cold of
the air. "Did you think," I say to him, "you'd take a little
swim perhaps? A little swim in the sea to make you young
again? Did you think you could wash something off?" I
stand there in front of him with my hands in my pockets
while his face runs. German soldiers walk along the prom-
enade of the city; no one pays any attention to us. "You
can't wash anything off, you old idiot," I say to him,
"there's nothing you can wash off. You old shit. Do you
think you're deserving of kindness now, because you're old
and pitiful? You're an old pitiful shit." He doesn't register

anything I say. Sometimes he's about to answer, but it's hardly ever comprehensible, and I have no reason to suppose it has anything to do with what I say to him. "Did you rack your brains," I ask him after a bit, "did you and the boys rack your brains at night there in the Chancellery, trying to figure out just how evil you could be? You must have racked your brains. You couldn't have just been born with such abysmal visions, is that possible? Racked your brains and when you came up with something terrible, you must have all said, But no, that just isn't quite terrible enough. Certainly we can think of something even more terrible than that. All the generals and bureaucrats and scientists racking their brains to think of things even evil incarnate would find freakish, even the Beast would cower before. Something with a modern touch." I shake my head. "Well somewhere out there," I say to him, nodding at the gray sea and the gray sky beyond it, "somewhere out there is a Twentieth Century that crushed you. Somewhere out there is a Twentieth Century that wouldn't abide you. That reached out of the hole, the collapsed center of its clock, and struck at you and pulled you down. So humiliated you that you felt no choice but to leap into the hole and fall forever. Somewhere that didn't care that it had devoured past and future, that didn't believe time and history and destiny could hold goodness hostage. You and me, old buddy," I say, "we're going to find that place. The Twentieth Century that doesn't exist, except in the sense that one needs to believe in it, as one once used to believe in God, that's where we're going. Pack your bag. We're going there, old man. You piece of old shit. You slime, piece of excremental slime. Bloody fucking piss-blasted fart from the intestines of history, you—" I stop, sputtering, breathing heavily, and look at him. I lean over and spit right in his face. He doesn't even blink. A big gob right in his eye; he doesn't even meet my gaze. He doesn't even feel my spit running down his cheek, it doesn't matter, his whole face is wet with cold, the tears and snot of him. "Shit," I can only say, and take his handkerchief from his pocket and wipe him. I lift him by the arm and we go back to our room; it takes us a long while to make our way up the street. In the dark of the room I carry him to his bed.

Before I get a chance to turn on the light, I know there's someone else in the room. Who is it? I say in the dark. I turn on the light and there are three of them, hunkered down in the corner. They don't have to say anything, I know they're Jews who broke out of the camp where the escape was yesterday. A boy and girl in their late teens who might be either siblings or lovers; there's an older man with them, about my age, perhaps a little younger though he looks older. We'll only stay tonight, the boy finally says, without explanation because he knows I don't need one. His mind's racing, trying to think what he'll do if I say no or try and turn them in; he knows they've put me in a bind, that I could get myself shot for keeping them. He knows that while he's much younger than I, he's nowhere as big, if it should come to that. I look at them and then over at Z on the bed; they look at the bed too. We all watch Z on the bed for a minute before I say, All right. I get this crazy idea in my head for a moment about the third, older man: I had a friend once, I say, who went to Paris. But the older man isn't Carl. That night I smuggle in some food for them. You've very brave and kind to do this, the girl tells me. Please don't say that, I ask her. After we eat, the girl goes over to Z and lifts him and begins to help him eat. I can't stand to see it. Please, I say, don't do that, don't help him like that. But he's an old man, the girl says. He's a piece of shit, I tell her. All of them now look at me in silent, hurt shock. Reproachfully, the girl continues to feed Z in defiance. No one speaks anymore of my kindness or courage, and in the pit of early morning, before dawn, the three are gone.

142

The German who runs the kitchen is constantly harassing us about the room and our work. Once, in the dead of winter, before a table of soldiers, he fires me and orders the old man and me to vacate the premises by nightfall. When night comes around, however, as I'm sitting there in the room trying to figure out what we're going to do next, there's a knock on the door and it's the German; he seems very strange. He says that he's changed his mind and we can stay if we want; the next day I'm back to the dishes. By the end of winter, I'm trying to figure out how to get the two of us out of Europe altogether. The captain of a steamer docked in Marseilles happens to come through one day and discreetly I take him aside and ask if we can ship out with him the next time he leaves. We haven't any money to speak of, I tell him, but perhaps we can work off the fare. He laughs in my face. But the next day he comes back to the restaurant; he seems to have returned for no reason other than to speak with me, though while he's at it he orders lunch. His demeanor has changed completely since the day before, though this isn't to say he's friendly; he says he's got a pal sailing for Mexico out of Wyndeaux, a small seaport on the western coast of France. I can leave that way if I choose, the captain says, but I have to take the old man with me. That's what he says. "You have to take the old man with you." Then he gives me two train tickets. I'm so surprised that all I can tell him, straight out, is that I'm not so sure we can get as far as Wyndeaux, the old man and I. Complications with the authorities, I blurt. The captain says, Oh I don't think you'll have any problem. He wipes his mouth with his napkin, and gets up and leaves, half his lunch still on the plate.

143

The trip to Wyndeaux takes two nights, and except for the fact I must constantly care for the old man, it remains uneventful. No one on the way asks about identification or papers. We arrive at the Wyndeaux train station the morning of the next day. Wyndeaux is a medieval city as blue as the one we left sinking in the Italian lagoon. In a beach cafe that glows like a lantern, I hunt up the captain who's going to sail us to Mexico. He's no more moved by our arrival than the German in Nice was by our departure, but he already understands the situation and has arranged things. We sail in forty-eight hours; until then, we're on our own. But we have no place to stay, I tell him; that's your problem, he answers. So we wander around the village streets half the day until I see the captain coming up the road toward us, to tell us we can stay with him. As with everyone else, there's no accounting for whatever's changed his mind. The morning we're to disembark, the old man and I are sitting on the docks waiting to board the ship when we're accosted by some soldiers who ask us what we're doing and who we are and whether we have papers. They start interrogating the captain, who makes it clear he'd be just as happy to leave us right there on the docks. This goes on a few minutes until a German officer of some rank shows up; as with the lieutenant on the train from Milan to Nice, he interjects himself. What's this all about, he demands of his soldiers. These old men don't have any papers, one of the soldiers exclaims, pointing to us. They don't have any papers! the ranking officer cries in mock alarm. But this can't be, he says, why, I'm certain Germany cannot survive such a thing. He's ridiculing the soldiers, who are baffled and flustered; he's hardly given me a glance. Let's say we not worry so much about old men without papers, the officer says. Let's say we find more significant ways to serve Germany and the Leader. The soldiers look at me and at each other, and salute the officer and leave. Only when they've walked away does the officer peer over his shoulder in my direction, and then at the ship's captain. The captain furiously gestures at us to get on his boat. We sail before the sun has crossed our heads.

1 4 4

We live in the cargo hold of the ship the entire voyage. It seems like a much longer voyage than the one that brought me over thirty years ago. It seems as though the sea's become much wider or the world more distant from itself, or perhaps it's that home, or anything resembling home, must, in my return to it, seem more unapproachable. Maybe it's just from living down in the cargo hold where there's no night or day. At first I'm afraid Z's not going to survive the voyage, but the cargo hold is quite warm, one of the boat's engines is just behind the next wall, and the food is better than the bread and coffee we've been living on in Nice for eight months. The old man doesn't get seasick either; he lives below the watermark of nausea. His own watermark, I mean. He's still among the living, or some kind of living anyway, the April night the captain calls me up on deck to point out, across the Caribbean before us, the harsh shores of the Yucatan.

145

We get ashore and there are more German soldiers waiting for us. No officer of rank needs to interfere, the soldiers just wave the old man and me on by. For a few days we live in a small abandoned hut on the northern outskirts of the port. A dirt road runs from the port up our hill and right past the hut. At night the old man crosses the road and sits on the edge of the cliffs watching and listening to his war taking place before him, up and down the coast of the Quintana Roo. In his face the sea flashes the green of coral and the red of bombs, and his eyes are still filled with the mad swirl of ancient birds in the hallways of the lagoon's sinking city. I'm not sure what to do next except try to get further into the Yucatan to Progreso, a large seaport that's divided between German and Mayan control. Each day a black cab drives up the road past us, the same guy at the wheel; sometimes he looks my way and waves. After a week I go down to the port to beg some food and see if I can find the black cab. I manage to talk the driver into taking the old man and me up the coast. I don't really trust him. I've seen him around the base transporting German officers and sailors here and there, and I don't understand why he would do this for me. I've made it clear I can't afford to pay him. But I'm thinking perhaps he's a spy for the guerrillas; he isn't Mexican but he isn't German either, Brazilian perhaps, latin but fairer than the Indians of the area. In other words, a German's idea of an acceptable latin. I sit in the front of the car, Z in the back. We drive slowly up the winding coast. I don't know where we're going and the driver doesn't either though he seems perfectly willing to take us there. I watch the Caribbean through the splattered insects on the windshield and after a while I fall asleep as the twilight rushes in from the western hills. When I wake, the driver's just sitting there in the same place, with his eyes open and a line of blood written across his throat as black as the cab itself; he doesn't look so fair now. The car's parked off the road among a circle of trees, and standing around are a lot of people with guns who definitely don't look like Germans.

146

The guerrillas live in an old Indian ruin that lies hidden in a mahogany forest at the tip of the peninsula. The old man and I stay through the early weeks of summer, which is when it rains in the Yucatan. The ruins are carved out of gray limestone and not much is left except the walls. The guerrillas sleep in hammocks strung high above the ground, under the hot rain of the skies above them; parapets have been constructed nearby. The woman in command, around twenty-eight years old, was born in the city of Merida and trained in America; she's hard and determined, and her name is Lucia. The guerrillas from the first regard me with extreme suspicion. They don't understand what two old men were doing in the company of a driver who was known to work for the Germans, in a car that was heading up the coast. There's continual discussion, even a month after we've been here, of whether I'm a German spy using a senile old man as a cover, and what should be done with me. I have no explanation other than that we're Austrian refugees who escaped through Italy and France; it only sounds more preposterous to them. My American English is all the more unsettling. When I tell them I want to get to America they only shrug, But you're already in America.

The guerrillas are traveling to Progreso too, where they'll blow up the railroad that links the seaport to German Merida. We travel at night, negotiating the underground pools and long mean swatches of jagged coral on my crippled feet, crossing the dark smoking henequen fields that have been strafed by German Stukas overhead. The ruins and abandoned Spanish plantations of the countryside are the bastions of the Mayan Resistance. Lucia says, The Americans bring in their own troops sometimes but the truth is they don't understand the territory much better than the Germans. Better, she says, that they airdrop the supplies and guns, or ship them across the gulf, and let us do the fighting. Let the Yanquis worry about defending Des Moines. I think she's trying to make an impression on me, so that if I am a German spy I'll understand that no matter how many Germans there are, or how big the guns and planes, or how many miles of the peninsula the Germans believe they control, there will always be the Mayans who know the Yucatan better and will engage the Germans until the last one's sealed up in a Viennese wall or has returned to Berlin to get drunk in his favorite beer garden. Sometimes I want to tell Lucia that my mother was an Indian; but there aren't many Austrian refugees with American Indian mothers, and I don't want to get caught in even the most harmless lie. During our time with the guerrillas, the old man and I live through two battles and several skirmishes. Z sits in a gully watching me load weapons for the purpose of shooting his army. Often I'm shaken awake in the night and must arouse the old man so we can pull out because a German patrol is close by. It's the guerrilla strategy to retreat whenever possible, never to be drawn into a battle for which the guerrillas themselves didn't plan and prepare. We wind our way though the forests across the limestone flats, always to another crumbling palace where we meet up with other rebels. Few of them ever speak to me, though they're always kind to the old man, feeding him soup and finding him the softest and most secure hammock. They blame me for having brought him into the situation, and of course they don't understand when I almost beat him to death one night in a small devastated village half a day south of the railway that runs to the sea.

147

It's the sight of the little girl that does it. We come into the village late at night, past midnight; a mile outside, the rebels know something's wrong. There's an odor in the air and a low din, which turns out to be the flies. The flies are everywhere in the village; the bodies of the villagers are black with them. Even for the guerrillas who've seen such atrocities, it's shocking; but for me it's more, the manifested vision of everything I've known but never had to see. The guerrillas stealthily sweep the village to make sure Germans aren't waiting. Lucia must decide whether to burn the village and the bodies or take the time to bury them. She opts to bury them. She sends a two-man scouting party on to the next village to see if there's a priest. It's as the men are digging that I come across the dead little girl. I don't want to talk about her. I don't want to tell what they've done to her. I . . . it's enough to explain that someone has pinned to her a note, which says, as far as my own German can translate, "Another virgin for the Leader." The girl, she must be all of eight. She's small enough that it's not so difficult imagining Courtney that age, if she'd lived a little longer to become that age. I turn my back on the girl. I can't even bring myself to remove the note, to pick her up and carry her in my arms to the graves. I turn my back on her and go out beyond the houses of the village to where I've left the old man lying in a clearing. Another virgin for the Leader, is all I keep saying to myself; I guess I'm still saying it when I find him lying there in the clearing. Silently, without a word, I just begin to beat him. I beat him and he's staring up at me with his eyes popping out, and the guerrillas come along and pull me off him when I'm within an inch of his life. They pull me off and it's clear that, in their own rage over the village, I've become to them the German who murders old people and children. You vicious bastard, Lucia says to me, while the others hold me back and someone tends to the old man. Another of the guerrillas, a short stocky Mayan who's second in command and hasn't spoken a word of English the entire time I've been around, speaks it quite well now. He says now, This man's like the rest of them. They stare at me; if they've ever considered shooting me, it's never seemed a more reasonable solution than at this moment. The old man lies at my feet bleeding from his nose and ears. For a moment I'm about to tell them. I'm about to tell them who he is, whether they'll believe it or not, and I don't suppose they would, but I'm about to tell them because I've been waiting to tell someone. And then I know I won't tell them. I won't because I believe it's better they villainize me, a big violent man my whole life, than an old weak sick man. Because there's always the one awful chance that they will believe me, that they'd look into his face and eyes and see that it's true, at which point the pure righteous wrath of their fight would have to accommodate the humanity of his evil. They're fighting for an age in which the heart and consciousness have not been stripped of the reference points that have become denied to time and space: they've stared into the bloody rorschach of the Twentieth Century and seen the budding of a flower. You can't do that to them, I say to myself. If you do one good thing in your life, I say to myself, let it be this, that you leave them their faith, that in your monstrous form you reaffirm their vision of what's monstrous, and what's therefore to be defeated; and that in his weak helpless form you reaffirm their vision of what's weak and helpless, and therefore to be defended. With one shudder from my torso up, I retrieve what havoc I need to shake the guerrillas free of me, and hope that in the process I provoke them to shoot me. They almost do. But Lucia barks a command within an inch of my own life, and instead throws me a shovel. With the others I return to the village to dig. I remove the note from the little girl's body before anyone can see it, and bury her myself.

1 4 8

Not long after that we're in Texas, or to be more precise, we're just below what used to be the border of Texas. I . . . I'm not sure how this happens. It's probably all that prevents my execution at the hands of the guerrillas; in the ambush that comes the day following our discovery of the massacred village, it's a German bullet that saves me. The ambush is fast and overwhelming, at the bottom of a ditch. In the midst of the scant three minutes it takes place, I remember the short stocky second-in-command taking aim at me; I turn at the last moment to read it in his eyes. If anyone's not getting out of this alive, his eyes say, it's you. And then the eyes flinch with annoyance as though he's just been stung by a mosquito, except it isn't a mosquito; he just drops. A second later I'm dropped as well by a blow I never see. In the hours to come I'm only fleetingly conscious; I'm aware of the back of a truck, where I'm bound at my hands and feet and jostling with other prisoners. I assume the old man's here too but I don't see him. Lucia's several bodies away from me, also bound; she may be alive or dead. When I come to again, I'm lying still bound on the open deck of a boat, bombs and gunfire in the distance; it's nightfall and I crane my head above the edge of the boat to glimpse in the full moonlight the waters of what must be the gulf. I'm cognizant enough to think to myself that perhaps it isn't the brightest thing to be sailing hostile waters in full moonlight. On the other hand, maybe that's the idea. I don't spot Z anywhere. Before slipping back to the deck, however, I do see those ancient birds of the blue city circling the dazzling lethal lights of the gulf as though they're coming home; I wonder if the old man, who's watched in his mind those birds night after night since we left, has sprung them loose by raising his eyes to the sky and opening them like cages. I rush to sleep before this boat is blown from the water. I'm surprised to wake at all, and a little more surprised to find myself sleeping next to a dying fire, the old man dozing right beside me, on a morning beach right outside of Brownsville.

149

We spend several days getting up to Galveston. On the streets of Corpus Christi I panhandle bus fare while Z sits on the curb moaning a strange unearthly sound that seems to come from some place other than his mouth. I know he's barely alive. Sometimes someone will give us a ration coupon for some food, but the shelves in the grocery stores are always empty. One day a woman tells us about a relief center for people who've been dispossessed by the shelling, but after I coax the old man three hours over four city blocks, I find a hopelessly huge crowd outside the center and I know we'll never get through. I must remind myself that the soldiers on the corners aren't Germans but Americans. I must also remind myself that it may not matter, it may even be worse. On a government bus that runs refugees north, I see the internment camps for enemy aliens. After a week we're in New Orleans.

According to the newspapers it's July 1970. Every day is a struggle to get coupons and hope we find a store with whatever items our coupons specify. Our last day in New Orleans we're lucky; someone's dropped a whole ration book on the sidewalk. I redeem some of them for canned fruit which I must feed to Z like a baby. Coffee's impossible because the Germans have cut off the flow from South America. I trade the rest of our coupons to get us back on the road. All along the highway up through wartime Louisiana I can see the barbed wire that runs along the bayous. The heat's terrible; the Negro bus driver scolds me for taking an old man on such a trip. Another old man on the bus gives Z a green baseball cap to shield his face from the sun that comes through the window. Every once in a while Z eats a can of something, whatever he can chew and digest, tomato broth or tapioca pudding. We get off the bus at each stop and I take him to the toilet, hoping we'll get back fast enough before the bus driver pulls out. The bus cuts up the south side of the Appalachians, through Montgomery and I think Atlanta, though I sleep through Atlanta, so I'm not sure. Z's still moaning in that way and the other people on the bus watch him. I'm still compelled by whatever force it was that smuggled us from the Italian lagoon in the first place; I've dreaded the truth of the matter so long that I've come to dread the dread more, and therefore must now admit the truth, which is that all this has been allowed by someone. It's too ridiculous to pretend I've somehow actually spirited out of Europe on my own the most powerful man in history, all the way from Italy to America without papers in the middle of a global war. Someone or something unseen directed us past the lieutenant on the train from Milan, the owner of the German kitchen in Nice who suddenly changed his mind about evicting us from our room, the captain from Marseilles who suddenly changed his mind about arranging us passage out of Wyndeaux, the cabbie in Quintana Roo who drove us up the coast for no reason at all, the ambush in a Yucatan ditch that brought us onto first a truck, then a boat that deposited us on an American beach without a soul asking questions and with a fire to keep us warm until we were up and on our way. I've been allowed by someone or something unseen to smuggle into the very heart of America the enemy, the withered dying husk of an old man who will soon break apart only for bits of him to blow across America and settle in its land and take root. What have I done, I cry out to myself there on the bus in the dark. I marvel at how everything I touch is marked with malevolence. After several days on the bus we're forced to spend more time begging in Raleigh before we can move on. When we come into Washington it's so black from martial law that the old man actually stops moaning a moment, his face alight, as though he recognizes in the black the same home seen in the lights of the gulf by the ancient birds he released from his eyes.

150

Near the end, in his last days, the moan that comes from him is unbearable. It's as if the soul of him, slipping into its final damnation, is already howling back through an open door. As it becomes a greater and greater moan, a greater howl, I begin not only to hear but to feel it; it ripples through me from the part of his soul that's attached to mine. Walking in the streets of Washington the people who pass look at us in the way one looks for the direction of a siren; they know it's somehow coming from us but they don't know how. I can so barely stand it that sometimes I just walk on ahead, leaving him behind. The howl then soars to stop me in my tracks; I turn back to him, expecting to see him staring after me and screaming at his abandonment. In fact he's not staring after me at all. I stride back to him and see how his body shrinks behind its features, disappearing until the only things left of him are his various grotesque appendages, the nose, the ears, the fingers. On a wall beside him is a poster which is old and shredded around the edges, curling at the corners: it's a poster of him. As on the German television broadcasts, the image is of the man nearly forty years ago, and printed across the image is a large black X. Beneath the image and its X is the single word, in large black letters, NEVER. The old man, now virtually dying before my eyes, stands peering out from beneath the rim of his green baseball cap at this picture of himself. I don't know if his howl is for the X across the image, or for the image itself. I pull him away and the humid swampland of the city breaks open in a summer storm. As the streets become small rivers he whimpers at my side. It's an improvement over the moan.

His last thirty-six hours are spent in New York City. I can barely remember why I left it, though I know the reasons were quite momentous at the time. I also know it's not the same New York City. We spend some time in Washington Square and walk, two ragged bums, up the great boulevards. There was a time once when he dreamed of marching up the great boulevards of New York with a conqueror's contempt, as when he marched up the boulevards of Vienna and Paris and London. Whose bodies would he have sealed up in the walls of Park Avenue? After a while it's not possible to move him anywhere on his own power. We catch the subway; he sits beneath a maelstrom of graffiti. Some teenagers torment him, knocking his cap this way and that, pulling it down over his face; when the doors slide open at Lincoln Center they grab the cap and take off through the turnstiles. At 72nd Street we get off. Every step up the stairs is an effort for both of us. His moaning ends, exhausted. I'm at the point where I must will myself beyond my lameness, the lameness barely accommodated by what's compelled and brought us this far. Not much further, I tell him now: I know exactly where we're heading.

We're heading for the small room where I first began to chronicle the adventures of old loves. Amanda and Molly. I'll bet they thought I'd forgotten them. It takes me only most of the morning to find the block, only most of the afternoon to get us to the building. The building hasn't changed, not outside anyway. When we enter the lower lobby I'm practically carrying the old man, I might as well sweep him up in my arms like a bride. I carry him into the lift, and at first I get the floor wrong. We go up and down a couple of times, and then I decide maybe I had the floor right after all. It had to be this particular floor. Right before the lift door slides open, I believe I'm going to look down the same hallway I looked down years ago, and see the door of my room. But the lift door slides open and where my room used to be is an office. I open the door of the office and no one's there. There's dust everywhere and mail on the floor that hasn't been collected. The blinds have been drawn many years. The papers on the desk are old and brittle. It's disappointing, I thought I'd see the old place. The old scene of the crime. The table where I wrote and the shelves that held old coffee grounds. I take him into the room and set him in the chair behind the desk; the air he exhales is startling, it seems like more air than his withered body could hold. His hands flop onto the flat top of the desk before him; at his fingertips is an old blueprint someone left behind. I walk over to the window and turn the blinds, walk back over to the door to pick up the mail, twenty blank white postcards that, from the postmarks, were all sent nearly two decades before. Nothing's written on the cards, but the addresses on the front are all in the same hand. I look around the office for a moment; it's utterly ordinary. I'm thinking maybe it's not the right floor after all, maybe it's not the right building. Maybe it's the wrong street. Studying the old blueprint in the light through the window, I find nothing extraordinary about it either; it's a house. It has a main floor and a floor upstairs and a basement, and all the usual rooms of any house. It could be the sound and certain house I grew up in, the one I burned to the ground. The only thing slightly curious about it is a room in the corner of the basement; its lines have emerged literally out of brown age, as though it was always there but only the actual passage of time would reveal it. It could have appeared any time in the last twenty years. I'm standing there in the light of the window looking at the blueprint when I realize he's dead.

1 5 1

I just realize it. I wouldn't make more of it than that. It's
not as though the part of his soul attached to mine has
given it a significant little tug. I just think that when you're
in a room with a dead person you instinctively know it,
although just as instinctively I know that isn't necessarily
so. I turn and there he is, nothing about him looks different
from the way he looked in the bottom of Giorgio's boat or
the way he looked sitting on the cliffs of the Caribbean
watching the war. I just know he's dead, and I walk over
and feel his pulse only because I don't trust my own in-
stincts anymore. Soon his eyes will roll up into his head;
I'll be damned if I'm going to close them. I'll be damned if
he deserves that kind of dignity. Still, I think I'm supposed
to say something. I think I'm supposed to let someone
know, before he breaks open and bits of him fly out over
the world. I'm supposed to call someone on the phone and
tell them the man they're looking for is here in the West
Seventies of Manhattan. By my calculation, which is certainly suspect, he's eighty-one. I leave him as he is, there
in the chair, the gold slits of twilight striping him through
the blind. I tear from the blueprint the emergent room in
the basement corner and pin it to his shirt. In the middle I
write not an explanation or an epitaph or an excuse, just a
mystery for someone better at mysteries, any random investigator who passes this way. It reads: "Aber ich liebte sie.
(But I loved her.) A.H."

152

I followed the postmarks of the blank white cards west. In Pennsylvania I saw a burning house. In Ohio, in the flatlands, at the Mississippi, I looked for every sign of him, every sign of any bit of him that had blown and settled and taken root. When I found him, I pulled the root up. Fingers of him, the hairs of his mustache curling up out of the soil, the veins of him scaling walls like vines, I cut them all down. I struck down his evil no matter what name it took for itself, no matter that it called itself history or revolution, America or the son of God, no matter that it called itself righteous, a righteousness that presumed the license to bind the free word and thought, that presumed the wisdom to timetable the birth of a soul, that presumed the morality that offers its children up to the plague rather than teach them the language of love. A thousand righteous champions calcified into something venal and mean by their presumptions of something sacred and pure and undirtied by the blood and spit and semen of being human: I recognized all of them by the bit of him they carried, sometimes in one eye, sometimes under their nails. I did not turn my violence on them. I didn't scorn them or call myself finer. I named them by what they were, sometimes in a place no one heard me, in a language no one knew; I named the evil that calls itself righteously destined. On the other side of a river that seemed to have no other side, I took a ride with a boatman who looked as though he'd seen one big man in his life too many.

1 5 3

I walked into town with the rest of the tourists and took a room at the hotel on the main street. The Chinese woman who ran the hotel sat in a back room; when she failed to acknowledge me, I slowly went up the stairs and found the first door that opened for me. The room was like many rooms I've lived in. I lay down on the bed and waited for someone to discover I was here. A bowl of rice and pork was sitting on the table by the window when I woke. Since then, every twilight when I've awakened, rice and pork wait for me on the table.

She and her son live several doors down the hall from mine. After I'd been in my hotel room for a month, during which time no one spoke to me or asked who I was or what I was doing, I got up one night and walked up the hallway and stood before their door. This was the place and moment to which I'd been compelled by his defiant birth. Now, years later, I'm still compelled there because I haven't yet found the courage to do what I came to do. Now, years later, I still stand before their door having come to the door that first night and then the next, and then the next, and every night after that for a week and then a month and then a year, and then two years, then five, then ten. Always I believe the courage will come to me at her door. I will not die as he did, never begging someone's forgiveness. That she would not or could not give forgiveness isn't what matters; what matters is the act of my begging. Every night I raise my fist to the door, about to knock; sometimes I hear her or the boy turn in their sleep on the other side. Many times I stand there the whole night for hours on feet that are racked with pain. When the dawn light drifts up from downstairs, when I see the top of the stairs fade to a softer blue, when I hear someone stir on the other side of their door, my nerve collapses altogether; I return to my little room and close the door and wait for the next night, when I try again.

154

It's now been seventeen years since I came to this hotel. Seventeen years of nights I've stood at her door with my hand raised. I see her sometimes from my window, when I have the courage to look out. Occasionally I believe she looks just as she did when she watched me from her own window that day in 1937, '38, I don't remember anymore. She spends much time in her own room caring for the boy; sometimes, when the boy's out playing somewhere, I smell the liquor in the hallway. I would have a drink with her, if it was possible; fortified by it, I would say all the things. All the things to say. We would, after all of it, become drinking pals in our old times. From my window I watch the boy too, whitehaired embodiment of the willful love of hers that defied all our terrible power. When the rains come one autumn she runs from the hotel looking for him as the island floods; the waters rush down the mainstreet with a terrible power of their own. After neither of them has come back, I pull on my coat and climb with difficulty down the stairs and out the hotel's backway. In the rain and wind I slowly trudge up toward the northern end of the island where the cemetery lies; there, huddled beneath a wooden shack, I can see the boy trapped by the storm as the graves bubble up around him. I wade out to him. By the time I reach him the downpour is such that almost nothing's visible but rain; I spot him by his hair. He's nearly unconscious. I pull him up from the water and for a moment, as he's caught in my hands, I have that old urge to avenge my wife and child who I can barely remember anymore; all I remember is vengeance. I have that old urge. But I pick him up out of the water and hold him to my chest and wade back to town. I come back to the hotel and up the stairs. I'm wondering what I'll say to her when I carry the boy through the door. But she hasn't returned yet and so I lay the boy on his bed and pull the blanket up around him when I hear the door downstairs, and I've only returned and closed the door of my own room when I hear her footsteps in the hall. She's lived a whole lifetime not to hear my footsteps behind her anymore. I hear her call his name at the sight of him, the noise of love's weapon fired years ago from the moment she bore him.

155

Seventeen years I slip in and out of the hotel back door in the dead of night and storm. Except for the unknown stranger who brings me my food, I am unknown and strange to the rest of the town. I've fallen out of time, it searches for me and I hide like a rebel in the ruins of Mexico. If it's found me out, it's left me to my delusions. From the window I watch the tavern, the woman who runs it, the Chinese carrying their dead north; I hear ice and its machine, crackling in the distance. Sometimes I like to pretend she's the one who brings the rice and pork. Sometimes I believe I wake to the smell of liquor in my room; I leave such a conviction to my delusions as well. I don't have much time.

156

I don't have much time.
Dania. Forgive me.

157

A moment ago my heart woke me. I look around and it's dark but still early, I hear the tourists in the tavern across the street, which means the last boat hasn't yet left for the mainland. I can barely move from the way I'm stricken, from beneath the weight. I'm angry with myself for having gone seventeen years without ever finding the courage. I don't have any time now. Time knew I was here all along. Now I have only moments. I have only one last burst of havoc in me. I stagger from my bed and lurch across my room to the door. In the hall it seems to take forever to get to her door. Maybe it is forever. Maybe it's the moment into which one's whole life falls. At her door my hand slides across the surface when I try to manage a knock, I cannot manage it. I can barely manage the knob. When the door opens, she's standing there in the middle of the room; no son or lover waits with her. She turns to look at me. Her face when she sees me is inscrutable. I look for a signal but she gives none.

Forgive me?

Lying there on the floor at her feet, I'm aware of the boy coming into the doorway. He stares at me in shock. Is it simply the sight of a dead man, or is it any man at all in his mother's company? Does the part of my soul attached to his give it a small tug? Does he feel the times I nearly killed him? Does he feel the times I finally saved him? Does he recognize in me the darkness from which I tried to create him? He looks at me, at his mother, and bolts. And somewhere, even in the silence of a forgiveness that never was given, the two parallel rivers of the Twentieth Century, which forked the only other time she ever saw me, flow back into one.

1 5 8

For an hour or so there's some confusion as the room fills with townspeople and tourists from the tavern across the street. A doctor confirms the news they're all waiting for, which is that I am indeed dead. But who is he? everyone's asking; no one remembers me from the tavern or coming over on the boat earlier that day. "How could anyone not notice him," the doctor says, "the man's a giant." I've never seen him before in my life, she tells them, still inscrutable. You remember me, I'm thinking, looking up at her: Vienna. In the window. The townspeople accept my anonymity with solemn resolve; it takes twelve of them to drag me out, after the tourists have gone their way. They're none too delicate about it either. My head bounces down the stairs like a bowling ball. For a moment I thought she was going to stop them, but she didn't; for a moment I think the woman who runs the tavern is going to stop them as well, but she doesn't either. They drag me down the street and through the thicket outside the cemetery marsh

until my backside's raw; if I were alive I'd crack the little
fuckers' skulls together like eggs. In the cemetery at the
edge of the island, before the wild night, they must bend
the tree all the way over to the ground in order to fasten
me to it, since they can't lift me; when they release the tree
I think I'm going to be catapulted into space. But the tree
only groans back to something midway its original height,
the last thing on earth that will ever succumb to the size of
me.

1 5 9

I'm up here eight days. It's not at all bad, truth be told.
The weather's fine and I watch out over the wide blue river,
fascinated with the red train that crosses high over the
water on its endless track. It reminds me of being on the
ferris wheel in the Praterstern. I'm warm in the sunlight
and birds visit my arms. I have this one melancholy fantasy
that she'll come to me one day and look up and say, I
forgive you. This doesn't happen but on the other hand it
could happen at any time. She could be on her way here
now, coming to say, I remember you from that day, before
the candleshop.

This doesn't feel like damnation.

I keep waiting for the damnation. As though it'll arrive
in the form of a black bird, and begin with the eating of my
eye. But the birds don't eat me, rather they seem content
to watch the river perched from me. So I wait for damnation; it's confusing that it doesn't come. I've expected it so
long, I spent so long earning it. It makes no sense that God
gives me this reprieve, I'd have thought he wouldn't waste

a second. I'd have thought he'd snatch me the first moment I slipped over, as though there wasn't another moment to lose. In my time, I have no reason but to believe that whatever God exists is the God of revenge.

The God of revenge in a century of revenge. It doesn't seem possible that this might have been the century of redemption after all. Not this century, not for me. After all the things, it doesn't seem possible that somewhere I committed some slight, insignificant act of kindness that redeems everything. One small act of kindness that wiped the rest of it away. And yet, in a century when time and space have liberated themselves of all reference points, perhaps one small good thing owns a universe unto itself, and a thousand monstrous worlds of evil must submit themselves to its love. I don't understand anymore. I'm only here at the end of an island where a river becomes one, waiting for God to come damn me, or for her to come forgive me; I wait for her to whisper my name from the window of her room. I almost killed him, really. I came that close. I held his little head in the palm of my hand and nearly popped it open the moment he was born; only a lapse prevented me. It wasn't that I was good or anything. It was only a lapse. I almost drowned him that day in the flood not twenty yards from here, from where I then carried him to the hotel; I didn't have the strength to kill him, was all. I meant to do it, hold him beneath the water until the last bubble up from the graves beneath our feet was his. That I carried him back was only weakness. Nothing good about it. Fuck the God who redeems me, I say.

But God doesn't believe me. I guess I don't believe me either.

Before his blue redemptive face above me, I've already forgotten the things I've cried out for, and the cry itself forgets its own name.

160

Every afternoon Dania leaves her hotel and goes down to the shore of the island to see if her son is returning. Sometimes she spots him lying face down, staring into the water from the edge of the boat captained by a man to whom she no longer speaks. Rejected in this way, she returns to town. After a week and a half, she goes to the cemetery.

The huge nameless man still hangs in the tree. Birds sit on his fingers and the top of his head, staring out toward the river. Each day several of the townspeople come by to hear if the man has yet cried out his name; each day the tree sags a little more beneath him. Dania holds her arms together with determination, as though she's waiting as well. She studies him each day. The Chinese quiz her constantly. She tells them she's never seen him before; she doesn't understand why they won't believe her.

By the tenth day she's begun to feel harassed. Also, the body's become an unhappy sight. She stands in the sunlight watching him awhile before she finally says, "His name was Banning Jainlight."

The Chinese who are present run into town to get the others. The others return and she says, still watching him, "His name was Banning Jainlight."

You're lying, someone says. Like you did many years ago about the woman you called Consuelo Garcia, you're making it up.

She says, turning, "Let him rot up there then." They call out after her as she walks back toward town. She shrugs, "Do what you want with him."

They cut down Banning Jainlight and bury him in the marsh.

1 6 1

My name is Banning Jainlight, a voice says to her fifteen years later; but it's only a voice in her head, after all, and she herself gave him that name. No dead man lies at her feet now. When she turns to the doorway and sees her son there, as she did fifteen years before, she has no reason to believe the voice she hears in her head speaks in his head as well. When the whitehaired rivermonk sees that the girl in the blue dress is not in his mother's room as he'd expected to find her, he bolts from the doorway just as he did the time before, his second such lapse, though this one cannot be said to interrupt a life of innocence. He runs back out into the street, stepping on the glass from the windows he broke in his evening's rampage. Greek Judy stands watching him from the doorway of her tavern. When Marc arrives at the boat, the passengers are still huddled in terror, waiting to be delivered back to shore; the journey is furious. At her tavern, Judy can hear the tourists' screams from out of the river's fog. Business is going to be off awhile, she thinks, or perhaps even says out loud, though no one else is there to say for sure.

162

After that, his fury subsided into a gentler sorrow. He never saw again the moment of profound isolation on the river. He went into the river, not long after his night on the island, to release from the boat's bottom whatever of the previous captain was still there; but there was nothing there. He always thought of going back to see his mother. Greek Judy brought him food and beer; she became tender toward his torment. One night about three years later she came to him with no food or beer but news, and he went onto the island for the last time. The street outside the hotel was filled with Chinese trying to get up to the hall outside her door, like scavengers waiting to pick over not his mother's possessions but the mystery of who she was: Over my own dead body perhaps, he told them, but not hers. At the top of the stairs her door stood open; for a moment he was about to call out, Mother, that she might hear him from her bed as he turned the door's corner. Instead he called her by her name. Turning the door's corner, there was a split second when he saw her white hair on the pillow and believed it to be his own.

Dania, he said. He saw her move slightly; he came to her side; his white hair tangled with hers. She looked up, very old and wrinkled, the scar that had always been at the corner of her mouth now just another of many lines. She put her hand on his face. In her eyes were theoretical tears. For a moment she was living very distinctly in the pain of bearing him. For a moment she was under the leaves of the Pnduul forest, the roof of the Vienna apartment, the tarpaulin of the boat on the river. What fell on her, however, what she heard about her, was not rain. It was a tapping; she knew what was tapping. She knew what now raised its fist to her door. Her son, clutching her, began to say something but she moved her fingers to his mouth to hold back his words. "I've already forgiven everyone," she said, her long exile finally finished. "Now it's their turn to forgive me."

She danced home.

1 6 3

No one was going to hang her in any tree; he knew that for certain. Yet over the years the cemetery marsh had become so occupied it seemed there was no place left for her, and so Marc buried his mother, wrapped in a white sheet, in the arms of the man who had come to her that night fifteen years before, though in fact nothing was left of him except bones and mud. He covered her and then he and the woman that his mother had named Judy Garcia walked arm and arm back up mainstreet where they drank alone in her tavern, not a tourist to be seen. Sorry I hit you that time, she mumbled near the end. Sorry I deserved it, he answered. When he smiled sadly she said, I don't think I've ever seen you smile, even a sad smile is nice. He leaned over the bar and when he kissed her forehead her face became buried in his beard. She laughed because it tickled her; he thought it was something else. He pulled on his old buttonless coat and started toward the beach at dusk, and when he came to his boat the girl in the blue dress, blond and unchanged and unaged since the last time he saw her years before, was waiting for him.

The rivermonk and the young girl sailed across the river where they caught the last bus into Samson. Halfway there Kara fell asleep on his shoulder. In Samson they ate in a diner and got a room at a motel five minutes down the highway; there were two beds and Marc said, Take your pick. She picked one and he took the other. The radio didn't work, the filament of the table lamp between them muttered on and off. Outside their door was a Coke machine that someone seemed to use every ten minutes. Marc didn't ask Kara where she'd been all that time or what she'd done. He didn't tell her of his mother because he figured she knew about that. They didn't make plans. He lay on his bed in the dark, listening to the sounds of the highway which didn't seem so unlike the sounds of the ice machine when he was a boy. He listened to her fall asleep, and sometime in the middle of the night, when he'd fallen asleep as well, he had a nightmare: it was about his father. He woke to find her stroking his forehead and soothing him. She went on soothing him beneath the breeze that came through the window from the highway, and when he fell asleep again this time he dreamed of her growing up in the midwest. From the porch of her teacher's house Kara named all the stars in the sky, and watched the leaves blow across the buried bridges of the plains. He heard the girl's voice in his dream, and felt the blue fabric of her dress against his face. He woke calling her in the morning, when the motel room was filled with sun; and in the middle of that sun her bed was empty. When he went to the motel office to pay for the room, a woman told him that Kara had left on another bus three hours before.

Living and migrating with the silver buffalo, he followed her trail seven years. The white hair on his arms grew longer and more savage, the hair on his face covered it so that no one would ever detect a sad smile again. On a mountain near the top of the world, he found her; she was living and working in an observatory, alone and happy. It was a place nearer the fiery field above her. He and the buffalo lived in the woods nearby. He didn't go to her, accepting that she had chosen to live by herself; he watched her stars with her, outside her walls, and though he'd discarded his coat long before, and though the coat had lost its gold buttons long before that, he now wagered them on which star she was studying tonight. The odds favored him. He fought off the beasts that came threatening her. Sometimes in her doorway, she called out, Who's there. He lay low until she convinced herself it was no one. After many more years had passed, he realized one day he hadn't heard or seen her recently, and with trepidation he invaded the observatory to determine she was in no danger. Almost as though she was asleep, she lay in the center of the arena under the observatory's open dome; the telescope was pointed at her as though the stars were studying her back. Because there was no way of giving her up to the field in which she belonged, he left her there. He'd seen enough burials anyway.

He migrated even further north with the silver buffalo; they seemed to know where they meant to go. Across the snowy flats, man and herd traveled in a steady vapor. The mining towns became more and more scarce, the signs of life fewer and fewer. They were running somewhere, and when they arrived at the place, the snow was falling. He knew he couldn't go further with them, that it wasn't his place. So he had to watch them leave him behind; he noted how they hurled themselves onward, and he pitied anything that fell before their path. Through the blinding falling snow he could barely see them disappear, but he followed their tracks nonetheless, and the sound of them, right up to the mouth of an arctic cave. As he stood there listening to them disappear into the dark of the cave, there roared into his face, from out of the darkness, an inexplicable blast of jungle heat.

Having exited the century at one end and entered it again at the other, the year was 1901 when he finally came to a village in northern Asia. He lived in the village awhile and when he understood that it was his time as it had been for others, he left to make his way down the mountains to the polar sea. He came to a bay clogged with ice. He plunged his old whitehaired body into the sea and swam to the first iceblock from where he spent the days remaining to him leaping from one block to the next, putting his ear to the surface of each. As with the ice he'd listened to as a boy on the island, the bergs in the sea were clearly ticking. What he now searched for was the one block of ice that melted in time to the beating of his own heart. He didn't have long to ascertain this about each one, since listening at any great length would freeze his ear to the ice, a prospect he considered no better than hanging from a tree. When he finally found the right one, he was too exhausted at first to feel much relief; only after he lay there some time, during which his fingertips and heels, and then the hair of his body, froze to the ice, did he feel some peace. He dozed. The ice, caught in a southward current, became smaller and smaller as it drifted off on its own course. For a while he allowed himself to remember everything; one thing after another came into his head, all the things he remembered of the years to come, until the ice had turned completely into the sea. Through the warm fog of his last breath, he watched the memories of a hundred ghosts drift skyward to finally and vainly burst.